AGE OF Ava

NEW YORK TIMES AND USA TODAY BESTSELLING AUTHOR

MELANIE MORELAND

BOOK 4

Dear Reader,

Thank you for selecting the Vested Interest: ABC Corp series to read. Be sure to sign up for my newsletter for up to date information on new releases, exclusive content and sales.

Before you sign up, add melanie@melaniemoreland.com to your contacts to make sure the email comes right to your inbox!
Always fun - never spam!

My books are available in both paperback and audiobook! I also have signed paperbacks available at my website.

The Perfect Recipe For **LOVE**
xoxo,
Melanie

Age of Ava (Vested Interest: ABC Corp #4)

Insta-Spark Collection written by M Moreland

It Started with a Kiss

Christmas Sugar

An Instant Connection

An Unexpected Gift

Harvest of Love

Men of Hidden Justice

The Boss

Second-In-Command

Mission Cove

The Summer of Us

Standalones

Into the Storm

Beneath the Scars

Over the Fence

My Image of You (Republishing Soon)

Changing Roles

Happily Ever After Collection

Revved to the Maxx

Heart Strings

Age of Ava
Vested Interest: ABC Corp #4

Copyright © 2021 Melanie Moreland
Registration # 1181588
ISBN eBook: 978-1-988610-55-9
ISBN Paperback: 978-1-988610-54-2 /
978-1-988610-61-0

MORELAND
BOOKS INC.

Edited by:
Lisa Hollett—Silently Correcting Your Grammar

Cover Design by:
Karen Hulseman, Feed Your Dreams Designs
Photo Credit:
iStock - PeopleImages

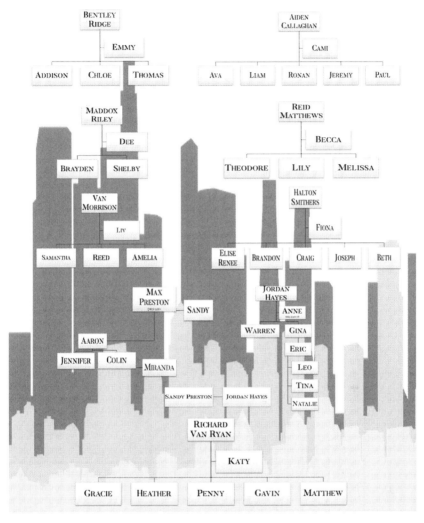

FAMILY TREE

The Contract VESTED INTEREST

NEW YORK TIMES AND USA TODAY BESTSELLING AUTHOR

MELANIE MORELAND

DEDICATION

For all the strong independent women I know.
You inspire me.

And for my Matthew, who sees every part of me
and loves me through it all.

CHAPTER 1

AVA

I parked the car outside the small town hall, shutting off the engine and reaching for the file inside my satchel. I flipped open the folder and double-checked everything, confident I was prepared. All the proper paperwork had been filed. The correct reports and architectural drawings, signed off by my brother Ronan, were in order. All the necessary documentation was in place, and we met every code. We'd done this hundreds of times, and this one was straightforward. We were going to knock down a dilapidated, deserted building and erect a new, efficient structure. It would house a blend of services needed within the community. The building would be run by one of ABC's divisions, the income expectation great for the bottom line of the company. Most of the time, we ran the businesses ourselves, but none of us had medical expertise, and this building would be dedicated to that industry.

I got out of the car, making sure to straighten my jacket and run my hand over my skirt. My hair was twisted up in its usual chignon. I headed up the stairs, approaching the door when it was flung open and a man burst through, almost knocking me down.

With a surprised gasp, I teeter-tottered on my heels, already feeling the impact of the cement on my ass, but the sensation of strong hands gripping my elbows held me up.

"Shit," a low, masculine voice muttered. "Dammit, I'm sorry."

I lifted my eyes, meeting the scowling countenance of a man. His eyes were piercing, the irises an unusual shade of light blue. We were so close I could discern a ring of darker blue around the rim, and they were set off by a set of long lashes. Our gazes clashed and held, and I caught my breath. There was something intense and stormy about his stare. It held me in its fury, his hand still grasping my elbow.

"Are you hurt?" he asked, stepping back.

I recovered my senses, shaking off his grip.

"I'm fine. You need to watch where you're going. People are on both sides of the door, you know."

He lifted one eyebrow, eyeing me sardonically. "Thanks for the lesson. I believe I apologized."

For a brief moment, I was once again speechless. With a small distance between us, I could see him fully. I judged him to be in his early forties. He had a head full of shaggy, deep-brown hair shot with silver, but his eyebrows were heavy and dark, his face all angles and sharp lines. His tightly trimmed beard showed off his chiseled jaw. A full, sensuous mouth and a straight nose were somehow both beautiful and masculine at the same time. His broad shoulders were covered in a thick plaid jacket that was open to reveal a tight white T-shirt, and dusty, torn jeans sheathed his long legs. He was about six foot three or so, well-built, but unlike the thick men of my family, his torso led to a trim waist and narrow hips. His feet were encased in a set of Doc Martens, muddied and worn from use. Everything about him screamed sex. A silver fox, I knew my cousins would call him.

With a start, I realized I had been staring. He was watching me, a slight curl to his lips as if I amused him. As if he knew exactly what I was thinking. I lifted my chin, meeting his gaze. "Apology accepted."

"Well, thank you. I'll sleep so much better tonight knowing I haven't offended you."

"I didn't say you weren't offensive. I simply accepted your apology."

This time, his lips quirked. "Really, I'm sorry." He held up a sheaf of papers. "Bureaucracy pisses me off. I had to get out before my fist went through a wall."

"Better than somebody's face."

He smirked. "I suppose. Not as satisfying, though, to be honest."

I had to laugh, because he was right. I held up my own file. "I feel your pain."

He laughed, a muted, brief sound of amusement that relaxed the frown between his eyes and made him infinitely more attractive —something I didn't think was possible.

He leaned down, his voice pitched low. "Maybe I could buy you a drink after? We could share our pain over paperwork and BS?"

I was tempted. So tempted. But I didn't go for drinks with strange men, and I had an evening of work ahead of me.

"Thanks, but I'll have to pass."

3

A flash of something went through his eyes, but he shrugged. "Pity." Then he held open the door. "I hope you have better luck in there than I did."

I walked past him, feeling regret. Part of me had hoped he would try—cajole me a little. But he let me walk away, and when I turned to peek over my shoulder, he was already at the bottom of the steps and heading away, his long legs eating up the distance quickly.

I straightened my shoulders and shook my head. I was here to do a job, not pick up a stranger. I needed to focus on that.

Glimmering blue eyes rimmed in indigo flashed through my mind. The curl of a sensual mouth half amused, half exasperated was in the forefront of my head.

I ignored them.

———

Twenty minutes later, I was in agreement with the stranger, except I would have preferred to punch the face of the man standing across from me, his condescending tone dripping with false politeness as he spoke.

"As I said, there have been some delays with your paperwork."

"And as I said, I need you to tell me exactly what the problem is so I can rectify it."

He smiled, running a hand over his slicked-back hair. His jowls moved as he swallowed, his beady eyes overly bright and eager.

He tapped the file in front of him. "So many issues," he tutted, cocking his head to the side. "Perhaps you should let one of your superiors handle it?"

I had been upset to discover that Milly Johnson wasn't in the office, but it explained the lack of response I had gotten to my inquiries. Instead, this middle-aged clerk, who was somehow drunk on what he thought was power, was now in charge of the department. Milly and I had had a great working relationship. She knew her stuff and was no-nonsense and direct. And I was very good at my job and rarely missed any required documentation. Our permits and licenses were usually a smooth transaction. Any changes needed were handled quickly so the projects we were working on went ahead. I made sure of it. I took great pride in my job and representing ABC Corp. I had been top of my classes at school, and my "grandfather" Jordan Hayes had taught me well before he retired. I was organized, detail-oriented, and driven. I never allowed my gender to come into play. I was a woman in what was typically still a man's world, but I refused to let that stop me. My father had instilled that in me, and my mother's work ethic was part of my makeup.

And now, this little man had mistaken me for a pushover and was trying to hold up my work. I studied him, wondering his endgame. He fiddled with the file, his fingers worrying the edge of the thick folder encasing the papers.

"Superiors?" I repeated.

"Maybe your boss. I could speak directly to him. I'm sure we could come up with a...mutually beneficial solution."

It hit me. This asshole was actually attempting to bribe the company. He was going to hold up the necessary documentation and extort money before he rubber-stamped the paperwork.

I wanted to laugh at the absurdity of it. He had no idea who he was dealing with.

"Where did you say Milly was?" I asked.

"On leave."

"Will she be back?"

He shrugged. "Not soon enough to help you with all these problems." He shook his head as if saddened by the fact. "So many, many issues with this file."

"But *you* could help," I said slowly. "Help resolve the issues," I added, as if relieved.

A calculating look flashed through his eyes. "I could be persuaded. Off the record, of course."

"Maybe I don't have to involve my superiors." I tapped my chin as if thinking.

His gaze became predatory and I wanted to reach across the counter and use one of my karate moves on him, but I refrained.

"I am sure we could, ah, satisfy each other."

"I need to make a call. Check my, ah, figures."

"You do that."

I stepped over to the window, tapping out a text. I was fuming. I hated assholes like this. Macho, small-dicked assholes who tried to buck the system. I planned to take him down a peg or two.

I was startled as I waited for a reply to my text to see the silver fox walk in the door. He met my gaze, his eyebrows lifting in surprise at seeing me again, while mine did the same at the sight of him. But he ignored me and went to the counter. He asked the asshole I'd been talking to a question, and it was obvious they'd already had dealings. I understood his bad mood earlier. The clerk wiped his hand over his head, shaking it despondently. "As I said, you will have to refile the paperwork and repay the fees."

"And I told you that was BS. I checked and double-checked everything in my truck. It's all in order. I want to speak to your manager. Now."

The clerk sighed. "I am the manager. If you wish to make a complaint, you need to fill out this form."

The fox grabbed it from him, muttering, "Right. Like that will go anywhere."

He crossed the room, slamming his file onto the table beside me. He looked over the form. "What a bunch of horseshit."

"Yep," I agreed in a quiet voice. "But wait a few moments. Things might get better."

He frowned, but before he could ask me, the mayor, Darren Thomas, walked into the office. He spied me by the window and came forward, beaming. "Ava, my dear, how good to see you."

The clerk's face turned white.

I accepted the mayor's hug. "How's Norma?" I asked. "Her hip doing okay?"

"Very well. And that soup basket you sent was much appreciated." He laughed dryly. "You know I can't cook. It came in very handy."

"Excellent."

"Now, what can I do for you? You said you have a problem? Something about a permit?"

I frowned. "Yes. Mr. Smith here seems to have an issue with the documentation but is unable to tell me what exactly. I thought maybe you could have someone else look it over."

Darren laughed. "*You* have incorrect documentation?" he teased. "Has hell frozen over and no one told me?"

I smiled, then became serious. "I was shocked as well. Even more shocked when Mr. Smith offered to help me out—off the record."

Darren's face went slack with shock. Mr. Smith sputtered.

"I-I think you mistook my words. I was only saying I would help you. Nothing-nothing more."

Darren looked between us, his eyes narrowing. "Those are serious charges, Ava."

I met his gaze. "I am aware. That's why I would like a second set of eyes."

He held out his hand to the clerk. "Give me the file."

Mr. Smith's hand shook as he grudgingly pushed the file Darren's way. "I was just doing my job," he muttered. "Making sure everything was in order."

"I wasn't aware that extortion was listed as part of the job description," I remarked. "You should eliminate that when reposting the position."

The silver fox barked out a laugh from the corner. The mayor glanced up. "Do you have something to add?"

"Yeah, your man was trying to shake me down too."

Darren shut his eyes. "Please leave this with me. I'll be in touch with both of you very soon." He sighed. "Ava, I have your information. Leave me yours, sir, and I will be in touch personally." He paused. "I would like to keep this private for now."

"I have no wish to bring you more trouble, Darren," I murmured. "I just want my permits. How you clean house is up to you." I paused, meeting his gaze. "It is very dusty in here."

The stranger walked past me, handing Darren a piece of paper. "Yep. Swiffer time."

I met Darren's eyes. "I'll hear from you soon."

He nodded. "Tomorrow, Ava."

I smiled and walked out.

My work here was done.

CHAPTER 2
AVA

I reached my SUV before my legs began to tremble. I leaned against the vehicle, taking in some deep breaths of the spring air. Despite my bravado, I detested confrontation. I had to handle it daily in my line of work. I dealt persistently with bureaucratic red tape, foremen not wanting to take directives from a woman, male clerks and suppliers looking down their noses at me because I had breasts.

I could also run circles around them discussing building plans, licensing issues, problem solutions, what type of wood worked best in any situation, and how a building was designed from paper to execution. I had learned from the best, and I knew my stuff. As project manager and coordinator for ABC, I had to.

Many of them disliked that fact. Many of them enjoyed trying to prove me wrong. Most of them failed.

I did my job and I did it well, and for the most part, I loved it. The energy of working at ABC, the enthusiasm of my fellow coworkers, and the talent they had—plus the fact that they were my family—made the days enjoyable and fun. We fed off each other and loved what we did. It was days like this that I disliked. Underhanded dealings. BAM and ABC were well known for their excellence. Their reputation was outstanding, and the companies were highly successful. Sometimes people decided they deserved a piece of that success, even if they had nothing to do with it. Such was the case today. A middle-aged clerk pushing papers who decided he should get a reward for doing his job. That sort of attitude made me want to punch something. Or, as the sexy stranger said, someone.

As if I had conjured him up, suddenly he was in front of me. Muddied Doc Martens appeared in my line of vision as I stared at the ground, feeling tired. I looked up, taking my time, perusing his strong thighs encased in tight jeans and the way his T-shirt stretched over his chest and abs. His lips were curled into a smile, and I met his eyes, the unusual color once again hitting me. How could the color of an eye seem so cool and impersonal, yet penetrating and on fire at the same moment?

I realized he was talking, and I shook my head. "I beg your pardon?"

"I asked if you were okay. You've been standing here for ten minutes."

I had?

"I'm fine. I was just thinking."

He crossed his arms, the movement tightening his shirt even more across his chest. "Quite the show you put on back there."

"Had to be done. He can't get away with shaking people down." I frowned. "I've never seen him before. The lady who is usually in that department was always great to deal with."

He rubbed the back of his neck. "I guess I owe you. He's been giving me a hassle for the last week." He lifted one eyebrow, his expression sardonic. "Must be nice to be on the mayor's good side."

I waved my hand. "I babysat his kids for years. The company I work for does a lot of building. I knew he wouldn't allow that sort of thing to be going on."

He pursed his lips. "Usually these things start at the top and work their way down."

I narrowed my eyes. "Not in this case. He is an honorable man. A great mayor."

He held up his hands. "Okay, Little Dragon. You've breathed enough fire for the day. No smiting me too."

I laughed at his words, the sound feeling good as it burst from my throat.

"Now, how about that drink?" he asked, grinning.

"I think I said no."

"That was before you put that little weasel in his place. Surely you need a drink now." He leaned closer. "Your pretty throat must need to be refreshed."

He was near enough that, once more, I lost myself in his gaze, fire and ice blending and holding my eyes. I could smell him. Fresh-cut wood and citrus. I felt the warmth of his body, and heat pooled in my stomach. He was intense and rigid. Determined and sexy. I needed to avoid that combination at all costs.

But I found myself nodding. "Sure. One drink."

He straightened, looking as surprised as I was. Neither of us had expected me to agree.

"There's a bar on James Street—The Tavern. Do you know it?" I asked.

"Yes."

"I'll meet you there."

He backed away. "Meet you there."

I slipped into the driver's seat, hoping I looked calm. Something about that man made me feel anything but. I felt like a schoolgirl, nervous and fluttery. My legs trembled and my hands shook. I felt off-kilter.

I started the car with a shake of my head.

It was simply the aftermath of the confrontation. Nothing more.

It had nothing to do with fire-and-ice eyes, a lean body, and a voice like melted chocolate.

Nothing.

He waited in the mostly empty parking lot at the back of the bar, leaning against his truck. I was used to men driving trucks, but this was a large one. Black and massive, it took up a lot of room. I was average height but my legs were long, and I was certain I would have trouble scrambling into the cab. I slid from my SUV, leaving my jacket inside. I stepped out, grabbing my purse, and we rounded the building to the door and stepped inside.

I had to blink at the sudden change in light. The bar was dim, the heavy paneled walls dark from years of use. Scarred tables and booths filled the room, and a long wooden bar ran the length of the space. The overhead lighting was dull, the back half of the bar full of pool tables. The sound of the balls hitting the pockets, muted conversations, and the country music playing on the jukebox met my ears. It wasn't overly busy yet, but I assumed as the hour grew later it would fill up. I knew on occasion my brothers and cousins came here for drinks and to shoot pool for a change of view. I had only accompanied them once or twice.

We slid into a booth, and the waitress appeared instantly.

"Hi, welcome to the Tavern. What can I get you?"

I smiled. "Creemore?" I asked hopefully.

She nodded, and the silver fox looked surprised. "Beer?" he asked.

"It's awesome," I assured him. "Made in Ontario."

"Okay, make it two," he ordered. "And some nachos. I'm starving."

She scurried away, and we looked at each other.

"I'm Ava." I offered my hand. "If we're going to share nachos, I should at least introduce myself."

His grin was slow and lazy as he shook my proffered hand. The smile pulled up one corner of his mouth, bringing out a dimple in his cheek. "Never said I was going to share."

I had to laugh. "I'm certain you're gentleman enough to do so."

The waitress brought over our beers, and he lifted his, clinking the neck with mine. "No one has ever accused me of being a gentleman before." He paused. "I'm Hunter."

Hunter. With those wicked eyes, the name suited him. A couple of times when he looked at me, I felt like prey. I laughed internally at the thought. How ridiculous.

I took a swallow of the cold beer, the icy liquid soothing my throat. Hunter had been right. I needed this to put out the fire.

I sighed, rolling my shoulders.

"Was that a hard thing for you?" he asked. "Acting like a bitch?"

"I wasn't acting like a bitch. I was dealing with a problem. One you benefited from, I might add," I snapped, my good humor evaporating. "Just because a woman stands up for what is right doesn't make her a bitch."

He held up his hands. "Sorry, wrong word. But for the record, I liked it. I like strong women. You were—" he paused as if searching for a word "—magnificent."

"Oh." That word took the anger away.

"In control, direct, assertive, and yes, a bit bitchy. The perfect combination to take down that little fucker."

"It's not something I enjoy," I admitted.

"But something you had to do. I get it."

The nachos arrived, and with a wide smirk, he handed me a plate. "Dig in, Little Dragon. No need for any more fire today."

"Stop calling me that," I protested, even though I had to admit, said in his low voice, I sort of liked it.

"It suits you."

I rolled my eyes, refusing to show my pleasure. No one, aside from my dad, had ever called me by a nickname until now.

We were quiet as we ate, the spicy jalapenos cooled by the sour cream. He ordered us another beer, and I sipped the smooth ale gratefully.

"You live around here?" he asked.

I nodded. "All my life." I wiped my mouth with a paper napkin, pushing away my plate. "You're new to the area?"

He looked over my shoulder, a faraway look on his face. "Just passing through. Visiting some…old memories," he finished, his voice rough.

I felt a flash of disappointment. "So, you're not staying around?"

He met my eyes over his beer bottle. "No, I'll be gone soon, I think."

"So, what did you need plans for?"

He drummed his fingers on the table. "To fix an investment. Once it's done, I'm gone."

"I see."

He barked out a laugh. "I doubt it."

He studied me for a moment, then crossed his arms and leaned across the table. "I have a room upstairs. Come there with me."

I blinked. "What?"

"Come upstairs with me. Spend the night."

I shook my head. "I don't sleep with people I just met. Especially ones who aren't sticking around long."

He sat back, running his finger along his lips. "Do you always deny yourself what you want?"

"I don't recall saying I wanted you."

"You didn't have to. Your body and your eyes said it enough."

"Think a lot of yourself, don't you?"

He shrugged. "Not really. But I certainly think a lot of you every time our eyes meet. I see what you're thinking, and you want me as much as I want you."

"You really should have checked your ego at the door," I said dryly, even as I clutched my hands into fists on my lap because he was right.

I did want him.

I wanted to feel his lips on mine. Find out how hard those thighs were. The strength of the muscles I could see flexing on his chest. When he had pulled off his jacket before sitting down, the way his arms bulged was sexy. I wanted to see how the ice-blue of his eyes would burn with passion.

He shrugged. "Your choice." He sat back, perusing me with those dangerous eyes. "What a shame. I bet we'd be an inferno."

I stood, brushing off my skirt, hoping I looked calm. Inside, I was anything but. His words had stirred up the fire, and I wanted nothing more than to yank his face to mine and kiss him. But I didn't do that sort of thing.

I regretted letting my guard down in the past. I had learned my lesson.

"As you said, I've breathed enough fire for the day," I quipped lightly. I reached for my purse, but his hand on my wrist stopped me. I looked down where his long fingers encircled my wrist, barely touching my flesh, yet it felt as if he had branded me with the heat of his hand.

"My treat. The least I could do for you for helping me."

I nodded, feeling strangely upset as I stuck out my hand. "Nice to have met you, Hunter. Thanks for the beer."

He tilted his head, studying me, then shaking my hand and dropping it. "Thanks for the company."

I nodded and walked out of the bar, the sun still in the sky but not as bright. My footsteps were slow as I headed to my SUV, tossing my purse into the passenger side. I paused before getting into the vehicle, something tugging in my chest. Once again, I leaned against the side, letting the warm air drift around me, trying to find my center. It was several moments before I opened my eyes.

Hunter appeared around the corner, his gaze locked on mine. Even across the parking lot, I could feel him, his intensity evident in his walk and the way he carried himself. A tremor went down my spine as he headed my way. He stopped inches from me. His gaze burned me with its intensity.

"Are you following me?" I asked.

He indicated the stairs to the right. "The rooms of this fine establishment are accessible only from the back. I was headed upstairs."

"Ah."

"Not much of a hotel selection around here."

I didn't tell him that would be changing once ABC was done with their projects. I only hummed in agreement.

Our gazes locked, the heat building between us once again. I felt his stare deep inside me, desire unfurling in long, tugging ribbons.

"Are you always this stubborn?" he asked.

"Yes."

"Good."

I wasn't sure who moved first, but the next thing I knew, my arms were locked around his neck, and he held me tight to his chest, his lips crashing down on mine.

His hold was too tight and aggressive, his mouth ruthless as he took mine.

It was perfect.

CHAPTER 3
HUNTER

The moment I saw her, I wanted her. There was something so undeniably sexy about a woman in a business suit. Her skirt was knee-length, her jacket done up, and her hair swept away from her face—nothing at all obvious or eye-catching.

Except, with her, everything was.

Her beautiful eyes, creamy skin, the hints of purple I could see twisted into a knot on her head. And that mouth.

That sassy, full mouth that taunted me immediately.

I had been so pissed off coming out of the town hall, needing to get even more damn paperwork from the truck, I hadn't seen her. I was glad I hadn't hurt her.

Now, I had her in my arms, and my hips were pinning her against the side of her car as I kissed her passionately.

Her mouth was hot and spicy, the same, no doubt, as mine, but there was something else, something uniquely Ava. It was addictive, and I pushed closer, wanting more.

At six foot four, I guessed her height around five seven or eight. I still towered over her, but she wasn't so short I had to bend. She made the softest noise in her throat—almost a purr—and I wanted to hear more of it. I wanted to know what she sounded like in the heat of passion.

With me.

I dragged my mouth to her ear. "Upstairs. Come upstairs with me."

She turned her head, pressing her mouth to mine again, and I let her lead, enjoying the strokes of her tongue and how she explored me. I wanted her to explore every inch of me. I wanted to do the same for her.

Then a car pulled into the parking lot, honking its horn loudly. "Woo-hoo!" some asshole yelled out, banging on the side of his vehicle. "Free show!"

Ava pulled back, startled, looking around, blinking and confused. I couldn't help but smile at her bewilderment.

I tugged her hand. "Come on."

She looked at me, her eyes now clear and panicked.

"No," she said emphatically.

Immediately, I dropped my hands, holding them up. I stood back. "Okay," I agreed.

I knew no meant no, and I wasn't the sort of man that thought otherwise.

"I'm sorry. I mean, I can't. I don't..." She trailed off. "I don't do this."

I rested my hands on my hips. "If it makes you feel any better, neither do I." I studied her for a moment. "You seem to be the exception, Little Dragon."

She drew in a deep breath. "It's just hero worship."

I lifted one eyebrow. "Beg your pardon?"

"Back there, at city hall. I helped you. It made me, ah, attractive."

I threw back my head in laughter.

"What happened back there was a spectacle worth seeing. But that's not what made you attractive. You need to look in the mirror more."

She furrowed her brow, and I backed up. "You sure?" I teased, knowing the moment had passed. Regretful, but that was how it went sometimes.

"Yeah, I am," she said, but I heard the trace of remorse in her voice.

"No problem." I turned and headed toward the stairs. "Nice encounter with you, Ava."

"Is that what you'll call it?" she asked, sounding curious.

I paused and looked back at her. Her cheeks were flushed, her mouth swollen from mine. Her hair was no longer perfect, one long strand hanging on the left side to her shoulder.

"No." I winked before I walked away. "I'll think about it as one of the greatest kisses that got me nowhere—ever."

I didn't wait to see how she would respond. I bounded up the stairs and turned the corner before I could change my mind and ask her again.

I wasn't the begging sort.

I waited and heard the sound of a door closing and a car backing away. I peered around the corner, watching her leave, the taste of regret strong. I headed to the room I'd had for the last few nights, avoiding my final destination for as long as I could.

Inside the room, my one real constant waited for me. He lifted his head, his tail wagging fast as I walked in. He leaped off the bed, greeting me enthusiastically. I patted his head, his amber eyes gentle and patient.

"Hey, boy. You ready for a walk?"

His tail went faster. I chuckled and reached for his lead. "Let's go. Have I got a story to tell you."

AVA

I leaned against the window, my arms crossed, gazing down at the floor. Behind me, the rain beat on the glass, the cool air outside making the window chilly. I studied my feet dispassionately, unable to settle into my usual routine.

I had tossed and turned all night, replaying my encounter with Hunter. The way his mouth felt on mine. The intensity of his stare. I had never seen eyes that color before now. Gracie's husband's eyes were a light blue, but Hunter's were so pale, they were almost silver at times. With the dark rim in indigo around the irises, they were startling in their beauty. Set in his rugged, handsome face, they were astounding. His mouth, his kiss had been exactly what I expected, yet not. Powerful, passionate, searing. I could feel his strength in his grip, the power of his arms, and the hardness of his body against mine. Yet underneath had been a gentleness. The way he cupped my face, how soft his lips felt on my skin, the way he whispered in my ear.

How quickly he backed away when I said no.

There had been no rancor, no anger. Instead, he teased and accepted my decision.

A huge part of me hated seeing him walk away. I swore I felt the pressure of his mouth on mine for hours afterward. I ran my fingers over my mouth. I still did.

"Ava?"

With a jerk, I stood, realizing I had been leaning on the cool glass the same way I had been pressed against the side of my car by Hunter yesterday. I blinked and cleared my throat, smiling at my brother. "Hey, Liam."

He pushed off the doorframe, his massive shoulders filling the space. "Hey, you okay?"

"I'm fine. Why?"

"I've been standing there for five minutes. You've been so lost in thought, you didn't even notice." He smirked, his hazel eyes dancing. "And I'm sort of hard to miss."

I sat, waving off his concern. I looked down, brushing off my skirt to have a few seconds to collect my scattered thoughts.

"Is this about yesterday?"

My head snapped up. "Yesterday? How did—" I stopped and shook my head. "Oh, the clerk in the office."

He frowned. "What did you think I meant?"

"Nothing. I was thinking about something else. I'm fine."

He frowned and hunched forward. "You're distracted. I know you hate shit like that."

"I do. But I dealt with it, and I expect we'll be back on track quickly."

He nodded. "That's good."

"So, what's up? Are you here to plant more stuff or just check on me?"

He rolled his eyes. "I had breakfast with Dad and Maddox this morning. They heard from Mr. Owens's lawyer, and the offer has been rejected."

I felt a frisson of sadness in my chest. Mr. Owens owned the last piece of property connected to the BAM compound here in Port Albany. We had lived here all my life, and now our head office had recently moved here as well. They had tried unsuccessfully to purchase it while Mr. Owens was alive, but he rejected every offer. When he passed away in December, the house was closed up, and no one had appeared to move in. BAM had contacted the lawyer with a generous offer to purchase the land.

Despite his gruffness, I had liked Mr. Owens. I was one of the few people he allowed on his property, and I checked on him often. He had a stroke last year but recovered, though he had gotten frailer as the months went on. He refused to leave his house, and unbeknownst to him, BAM had paid for extra staff to care for him. He thought it was covered under the health care system, and I never dissuaded him. I had a feeling he would refuse the help because of who it came from. He disliked most people, it seemed, and especially the BAM boys, thinking they only wanted his property and nothing more.

But everyone remembered him from when we were kids and his wife, Gail, was still alive. He had been friendly and kind. My grandparents recalled a daughter but had no idea where she had disappeared to. Being the men they were, BAM made sure he was looked after. I would spend some time with him when he allowed, but I was never invited inside. I sat on the porch with him, and he would talk about Gail, the sunset, the water that we could watch from his porch, or whatever he felt like discussing. My family was off the table. No BAM talk. Nothing personal, aside from his wife and how he missed her.

I was sad when he passed, but I knew he would be happy to be back with "his Gail," as he called her. As per his instructions, there was no funeral, and he was cremated.

The news about the offer being rejected somehow didn't come as a shock. I shrugged. "He was adamant that BAM wouldn't get the land. I wonder if he'll sell to someone else."

"His lawyer says it's going to family."

"Oh. Well, maybe the daughter will reappear. Maybe she'll move in."

"No idea. Shame, though. I know you love that view. Dad was going to build two houses there, and one was for you."

"I know. It's fine. I love my little place."

I lived in the BAM compound in the smallest house we had. It was still generous, but it was more of a cottage than a house. It was tucked into a small break in the woods and had a simple floor plan. Two bedrooms, a lovely bathroom, an open concept living room/kitchen area, and a wide, screened-in porch I liked to sit in during the warm weather. I could see the water, but not the way you could on the bluff. The scope there was vast and mesmerizing.

He nodded. "Okay. I am off to 'plant some stuff,' as you say. Then I need to head home and see my girls."

"How are they?"

A warm smile crossed his lips, and his eyes were soft. "Awesome. Hal has all the adoption stuff started. Soon, they'll both be mine legally."

I smiled at his words. Liam had met Paige when our brother Ronan had started dating her roommate, Beth. He fell hard and fast for Paige—and her little girl, Lucy—and, to everyone's shock, had married her and moved them into his house at the compound in a short period of time. He had been steadfast in his determination, and I had to admit, I had never seen him happier. He was settled and calm. He loved being a daddy to Lucy, and she adored him. Paige was already pregnant, and he was so excited about welcoming a new baby into their lives. Our parents were over the moon. Grandbabies, Ronan's wedding, plus two more to follow, I was certain, with Paul and Jeremy both finding women they loved. Our family was expanding rapidly with my siblings all settling down.

That left me the single one of the group. It didn't bother me, although at times, seeing the closeness Liam shared with Paige, or Ronan with Beth, I felt a little tug in my chest. But the fear of opening myself up again was too great. I liked being single, answering to no one. One serious crash and burn was enough. I'd had a few relationships since then, but they were casual and ended amicably. I never let my heart get involved again.

"I'm happy for you."

He stood. "Come for dinner one night. Just you. I mean, family is great, but—"

I laughed. When we were all together, it was loud and crazy. Lots of voices talking, raucous laughter, and tons of teasing. And that was just my immediate family. When other households in the compound joined in, it was nothing short of chaotic. It was nice to do the small gatherings on occasion.

"I'll call Paige. I'll bring dinner too, so she doesn't have to cook."

He grinned. "DoorDash, you mean?"

I laughed with him. I wasn't much of a cook, except breakfast and spaghetti. Those, I did well. The rest of my repertoire was simple and limited. So, Liam was right. DoorDash and I were great friends.

I held up my finger. "This wields great power."

He laughed as he walked out of my office.

"That it does, my sister. That it does."

CHAPTER 4

AVA

Saturday afternoon, I wandered around the beach. The sun was high in the sky, its warmth welcome as I strolled. I headed to the far edge, disappearing around the outcropping of tall rocks. The beach became stonier, large boulders and huge rocks piled up, tossed around like feathers in the water and ending up in this cove over hundreds of years. BAM chose to leave this portion wild and let nature do her thing. As kids, we had spent many happy days exploring the rocky expanse, but now I used it to sit and watch the water, a private place. I knew a lot of us did the same, yet we rarely ran into each other here.

It was also the break between us and the Owenses' property. BAM owned the stretch of beach, but at the end was a rarely used trail that led up to Mr. Owens's place. It was overgrown but still passable, or at least, it had been last year when I would go to visit. I usually took the easier route, skirting the two properties, when I would go to visit him, but occasionally I would take the shorter way of crossing the rocky beach and climbing the hill.

Perched on a flat rock, I enjoyed the view of the water and sipped from an insulated cup of coffee, appreciating the smooth flavor. Jaxson, Gracie's husband, had turned us all on to his favorite brand of coffee, and I especially loved it.

I lifted my face to the sun, letting the warmth soak into my skin for a minute. The muted sound of music drifted in the air, and I frowned, tilting my head, unsure where it was coming from. It stopped and I shrugged. Dad was probably testing some new speakers around the pool area, although usually you couldn't hear them this far away. I pulled off the sweater I had wrapped around my waist and rolled it, tucking it behind my head and leaning back against the boulder, breathing in the fresh air deeply and letting the week drift away. I planned to do nothing the rest of the weekend. Hang around my little house, do some laundry, sleep in tomorrow, and hopefully poach dinner off my parents. I was sure they would be grilling something delicious since my dad loved to barbecue. Maybe if I was lucky, he and Maddox would have decided to use the smoker and do some ribs or brisket. I'd luck out with dinner and leftovers.

Another sound met my ears, and I sat up as the music started again—faint, but it was there.

I began to stand, freezing as a big golden retriever came into view. He stopped briefly upon seeing me, then his tail began to wag and he jogged over, his tongue hanging out. He greeted me with a low woof, standing in front of me, waiting.

Unsure, I held out my hand, and he sniffed it then came closer, head-butting me gently. I patted his large head, gazing into his gentle amber eyes.

"Hey, you. Where did you come from?"

I got another low "woof," his tail wagging furiously.

"Are you lost, boy?" I asked, running my hand over his long back. He was well cared for, his coat shiny, his eyes clear, and it was obvious he was well-fed. He was strong and agile.

But where had he come from?

I ran my hand over his neck, but there was no collar.

A flash of light caught my eye, and I looked toward it. It came from the bluff. Mr. Owens's place. I looked down at the dog, who was watching me happily, not joining me in my concern for his misplaced whereabouts.

Obviously, someone was at Mr. Owens's place. Maybe his daughter had shown up. That would explain the music and the dog. I huffed out a breath in irritation. How irresponsible not to keep him on a leash. He had wandered down here, but he could have walked off the bluff or into the water. Someone could have picked him up and taken him. He was a beautiful, friendly dog.

I shook my head. "Let's go, boy."

I made my way across the rocky shore, carefully scrambling over the damp stone and moss-covered areas. I cursed my sandals that slipped at times.

"If I had known you were going to show up, I would have worn sneakers," I griped to the dog, who followed me, his tail wagging, not at all bothered by the treacherous stretch of beach. He loped and sniffed, returning to my side every few moments. We reached the overgrown path leading up the side of the bluff, and I eyed it speculatively. Had it always been that steep?

I shook my head and began to climb. Twice, I stumbled, once going down hard on my knee. I cursed under my breath and wiped off my jeans, muttering when I discovered a hole in the fabric.

"Dammit, I liked these jeans," I muttered, but I kept going.

The music was getting louder and clearer. Garth Brooks was belting out one of his catchy tunes, and I could hear the sound of a saw being used. Work was being done on the house, and I wondered if that meant it was going to be for sale or we would have a new neighbor.

As we got to the top of the bluff, the dog raced ahead of me, wagging his tail. I stood for a moment to catch my breath, and he stopped, as if waiting. I cocked my head to the side, studying the large black truck in front of me. It was familiar. My stomach clenched as I moved toward it, recalling why it was familiar.

Intense fire-and-ice eyes came to my mind. Strong arms and a wicked, passionate mouth that was possessive and gentle poked at my memories.

I rounded the back of the truck and stopped, the dog sitting down beside me.

There he was.

Hunter.

He didn't see me at first. I didn't interrupt him.

He was too busy dancing. I was too busy staring.

His jeans hugged his ass. His T-shirt was stretched tight across his back and arms. His hair glinted in the sunlight.

And his hips moved. Gyrated. His torso bent and swayed. His arms rose and fell with the beat of the music. He sang, his voice rich and deep, his feet and body keeping perfect rhythm with the song. He spun on his heels and froze. Our eyes locked and held.

And, unexpectedly, he smiled. Wide and carefree. He held out his hand.

"Dance with me, Little Dragon."

I found myself taking his hand. Joining him under the sun. Letting him lead me, spin me around, pull me to his hot, sunbaked chest as we moved. He crooned in my ear, making me laugh. He joined me, the sound of our shared amusement fading away as the song ended and we broke apart. Slowly, carefully, as if neither of us wanted this moment to end.

I turned to face him, my breathing ragged. I was out of shape, obviously, since that was the only acceptable reason for my short-ness of breath. It had nothing to do with his close proximity. Or the way his eyes were slowly devouring me. It especially had no bearing on the fact that I had been held against his hard, firm body and I wanted to be back there again.

Nope.

I blinked and cleared my throat.

"Um, hello."

He laughed, the sound loud in the sudden quiet.

"Hello, Little Dragon." He looked around. "Am I missing some-thing? Is a crime being committed, and you're here, once again, to foil the evildoers' plans?"

A smile tugged on my lips, and I tried not to laugh.

"The crime is that I found this dog on the beach down there." I pointed over the bluff. "Shouldn't he be on a lead?"

He frowned and tapped his leg. "Cash, come here."

The dog trotted to his side, gazing up at him with adoration. Hunter crouched down, running his hand over his neck. "How did you get off your leash?" Then he shook his head. "Where the hell is your collar?"

"That's what I was wondering. He could have been hurt or taken," I reprimanded him.

He narrowed his eyes. "He has one. He keeps getting off it, dammit." He walked toward the huge oak tree closer to the house. He bent and picked up a long lead, a collar dangling from the end. "How is he doing this?"

"You didn't notice he was gone?"

"When I checked him fifteen minutes ago, he was asleep on the porch, collar intact. Nothing indicated he had moved." He narrowed his eyes at Cash. "You little bugger. That's twice." He glanced up at me. "I caught him yesterday and tightened the collar." He held it up, and I took it from his hands, examining it.

"Um, this bit is broken." I showed him. "It looks like it's fastening, but all he has to do is yank it, and he's free."

Hunter stood and shook his head. "Well then, I guess he's housebound until I get a new one."

As if he knew what Hunter had said, Cash flopped down onto the ground, exhaling a long, low whimper.

Without thinking, I unbuckled my belt and pulled it from the loops. I bent and wrapped it around Cash's neck. "If you cut this and add a hole here, this would work temporarily. You can clip the lead here."

Hunter frowned. "It would ruin your belt."

I laughed. "It's old, and I don't care." I patted Cash's head. "I hate to think of him cooped up in the house on such a great day."

For a moment, Hunter said nothing, then he stopped and took the belt. He walked away, and I watched him covertly, admiring the way his jeans hugged his ass and thighs. He grabbed some tools from his truck and returned a moment later, the belt cut, a new hole in place. He fastened it around Cash's neck.

"Say thank you to Ava. The Little Dragon saved you from being locked inside, you pain in the ass." But his words were said without venom, and he stroked Cash's great head, his touch gentle.

He stood, his gaze lingering, then he frowned. "Why is there blood on your jeans?"

I glanced down. "Oh, I tripped coming up the path."

One moment, I was standing. The next, I was in his arms, being carried to the back of the truck.

"What the hell are you doing?" I yelped, clutching his shoulders.

He sat me on the edge of the open truck bed, pushing up my jeans. "Jesus, that's a deep cut," he muttered. He leaned across me, pressing me into his body as he rummaged behind me. His heat soaked into me the same way it did the other day. His scent filled my nose, warm and rich. I tried not to whimper.

He opened a first aid box, muttering the whole time. He refused to let me move as he cleaned and dressed the scrape. I gasped when the iodine hit my skin, and he muttered a terse apology, bending low and blowing on my knee. The pain faded as he lifted his gaze and our eyes locked.

He stilled, his eyes becoming liquid fire. They mesmerized me, stopping all coherent thought. Who he was, why he was here, didn't matter. All that mattered was he was close and I wanted him closer. As if he knew what I was thinking, he stepped nearer, his body crowding between my legs. He settled his hands on either side of me, trapping me fully with his body.

"Should I kiss it and make it better?" he murmured, his voice raspy.

I lifted my arms, draping them over his shoulders. I slid my fingers into the thick hair that swept the back of his neck. He shivered and pushed closer, his mouth hovering over mine. "I think I need to make sure everything is in working order."

I pulled him to my mouth. "Yes, yes, you do."

His lips touched mine, and everything else disappeared.

He wrapped his arm around my waist, dragging me close to his chest as he kissed me. He tasted of coffee and mint, his lips slightly damp and salty from sweat. His tongue stroked along mine, exploring and possessive. He spread his hand wide on my back, his fingers pressing into my skin. He slid his other hand under my ass, lifting me closer. I felt his need pressing into me, driving my own up into a frenzy. Our tongues dueled and fought, retreated, and met again. He groaned low in his throat, and I whimpered as his hand slid closer to my center, the heat pooling and swirling in a whirl of desire. I gripped his neck, tugging on his hair, craving I had never experienced making me crazy.

Until a long, low howl came from the porch, and Hunter startled, stepping back. Our eyes clashed, desire burning. He ran a hand through his hair and cleared his throat. He broke our gaze to look over at Cash, who had somehow wrapped his lead around the broken post column and was trapped half on and half off the porch.

"You crazy mutt, why don't you ever stay where I put you?" he muttered and headed over to free him.

I slid off the truck end, my legs shaky and breathing uneven. What the hell was I doing kissing Hunter?

Again, a little voice in my head whispered.

I had no idea who this man was. Or why I kept letting him kiss me. I knew better. The man was a stranger and, for all I knew, trespassing.

Reality returned, and I marched over to him. He straightened as I approached, my belt in his hand, Cash lying on the porch, looking happy to be free of it.

"Who are you anyway?" I demanded. "Why are you on Mr. Owens's property?"

He narrowed his eyes. "I think the question is, why are you on my property?"

"*Your* property?"

He settled his hands on his hips. "My property. I inherited it from my grandfather." He glanced in the direction I had come from. "The beach down there is private property as well. Why were you on it?" His narrowed eyes became a fierce glare. "Who the hell are *you*?"

Mr. Owens had a grandson?

"I'm Ava Callaghan. I knew your grandfather," I offered, trying to understand.

"Callaghan?" he repeated. A deep frown crossed his face. "You're *her.* You're also one of *them.*" He shook his head. "The property isn't for sale. Stop snooping around. Get off it."

You're her? What the hell did he mean by that?

"*One of them? Snooping around?*" I gasped. "I was bringing your dog back to you!"

"Well, you've done that, so you can leave now." He turned his back, clearly dismissing me. His voice had gone from low and warm to furious and cold. His shoulders were stiff with tension, and he walked away. "You're not welcome here, Ms. Callaghan. Leave my property," he called over his shoulder. "Don't come back."

Furious, I stomped away, not looking back.

What an asshole.

I stopped at the top of the pathway. "If I had known who you were the other day, I wouldn't have helped you!" I yelled.

"I wouldn't have let you either," he snarled back.

"I damn well wouldn't have kissed you," I mumbled, somehow knowing that was a lie.

I muttered all the way down the path and across the beach. I was so angry, I did it in record time, not slipping once. When I reached the large rock that jutted out and separated the two coves, I turned, surprised to see Hunter standing on the bluff, watching me.

No doubt to make sure I left and wasn't *snooping around.*

What an asshole.

I flipped him the bird and rounded the rock onto the sandy beach.

Obviously, our new neighbor wasn't going to like us any more than the old one had.

I dismissed the feeling of sadness that welled up inside my chest at the thought.

CHAPTER 5
AVA

Later that afternoon, I went over to my parents' house. They were on their deck, enjoying the sun. Bentley, Maddox, Emmy, and Dee were with them. Bottles of wine were open, and a large platter of antipasto sat in the middle of the table. The fragrant aroma of the spicy meats and cheeses was too much to resist, and I grabbed a plate and filled it. My dad slid a glass of crisp, delicious Riesling my way, and I sipped it in appreciation.

It always amazed me that the three men who worked together every day still hung out with one another during their off time. But they were incredibly close, and their friendship was legendary. Their wives had been best friends before marrying each of the men, and they were the rocks of our little community. I had loved growing up in Port Albany. The water, the fresh air, the endless scope of the horizon. My brother Liam was the same way. Ronan, one of the triplets, loved it here as well. Paul and Jeremy—the other two-thirds of the triplets—preferred the bustle of Toronto but spent a lot of weekends and holidays here. Our parents were thrilled whenever we were all together. All the families that lived here had those who came and went. Some stayed, some visited, but it was the nucleus that kept us all grounded.

Just after I sat down, Sandy and Jordan appeared, hugs and kisses happening with everyone. They were our adopted Nan and Pops and were adored by everyone. My dad watched Jordan carefully maneuver the deck with his walker and sit down.

"How's the knee?"

Pops patted his leg. "Better every day." He regarded Sandy fondly. "Someone is taking great care of me. Making me do my exercises and keeping me off my boat."

Dad laughed. "The boat will be there when you're ready. Far too unstable with your recent surgery." He winked at Sandy. "Good job."

She laughed, accepting a glass of wine. "Pain-in-the-ass patient."

Her words reminded me of this morning, and I spoke.

"I met our new neighbor today."

All eyes turned to me.

"His dog got off his lead and was wandering the beach. I returned him," I explained.

Bentley frowned. "His? Not the daughter?" He glanced at Sandy. "What was her name?"

"Nina."

I shook my head. "Her son, I think." I barked a laugh. "He takes after his grandfather. Ordered me off the property. He said he inherited it."

Sandy pursed her lips. "I had heard the daughter died years ago, but I never knew if it was true. After Gail—Mrs. Owens—died, Jack shut down." She smiled my way. "You probably don't remember her."

"I have a vague recollection. She always had cookies."

Sandy nodded. "Yes. They were private, but friendly. Nina was wild when she was young, and they struggled. She left home before she even graduated. I think it broke her mother's heart. They became distant. Once Gail died…" She stopped talking. "Well, things were never the same. Jack closed himself off."

"Well, the grandson is pretty closed off as well."

Unless he's dancing in the sun. Or kissing me, I added in my head.

"Maybe once he settles in, he'll be friendlier. Unless he's not planning on staying?" Maddox asked.

"I have no idea. He was at city hall the other day trying to get some planning permission, so obviously, he is fixing the place up. To stay or sell, I have no idea."

Bentley picked up his wine. "Darren Thomas called me." He smirked after he swallowed, regarding me over the rim of his glass. "He assured me our permits will be ready this week. He also said you were a force to be reckoned with and wants to put you on his payroll."

I laughed. "Not interested. Is that dreadful man gone?"

He nodded. "He came from Toronto to fill in while Milly was away on sick leave. Darren thinks his superiors wanted him out of Toronto and pushed him his way as a *favor*." He lifted his fingers in quotations. "Darren ended his contract, launched an investigation, and was told it would be handled."

Maddox snorted. "Typical government. Pass the buck."

Bentley nodded. "As long as we don't have to deal with it. I told Darren I would put out some feelers in Toronto at city hall." He sat back with a grin, laying his arm over the back of his chair so his hand rested on Emmy's shoulder. "I assured him I had some influence there. That man needs to be removed from any job where he has a chance of doing that shit."

As he spoke, he tugged the shawl on Emmy's arm higher to her shoulder, tucking it tight. It was an unconscious move on his part, a tender act he performed without thinking. She let him fuss over her, a small smile on her lips. I loved seeing his gentle side with her and his family. It was vastly different from the tough businessman he was during the week.

"How old is the grandson?" Mom asked.

I shrugged. "Older than me. Younger than you. Forties, I guess?"

"Maybe we should invite him for dinner," Emmy mused.

I barked a laugh. "Don't bother—he won't come. He called me 'one of them' and told me to leave him alone. I think we'll probably see about as much of him as we did Mr. Owens. Even less. He has no interest in being neighborly."

Dee and my mom shook their heads. "How sad."

I thought about the way he looked when he was dancing. His smile. How his mouth felt on mine. The way he had fussed over me when he saw the cut on my knee. How incredibly right it had felt to be in his arms. The fact that I doubted I would ever feel that again. I doubted I would ever see him again unless it was as a distant figure on the bluff.

I had to agree—it was sad.

Sunday morning, I slept in. I gave myself every Sunday to just be Ava. After getting up, I lounged around all day, wandered the beach, and relaxed. I soaked in the huge tub my dad had installed for me, read romance books, and indulged in chocolate, coffee, and watched the water. It was my day to unwind and rejuvenate. Prepare for another week of being a woman in a man's world and having to be on guard all the time. I left my hair loose, painted my toes, wore frilly blouses and torn jeans, and enjoyed the quiet.

The sky was duller today, but it was still pleasant. I carried a cup of coffee to the beach and sat in a chair on the sand, enjoying the breeze on my face. I waved at Ronan and Beth on their deck, spied a few other people around, but stayed in my little spot close to the rocks. I would see people later. I didn't venture to the rocky side of the beach. No doubt Hunter would accuse me of spying or some such nonsense. The sun broke through the clouds, its appearance welcome. With a long sigh, I wound my hair into a loose knot, tilted my head up, letting the sounds of the water and the wind wash over me. I enjoyed the quiet and solitude, slowly drifting until the feel of a cold, wet something touched my hand, and I jumped in fright. Sitting beside me on the beach was Cash. His great head was cocked, and he studied me, his tail slowly thumping on the packed sand.

"What are you doing here?" I asked.

He inched closer, laying his head on the arm of the chair, looking up at me. Unable to resist, I stroked his fur, running my hand over his neck.

"How did you get out of your collar again?" I murmured.

He issued a low "woof," and I shook my head.

"I don't speak dog." I rolled my eyes. "I suppose your master is going to come for you and accuse me of kidnapping you or some such nonsense." I pointed in the direction of the bluff. "Home, Cash. Go home now!"

He stared at me, his expression almost comical. He huffed a low whine and flopped on the beach, resting his head on his paws.

"Dammit," I cursed. "Go see Ronan or my dad. They can take you home." I'd let them figure out where the dog belonged.

He thumped his tail, not moving.

"Stubborn as your master, I see."

He exhaled.

"Why does he dislike us? My family, I mean? Well, I guess he dislikes me too, except for the kissing part—" I stopped. "Holy shit," I muttered. "I'm talking to a dog. *His* dog, no less."

I stood. "Come on, boy. I'll show you the way home."

With a happy bark, Cash stood, waiting.

"You are such a pain in the ass," I told him. "Just like your owner."

I swear he grinned at me.

Five times I stopped while crossing the rocky beach. I pointed to the bluff where I could see the truck. "Home! Go home!"

Cash would stare at me and sit. If I tried to turn around, he followed me. I was at a loss for what else to do, so I led him to the path up to the bluff.

I pointed. "Go!"

He trotted ahead, and satisfied, I pivoted, planning on heading back to the beach. Cash barked, bounding back down the incline. I dropped my head, huffing in vexation.

I followed him back to the trail and stayed behind him. As soon as he saw Hunter, he'd forget about me. I waited until he was almost at the top, and I stopped, then turned to go.

Cash halted, barking loudly and heading back toward me. I met him partway up the slope.

"Look," I said, dropping to my haunches. "Your mean master doesn't want me around. If I show up, he'll probably throw me off the bluff. Now, *go* home." I pointed. "*Now.*"

Cash licked my face, and I pushed him away. "Again like your master. Licking me. Eww."

"You weren't saying 'eww' yesterday." I startled at the sound of Hunter's low voice. "Unless your moaning was covering it up."

Cash bounded up the trail, his tail wagging. Hunter looked down at me from the top of the bluff, his arms crossed.

I braced myself for his wrath.

"He showed up on my beach. I didn't encourage him. I was trying to get him home."

"I know," he surprised me by saying. "I watched you ineffectually leading him this way." He shook his head. "How is it you can put some asshole clerk in an ill-fitting suit in his place and not be able to send my dog home?"

"I tried." I crossed my arms. "He's as pigheaded as you are."

He lifted one eyebrow, regarding me in silence. When he spoke, I swore he was trying to hold in his laughter.

"I don't appreciate you disparaging me in front of my dog. He'll lose respect, and I'll have to rebuild his trust."

My lips quirked, and I tried not to laugh.

"I speak only the truth. He refused to come without me."

"Well then, I suppose I owe you a cold drink for your efforts." He held out his hand. "Come on up."

I blinked and looked around. I peered over the edge, wondering if he was drawing me closer so he could indeed throw me off. He laughed at my hesitation.

"I'll behave."

"I haven't seen much evidence of that so far," I muttered, slowly walking up the incline.

I accepted his hand nearer the top and let him pull me the last few feet. I stumbled a little, and he gripped my arms, holding me upright.

"Okay?" he asked.

"Yes, I'm fine." I indicated Cash, who was lying on the porch, looking innocent. "How did he get off the lead?"

Hunter scratched his head. "I can't find it. I swear the little fucker hid it. I tied him to the porch, and he got out."

"Maybe you should change his name to Houdini."

He chuckled. "I'll go buy a new collar tomorrow. After you leave, I'll lock him in the house." He pointed to the chairs I used to sit in with Mr. Owens. "I'll get us a cold drink. Sit."

I sat down, grateful for the canvas overhang. I peered up at it, noticing it was getting threadbare in places. It would have to be replaced soon.

Hunter came out and handed me a lemonade, the glass filled with ice, clinking against the rim. He pushed his hair off his forehead, only for it to fall back into place.

"I have this or water."

"I figured you for a beer guy."

"I'm out."

"Ah." I sipped my lemonade, absently scratching Cash's head. He'd come to lie beside me on the porch, one paw draped over my feet.

Hunter looked down, pausing before he took a swallow of lemonade. He scratched at the back of his neck.

"Nice toes."

I glanced down and shrugged. "I like pretty colors on my feet." Last night after my bath, I had painted my toes a bright cherry red and added sparkles to the big toe. I wiggled them so the light caught the sparkles. "Want me to do yours?" I asked playfully.

Hunter snorted. "Yeah, sure. Maybe we could do each other's hair too."

"And I'll wax your eyebrows," I said seriously.

He blinked. "I don't think so."

I giggled at his incredulous look. "Teasing," I assured him. "Your brows are fine." I paused. "But your hair *could* use a trim."

He actually chuckled at my remark. "I know. I need to find a barber."

"Avoid the one in town. My brother tried them last year. It took almost six months until his hair grew back normal." I smirked at the memory. Liam had looked as if he had done it himself, in the dark, with dull scissors.

He grunted, pushing his hair off his forehead again.

"You finding everything okay?" I asked, determined to be friendly.

He leaned forward, resting his elbows on his knees. "It's a time capsule in there," he admitted. "But I'm figuring it out."

"Oh?"

He sipped his lemonade. I tried not to notice how his neck muscles worked as he swallowed.

I failed.

"It feels as if I am still five, walking through the door. I don't think much changed inside since I lived there."

"You lived with your grandparents?" I asked, shocked. No one had ever mentioned that fact.

His face became shadowed. "Briefly. More of an extended visit."

He abruptly changed the subject. "What did Cash interrupt? Will your burly boyfriend be following you shortly to find out where you are?"

I laughed. "I was sitting on the beach, enjoying the breeze and the sun."

His gaze flickered over me. "You don't burn? Your skin looks as if it would."

I shook my head. "I wear strong block."

"And the boyfriend?" he prompted.

"No boyfriend, burly or otherwise." I met his gaze. "Do you think I'm the sort of woman who would kiss someone while she had a boyfriend?"

He shrugged. "I have no idea what kind of woman you are."

"Well, I'm not," I snipped.

"Good to know." He paused. "But you are the sort of woman who paints your toenails and puts purple streaks in your hair."

"I like them. My mom has them as well. It's fun."

For a moment, there was silence. I looked up to find his gaze on me. Steady, intense blue fire studying me.

"I want to see."

"Pardon?" I whispered, my throat suddenly dry.

His voice was no more than a murmur on the breeze. "Let your hair down. I want to see how it looks."

I swallowed. "I'll show you if you let me cut your hair."

He narrowed his eyes. "Cut my hair?"

He kept fidgeting with his hair, brushing it off his face and lifting it off the back of his neck. A few snips of the scissors would erase that uncomfortable feeling. And if I was honest, I was dying to feel the silky strands under my fingers again.

"I know how. It would save you a trip into Grimsby to find a decent barber. Do you have scissors?"

He drained his glass, pursing his lips in thought. "Fine." He went over to his truck, digging in the large tool chest. He held up a pair of sharp-looking scissors, still in their case. "Will these do?"

I examined them. "Yep."

"You're going to cut my hair, not my neck, right?"

"Unless you're overly critical."

He lifted one eyebrow. "I can be pleasant."

I snorted. "We'll see. Go wet your hair and bring a chair."

He hesitated, then nodded, disappearing into the house.

I clasped my hands on my chest. After the argument we had yesterday, I shouldn't even be here. I should have returned his dog to him and left. But there was a draw between us I was unable to ignore, no matter what I tried. I shook my head in frustration. I wasn't acting like myself.

What the hell was I doing?

He reappeared, carrying a yellow-vinyl-covered kitchen chair. His hair was wet, and he had a towel draped over his shoulders and chest.

His bare chest. His sweats hung low on his hips, offering me a tantalizing glimpse of his vee.

I swallowed the last of my lemonade, choking and sputtering. He frowned and came over, awkwardly patting me on the back.

"You okay?"

I nodded, unable to speak. Finally, I managed to clear my throat. "Need a comb."

He dug into his back pocket and held one out. "Got it."

He lowered himself into the chair, and I blew out a long breath. His chest and abdomen were a road map of muscles leading down to a trim waist and lean hips. Tight ridges and thick cords rippled under his skin. His biceps flexed as he rubbed his hair.

I circled the chair slowly, pretending to look at his hair but drinking in the sight of him instead. His shoulders were broad, his back muscular. His chest and arms were dusted with hair, but it was light in color. His skin was tanned from all the time he spent outdoors.

He was gorgeous, and my fingers itched to touch him.

I plucked the towel from his hands and rubbed it over his head, then draped it over his shoulders.

"A trim," he stated firmly. "I don't want to resemble that description of your brother."

I ran the comb through his hair, and he grasped my wrist, lifting his head and meeting my eyes.

"I'm trusting you, Little Dragon."

I could only nod.

For a moment, there was silence. I combed and snipped, being careful to only take a little. Slowly Hunter relaxed, his shoulders losing their stiffness. I hummed as I worked, enjoying the chance to touch him freely, tilting his head to the side, laying a hand on his shoulder as I studied the result, lifting up his chin to make sure the length was equal. He watched me with his intense gaze as I edged closer to work on the top. I nudged his legs, and he opened his knees widely, letting me step between them. I stilled briefly as he rested his hands on my hips. I felt the heat of his touch through the loose linen drape of my pants, but when I glanced down, his eyes were closed.

"Not too short," he murmured.

"Nope," was my breathless retort. I cleared my throat. "What did you mean yesterday when you said 'You're her'?"

There was a pause before he spoke. "I had heard your name."

"That's it?"

"Yes."

I could tell he wasn't going to say any more, so I shut up. I really didn't want to argue with him again. I'd find out eventually.

I concentrated on the task at hand, finally ending up at the crown. "How short do you want the front?"

"Short enough I can look at you clearly," he rasped. He opened his eyes, his focus powerful. Icy fire burned me. My breath caught in my throat. My hands froze. In one swift move, he wrapped his arm around me, shifted his legs, and lifted me to his lap.

He plucked the scissors from my hand, tossing them to the ground. He spread his hand wide across my back, pulling me close. "Do you have any idea how good you smell?" He groaned. "How I can feel your body move, sense your heat?"

I whimpered, sliding my hands around his neck and into the shorn hair at the nape.

"How fucking good your little fingers feel on my skin?" He yanked me tight to his chest, his heat soaking into my skin, the sheer strength of him pressing on me.

"You owe me something," he growled.

I stared at him.

"Take down your hair."

I reached up and loosened the clip, letting my hair fall. He wove his hands into it, tugging on the strands and bending my neck back. He dragged his mouth along the column of my throat.

"Sexy," he groaned. "You are so fucking sexy, Little Dragon."

He pulled my face to his and covered my mouth. He caressed my skull, cupping my head in his large hands. His tongue stroked along mine, the taste of him overwhelming my senses. I was adrift on a sea of sensation. His body against mine. The sun on my back. His hands in my hair. His low groans. His erection pressed between us. I shifted, wanting closer. Wanting more. He cursed as I rose, slipping my hand under his waistband.

He was commando.

His erection filled my hand—hot, hard, and rigid. He cupped my ass, a low rumble of satisfaction in his chest. He kissed me harder. Deeper. Possessive was the only word echoing in my mind. I stroked him, velvet over steel, running my thumb in circles over the head. He bucked, his mouth never leaving mine, his kiss becoming so desperately erotic I thought I would explode. I had never been kissed so carnally. It was as if he were fucking my mouth, his tongue doing things I had only ever read of.

He said my name. Repeated it louder.

Reality hit me. That wasn't Hunter talking. The voice saying my name was shouting, and it belonged to my brother.

I leaped back as if I'd been burned. Hunter startled, reaching for me. "What—"

Then he heard it as well and stood. I hurried toward the edge of the bluff and waved at Liam.

"Jesus, Ava," he yelled. "I've been looking for you. Your chair and sunglasses are on the beach, your hat is in the water. You fucking scared me!"

"Sorry," I called down. "I was returning the dog." I patted Cash's head when he appeared beside me. "Hunter gave me a glass of lemonade. I'll be right there!" I added as he moved closer. This was not the right time for those two to meet. I glanced over my shoulder where Hunter stood, a fresh wave of desire hitting me.

"I have to go," I said.

He nodded and called for Cash, who trotted over. I waited until they disappeared into the house, and I headed down the incline to join Liam on the beach.

"Sorry," I panted. "I lost track of time."

"You're out of breath."

"I was playing with the dog. Throwing the ball and such."

Or playing with Hunter's balls.

Same thing, really.

"So, we have a new neighbor?"

"Yes," I said shortly.

"And the dog?" Liam questioned. "He biting your neck and mussing your hair, Ava?"

I tossed my head. "Shut up. Leave it alone, Liam."

"Whatever. You fucking scared me. Don't leave your stuff that close to the water and disappear."

I tucked my arm into his and squeezed. "I'm sorry."

He flung his arm over my shoulder and hugged me. "I'm glad you're okay. And sorry if I, ah, interrupted anything."

I couldn't tell him what he had interrupted. Or that it was probably best that he had. Things had progressed fast with Hunter. Far too fast. It seemed as soon as we were close, we both lost whatever common sense we possessed.

Still, I felt a small quiver of sadness when I glanced back and saw him standing on the bluff, watching us walk away. I wondered if he was relieved or was feeling the same pang of regret that we were interrupted?

Would he finish what I started?

I had to cover my laugh with a cough.

I might have to ask him next time.

CHAPTER 6

HUNTER

I picked up the building permit Tuesday morning. There was an older woman in the office now, and she was friendly, introducing herself as Milly and answering the few questions I had. I stopped at the pet store, selected a new collar, then bought a few groceries. I sat in my truck, using the information Milly had given me, and arranged for a disposal bin to be delivered by Thursday. I had to start cleaning out the house. It was going to take me a while to go through everything that my grandfather had squirreled away in the place. I hadn't been kidding when I told Ava the house was a time capsule. I doubted much had changed since I had been there as a child. As fuzzy as my memories were, some things were very familiar as I walked through the house.

I grabbed lunch at the small diner in town. It was still early, and the place was quiet. I decided on the all-day breakfast, and I opened the folder with the lists I had made of everything I needed to do back at my grandfather's house.

Or mine now, I supposed. It felt odd thinking of owning something. I wasn't staying, but I had plans to renovate and use the property for income. I never stayed anywhere very long. I rubbed my eyes, not wanting to think too deeply on that subject today. I didn't want to think about anything, especially not the one thing I couldn't seem to get out of my mind.

Ava.

From the moment I had first seen her, she had fascinated me. Intrigued me. Our last two encounters had only cemented both sensations. Kissing her was dangerous. Having her close was an enticement I found too difficult to resist. That smart mouth of hers tempted. Her sexy laughter was an invitation to trouble. Even knowing she was part of the BAM family hadn't diminished the draw I felt toward her. After what happened on Sunday, I knew I had to stay away from her. I had the feeling she could throw my entire world into chaos.

It didn't stop her from popping into my head frequently, though.

I recalled the day I arrived in town and went to the lawyer's office. He went over the will, explaining the house and property as well as a small inheritance that was involved. I had been shocked enough finding out about my grandfather, never mind that he'd left me some money.

"What are your plans?" he asked.

"Do I have a choice?"

"Many. Keep it, fix it up and rent it, sell it." He shrugged. "It's yours now to do with what you want. But there is an interested party."

"Interested party?" I asked.

He only nodded, but I heard his secretary, Natasha, mutter something. She was younger than me, pretty, but there was a hard edge to her expression, as if she'd been wronged once too often.

Whatever she said, he ignored, and he handed me a copy of the will. "Your grandfather added a codicil not long ago, although it's a moot addition now. You can read this over. I'll make myself available for any questions you might have."

I left, standing outside, unsure what to do next. Go see the property and decide, perhaps. That seemed the best course of action.

Natasha came out, handing me a card, distaste in her voice. "Mr. Daniels asked me to give this to you. This is the company that wants the property if you were interested." She sniffed. "Your grandfather disliked them."

I glanced at the logo on the card. BAM.

"Why?" I asked.

"They pressured him. Always snooping around the property, making up excuses to be on it. He complained to me more than once." She leaned close. "Rich, entitled snobs, they are. Too good for any of us around here. Always throwing their weight around. They own all the land around yours, and they wanted more." She shook her head. "They always want more. Your grandfather was sure they would ruin the entire landscape with their plans. He held firm."

I hated high-handed tactics. I had seen them too often in the various jobs I had held. If that was how this company worked, I wanted no part of them.

Yet, Ava didn't seem to be that way. But I didn't really know her. And I never would.

I shook my head from my thoughts and returned to studying the lists on the table. Someone slid into the booth across from me, and I looked up, surprised to meet the beautiful eyes of none other than the woman herself. Ava Callaghan. She was in full business mode, a dark green suit hugging her torso, her hair swept into a knot at the base of her neck, the purple streaks barely visible. A silky-looking white blouse peeked out from under her jacket, and her makeup was minimal.

She was stunning.

"That seat is taken," I said dryly.

Her eyes danced in the sunlight filtering through the windows. "It is now."

My waitress came over and placed my meal in front of me. She smiled at Ava. "Coffee?"

"No," I said at the same time Ava nodded.

"Please, Connie. And some rye toast."

Good God, was there anyone this woman didn't know?

Connie looked between us and shrugged, walking away.

"I don't remember asking you to join me."

She grinned, not at all put out by my tone. "I felt it. It's one of my superhero talents. I can hear your inner voice."

I picked up my utensils. "I hope you can hear what my inner voice is saying right at this moment. In case you're unclear, that's not 'hey, you.'"

She giggled. A full-out, girlie giggle that seemed so out of place given her outfit and the vibe she was putting off.

The sound made me want to smile.

Which pissed me off and I deepened my frown.

"Don't you have corrupt city officials to bother instead of me?"

"Nope, I'm all yours."

"Lucky me," I said sarcastically.

"Where's Cash?"

"Locked in the house, no doubt trying to figure out how to pick the lock and escape."

She grinned. "I'm sure he'll figure it out. He'll know how to hotwire the truck soon."

I had to chuckle.

She snagged a home fry off my plate, chewing it slowly.

"Hey, stop that," I snarled, trying to smack her hand when she reached for another one.

"I love their home fries," she protested.

"Get your own."

"I like yours." Then she snuck a piece of my toast.

Little thief.

I rolled my eyes and cut into the omelet. It was filled with ham, mushrooms, onions, and dripping with cheese. I closed my eyes briefly as I chewed. It was delicious, and I was starving. I wasn't much of a cook, and there was little in the way of food at the house.

Ava hummed across the table, and I opened my eyes, shocked to see her nibbling on a piece of my bacon with my coffee cup in her hand.

"What the hell are you doing?" I reached across the table and snagged the cup back. I was too late to grab the bacon. "That's mine."

"I love bacon," she informed me, as if that made it okay to steal it off my plate. "And I needed a sip. I don't see the problem. We've shared spit already."

I almost choked on the mouthful of coffee I was attempting to swallow.

My God, she had a smart mouth and the balls to use it.

Luckily, Connie came over and put the toast in front of Ava, plus her own cup of coffee, then refilled mine.

"Get her an order of bacon," I said. "Please," I added.

"I'm good." Ava waved her hand.

I met Connie's eyes. "Another order."

She was laughing as she moved away. I had to bite back a grin as Ava put a slice of her toast onto my side plate to replace the one she'd eaten. I had a feeling she'd take it back soon enough.

"You finished your hair," she observed, stabbing another potato on my plate.

Where the hell had she gotten that fork?

I glared at her. "Stop eating my breakfast." Then I turned the plate so she could get at the potatoes easier. She wasn't going to listen to me anyway.

I decided to give as good as I got.

"I finished everything you left incomplete," I said, eyeing her over the rim of my coffee cup.

She sputtered into her cup, setting it down and coughing into a napkin.

"I see. I hope it was satisfactory for you."

I tried not to smirk. It had been more than satisfactory. With the scent of her still on my skin and the taste of her in my mouth, there would have been only one thing better.

Being inside her.

As if reading my mind, she spoke. Her voice was quiet. "I'm sorry we were interrupted."

"I assume that was a brother?"

"Yes. Liam."

I grunted, eating more of my breakfast. She picked at the potatoes, which I had to admit were awesome with tons of onions and paprika in them. Her bacon arrived and she pushed it my way, and we ate it between us.

"I love bacon," she mused. "It should be its own food group."

I chuckled.

"It's best we were interrupted," I said finally, pushing away my empty plate.

She tilted her head. "Oh?"

"You're complicated, Ava. I don't do complicated."

"What makes you say that?"

I waved my hand. "Oh, let's see. A huge, rich family that owns all the land surrounding my property and wants to get their hands on it. You have a complete lack of respect for personal space and a habit of turning up in the oddest places. I value my privacy. I don't need your family or you pushing yourselves into my life. I'm here to work on the house, and that is it. I'll be gone in the not-too-distant future, so there is no potential for us."

I didn't know what I expected, but her reaction surprised me. She wasn't put out by my words. She shrugged.

"My family is huge, yes. Rich, yes. I'm not. I work hard and earn my money just like everyone else does. As for your property, they would like to buy it if it was for sale, but you've made it clear it is not, so they won't bother you about it. They made your grandfather very generous offers that he declined. They tried to be good neighbors, although he made it difficult at times." She paused, as if contemplating her next sentence.

"I understand wanting privacy. I like mine as well. I don't recall asking you for a future, nor planning one with you. Let me remind you that you asked to sleep with me first, not the other way around."

"I did," I acknowledged, falling silent as she kept talking.

"You seemed to be just fine with my lack of respect when your cock was in my hand and your tongue was down my throat."

I blinked.

Jesus.

She had a point, though.

I cleared my throat, tamping down my amusement. "But it's best nothing happened. In the long run, we'd both regret it, I think."

"I see," she said. "So, you have no desire to have sex with me anymore."

"It's not that. Not at all. Frankly, I'd give my left nut to have sex with you."

"Your *left* nut?" She frowned. "Are you left-handed?"

"No."

Her eyes twinkled. Danced with mischief.

"So, you wouldn't give your more predominant nut—the right one—to have sex with me. Only your slightly useless left one."

For a moment, I stared. Then I began to chuckle. The chuckle became a guffaw, which turned into a deep laugh. The kind you have to hold your stomach while emitting. I bent over, gasping for air as I shouted my amusement into my hand.

Who was this crazy, outspoken woman? And how did she make me feel this way—lighter and more relaxed than I could recall feeling every time I was in her presence?

Finally, I wiped my eyes. "You're a strange girl, Ava Callaghan." I swiped at my mouth with a napkin and stood, looking down at her. Before she could say anything, I bent down and kissed her briefly. Hard. Not caring who was watching.

"And yes, I'd give my right nut." Then I winked and tossed a couple of twenties on the table. "Breakfast is on me."

I was still laughing as I walked out of the restaurant.

My smile faded as I pulled up to the house, finding a car full of women waiting for me. I climbed out of the truck, grabbing the bags.

"Whatever you're selling, ladies, I'm not interested. And if you're some sort of welcome wagon, consider your job done."

I walked past them, nodding. "Have a good day."

"Oh, Ava didn't mention how handsome you were."

I stopped short at the sound of her name. "Ava?" I asked, narrowing my eyes. "Did she send you?"

The eldest woman stepped forward. Her hair was snow-white, her hazel eyes intelligent, and her voice clear.

"No, Ava didn't send us. In fact, she informed us you were private and to stay away. But seeing as you are our new neighbor and on your own, we wanted to welcome you and introduce ourselves."

Another woman spoke up. She held a covered dish in her hand. "That's what neighbors do." She eyed me speculatively. Her green gaze was bright, as was her smile. Her purple streaks and facial features let me know she was Ava's mother.

"I'm not here for long."

Another woman holding some sort of container laughed. "You're here now."

I hesitated, wanting to tell them to go away. I didn't do neighbors. I didn't do anyone. I preferred to be alone. That was what I knew. It was all I knew.

"I'd offer you coffee, but I'm afraid I have no way to make any. Maybe another time," I lied.

"Your grandfather sat outside drinking coffee all the time."

"I found a carafe," I admitted. "But no coffeemaker. It must have broken."

The older woman shook her head. "Stubborn like Jack, aren't you?" She stepped forward. "I'm Sandy Hayes. These ladies are Ava's mother, Cami, and her aunts, Emmy and Dee. Now open the door, young man, and I'll show you where the coffeemaker is."

I was going to argue but realized it would do me no good.

"I have a dog."

"We love dogs," Emmy insisted cheerfully. "And we brought scones."

Dammit. I loved scones.

"Fine," I said through gritted teeth. "Follow me. Watch Cash doesn't knock you over. He's crazy."

Twenty minutes later, it was as if a hurricane had torn through the kitchen.

Sandy had laughed when I'd shown her the carafe, and she had opened a cupboard, finding a plastic cone and filters. "You add the coffee here and pour boiling water over it," she explained. "It's called a drip coffeemaker."

"There's no kettle either."

"Your grandfather boiled water on the stove."

"I have no idea how to use the stove. It's propane-based."

"I'll show you," Dee insisted. "That's what we had before we had electricity and gas lines added to the houses."

While she was doing that and showing me how to use the ancient equipment, the other ladies performed some sort of miracle. The counter was cleaned, some containers of food put into the refrigerator after they explained each had instructions to reheat or cook. They unpacked the groceries I'd bought, clucking at the store I had been to.

"There is a much bigger one about twenty minutes from here. Better prices and selection," Emmy said.

"Okay," I mumbled.

The kitchen table with its plastic table cover was cleaned off, and mugs and plates for scones were set out. They had brought jam and butter with them, already in doubt, it seemed, over my ability to have items such as those on hand.

They were correct.

Cash made a huge liar out of me, greeting them calmly, lying down, and accepting their attention with a wag of his tail. He ate up the attentiveness and cooing, making me roll my eyes.

Then the women all sat and waited for me to join them. I had no choice but to pull up a chair and sit, wondering how the hell to get them out of the house—fast.

"So, Hunter. Ava says you're doing some work in here?" Sandy asked, looking around. She leaned forward. "I haven't been inside this house in twenty years, and it looks exactly as I remember it."

I snorted. "It looks the same as I remember it from thirty-plus years ago." I stopped talking, picking up my coffee. I had to admit, the carafe and filter thing were old, but the coffee tasted good. I might spring for a kettle, though.

"Yes, you stayed with your grandparents for a short time," Sandy mused. "Your, ah, mother…?" She trailed off.

"Dead," I said shortly.

All the women looked horrified at my terse answer.

"We weren't close," I stated.

"I see your truck has Alberta license plates on it. Is that where you live?" asked Cami, tilting her head and studying me. She looked like Ava, although Ava's eyes were unique and her expression was more mischievous.

"I've been there a year or so."

"And before?" she asked.

I waved my hand. "All over. Look, ladies, I appreciate the visit and all, but I'm not one to talk about myself, and I have a lot of work to do. I'll save you some time. The land isn't for sale. Not to you, not to anyone. At least, for now. If I change my mind, I'll let you know. No amount of baked goods or premade meals is going to sway my decision."

They exchanged glances, and Emmy laughed. She was a pretty lady with golden hair and warm, dark eyes.

"You have us confused with our husbands. We aren't interested in your land. We tried to befriend your grandfather, but he didn't want that. Sandy knew your grandmother a little, but once she passed, that was the end of being neighborly. The only one who got even remotely close to him was Ava. She checked on Jack every so often and made sure he was okay. He'd let her sit on the porch on occasion, and other times, he'd tell her to go away. But she always returned."

Somehow that didn't surprise me. Any of it. The part about my grandfather or Ava. Emmy kept talking.

"We have no desire to talk business with you. All we wanted was to say hello, let you know we're right over the bluff, and you're welcome anytime."

I felt a rush of guilt for being rude, and I cleared my throat. "Sorry, I'm not used to company."

Cami patted my hand. "We understand. But we're close should you change your mind or need anything." She paused. "So, you've met Ava."

I swallowed the mouthful of scone, wondering what she had told her mother.

"Yes."

"She mentioned you were applying for some planning permission."

"Yes. It needs some improvements." I cleared my throat again, feeling as if I should say something. Something nice about Ava. Probably telling Cami I would like to fuck her daughter would fall outside the realm of polite society acceptance. "She was, ah, very helpful."

Cami nodded. "She is very good at what she does."

"She's very mouthy," I said without thinking. "And she's bossy."

They all laughed. "That's my daughter," Cami agreed. "Her father's mischievousness and my outspokenness. It's a bad combination."

"She steals potatoes and bacon off my plate too," I grumped, then realized what I had said when they all looked at me.

"Ah, I ran into her this morning."

Cami grinned. "Potatoes *are* her favorite food—along with bacon. But I thought I taught her better manners than to take food off a stranger's plate."

"We're hardly strangers," I snorted, then wanted to smack my head on the table.

How the hell were these women getting me to say this shit?

"I mean, she helped me at city hall, and she returned Cash to me when he got off his lead," I said, sounding lame even to my ears.

They all exchanged glances I was certain had meaning. And had something to do with me. I picked up my mug and drained it, wanting to curse. This time, though, I stayed quiet.

Emmy glanced around. "How do you plan on doing all the work?"

I held up my hands. "With these."

"You can't do it all by yourself. We have lots of strong men in the family. If you need anything, all you have to do is ask," Dee informed me.

They all nodded again, having a silent conversation between them with their looks. I didn't like it.

I didn't tell them that wouldn't be happening. I preferred to work alone, and if there was a job I needed help doing, I would hire someone. I remained silent.

They took my lack of response as their cue to change the subject. I ate a couple of scones and complimented Emmy on how delicious they were. They chatted about the area, and I pushed myself to remain polite. They were all kind, lovely women.

Mothers. Caring and concerned, wanting to help. I mentioned I planned on shopping for a grill, and they recommended a place close to the grocery store they had mentioned. They told me about a great mechanic, where to shop for pet supplies that had a greater selection than the store in town, and a whole host of other information I didn't ask for and had no idea I needed to know. But I smiled and nodded, allowing them to write down their phone numbers and email information. They didn't force the issue when I didn't offer mine in return.

Then in a flurry of goodbyes and hugs I wasn't prepared for, they departed. I walked back into the house after waving them off and looked down at Cash. The house somehow seemed darker, duller since they left, which felt odd. Too quiet.

I preferred the isolation and the silence. I always had. It was all I knew.

"I don't think we're in Kansas anymore, boy."

He woofed and thumped his tail on the wooden floor, seemingly agreeing with me.

I shook my head at the strange thoughts.

CHAPTER 7

HUNTER

The rest of the week passed in a haze of days that bled into one another. I emptied one of the spare guest rooms which was the least full, but it still filled a quarter of the dumpster I had rented. The floors under the old, worn carpet were in good shape, so I planned to rent a machine and sand them, leaving the wide pine planks natural and adding a layer of varnish once I had done the same in the other room. I would paint both rooms in a light color to brighten them up. For now, I left it, reassembling the bed frame and adding in a new mattress I'd ordered online. I was getting tired of sleeping on the couch. The first thing I had done when I arrived was to take the mattress to the dump. It was old, lumpy, and musty, and I had no desire to use it. I even bought a set of sheets, grateful that the laundry machines, ancient as they were, still worked. I was looking forward to sleeping in a comfortable bed again.

I stayed busy morning until night. There was enough work to be done, I never had to worry about running out of things to keep my hands and mind occupied.

Still, *she* was there. On the fringes of my awareness, poking around the corner, the memory of her smile, her laughter, the way she teased me, stole food from my plate. Cut my hair. Kissed me back.

Ava.

The worst time was at night, when my body was tired from work, but my mind still awake. I would replay the hours I had spent with her. It didn't matter who she was—or who her family was. All that mattered was how she felt in my arms. Tasted. The scent of her skin as I kissed her throat. I couldn't seem to shake thinking about her. As I lay on the old but surprisingly comfortable couch, the moments in her company played on a loop in my head. The way it felt as she combed my hair and cut it. The intense look of concentration as she focused on the task at hand. She narrowed her eyes, and her tongue pressed on her bottom lip, her small white teeth worrying the edge of it as she worked. It was quite…adorable.

I didn't do adorable.

But I couldn't stop thinking about her. It was useless to do so. Ava was everything I admired in a woman and, at the same time, the very thing I avoided.

She was smart, witty, intelligent, and funny. Her smile was contagious and her laughter intoxicating. She was warm and personable. Bossy. Direct. In charge and in control.

She was also sexy as hell. In her power suits and heels, she was elegant and refined. Sure of herself. But dressed down, with no makeup and simply Ava? She was stunning.

I tried to ignore the picture of her sitting on the porch, relaxed and happy, that kept coming to my mind. But it wasn't the porch the way it looked now, run-down and creaky. It was solid and sturdy, with a massive swing piled with pillows hanging to the right of the door, where the view of the water was amazing. I was beside her, our hands entwined, and the sensation I felt every time that image snuck into my head was one I couldn't recall ever feeling in my life.

Contentment.

Where that came from, I had no idea, but I pushed it aside every time it hit me, and I ignored the little voice in my head telling me it was going to happen.

Obviously, I needed to get out of here for a while. Even I had taken being alone to the next level.

My phone buzzed, and I checked the voice mail, pleased when I heard that my permit was ready and I could pick it up. I glanced at the time and decided I would grab it this afternoon, then head to the bar for a couple of hard-earned drinks and a meal.

Maybe I would pick up something else.

Milly Johnson handed me the document. "There you go, Mr. Owens. All set."

"Great."

"The new porch will be a lovely addition."

"I think so."

"You have a lot of plans for the house."

I nodded. "It needs some serious updating. I have no chance of renting it the way it is right now." I chuckled. "It's a time capsule

—and a bad one, at that. As soon as I have the plans drawn up, I'll be back."

She smiled. "You plan on renting it, then? You aren't staying?"

"No. It will be a good rental income. I'll come check on it every so often."

"With the view and the area, I'm sure it will do well."

I smiled in thanks and picked up the file. My mind was already planning, thinking of the lumber I would need for the addition, the machines I would have to rent, the roof extension. I was so busy thinking, I almost missed her. I pushed at the door leading out as she pulled, and we both froze as we recognized each other.

Ava was dressed in slim-fitting slacks, a purple blouse peeking out from a tailored vest that hugged her torso and looked anything but masculine on her frame. Her hair was twisted up away from her face again, and her makeup was skillful and light. The heels she wore made her legs look long and sexy.

But it was the expression on her face that caught my attention. She looked tired. Defeated. Her shoulders were bowed, her eyes dull today. She smiled in greeting, but it didn't reach her eyes— they remained leaden and distant.

"Hello, Hunter."

"Ava."

"We need to stop meeting like this," she said, although the humor sounded forced.

I chuckled. "A trip to city hall isn't complete without running into you, Little Dragon. Here to chap some asses?"

She shook her head, the action causing the small purple studs in her ears to twinkle. "Just dropping off some more paperwork."

I stepped aside. "Don't let me hold you up."

She sidled past me, the scent of her drifting by. It was floral but not heavy, with an undertone of something citrusy and light. It was lovely and suited her well.

"Thank you," she murmured and kept walking.

I stared after her, shocked.

No quips, no needling, no teasing. She was withdrawn and...*sad* was the only word I could think of.

I was surprised how much that bothered me.

I headed to the truck and climbed in. But I didn't start it. I sat, watching the door for some reason.

Waiting, I realized with a jolt, for Ava to reappear.

When she did, I observed her. Even her walk was different today. Slower, as if the act of moving forward was almost too much. Before I could stop myself, I was out of the truck and by her SUV.

"Ava."

She looked up, blinking, surprised to see me there.

"Hunter?" she asked. "Is there something I can do for you?"

The tone of her voice told me everything. She'd been doing things for everyone, and she was more than sad. She was exhausted. Drained.

I stepped closer. "Yes."

I saw her struggling to stay polite. Be kind. Because if there was one thing I knew about her, it was that she was always kind.

"What might that be?" she asked, trying to sound upbeat. "I don't have much to give, but I can try."

"Have dinner with me."

"Pardon me?"

I stepped closer. "Have dinner with me."

"Why?" she breathed out.

I couldn't explain it to her. I had no idea how to tell her what I was feeling. That seeing her this way, fatigued and weary, made my chest ache in an odd way. It brought out a sensation of wanting to help her. Something I had never experienced until this very moment.

"I felt like Chinese, and it's never fun eating that alone. I like to have a few dishes. Come eat with me. Relax a little. You look like you could use it."

She glanced at my casual clothes and down at her outfit. I laughed. "You can go change if you want. Or stay dressed up. I don't mind."

Suddenly, her eyes were bright again, the fog from earlier disappearing. "Hold up." She rounded her little SUV and opened the trunk. She reached in and pulled out a pair of flat shoes, kicking off her high heels. She undid the buttons of her vest, sliding it off and tossing it in the trunk with her discarded heels. She pulled the silky fabric of her blouse out of her waistband, letting the material hang loose around her hips. Then she reached up and unclasped her hair, running her fingers through the dark silk that hung straight to her shoulders.

She sighed in happiness and looked at me, lifting her arms. "Will that do?"

She was artlessly sexy, her hair not perfect, her blouse wrinkled, and her pants a touch too long with the flats. But her shoulders were straight, the light back in her eyes, and she was smiling.

"Perfect," I assured her. "I assume you know a good Chinese place?"

"The best. You want to follow me?"

"Yeah, Little Dragon, I'll follow you."

She paused before sliding behind the wheel. "Hunter?"

"Hmm?" I asked, looking over my shoulder.

"Thanks." She smiled at me, the wattage that of the bright afternoon sun in the summer. Its warmth hit my chest, lighting me up.

I got into my truck, shaking my head. Adorable didn't begin to cover it. Neither did sexy.

Dangerous, maybe. Addictive, for sure.

What the hell was I doing?

The restaurant was about fifteen minutes away, hidden away in a small strip mall. You would miss it if you blinked. I pulled up my truck beside Ava's and slid from the vehicle, eyeing the small weather-beaten sign.

I scratched my head. "You sure this is the right place?"

She tugged on my hand. "Trust me."

We walked into the restaurant, and the aroma hit me. Spice, garlic, ginger, and soy. Pungent and rich. There were only six tables and the two sides lined with eight booths. A couple of tables were taken, but Ava headed to the far side and slid into a booth. I followed her, my stomach growling. If the food tasted half as good as the place smelled, I was going to enjoy our dinner.

Ava plucked a plastic-covered menu from the holder and slid it my way.

"The dinner for two is good, but I usually order the dinner for four. The spicy one."

I glanced at the list. Hot and sour soup with sizzling rice, spring rolls, sliced barbecue pork with hot Chinese mustard to start. Sizzling spicy beef, General Tso chicken, vegetables with almonds, crispy house noodles, and salt and pepper shrimp were the main dishes.

My mouth was watering.

"You take it home and share it with your family?" I guessed.

She shook her head. "I take home the leftovers, but I eat in usually. I prefer it hot and fresh." She wrinkled her nose in amusement. "I love it when they drop the sizzling rice into the hot and sour soup. It makes lots of popping noises."

I gaped at her. "You order a dinner for four just for yourself?"

"They're my favorites." she defended herself. "I take most of it home. And Mrs. Yeo only brings me one soup. She packs the rest of them up for me to take home." She grinned. "Trust me, if I'm taking it home to my family, I need at least double that order. My dad could eat most of the one dinner by himself."

I had to laugh at this crazy woman. She was so natural. She liked all the dishes, so she ordered a dinner for four by herself. She didn't care. I couldn't think of another woman I'd ever known who would be so carefree about something like this. One woman I'd dated used to count the number of bites of everything she ate. It drove me crazy since she'd rather starve herself or waste the food than take one more bite. We hadn't lasted long. No one ever did.

Not that this was a date.

Having dinner with Ava didn't count as *dating* her. I was simply returning the favor from the other day. That was all, I assured myself.

I slipped the menu back into the holder. "Sounds good."

A young woman appeared by the table. "Hi, Ava." She glanced my way, and her eyes widened. "And hello, stranger."

Ava chuckled. "That's Hunter. Hunter, this is Jade." She turned to Jade. "How is your mom?"

"Much better. She'll be back soon. Her hip is healing well." Jade smiled. "Thank your family again for the gift basket and the meals. Mom said she was spoiled."

Ava waved her hand. "It was our pleasure. She's cooked enough meals for us, it was nice to give her a treat."

Jade looked pleased. "Do you know what you want?"

Ava nodded. "The usual, but two soups."

"I'll probably eat two bowls," I interjected. I loved hot and sour soup. "And bring all the appetizer things."

Jade laughed. "Okay, then. Drinks?"

"White wine, please," Ava said.

"Beer. Whatever is cold," I added.

"Coors?"

"Good."

Jade walked away, and I studied Ava. She still looked tired, but she was more relaxed. "Hard week?" I asked casually.

A shadow crossed her face. "A long one. Nothing new or different." She traced her finger over the worn surface of the table. "Some feel longer than others."

"What do you do, exactly? I mean, aside from the superhero gig?" I asked, trying to keep the mood light.

"I oversee all the planning and paperwork on every project we handle. I coordinate all the departments, secure the permits, deal with the various foremen, and work with the leads to stay on budget—" She frowned. "Among other things."

"You deal with a lot of red tape."

She paused before answering, letting Jade set down our drinks, and sipping her wine. "Yes, I suppose I do."

"You must be very good at it."

Her eyes focused on the table for a moment. "I try."

I sensed we were heading down an unhappy path. "I think you do more than try." I nudged her foot with mine. "You're humble."

That made her smile. "That almost sounds like a compliment, Mr. Owens."

I chuckled and shook my head. "Never. Here comes your soup."

That made her sit up. She smiled widely. "Oh."

———————

The soup was delicious. I could understand why Ava enjoyed the sizzling pucks of rice being dropped into the hot broth. It popped and steamed, blazing with heat. The rice added another element to the soup, and I ate two bowls. Everything that followed was amazing. Including watching Ava eat, which was a total turn-on. There was nothing put on or fake about her. She picked up the pork with her fingers, dragging it through the hot mustard. She cursed at the heat, chugging water, then went right back for more. She licked her fingers when the plum sauce on her spring roll dripped. She slurped the noodles, catching the sauce that dribbled on her lips with her tongue. She snagged the mush-rooms I pushed to the side of my plate with my chopsticks, not caring if I disliked them or was saving them for later. She moaned low in her throat as she ate a shrimp, biting into the crisp, spicy coating with gusto. We played chopstick war over the dish of vegetables when I realized she was sneaking all the crunchy almonds out of the dish. We talked about nothing and everything. The small town. The area around it. Toronto in general. Her little SUV and how minute it looked beside my large Ford F-150.

"Why do you need such a large truck?" she asked, eating the last of her spring roll.

"I move around a lot. I carry my tools with me. My life is in there." I shrugged. "Sometimes I sleep in it when we're on the move."

"Does Cash like the truck?"

I chewed a piece of the sizzling beef, swallowing the delicious mouthful.

"I found Cash wandering by the road a few years ago. He was barely more than a pup. He had a limp and was pretty thin—it was obvious he'd been alone for a while. I pulled up beside him, and he came right to me. He had a huge piece of glass stuck in his paw, and it was infected. I found a vet and got him fixed up. He had no collar, no chip, nothing. No dogs like him were reported missing. It was fall, and the vet figured he'd been abandoned."

"That's awful," she whispered, her eyes bright with unshed tears.

"He said it happened a lot. People got a pet for the summer, then when they headed back to their life in the city, they left the dog or cat behind." I shook my head. "I couldn't leave him, so I took him with me." I paused, taking a sip of my beer. "To answer your question, I think Cash associated the truck with me, so he loves it. He knows he's safe." I didn't meet her eyes. "And he is my most loyal constant."

She regarded me quietly, then laid her hand on mine on the table. "You're a good man, Hunter Owens."

"Don't spread that around."

"Your secret is safe with me."

I sat back and regarded the table. We had done a pretty damn good job eating the food. There was lots left, but I was shocked at how much we'd consumed.

"I was hungry," I commented.

"Me too."

"I know."

Jade came and brought us takeout containers, which we filled. She added the extra soup and cleared away the dishes. I crossed my arms on the table and studied Ava. She had more color in her cheeks, and her eyes were brighter.

"I liked watching you eat," I said.

"Really?"

I nodded. "You're not pretentious. You enjoyed the food, and you didn't try to hide it."

She lifted one shoulder. "Life is too short to deny yourself. Food was an important part of growing up. My father and brothers had voracious appetites. I liked food, and my dad always insisted I eat to enjoy it and fuel my body. Not to deny myself. I work hard and I need it."

The bill appeared, and before Ava could move, I slid it my way and offered her the plate of orange slices and fortune cookies.

She narrowed her eyes. "We'll each pay."

I shocked myself when I shook my head. "Next time. Tonight is my treat. Now take your fortune and read it out loud."

"Do I have to add 'in bed' at the end?"

"What?"

She chuckled. "My family always adds the words 'in bed' at the end. Makes it fun." She cracked open the cookie and read the small slip of paper.

"You will do amazing things—" she paused with a grin "—in bed."

I laughed and opened mine.

"You are a great leader—" I lifted my eyebrow and waited "—in bed."

The air shifted around us, growing warm. I ate the crunchy cookie, and Ava picked up an orange slice, biting into the fruit. A small river of juice ran down her chin, and I had the craziest desire to pull her closer and lick it off, then kiss her until she begged me to stop. Or to take her home.

She laughed and swiped at her chin, slipping her finger into her mouth and licking it off. Our eyes met and locked. I broke open another cookie and spoke.

"Dance with the man across the table." I swallowed. "In bed."

Her eyes widened. "That's not what the cookie says. You didn't even read it."

"Because I already know what my fortune is. You. Coming home with me tonight."

"I don't do relationships. And you said you don't do complicated."

"So, we'll keep it simple. I want you, Ava. I want to feel you against me." I leaned closer. "I want you under me. I want to feel how you move with me. You've been on my mind since you walked away on Monday."

Her cheeks flushed, and her breathing picked up. "Birth control," she whispered. "I'm not on any."

"My responsibility. I'll pick it up on the way home."

"It's been a while."

"Me too. All the sweeter when we're together, Little Dragon." I dropped my voice. "Say yes. Life is too short to deny yourself," I said, covering her hand on the table.

She flipped her hand over, our palms smoothing together.

"Yes."

CHAPTER 8

HUNTER

I followed Ava outside to her SUV, waiting as she opened the door. She looked at me, her hesitancy winning out.

"Don't change your mind," I pleaded quietly. "This has been brewing between us since we met. You know it has."

"Just one night," she whispered.

I had a feeling one night wasn't going to suffice when it came to her. I didn't think I could get enough of her, but I nodded in agreement. "Just tonight. Neither of us wants to be alone."

She still looked torn, and I covered her hand with mine, slowly leaning down, giving her a chance to say no. She edged closer, running her hand up my chest and gripping the material of my T-shirt in her fist. Our lips touched and released. Touched again longer. Harder. I slid my arm around her waist, pulling her close, settling my mouth on hers. I stroked along her bottom lip, groaning as she opened for me. I only meant to kiss her softly, to assure her. But that idea went out the window as soon as our lips melded. I angled my head, kissing her passionately. I stroked my tongue along hers, tasting the sweetness of the cookie and the tartness of the orange. The lingering tang of the wine. The sweetness blending them all together that was Ava. In seconds, I had her pressed against the back passenger door, desire and need overwhelming any common sense I might have used. I wanted closer. I wanted more of her. I wanted fewer clothes and more skin. I wanted to taste her all over and know how different parts of her felt on my tongue.

A car pulling into the lot broke through my lust-filled brain, and I eased back, protecting her from being seen. I dropped a fast kiss to her mouth.

"The door is open to the house. Go there and wait for me. I'll be right behind you."

She gazed up at me, her lovely eyes dazed and fogged—this time with the same desire I was feeling.

"Okay."

She slipped into the SUV as I headed to the truck, determined to find the closest drugstore and get to the house not long after her. I didn't want to give her enough time to change her mind—just the thought of her walking away made my chest ache. I reversed out of the spot and followed Ava, trying not to laugh when she slowed down, putting on her blinker, indicating a small drugstore as we approached the center of town. I flashed my lights at her so she knew I understood and hurried inside to buy what I needed as she drove away.

I was almost giddy over the fact that she now seemed as certain as I was.

It promised to be a good night.

I pulled up next to her small SUV. She was in the yard, throwing a stick for Cash. He bounded over, his tail wagging back and forth like a pendulum on a clock—fast and steady. I knelt down, stroking his head, running my hands over his thick coat.

"Hey, boy. Relax, just relax."

He woofed and headed back to Ava. I followed him, stopping in front of her.

"Did you, ah, get it?"

I held up the bag. "Some old lady was behind the counter. I felt like I was fifteen, buying condoms to fool around with my girl in the back seat. She said an awful lot without saying a word." I smirked.

"That would be old lady Beechmore. She'll be talking about you in her coffee group tomorrow."

I stepped closer, easing my arm around her waist. "Oh yeah? And what will she be saying, Ava?"

"She'll talk all about the sexy stranger dropping in for love gloves. How hot he was with his newly cut hair and his tight jeans."

I dropped my head to her neck, laughing. "Love gloves?"

"That's what my dad always called them. Told the boys to always glove up."

I chuckled, running my lips up her neck, enjoying the shivers. "What else, Little Dragon?" I nipped her ear.

"She'll tell all the ladies you winked at her. Said if you didn't have plans already, you'd take her for a turn or two on your drill."

The amusement she always seemed to bring out in me slipped free, and I laughed, yanking her to my chest. She giggled, and I wrapped her in my arms. She felt right settled against me, her head the perfect fit under my chin. For a moment, I held her, and I felt her loosen and relax.

"Want a drink?" I murmured.

"Sure."

I drew back and cupped her face between my palms. I kissed her slowly. Sweetly. I traced her lips with my tongue and kissed her again. I held my mouth to hers, my lips not moving until I felt the trembling in her lips stop and she sighed, her breath fanning over my skin.

"Stay there," I instructed, bending over and picking up the bag I had dropped when I embraced her.

In the house, I turned on a lamp beside the bed. The room was empty aside from the night table, a small dresser in the corner, and the bed. I was grateful for the new mattress and sheets. I would break them both in right.

I stopped and grabbed a couple of beers and my old boom box and headed outside. I handed Ava the beers and fiddled with the buttons until the sound of soft music began to play. I followed Ava to the edge of the bluff, looking over the water.

"Isn't it beautiful?" she whispered.

I wasn't looking at the view when I replied, "It is."

"It's my favorite. I find peace with the vast expanse. The separation."

Her words made me frown. I turned to face her, tucking a long strand of hair behind her ear. "You don't find your life peaceful?"

"Does anyone these days?" she replied. "Cell phones, laptops, watches that record your moves, all have the ability to reach you anywhere. Sometimes I just like to get lost, forget about the crazy world of ABC." She smiled at me, but her eyes were sad. "That's what drew my dad here. The peacefulness. The break away from Toronto. He spent more and more time here. He says it is what saved him." She laughed quietly. "Well, this place and my mom." Her eyes stared over the vista in front of us. "I love it here. I was so glad when we decided to move our headquarters here."

"But you go into Toronto a lot?"

"Just finishing up some projects. I'll be here all the time soon."

One of my favorite songs began, and my foot started to tap. She glanced toward me.

"Joe Cocker?" she guessed.

"Yep," I replied, oddly pleased that she recognized the song so quickly.

"You love 80's music."

"My mom was hooked on it. It was all I heard growing up. No matter where we were, what we were doing, or our circumstances, that boom box and her mixtapes came with us." I swallowed then spoke again. "I don't have a lot of good memories of the past, but this music is one of them."

"Your mom—?" she asked, opening her mouth to keep talking. I cut her off, taking the beer bottle from her hand and spinning her toward me.

"Dance with me, Little Dragon."

I held her close, and we moved under the dark sky. One 80's love song bled into another, the tape showing its age at times, but we ignored it and kept dancing. I liked having her in my arms, twirling her away and pulling her back. We moved together well, and I knew that would work the same in the bedroom.

Cash lay on the porch, regarding us. Eventually, he nosed open the screen door and went inside, bored and out of sorts that he was being ignored.

"Careless Whisper" began to play, and I pulled her close, humming the song into her ear. She slid her arms around my neck, letting me tug her nearer so our bodies moved as one. Her breasts pressed into my chest, the softness melding into my tight muscles. Her nipples hardened as I ran my hands up and down her back, dropping my head to her neck and running my mouth over the elegant column. She tightened her grip on my shoulder with her fingers, while the other hand played with my hair. I trailed a line of gentle kisses over her cheek until I reached her mouth, hovering over it for a moment. Her breathing picked up, matching my short intakes of air. She sighed as I settled my mouth on hers, opening for me right away. Our tongues stroked together, teased, and explored. She whimpered, tightening her fists, yanking on my hair. I growled in return, fisting her thick strands and kissing her harder. Lifting her onto her toes as I deepened the kiss, the sensations rising within me powerful. I was intoxicated by the feel of her mouth. The softness of her tongue. The heat of her breath mingling with mine. My body was tight, my cock hard and pressing against my zipper. I wanted to feel her supple skin against mine. Know the curves of her body—learn them with my hands and mouth. Know how she tasted every-where. The need to have her, make her mine, claim her, took hold, and I was powerless to stop it. I slid my hands under her spectacular ass and lifted her, walking toward the house.

She gasped into my mouth, and I stopped. I pulled back, already missing her mouth on mine.

"Do you want this?"

"Yes."

"Are you sure?"

"Yes."

"But…?" I asked, sensing reticence. I wanted her one hundred percent sure. I wanted her to want me as much as I wanted her. More than her next breath. More than anything else.

"It might rain, and your boom box…" she whispered, pointing behind me. "I don't want you to lose that."

Something akin to tenderness blossomed inside me. She was worried about my losing something she knew was special to me. I set her down carefully, cupping her face and kissing her in a gentle caress.

"I'll get it. You go inside. Maybe you'd, ah, like a moment?"

She nodded, and I kissed her again. She seemed vulnerable, not at all the way she projected herself normally. I rather liked that she allowed me to see this side of her. The same way I had felt safe enough to share the history of the boom box. There wasn't another living soul on this planet who knew that fact.

"Go inside. I'm right behind you, Little Dragon."

AVA

I stepped inside the house, looking around me in awe. Hunter hadn't been lying when he said time capsule. Plaid couches, wood paneling, and an orange shag carpet covered the floor. I spied a Formica-topped kitchen table, surrounded by yellow-vinyl chairs I recognized from the other day. I didn't stop to examine anything. In the hallway, I peeked to the left and right, following the dim light I could see coming from the end of the hall.

Hunter's bedroom contained a bed, nightstand, and a dresser. A duffel bag sat on top of the dresser, the zipper undone, clothes piled inside. A braided rug graced the floor, and Cash was curled on the frayed mat. He wagged his tail as I went close, stroking his head. He gazed up at me, his amber eyes gleaming in the dull light.

"I don't know if you want to be in here for the next while," I murmured. "I think your master is gonna get down and dirty with me."

"I'm hoping to," Hunter said from the doorway.

I looked at him over my shoulder, swallowing hard. He'd already removed his shirt, his shoulders broad and his toned arms crossed over his chest. His jeans were undone, hanging low on his hips. His erection was obvious and I tried not to stare, but as usual, I failed. I focused on the prominent bulge that seemed to grow under my gaze. He cupped himself, his fingers curling around the taut denim.

"See something you like, Little Dragon?"

I think I squeaked. I wasn't sure what the sound that escaped my throat was, to be honest. He grinned and slapped his leg.

"Cash," he commanded, his voice low and gruff. "Come."

I was sort of glad he had made sure we knew it was Cash he was directing. I was so tightly wound, I might have obeyed him myself. My body felt taut and needy. I ached with desire for the man smirking at me from the door as if he had guessed my thoughts.

Cash went to him, wagging his tail. Hunter disappeared with him, and I heard him crooning to him quietly. There was the sound of food being put in a bowl, and Hunter told him to sleep on the couch. "It's your favorite spot anyway." He bribed the dog. I tried not to laugh at his words as he made sure the dog was out of the room before we began…whatever it was we were about to do. I hoped it contained us naked and lots of orgasms.

I stood, looking at the bed as I kicked out of my shoes. The frame was old, wrought iron and wood, but I could tell the bedding and mattress were new. A tag stuck out on the end, and the bedding looked pristine. I walked over, running my hand along the smooth expanse of cotton.

"Have you changed your mind?"

I turned to find Hunter had returned. He had pushed the door closed behind him but hadn't advanced toward me.

"No."

"You're still dressed."

"I thought you might, ah…"

He grinned. "Oh yeah, I want."

He stepped closer, laying his hand on the side of my neck. "Your pulse is racing," he murmured.

"I know."

He ghosted his lips over my cheek to my ear. "So is mine."

I rested my palm on his chest, feeling his racing heart.

"Are you nervous, Little Dragon?"

"Would you think less of me if I said yes?"

He shook his head, his expression tender. "No, I'd feel honored."

I shivered as he tugged my blouse over my head. He smoothed my hair back, then slowly trailed his fingers over the lace covering on my breasts. My nipples ached for his fingers. His mouth.

"So beautiful," he murmured against my skin, making short work of the clasp and freeing me. He kissed my collarbone, sliding down to take one nipple in his mouth, teasing and sucking. I grasped his hair, groaning in pleasure. He slid his hands to my waistband, unzipping and pushing down my pants and underwear, the cool air hitting my skin and making me shiver.

"I'll warm you," he promised, running his hands up and down the backs of my thighs. "You're going to be burning soon."

I slid my hands to his neck, cupping his face, feeling the scratch of his bristles on my palms. "I already am, Hunter. I want you so much."

"Good." He covered my mouth with his and lifted me, placing me on the bed. He stood back, tugging down his jeans and kicking them away. He was aroused, his cock heavy and thick as he stroked it, his chest moving rapidly.

"Look at you," he growled. "Lying on my bed, waiting for me. Dammit, Ava, you are gorgeous."

His words relaxed me. Made me brave. I slid up the bed, reclining against the pillows, and let my legs fall open. "I'm waiting, Hunter." I bit the end of my finger. "And I don't like to wait."

He was on me in a second. Our mouths fused together, our kiss heated and desperate. His chest hair was rough on my breasts, his weight on top of me warm and welcome. We explored each other, licking, kissing, touching, and learning. I discovered two dimples at the top of his buttocks. Felt the strength of his shoulders as he flexed over me, my hands gripping his sinewy back. His hair was as soft as I remembered, and he loved it when I ran my fingers through it. I rolled on top of him, exploring his torso, running my tongue along the ridges of his abs, his flat brown nipples that were hard under my mouth. I cupped him, his cock hot and silky in my hand. He groaned as I teased the crown but stopped me from putting my mouth on him.

"It'll be over before it's begun, sweetheart. Save that for later."

Then I was under him again. He made short work of the condom and settled between my legs. Gripping my hip, he brushed the blunt head over my opening, easing in. He braced himself on his elbows, pressing his forehead to mine as he groaned in complete satisfaction.

"Fuck, you feel good."

"*More.*" I arched my hips. "I want all of you."

He gave it to me. One snap of his hips and he was lodged inside, the feeling of being claimed and possessed filling me. I gasped his name, and he took my mouth, beginning to move. He didn't hold back, his strokes powerful and intense. I was awash in sensation. His heat soaked into my body and his scent filled my head. He moved inside me, the pleasure spiking fast, and I gripped at his shoulders.

"That's it, baby. Come fast for me, then I'll take you there again." He slipped his fingers between us, stroking my clit, and I exploded. My muscles clamped down and I cried out. He kept moving, gripping the old headboard as he grunted and cursed.

"You feel so good."

"Fuck, never—it's never…"

"Grip me. Yeah, just like that, Ava. Jesus, you are perfect."

"I can't… Come again, Ava. Come with me."

I shivered, feeling another orgasm barreling down on me. I wrapped my legs tighter around him, and he hitched them higher, driving deeper and chanting my name in a low, throaty growl. He stiffened and dropped his head, letting out a long, deep cry. I shattered again, my body shaking, my muscles gripping him. He kissed me, long, slow, and sweetly as our bodies finally eased. For a moment, he dropped to my chest, and I wrapped my arms around his shoulders, stroking the back of his head. There were no sounds aside from our erratic breathing and the rustle of the bedding under us.

He lifted his head, the silvery blue of his eyes now a banked fire. He smiled and took my hand, kissing the inside of my wrist.

"Little Dragon," was all he said in a whisper. "Thank you."

I felt an odd sense of loss as he rolled off me and left the room. He returned quickly, scooping me up and lifting the covers. He joined me under them, then paused before turning out the light. "You're staying, yes?"

"If you want me to."

He snapped off the light and reached for me, pulling me to his chest. "I'm not done with you yet, so yes, I want."

I smiled against his skin. He began to run his fingers through my hair, his touch light and gentle. "Sleep for a while."

I was too tired to argue. I nestled closer, my smile getting bigger as I felt him tighten his arm. A few moments later, his deep breathing told me he was out. I slid my arm around his waist, anchoring myself to him, and let sleep claim me too.

I woke up on fire. At least, I thought I was on fire. It didn't take me long to figure out why. Hunter was wrapped around me, his chest pressed to my back, his body like a furnace. Cash was asleep, draped over our feet at the end of the bed, snoring away. He emitted enough warmth to heat the entire room. Between the two of them, I was suffocating. I blinked in the early morning light. There was a towel on the floor, dropped from Hunter chasing me into the room and yanking it from my body.

He had woken me only a couple of hours after we'd fallen asleep, his mouth on my neck, his hand stroking me. He'd pulled back my leg and entered me from behind, moving in long, slow thrusts, caressing my sensitive clit until I exploded around him. Then he took me to the shower, and we kissed and explored each other as we washed and rinsed. I'd dropped to my knees and taken him in my mouth as he let his head fall to the faded tile wall and groaned out his pleasure.

After the shower, sitting on dry towels, we'd eaten leftover Chinese food right from the containers, laughing at his attempts to use chopsticks. I fed him from mine, secretly suspecting he could have done fine on his own, but I did enjoy feeding him.

After we'd eaten, he'd chased me back to bed and returned the favor, his mouth and fingers working in tandem to coax two more orgasms out of me.

Then we'd curled up again and slept.

Carefully, I eased out from beside him, sliding my feet out from under Cash's great weight. Cash opened his eyes, huffing a sigh as I rubbed his head. I quietly picked up the towels, hung them in the bathroom, washed my face, and pulled Hunter's discarded T-shirt over my head.

In the kitchen, I looked around, finding the old coffeepot. I boiled the water on the stove and poured it slowly through the drip, exploring as I waited for the coffee to finish. I doubted the kitchen had changed since the house was built. Wooden cabinets showed the age, the varnish worn away around the handles that were dull with use. The countertop was chipped and stained, the linoleum floors dull from years of use. Even the dishes were old, the CorningWare design faded on the white glass of the mugs. I peeked in the cupboards, seeing most of them were empty aside from dishes, glasses, and pots.

The table was covered in plans and notes, various pieces of paper scattered all over it. I glanced at the rough sketches, looking at the improvements Hunter planned on making. He had some great ideas. I had to fight against the urge to sit and organize it all. Instinctively, I knew Hunter wouldn't like that.

I poured my coffee and was glad to see there was cream in the fridge. There were a few covered containers as well as a bag of scones in the freezer, but otherwise, not much else. It was as if Hunter only stocked enough food for a few days. As if he only planned ahead that long.

I felt a wave of sadness in my chest at that thought. I grabbed an old afghan off the sofa and headed outside and to the edge of the bluff, pulling the blanket around me and sitting on the flat rock by the edge. The sun was coming up, the sky lightening. Soon it would reflect on the water, its glittering rays dancing across the waves.

I loved the view here. The higher elevation showed the wide expanse of water, the sky stretching over it like a blue blanket. Far across where land met the shore again seemed days away, even though you could cross in a boat fairly quickly. On sunny days, the water dappled in blues, greens, and turquoise. On stormy days, the white peaks of the waves were froth on a dark bed of gray and navy. We had a few higher elevations on our property, and I loved to sit and watch the water from those vantage points. But because this bluff stuck farther out, its view was unobstructed. The direction it faced, no one else was around. It was isolated, untamed, stark in its beauty. Unprepared to give up its secrets to the never-ending scope within.

Very much like the man who occupied the house behind me. He was a study in contrasts. Grouchy, unapproachable, removed. Sweet, funny, and caring. He insisted he needed no one and nothing, yet his actions said differently. His lovemaking had shocked me. I had expected hard and fast. Dirty and self-contained. A means to an end. I had anticipated being asked to leave once we had finished, for him to push me away, but to my shock, he wanted me to stay. And he'd been a giving lover, as intent on my pleasure as his own. There was no doubt he was holding back as he took me. I was used to strong men—the males in my family were all fit and used to working out. But Hunter's strength came from daily, hard work. His muscles were carved of stone, the power in his body undeniable. Yet he touched me with an unexpected tenderness I wasn't prepared for. His eyes changed, becoming molten blue fire that spoke of unsaid words and needs. There was a quiet vulnerability in his gaze, a softening of the usual icy glare. It was as if, in those unguarded moments, he allowed the real Hunter to be on display.

I wasn't sure if he was even aware of that fact. Part of me wondered how often anyone even noticed. I was certain this side of Hunter wasn't something many people witnessed.

I startled as Cash appeared beside me, huffing as he sprawled on the ground. When Hunter slipped behind me, pulling me back to his chest, I felt a warm satisfaction in his actions. He still wasn't pushing me away.

"I woke up and you were gone," he said simply.

"I wanted to come enjoy the view."

"Wake me up next time." There was a pause. "I didn't like it."

His words surprised me. *Next time* spoke of a future. One he said we didn't have. One I had told him I didn't expect.

"Okay," was all I said.

He reached around, taking my coffee cup and draining it. His long legs extended beyond mine, the heat of him soaking through the afghan and into my back.

"It's like you're all alone up here," I commented. "No one for miles."

"I know. Great privacy." He dropped his head to my neck, his mouth hot on my skin. "No one can see anything here."

My breathing became shallow as he tugged away the blanket and pulled aside the neck of the T-shirt. His tongue traced a path up my neck, swirling in long, slow circles behind my ear, making me shiver. He slid a hand under the shirt, cupping my breast and rolling my nipple between his fingers.

"Just us," he murmured.

"And your dog," I uttered.

"He's gone."

I glanced to the side to see Cash had left. He was rolling in the grass farther away, ignoring us.

"Ah," I croaked, gasping as Hunter pinched my nipple, then slid his other hand inside the shirt, mimicking the action. He stroked and teased, worshiping my neck with his tongue, playing with my breasts. I squirmed against him, feeling his arousal pressing on my back. He hooked his legs underneath mine, spreading them wide. The cool air hit me, and I whimpered as he glided his fingers along my legs.

"I woke up hard and ready for you, Little Dragon. We're all alone up here. You gonna give me what I want?"

"What do you want?" I gasped as he delved between my legs, stroking my clit in light, unhurried passes.

"I want to take you here. Outside. I want to watch you ride my cock with the vast expanse behind you and my hands and mouth all over you. I want to watch you come and hear you shout my name into the wind."

I shivered, moaning as he touched me. I bucked up, wanting more. Needing him to touch me harder. Fill me. He laughed lightly in my ear. "Not until you say yes."

"Yes, yes, yes," I chanted.

He showed his strength in the ease with which he lifted me, shifting me around so we were nose-to-nose. My legs wrapped around his waist. His already-sheathed cock nestled against me.

"All prepared, were you?" I teased.

"The Boy Scout in me."

"Why doesn't the Boy Scout get in me, then?"

He lifted me, and for a moment, our gazes locked. The fire was back, icy and hot. His eyes fluttered shut as I grasped him, guiding him inside. We both groaned as I sank down on him, the fullness welcome, his hands gripping my hips.

I grasped his shoulders, moving slowly. Taking him in, withdrawing and sliding back to the hilt. He cursed and groaned, his gaze flickering to where we were joined then back to my face.

"I've never seen anything so sexy," he growled. "Ride me hard, Little Dragon. Take me."

I leaned back, resting my hands on his hard thighs, and did exactly what he asked. He spread his hands wide on my back, sucking my nipples through the T-shirt as I rode him. I let my head fall back, my hair brushing his legs. Upside down, the horizon bobbed and moved. Pleasure built, narrowing down to the point where we were joined. I ached with the need to come, to find my release. It was a low, slow fire building, threatening to consume me. He suddenly jerked me to him, burying his face in my neck, his thrusts hard and powerful. I exploded, shaking and crying his name. His body was taut, his muscles granite under my hands as he groaned, swelling inside me and releasing. He held me so tightly I wondered if he'd leave bruises, then he shuddered and stilled, his grip never lessening.

For moments, we stayed locked together. Around us, the world returned to normal. The breeze ruffled our hair, the sun warmed our skin. He stroked his hands up and down my back. He turned his head, kissing my cheek, pulling back to cup my face and kiss me. His touch was gentle, his mouth soft as he held me and said a thousand words without speaking.

"Spend the day with me. Just us."

I nestled closer. "Yes."

For the second time in less than a day, I found myself in a shower with Hunter. He soaped my body, making sure I was very clean.

"I wasn't aware my breasts were that dirty," I mumbled, watching his large hands cup and lather them repeatedly.

"Oh, they are. So, so dirty," he assured me. "All of you needs a good scrubbing."

"Is that a fact?"

He laughed, kissing the end of my nose in a surprisingly affectionate gesture. When he decided I was clean enough, he soaped himself up as I rinsed off, watching him discreetly. He handled his powerful body with ease, gliding the soap over his skin and scrubbing his head roughly with the shampoo. He was fascinating to watch—the way his muscles rippled, the flex of his arms, the tight band of strength that stretched over his back. His butt was sculpted, and the two dimples I had discovered last night were deeply embedded above the tight buttocks. He had a matching pair at the base of his neck. I reached over, trailing my fingers up his skin, loving his instant reaction to my touch. He turned with a frown, trying to look stern and failing.

"Don't start something we can't finish, Little Dragon. You must be sore."

His eyes widened as I dropped to my knees in front of him, running my hands up his thighs. "The question is, Hunter, how sore are *you?*" I pressed a kiss to his half-erect cock, unable to stop my smirk as it stiffened and lengthened. "I think I need to inspect the goods. Kiss it better if needed."

"You look so good on your knees in front of me," he said, cupping my chin. "I shouldn't like it so much."

"Neither should I," I admitted. I had never minded giving blow jobs and my partners had never complained, but with Hunter, it felt different. More intimate. I felt a power with him I had never experienced before.

He groaned as I engulfed him in my mouth. "Inspect him well, Ava," he grunted, weaving his hands into my hair. "He's had a hard morning."

With a wink, I gave him what he wanted. It didn't take long—I loved the feel of him in my mouth, and his cock apparently agreed. He leaned against the old tile wall, gasping and looking shell-shocked. I rose to my feet, rinsed off, and stepped out of the shower. I peeked over my shoulder to find him watching me, his silvery eyes narrowed and intense.

"Wherever you learned that, I don't want to know," he said, his voice low. "But you are amazing." He shook his head, turning to the water, muttering under his breath about *unexpected* and *not the plan.*

I shrugged, pleased. Then for fun, I reached behind him and turned off the hot water.

I was out of the small bathroom before he started to yell.

He came into the kitchen wearing jeans and a T-shirt. I glanced down at the clothes I had on from yesterday, and he smirked, lifting an eyebrow. I ignored him, making another pot of coffee. He reached into the freezer and pulled out the bag of scones I had noticed earlier and popped a couple into the old toaster.

"You have to watch this one," he said. "One second, it's fine. The next, your bread is on fire. These scones are too delicious to waste."

"My aunt Emmy makes awesome scones. Where did you get yours?"

He frowned. "From her. They were in the massive care package the ladies brought with them."

I gaped at him. "*What?* What ladies?"

He frowned and sat across from me, stacking up some of the files to make room for the plate he was carrying. "Your mother and aunts. Your grandmother too, I think?"

"When were they here?"

He looked startled. "You didn't know? They showed up Monday after I got home." He snorted. "Came in, decided I needed food and company, so they made coffee and stayed. They never told you?"

I shook my head. "I saw my mom on Wednesday, but she never mentioned it."

"Huh. I thought she'd tell you. How come you only saw her Wednesday—you all live in some sort of commune, don't you?"

I laughed at his description. "BAM owns all the land over there, yes. Many of us live there. Some have a place they crash on occasion. Others use it as a holiday spot. But it's not a commune." I paused. "Well, I suppose it is in many ways. But we all live our lives. We're not in one another's back pockets. We have family brunches once a month, and we are pretty tight, but we go our own way most of the time. I often only see my parents on Sundays at the Hub."

"The Hub?"

"It's like a rec center. There are too many of us to gather in anyone's house. There's a big kitchen and a massive living area. Downstairs, we have games and a gym. There's a pool and a little library. Sundays, the parents usually gather for coffee. I join them once I wake up." I paused and sipped my coffee. "I like to sleep in on Sundays. It's sort of the one day I keep to myself."

"What do you do once you get up?"

I sighed. "Nothing. That's the best part. I'm so busy all week, I never slow down. Sundays, I have a long bath, take walks, paint my toenails. Read. Nap. I don't have to deal with paperwork, people telling me why I'm wrong, arguing with foremen or crews." I smiled at him. "It's an Ava day."

"What about Saturdays?"

"I usually do stuff around the house, laundry, some grocery shopping, make a few meals so when I get home at night during the week, I'm not trying to figure out what to cook."

He looked surprised by my words. "What?" I asked. "Did you think I lived in the lap of luxury and had people do all that for me?"

"Yeah, I guess I did."

I shook my head. "My parents didn't bring us up that way. We were taught we had to work hard to get the rewards. We all had part-time jobs growing up. I waitressed at the diner you had breakfast in the other day. Ronan washed dishes there and was a busboy. Liam worked at the local garden center all through high school. Paul and Jeremy both worked for the nearby grocery store, stocking shelves and being cashiers. When they got older, they became bartenders. We all had to learn the value of money."

He didn't say anything for a moment. When he spoke, I was surprised by his words. "I owe you an apology, Ava. I assumed you were a rich kid and spoiled. I should have known better now that we're, ah—" I was shocked to see dull color saturate his cheeks "—better acquainted."

I snorted with laughter. "Is that what we're calling it? Better acquainted?"

"For lack of another word. I have no idea what to call—" he waved his finger between us "—this."

I shrugged. "Do we have to name it?"

He studied me. "Most women want that."

"Hunter, I'm not interested in a long-term relationship. You don't have to be worried about that. I'm not planning on moving in and setting up house with you just because we've had sex."

He finished the last scone, pushing away his plate. "Is that just with me, or in general?"

I laughed lightly, not wanting to get into it. "With anyone. I tried it and discovered it wasn't for me."

He stroked his chin, his long fingers brushing the gray strands slowly. "Not to put too fine a point on it, but why? You seem like the sort of girl who would want to settle down and have a family."

"Well, looks can be deceiving," I said, standing, not wanting to discuss it. Not wanting to remember the pain of that voice telling me how much he hated the person I was. How difficult I was to handle.

"You're just too much, Ava. You're always too much. I can't deal with it. We're over."

Hunter caught my wrist as I went past him. "Hey, I'm sorry. Whatever I just said that upset you, I'm sorry."

I shook my head, taking his empty plate. "It's fine."

I carried the plates to the sink and returned to my chair. I tapped the pile of plans and paperwork. "You have a lot going on here. Lots of ideas."

He nodded. "I plan on starting with the front porch next week— that was approved, and I got a great deal on the Trex I needed. That's the imitation lumber," he explained, then chuckled. "I guess you knew that."

"Yes. It's great. Easy to maintain and no splinters."

He nodded. "Someone returned an entire order while I was at the building center. They marked it down for quick sale. I grabbed it. I can use it, and what's left, I'll use elsewhere."

"Good plan. What's next?"

He hesitated, then spoke. "I need to get architectural plans drawn up for the extension and get them approved. A deck drawing, I can handle. I need proper specs for the extension."

I bit my lip to stop myself from telling him Ronan could whip him up a set of drawings. I had a feeling he wouldn't like that. "Can I see your plans?"

I saw him tense, his shoulders going back and his hands tightening.

"Hunter, just relax. You're jumping to conclusions. You remind me of your grandfather."

He snorted. "Whatever."

"I'm just asking as a friend. What do you think I'm going to do with them? Copy and sell them on the black market?"

"Tell your family," he growled in admission.

Suddenly, I was angry. "First off, if you'd been paying attention, you would know my family doesn't care what you do with this place—they're just trying to be good neighbors. The same way they did with your grandfather. Second, I don't discuss my private life with them because it is exactly that to me—private. And third, you're a presumptive asshole who thinks far too much. This isn't mission impossible, buddy. It's a damn house extension. No one is going to meet me at midnight and tell me the moon is rising on the Seine despite the clouds, so I tell them what you're planning."

I jumped to my feet, now furious. "Is that why you slept with me? Trying to have something over me so I don't tell my family you're doing some renos?"

He blinked at me then had the audacity to smile. "Now who's living in a movie? I slept with you because you're fucking sexy, and I wanted you. I didn't give a shit then or now who your family is. I have no plans to tell anyone about us either. And when you're all riled up and snarking at me like this?" He leaned forward, resting his elbows on his thighs. "I want to do some really wicked things to you, Little Dragon." He cast his eyes over my form, dark and tempting. "Really, really wicked."

"Well, good luck with that. I hope your hand is snarky enough for you." I marched past him, yelping as he pulled me to his lap. "Get your hands off me, you jerk!"

He looked down at me, his gaze dark. "Is that what you really want, Little Dragon?"

"Y-yes," I stuttered out.

"I think what you really want is for me to carry you to my room and return the favor from the shower." He ran his nose up my neck. "Then you want me to fuck you. Hard. You want me to help you forget all about last week, or anything else but us. Nothing but my mouth on your body and my cock deep inside you."

I glared up at him. "Asshole," I snapped, then pulled his mouth down to mine.

He was a presumptive idiot, but he was right.

That was exactly what I wanted.

CHAPTER 9
AVA

I lifted my face to the sun, enjoying the rays. Hunter was throwing sticks to Cash, who barked and chased them, returning them to Hunter's feet and waiting impatiently, his tail swishing in the air like a set of windshield wipers on high for Hunter to throw the stick again.

Hunter glanced at me. "He needs a walk. Feel up to going?"

"Sure."

I stood and joined them. Hunter had a leash he'd picked up, but he didn't attach it to Cash's collar. He smiled at my inquisitive look.

"He won't go far from my side, and if I call him, he'll heel right away."

We set off, and instinctively, I headed in the direction I always used when coming to check on Mr. Owens. Hunter followed me, not speaking. We both enjoyed the quiet, neither of us feeling the need to fill it with unnecessary chatter. When we reached the boundary between the two properties, we stood, looking at the view.

"Amazing how different, yet similar the two are," Hunter murmured. "The contrasts in the landscape."

"It's lovely anywhere along this stretch."

He nodded and turned to head back. I stopped him, laying a hand on his arm. He met my eyes. "What, Little Dragon? What has you suddenly so serious?"

I pointed behind him. "About five minutes through those trees is my house. I'd like to go change if you wouldn't mind."

He tensed and didn't say anything.

"No one would see us. My house backs into the trees. All the second gen are in Toronto today at an afternoon charity event."

"Second gen?" he asked.

I smiled. "We refer to Nan and Pops as Generation One. Our parents are Gen Two. I'm part of Gen Three. Gracie's little girl is Gen Four…" I shrugged as he lifted an eyebrow.

"You sure this isn't a commune, Ava? Or a cult?" he asked, but his voice was teasing.

"Maybe. If I get you in, I get bonus points because of the dog. We've never had one before."

"Oh yeah?"

I nodded. "Bringing the two of you into the fold means a new toaster oven. Cash guarantees me an air fryer one."

For a second, he stared, then threw back his head in laughter. "Lead on, then. If my presence gets you that, I hope I get to reap the benefits of it. I hear wings are good in those machines."

Still chuckling, we headed down the trail. It had been a while since I'd walked it, and it was overgrown. I stumbled at one point, and Hunter reached out to steady me. After that, he kept his hand wrapped around my arm, walking close behind me. I liked the odd sense of protectiveness I felt from him.

We walked up the steps to my back door, and I entered the number on the keypad. Cash trotted in as if he owned the place, collapsing on the kitchen floor with a long, exaggerated sigh. Laughing, I took a bowl from the cupboard and filled it with water. He lapped at it, looking grateful. I turned to Hunter. "There's water or soda in the fridge. Help yourself. I'll only be a moment."

He nodded, looking uneasy.

"I was only kidding about the cult thing. You know that, right?"

He flashed his teeth at me. "Yes."

"We'll be out of here in a few minutes."

He waved me off, pulling a bottle of ginger ale from the fridge. "Take your time."

"Back in a minute."

HUNTER

I looked around, curious. I had no idea how I had gotten here. Why I had asked Ava to stay last night and again to spend the day with me. That wasn't my usual MO. Then again, Ava wasn't my usual sort of woman.

I hadn't expected to end up at her house, but now that I had, I decided to explore a little. I wandered into the living area and turned to take it all in. Designed as an open plan, it was light and airy. The colors were muted greens, grays, and creams. The furniture simple and comfortable-looking. The kitchen had a lot of open shelving and tons of bottom cupboards and drawers. A large island separated the two spaces. A small two-seater table was tucked into the corner, situated under a window that overlooked the heavily treed back.

The front wall housed a nice-looking gas fireplace, the mantel made of rough stonework. I ran my hand over it, noting the craftmanship. A TV was higher up in an alcove fashioned for that purpose, all the wires hidden. My eye caught the wall opposite, filled with pictures, and I walked over, studying them. I recognized the older women as my visitors in many of the pictures and drew my assumptions about the men beside them as their husbands. There was a family picture of Ava with her parents and siblings. She resembled Cami a great deal, and she hadn't been kidding when she said her dad and brothers were huge. They all towered over her and her mother, and they resembled their father. There was a large photo which I assumed contained most of, if not all, of the family. I lost count of the number of people in the picture, but I recognized the water behind the group. It was professionally done, the families in small groupings within the photo. They were all smiling and happy, and something tugged in my chest. I often wondered what it was like to belong to a family. It was something I had never experienced and knew I never would. I wasn't built that way. My DNA didn't allow me the peace to settle somewhere or connect strongly enough with a person on an emotional level to want to even try.

Yet, there was a strange longing that drew me to the picture, and I studied it.

"That was taken last year," Ava said, appearing beside me.

I startled, looking down at her. She had changed into a loose shirt and some sort of drapey cropped pants with old, beat-up runners on her feet. With no makeup and her hair loose around her shoulders, she was stunning.

"You're not all related."

"By blood, no. But we're a family, nevertheless."

The words were out before I could stop them. "I don't understand."

She smiled, tracing her finger over the picture. "My dad didn't have a family growing up—not a good one anyway. Neither did Maddox or Bentley. They became their own family, and once they each fell in love, it grew. Most of us third gen grew up here. Some came and went, but they were always part of us. Part of holidays and good memories. I love them as much as if they were one of my brothers." She shrugged. "I can't explain it. They are all part of me. I would do anything I could to help them, and they would do the same for me."

That was a completely foreign concept to me. With a shake of my head, I turned. "You ready to go?"

If my abrupt change of subject startled her, Ava didn't show it. She stopped by the chair in front of the window and picked up a book. "Maybe I can read today," she mused.

"You like to read?"

"Very much. But lately, I'm too tired." She frowned. "I've been wanting to start this one for a while, but I can't seem to keep the words straight."

I plucked the book from her hands. "Historical romance?" I smirked. "I would have taken you for a murder mystery kind of gal."

"I love those too, but this is my guilty pleasure."

Before I could respond, the sound of heavy footsteps on the front deck echoed in the room. I met Ava's startled gaze.

"Stay quiet," she said, panicked.

But the sound of the footsteps, followed by the loud knocking, was too much for Cash. He began barking, rushing to the door, his tail wagging.

"Shit," Ava muttered. "Sorry. I think it's my brother."

She moved past me, and I had no choice but to stand there. I wasn't going to hide in the bedroom as if I were doing something wrong. Besides, the barking Cash did had blown any chance of a quick exit.

Ava opened the door, and a large man stepped inside. Cash went berserk, jumping up, wagging his tail, spinning in circles, beyond excited about a new visitor.

The man glanced between Ava and me, then hunched down, stroking Cash.

"Hey, boy. Aren't you a handsome dog? Yes, you are," he crooned.

"It's a girl," I snarked. "You just insulted her."

Ava shot me a look. "No, he's not. That's Cash." She pointed at me. "His dog."

The man stood and crossed over, Cash pressing against his leg. I had to roll my eyes—what a traitor my dog was.

"Ronan Callaghan," he said, holding out his hand.

Part of me wanted to ignore it, yet I couldn't. I took his firm grip. "Hunter Owens."

His eyebrows flew up. "Mr. Owens's grandson?"

"Yep."

He glanced between Ava and me. She smiled nervously. "I made friends with Cash last week. He got off his lead again and ended up in my backyard. His, ah, collar was caught on a branch, and I got him free. Yes, that's what happened. Hunter was just coming to find him. He just got here!" she rambled as she lied.

Badly.

Ronan pursed his lips, looking at the empty can of ginger ale on the coffee table, the book I had clutched in my hand, and Ava's flushed cheeks.

"Where's your car?" he asked.

"Um…" She trailed off. "In the garage?" she offered lamely.

"I looked as I went by. It was empty." He crossed his arms, clearly enjoying himself. "I noticed no lights on last night or any sign of you today."

"I went to bed early last night, and I slept in." She rubbed the back of her neck. "I meant in the garage in town. I'm going to pick it up soon."

"What happened?"

"Er…"

I had to step in. She was a horrific liar.

"Flat tire," I said. "She was just telling me. I offered to drive her into town to say thanks for getting Cash loose and looking after him."

"Well, that's neighborly of you."

I lifted my shoulders, dismissing his words.

"I'll take you, Ava. I have to head into town anyway," Ronan offered.

Her eyes widened to the point of hilarity. She glanced between us, unsure what to say.

"Ava is going to point out a few places in town for me, Ronan. I'd appreciate her help."

A smile tugged his lips. "Okay, then," he drawled out. "As long as you're all right, Ava."

"I'm fine."

He turned his attention to me. "I hear you're doing some work on the old place."

"Yes."

"I'm around. So are Liam and a few other guys. Happy to lend a hand if needed."

"He's looking for an architect," Ava interjected.

"Oh. Well, happy to help there too."

"You know someone?"

He smiled, big and wide, and I saw the same mischievous glint in his eyes that Ava had. "I am the architect."

"Oh. Well, thanks." I left it at that and didn't say anything else.

He seemed to clue in because he simply shrugged. "Okay, I'm off." He turned to Ava. "You coming to brunch tomorrow?"

"Yes, I'll be there."

He headed to the door, and I relaxed. We'd fooled him, or he really didn't care. Either way was okay with me. "Good to meet you, Hunter. Oh, and Ava?"

"Yeah?"

"You might want to cover your neck tomorrow. I doubt Mom and Dad will believe those marks on your throat are from freeing a dog from tree branches or anything." He winked in my direction. "I'll be seeing you around, Hunter."

"I doubt it," I said dryly.

He shook his head, his amusement evident. "Oh, buddy, you can count on it."

Then he was gone.

We were quiet on the walk back. I threw sticks for Cash, who trotted ahead of us, happy and carefree. I wasn't sure if I should bring up the subject of her brother or not, then decided to let it rest. When we got back to the bluff, I glanced down at Ava. She had been remarkably silent. I wondered if she was regretting agreeing to spend the day with me or if the fact that her brother knew something had happened between us was bothering her. I needed to know.

"Not too late if you want to head off and do your errands," I offered.

"You want me to go?" she asked. I detected the soft note of hurt in her voice, and I turned, planting my hand on her waist and pulling her close. I brushed my mouth over hers.

"No."

She rolled up on her toes and kissed me back. "Good."

"Okay, then."

She scrunched up her nose. "What are the plans?"

I gazed at her wordlessly, amused when color crept into her cheeks. "Again?" she murmured. "Isn't he satisfied?"

I smirked. "When it comes to you, apparently not, but we can save that for later."

She pushed against my chest, and I let her go but not before stealing another kiss from her pretty mouth. I had never particularly enjoyed kissing—it was more a means to an end—but with Ava, I couldn't seem to stop myself.

I rubbed my chin. "I was going to do some measurements for the extension, but we can do something else. You want to sit in the sun and read or something?"

She clapped her hands. "No, I can help you. I'm good with a measuring tape and recording."

She sounded so excited I didn't want to burst her bubble. I wasn't used to help—even on jobsites, I was known as a loner who got the job done. It was only a few measurements.

"Okay. I'll get the paper and the measuring tape."

"Great!"

Inside, I grabbed what I needed, changing into a pair of long shorts and a T-shirt. I grabbed a baseball cap, knowing the sun would be overhead, then picked up a second one for Ava. I walked out back, trying not to gape at the scene in front of me. Ava, bending over to pick up something, her long, bare legs set off by a pair of tight shorts. Her ass was full and round, and I recalled how it felt in my hands. Firm and perfect. I cleared my throat, and she straightened.

"Didn't you have, ah, pants a moment ago?"

She nodded. "I had these on under them. In case I got hot."

She was making me pretty damn hot. My cock was sweating already, and we hadn't even started the project. It didn't help that she had tied her T-shirt in a knot at her waist, the sliver of skin above her waistband tempting and sexy.

I shook my head to clear it. "Fine," I said gruffly. "I brought you a hat."

I groaned inwardly as she bent again, gathering up her hair and tucking it under the cap. A few strands escaped. She looked sexy, younger than her early thirties I guessed her to be, and happy standing in the sun, her creamy skin on display and dressed so casually. It was very different from what I was used to seeing with her.

"Will you burn?"

"Nope. I used sun block spray before I got dressed. I figured we'd be outside."

"Huh."

"What?" she asked, cocking her head in query.

"You're very easy. Not high-maintenance."

She laughed. "Let's see how you feel in a few weeks."

I had no clue what to say to that statement. It was rare that anyone would remain in my life for a few weeks. Yet her words only made me grin, so I let it go. "Let's get to work."

Half an hour later, I bent over the drawing Ava had made on graph paper I had given her. I stared at it with narrowed eyes. What I had seen in my head didn't seem to work on paper. She had been correct—she was great with a measuring tape and recording the figures. I had a template of the house already sketched out on several sheets so I could tweak as needed to take to an architect for the final renderings. I knew this might take a few attempts to get what I wanted.

I blew out a huff of air, looking around. Something was off, and I wasn't seeing it. Beside me, Ava sat quietly, her head bent over another piece of paper. I glanced over to see what she was doing, but she turned so I couldn't see. Amused, I pretended to turn back, and when she relaxed, I slid my hand over, snagging the paper. She gasped and lunged, but I was too fast for her, standing on the top step and holding it over my head.

She stomped her foot. "Give me that back!"

"I want to see it first."

"I'm not finished."

"I don't care."

She crossed her arms, looking down at the ground. "Fine."

Suspicious, I stepped back and glanced at the paper. I blinked and brought it closer, looking at what she had done. With a few extra strokes, the image in my mind had been copied to her paper. I looked at her in amazement. "What have you done?" I asked. "Explain this to me."

She hesitated and took the paper from my hand, sitting back down. I sat beside her as she explained. "I extended this piece, so the kitchen becomes bigger, as well as the bedroom. You can add another bath here if you want, and right here, you can install an outdoor hot tub. Imagine sitting outside at night with the view, the hot water bubbling around you, a glass of wine in your hand. It's so private up here, it would be amazing."

I tapped the corner. "An overhead trellis for some sun protection."

"Yes," she agreed enthusiastically. "Sliding doors off the bedroom. A wraparound deck you can access from the kitchen to the master bedroom. I know you said you plan to rent the place. That would be a huge draw."

I nodded, her vision spot-on.

I ran my finger along her lines. "Adding to the kitchen will change the inner layout." I had only planned on making the master bedroom bigger to attract holiday renters—add a small en suite. The front porch was already going to be bigger. I would paint and refurbish the kitchen but had planned on leaving it rustic. Cottagey-like.

"Yes," she agreed, her tone hesitant.

I glanced at her. "You have ideas?"

She didn't meet my eyes. "Maybe."

Recalling the way I had snapped at her last night, I couldn't blame her reticence. Except I wanted to hear her ideas. See the place through her eyes. I knew she had good taste—I had seen her home. And despite my better judgment and our angry words yesterday, I knew I could trust her. It was disconcerting since I rarely trusted anyone, but with Ava, it felt right. There was something so different about her—what it was, I didn't know, but it was there.

I stood and faced her. She looked up, her lovely eyes bright in the sun. I leaned down so my face was level with hers. I tucked a strand of loose hair into the baseball cap on her head and rested my cheek against hers so my mouth was close to her ear. "The moon is rising on the Seine despite the clouds," I whispered conspiratorially.

She giggled, the sound infectious.

"Show me your plans, and I'll show you something else rising over the Seine later." I pressed a kiss to her cheek, then the side of her upturned mouth.

The giggles became laughter, which became guffaws. I had to join in her amusement, once again filled with wonder at how she made me feel this way. Light. At ease.

I held out my hand. "Come show me your ideas."

She let me pull her up, still smiling and amused. I led her inside and waved my hand. "Talk."

CHAPTER 10
HUNTER

I shook my head in astonishment, staring at her accurate and detailed drawings. I tapped her forehead. "You had all that up there after only seeing this place for a few hours? You should be in design, not running the show."

She smiled, her cheeks flushed, her eyes dancing. "No, I like my job. But I'm around all the areas so frequently that I know just enough to be dangerous. A good designer like Liv or Heather could do better."

"No one could do better. Your ideas are amazing. I really like the concept for the kitchen. And reusing the wood panels."

She nodded enthusiastically. "Use drywall in the guest room and reuse those panels in the master bedroom addition." She ran her hand over the thick mahogany boards. "It's beautiful. Lighten up in here but strip it in the master and leave it natural. Seal it, but let the grain and color be the star."

All her ideas floored me. Pushing out the back wall and adding to the kitchen. Repurposing the cupboards and cutting out the center panels in the top doors and replacing them with glass. Adding shelves and a new island.

"Stock cupboards can be easy on the budget but painted and arranged to look custom," she offered.

"Stone work tops?"

She nodded. "You get more bang for your buck. But you might be able to find a deal on those too. Something with movement but not overly busy. I'd go darker since you're lightening up the walls." She glanced up. "You said you were doing a new roof. Maybe add in a skylight? Let in more light."

"Your ideas will give it the whole cottagey-but-modern look I wanted. It would appeal to renters looking to get away but who don't want to rough it."

For a moment, she looked sad, then nodded. "Exactly."

"I'll need to replace the furniture and rugs."

"There are always garage sales, Facebook Marketplace, Kijiji. We have…" She stopped talking, her cheeks flushing a dull red.

"We have?" I prompted.

"We have warehouses full of furniture, doors, windows, everything. Bentley's first passion was flipping houses. The company still does it. Liv is always staging places. She thins out the inventory and sells and donates things all the time. She keeps architecturally nice doors and newer windows." She didn't meet my eyes. "It might help the budget, but I realize you're probably not interested if it comes from my family."

I wasn't. Or at least, I hadn't been yesterday. But I didn't want to hurt her. She was too amazing to do that. "Little Dragon," I said, waiting until she looked up. "Thanks for the offer. I'll think about it, okay?"

She smiled so widely, it made me want to smile back at her. It felt as if the sun had just come out of the clouds and was blinding me with its brilliance. All because I hadn't rejected her idea. She was so easy to please.

"We can poke around places too," she said. "You never know what you'll find."

"Sounds good." I held out the thick pad of paper. "You want to take some measurements and jot down your ideas?"

She took the pad eagerly, settling at the table, and immediately began working. I watched her for a moment, then, without thinking, bent and kissed her head. She looked up with another smile, and I couldn't resist kissing her.

"Thanks."

She winked. "Sure." Her stomach growled and I chuckled.

"I'll rustle up some sandwiches then we'll go outside and relax, okay?"

"Sounds good."

I carried out a plate of sandwiches and some cold sodas. We sat in the sunshine and ate, not talking much but enjoying the warmth. I opened a bag of chips, and Ava took a handful, munching on them happily.

"I was thinking…" I started, watching her with enjoyment.

She paused, her cheeks full of food. I chuckled and tapped her face. "Squirrel-like behavior. I promise to feed you later, so no need to save a snack."

She chewed and swallowed, looking mischievous. "I love chips."

I tilted up the bag, adding more to her plate. "Good. I was thinking we'd throw something on the grill I bought this week if I put it together later, but I've got nothing aside from the last of the casseroles your womenfolk brought."

She snorted. "My *womenfolk*. I'll tell them you called them that— they'll love that."

"Your Gen Two or whatever. Needless to say, I still have nothing to grill." I grinned her way. "I wasn't expecting company."

"We can eat the Chinese food."

"Ah, Little Dragon, we finished that off in the middle of the night. You were ravenous."

She ducked her head with a small laugh. "Right. You were as well, if I recall correctly."

"For something totally different, yes. I ate to keep up the strength you kept depleting with your sexual demands."

She burst out laughing, tilting back her head, the sable color of her hair catching the light. I joined in her amusement.

"So, we'll head to the store and grab something. I can pick up a few things for next week while we're at it. You can too," she said when she stopped laughing.

I scratched my head. "Like grocery shop together?"

She rolled her eyes. "Would you prefer if I went alone? I'll grab a few groceries I need at the same time."

"No, you're right."

"Okay, we can go to Grimsby later. There's a bigger grocery store, and it's never busy Saturday in the early evening. We'll get a few things and grill whatever strikes our fancy later since we just ate the sandwiches."

I tamped down the feeling of worry. It was a grocery store. What could happen at a grocery store?

"What's the matter?" Ava asked from her perch on the steps.

I looked up from the small grill I was assembling. After lunch, she'd opened her book, enjoying a little relaxing time in the sun while I put together the grill. I had music playing in the background, humming under my breath as I worked. It was fairly easy, but the one piece was proving stubborn.

"This gas connector is refusing to cooperate," I grumbled. "It's an odd angle to get to."

She set aside her book and strolled over, peering over my shoulder. "Tight space," she agreed. "Your hands are too big."

I smirked up at her. "You know what they say about big hands and feet, Little Dragon." I winked and leered at her.

Laughing, she pushed me aside. "Yeah. Large gloves and shoes. They both match your ego."

Chuckling, I moved away. She bent and slipped her hand into the tight space and, a moment later, lifted her arm in triumph. "Ta-da!"

Without thinking, I spun her and dragged her to my chest, then kissed her. She flung her arms around my neck, enthusiastically returning my caresses. It surprised me how natural it felt— holding her in my arms, kissing her in the sunshine. Teasing her, laughing. Even working on a simple project as she read quietly in the background. I experienced no tension, no feelings of unease or that she was invading my solitude. I enjoyed having her with me—yet another surprise since I usually preferred to be alone. But somehow, her sitting on the porch, Cash lying on the grass, tunes filling the air, and me puttering around, felt easy and right. As if we'd done this a hundred times before. It was comfortable. It felt like—*home?*

That word drifting through my mind brought me up short. Home was a concept I didn't understand. I'd lived many places— far too many to count. Dwelled in apartments, houses, all sorts of horrid places—some worse than others. But they had all been a place to sleep, to escape the outside world. They had never been home.

But then again, Ava had never been there.

That thought stopped me cold. I lifted my head from Ava's tempting mouth and stepped back.

"What?" she asked, sounding breathless. Her hair moved in the breeze, fluttering around her shoulders, the sun catching the purple streaks. Her eyes glimmered in the sunlight, the color swirling and mixing the way it always did. I never knew what hue to expect, although I was slowly realizing the shade of her irises seemed to match her mood. Right now, they were a soft green, relaxed and at ease.

I shook my head, not answering her. Instead, as Hall & Oates began one of their catchy songs, I twirled her, enjoying her burst of surprised laughter. I began to move, dancing with her. That was something else I liked about her that astonished me. I had always loved to dance—I wasn't particularly good at it or polished. I just moved my feet and hands to the rhythm and stomped around, enjoying the movement and music, but it was something I only ever did alone. I liked dancing with her—she moved freely, and we somehow fit. We fit together in many ways —and I wasn't entirely sure how I felt about that fact.

I certainly wasn't prepared for it.

Yet, as I twirled her again, then yanked her back to my chest and kissed her in the sunshine, I couldn't find it in myself to care.

We pulled into the parking lot of the grocery store, and I was pleased to see it didn't look overly busy. Ava had been correct, which was good since it meant we could be in and out quickly.

She pulled out her phone. "Okay, got your list?"

I scratched my head. "List?"

She shook her head. "You didn't make a list?"

"No, I just pick up whatever I decide I might want."

She dropped her head to her chest. "God help me," she muttered.

I chuckled at her frustration. As I was discovering, Ava was highly organized in everything. After I'd grabbed a quick shower, I walked into the living area to discover she had taken all my piles of paper and organized them. They were now in color-coded files. I wasn't sure if I was more impressed at her swiftness or her brazenness. Both made me smile.

She glanced up, looking guilty. "I couldn't take it anymore, and I couldn't help myself. Now you'll know where everything is, and you won't have to search. Look," she said. "Permits, ideas and drawings, receipts—everything in its own file."

"And where did the folders come from?" I asked. I knew I had nothing like those in the house.

"In my SUV. I always carry extra file folders. I'll leave a few blank ones so you can make up new folders as needed." She paused, pursing her lips. "I can't leave you my label maker, but I could get you one."

That made me want to laugh. As if I would bother with a label maker.

"I'll use a pencil," I assured her. "Not as fancy, but it works." I doubted I would ever add to anything, although I had to admit her files looked good. At least the top of the little table was clear now. She picked up the completed files and slid them onto one of the shelves in the living room, the bright colors easily found. She gazed at me nervously.

"Are you mad?"

I met her eyes and slid my arm around her waist. "No, Little Dragon. I'm surprised you were able to rein yourself in for so long." I had seen her eyes return to the piles on the table many times, and now I understood why. It must have been driving her crazy.

She grinned. "It was difficult."

I kissed the end of her nose. "Try to refrain from reorganizing the store displays when we get there, all right? Maybe leave the label maker here."

"Okay."

I had only meant to tease, but I had a feeling she was serious. The thought amused me to no end—Ava reorganizing an entire store to make it more efficient. Chances were, she'd be right.

I undid my seat belt, still chuckling. "I'm a simple guy, Ava. Now that I have a grill, all I need is some meat to cook on it, some salad stuff, and a few staples."

Inside, I took a handbasket, and Ava grabbed a cart. She eyed the handbasket. "Your groceries won't get cooties sharing the cart with mine."

I really hadn't planned on getting much, but to make her happy, I put the basket in the bottom of her cart and took it from her. "I'll follow you since you know the place and I'm not getting much."

She nodded. "I have my list organized by aisle. It's faster."

"Of course it is." I hid my smile.

I had to admit, she was right. She knew exactly what she wanted, where to get it, and she didn't waste time. My basket contained a lot of meat, some odds and ends that caught my eye, snacks, and a large box of dog biscuits for Cash. A couple of bottles of wine because I knew Ava liked red wine. For some insane reason, I had picked up a little bunch of flowers, thinking they'd look nice on the table, and I knew Ava would like them as well. Luckily, she didn't notice and pulled me along quickly before I changed my mind. In Ava's part of the cart, I could see the meals she was planning. Spaghetti. A whole chicken. Short ribs. The ingredients to go along with them. Cereal for breakfast. Cream for her coffee, which reminded me I needed some as well. Our two worlds summed up in a grocery cart. One organized and methodically planned, one chaotic and barely thought-out.

We turned to the last aisle—the produce department—and Ava stopped, cursing under her breath.

"What?" I asked.

"Turn around," she hissed. "Just turn around."

I attempted to, but the cart hit the display, and some cans tilted, then toppled, rolling over and hitting the cart, then the floor, making a loud noise.

"Shit, damn, and blast," she muttered. "What are the odds?"

"Odds of what?" I asked again, picking up the cans.

"That."

I looked up and saw a familiar-looking man headed our way. There was a little girl with him, and he was frowning as he approached. For a moment, I thought it was Ronan, then realized it was actually another brother. It had to be, given the resemblance.

I stifled a groan at the thought of meeting yet another family member. They were bloody everywhere. Ava was right—what were the odds?

Her brother stopped, not speaking but staring. He glanced between us, then at the cart. The little girl looked excited, smiling widely.

"Auntie Ava! I told Daddy that was you!"

Ava bent and hugged the little girl. Her brother continued to stare. I cleared my throat and held out my hand. It felt as if I were doing that a lot lately. "Hello. I'm Hunter."

He shook my hand, his grip firm. A little too firm. "Liam Callaghan."

I withdrew my hand, resisting the urge to flex my fingers and get some feeling back in them.

"Hi! I'm Lucy!"

"Hi, Lucy." I grinned at her since she was hard to resist. "It's nice to meet you."

She beamed at me. She was adorable, with the biggest smile I had ever seen. I noticed she had a prosthesis on her arm and wondered what had happened. I would have to ask Ava later.

"What are you doing here, Liam?" Ava asked. "You usually don't shop this time of the day."

"Mommy had a headache. Daddy and I were making supper, but he burned the grilled cheese. So we had to come get something else," Lucy informed her.

Liam grinned, his expression loosening. "I ordered one of their deli pizzas. Paige and Lucy love them. I decided to get a few other things while we were here waiting. The grilled cheese is a lost cause."

Ava laughed.

Liam lifted one eyebrow. "I was wondering what you were doing here, to be honest." He eyed the cart. "Shopping for two?"

Before I could protest, Ava spoke.

"No. Hunter is Mr. Owens's grandson. He just moved here, so I'm showing him the best places to shop. I had to get some groceries, so we came together."

He rubbed his chin. "Jack's grandson. Hmm. Interesting. Ronan said he met you earlier—at Ava's house. And here you are now, together *again*." He nodded slowly, his eyes gleaming. "Yep. Interesting."

Ava's cheeks colored. "Just being neighborly."

"Ava helped me with my dog earlier," I interjected. "She mentioned she had to go grocery shopping. I asked her for another favor."

"Right."

"It's just groceries," I added.

"I'm not saying anything." Liam smirked.

"We both had to come. Saved taking two vehicles."

"Very *responsible* of you."

I waved at the cart. "We have two different orders."

"I see. Very circumspect." He winked. "I'll let you get on with your *neighborly* grocery shopping." He tapped the wine and flowers in my basket. "Enjoy your evening. I'll see you tomorrow at brunch, Ava." He began to laugh. "Or not." Then he met my eyes. "I'll see you around, Hunter."

"Not if I see you first," I muttered.

Then just like his brother, he smiled. "Count on it."

Why the hell did they keep saying that?

I could still hear his amusement as he turned down the aisle, Lucy waving as they disappeared.

Ava hung her head. "I am cursed," she muttered. "I've been coming here for years at this time and never once run into a family member until today. Ronan rarely drops over to check up on me." She peered up at me. "I'm sorry."

I could only shake my head. "It's fine. Let's finish up before your parents make an appearance. I don't think I could handle that today."

She sighed, and I slipped my hand over hers. "It's fine, Little Dragon. So, I saw your brothers, and they saw me with you. In your house, grocery shopping together. They can draw whatever conclusions they want. We know the truth, and that's all that matters."

She looked as if she wanted to ask something, then changed her mind. "Okay. Let's finish up."

I meant what I said. It was no one's business but ours. We knew what was going on between us, and that was enough. We were scratching an itch. Filling a void for each other for a short period of time. This was no different from any other relationship I had ever had in my adult life.

I tamped down the little voice in my head that asked if I really believed my own bullshit. It needed to shut up and mind its own business.

Ava was quiet in the truck. It wasn't unusual—I had noticed she wasn't given to idle chatter, a gift I appreciated. But this seemed different, as if the silence had a heaviness to it. She stared out the window, her arms crossed.

I pulled up to the house, shut off the engine, and turned in my seat to face her.

"Little Dragon."

She met my eyes, hers so indescribably sad, I was moved. "Hey, what is it?"

"I'm sorry about my brothers. I really had no idea—" She paused and swallowed. "I'll make sure they know not to bother you."

"It's fine."

"I know you like your privacy. I'll grab my groceries and clear out. But I had a great day, Hunter." She stretched her head and kissed my cheek. "Thank you."

She slid from the truck, and I blinked.

She was leaving?

I was out of the truck, stilling her hands before she could reach in the back for her bags. "Whoa, hold up. What exactly is going on in that pretty head of yours? I'm not upset. I know you didn't arrange for your brothers to see us. Shit, Little Dragon, it was just dumb luck." Realization dawned on me. "That's what you think, isn't it? That I think you arranged all this somehow." I barked out a laugh. "Not even you can be that meticulous."

"I don't want you thinking that I think there is more to this than there is. That I somehow was pushing—"

I cut her off and wrapped her in my arms. "I don't think anything. We ran into your brothers. Hell, Ava, you know people everywhere you go. They can all think what they want. I don't care. Just because your brothers ribbed me a little, I can take it. I don't want you to go."

"You don't?"

"You really think I'm that much of an asshole?"

"No. But I know how it looks."

I chuckled. "You were as shocked as me both times. If I hadn't knocked over the cans, we would have made the escape you were trying to engineer. Stop overthinking this. Everything is fine." I brushed a kiss to her head. "Stay. Please. I got wine and steak. I even bought potatoes because your mom said they're your favorite." I reached behind her and pulled out the small bunch of flowers she hadn't noticed since she'd been so preoccupied with the crazy thoughts in her head.

"And these are for you."

Her eyes widened, filled with shock. "Really?"

"If I give them to Cash, he'll eat them. And when I buy myself flowers to feel pretty, I prefer roses," I deadpanned.

She looked up, her lips quirking. "Red ones?"

"Peach, darling. I sprinkle them on the bed and roll around in them. I look *fabulous* in peach."

That did it. She threw back her head in laughter, and I had to kiss her. Long, thoroughly, and deep.

"Stay."

"Yes."

I winked. "Good."

CHAPTER 11
HUNTER

I sat back, replete. I picked up my wine and sipped the rich, heady red with appreciation. We had unpacked the groceries, stored Ava's in the bottom of the still mostly empty refrigerator, then I had grilled the steak and Ava had made some sort of potatoes and onions she put in foil and cooked on the barbecue. I had no idea what was in them, but they were delicious. I had once again witnessed her love of potatoes when she slid part of her steak onto my plate, then picked at pieces of potatoes I had left in exchange. Laughing, I had pushed the plate closer to her so she could get at them easier. She was rather endearing with her potato-stealing ways.

"Awesome dinner," I mused.

Ava smiled, picking up her wine. "Perfect summery meal." She sighed. "It would have been better with corn, but that won't be ready for a couple of months." She eyed me over the rim. "Will, ah, you still be here for corn harvest?"

"Depends on how work goes here. There is a lot to be done."

She looked at the worn table, running her finger over the faded top. "You have someplace else to be? Like a set date you have to leave?"

"No."

"You mentioned you were in Alberta before you came here. You have a place there?"

"No. I rented a room in a house with a bunch of guys. Before that, I was in a place outside town—a little trailer. I had a rented room in a boarding house prior to that, a small apartment for a while…" I paused, taking a drink of wine. "I can go on if you want."

She frowned. "You don't have a home? A base?"

"No. I never have."

Her shock was written on her face. "Never?"

I didn't really like to discuss my past. But I ran a hand over my jaw, scrubbing it roughly. "I have never had a place to call home. My mother never settled anywhere for longer than a few months. I don't know any other way to live. When I went out on my own, I just stuck with what I knew. I have my truck, my dog, and I go where the wind takes me."

"Just like that?" she asked.

"Just like that. I go where I find work. Usually construction. I stay until I feel the need to leave. And I go."

"Don't you…don't you get lonely?"

I met her gaze. "Getting lonely implies caring for someone. I don't do that, Ava. I don't get attached."

"You're attached to Cash."

At the mention of his name, he rose to his feet and trotted over, leaning on my leg. I rubbed his head, and with a sigh, he shut his eyes, enjoying the attention.

"He's the exception. I care for him because he was discarded. Much the way I was. Through no fault of his own, he was abandoned and left behind. We share that. So, I look after him. One day, he won't be around, and I'll be back on my own. And I'll carry on."

She stared at me, her eyes wide with disbelief. Seeing the pictures on the walls of her home, the little cluster of homes of the people she loved that surrounded her, I knew I had shocked her. She would be as adrift in my world as I would be in hers. Both were foreign concepts to the other. She was used to being surrounded by love and belonging. My life was a string of forgotten places and people.

"I don't know what to say to that," she admitted.

"Say nothing. I don't expect you to understand. Any more than I can understand your world. But that's okay. You're here right now, and I want to enjoy that. What happens next week or next month will happen. Enjoy the moment with me, Little Dragon. Try it."

She nodded and stood, taking her plate and lifting mine. She carried them to the kitchen and filled the sink with hot, soapy water. The evening sky darkened the window, the steam gathering on the glass. Her reflection was sad.

Oddly enough, it matched the way my own words made me feel.

After dinner, we wandered outside, watching as the last of the light faded. The air was cooler, the scent of outdoors fresh and clean. I had to admit, I liked it here. The way the house was situated, it felt as if you were alone in the world, tucked away from the craziness that existed outside the little bubble this piece of property offered. I slid another one of my favorite mixtapes into the boom box and, once again, took Ava in my arms. We danced under the dim moonlight, the stars slowly brightening in the night sky. We didn't talk, letting our bodies feel the gentle rhythm of the music and nothing else. Cash lay on the porch, bored and indifferent to us, his tail thumping slowly on the old boards.

The breeze picked up, and Ava shivered. "We should go inside," I murmured. "It's getting chilly."

Wordlessly, we entered the house. She curled into the old chair, and I sat on the sofa, Cash lying by my feet. Ava picked up her book, opening it but not really reading. I knew she was troubled by my earlier words. She couldn't comprehend them. A world without family, without love, and a place called home didn't sit well with her. I had to admit, I found her worry somewhat sweet. But I needed to break her train of thought.

"Not enjoying your book?" I asked.

"Oh, um, it's good." She rubbed her eyes. "When I get tired, I find it hard to concentrate." She offered me a smile. "I always need the weekend to recharge."

I had noticed yesterday she looked tired. She'd been brighter today, but I could see the exhaustion creeping back up. "You work too hard. You're under a great deal of pressure all the time."

She shrugged. "We all are. ABC is a busy place."

"Do you have help? An assistant?"

"If I need help, I ask."

I fought back my smile. "I bet you never ask." I relaxed against the cushion. "When's the last time you took a break?"

"I'm off every weekend."

"A holiday," I said patiently. "A long stretch of time away from the office and the responsibilities."

She blinked. "I took a few long weekends last year."

I snorted.

"What about you?" she asked.

"I took two months off and went up to Alaska. Me, Cash, a trailer, and the open road. No phone, no email, nothing."

Her eyes widened. "Really?"

"Yes."

"Was it wonderful?"

"It was great. I needed the break."

"I couldn't do that. I have too many responsibilities."

"Maybe you need to reprioritize. Ask for help at the office so you can live your life as well as work. You can't organize every minute of your life. You need to let some moments simply happen."

She didn't say anything. She looked small and sad. I didn't like it.

I stood, extending my hand. "Come to bed with me, Ava."

She hesitated.

"Bring your book. I'll read to you."

"Really?"

"Yes. I think you need to let me take the reins for a bit. I like reading out loud." I waggled my fingers. "Come on."

She took my hand and let me pull her from the chair.

"It's a romance book."

"Is it dirty?"

"Scarlett Scott usually is."

I pulled her in and kissed her. "Maybe I'll get some ideas. All-new ideas on how to ravish you."

She laughed, and I felt her relax.

My plan was already working.

AVA

I woke up, blinking and warm. Once again, I was surrounded by heat and the snores of both Cash and Hunter. I had to admit, Cash was far louder. Outside was still dark, although I sensed the light would soon break through the dawn.

I had let Hunter lead me to bed last night. He'd surprised me with his offer, and I assumed a few pages into the book, he would tire of the words and decide to get physical instead. But he had helped me disrobe, kissing my skin as he uncovered it, then slipped one of his T-shirts over my head and lay on the bed, patting his bare chest. I lay on his warm torso, his arm wrapping me close as he braced the book on his bent knee and began to read. He stroked my hair as he spoke, his touch light and gentle. I felt myself relax, sinking deeper into him, my eyes shutting of their own accord, suddenly too heavy to stay open. His voice was low and rich, and he read very well. He was an excellent orator, hitting all the marks well. I couldn't recall the last time anyone had read to me—probably my dad when I was a child—and I was shocked how much I enjoyed hearing the story out loud.

I fell asleep with his voice in my ear and his hand on my head. I slept dreamlessly until the feel of his mouth on my neck woke me, the darkness surrounding us, his hands stroking along my skin under the shirt he'd slipped over my head. Not a word passed between us as he caressed me, his mouth worshiping my skin, then settling on mine with a profound passion and need I sensed deep in my bones. I spread my hands over his bare, strong back, stroking along his spine, cupping his buttocks. I felt his erection, hard and hot, between us. I opened myself to him, letting him settle between my legs, suddenly as desperate for him as he was for me. His surge was sudden and fast, and I gasped his name, feeling the power of his possession. He gripped me, his fingers sinking into my hips as he drove into me, groaning my name and thrusting in long, steady movements. My orgasm was unexpected and swift, catching me off guard. He followed not long after, gasping and grunting, fisting my hair and shaking.

He collapsed on top of me, his breathing fast and heavy. He kissed the side of my neck and rolled away, disposing of the condom. He returned to the bed and pulled me into his arms.

"Sorry, Little Dragon. I tried to resist."

Still reeling, I shook my head. "Resist?"

He laughed lowly. "You fell asleep, but I kept reading." He paused. "You're right. That Scarlett writes dirty stuff."

I began to giggle. "You got turned on?"

"Yes. I tried to go to sleep, but you were right there. Your leg was over mine, and your hot little pussy was pressed against me. I couldn't stop myself."

I yawned. "I'm glad you didn't try."

He kissed me. "Go back to sleep. No more jumping—at least for tonight."

I had fallen back into sleep right away.

I slipped from the bed, careful not to disturb either of them. Hunter frowned, his hand searching the air, and I shoved my still-warm pillow toward him. He buried his head in the fluffy material and fisted the edge, settling back into sleep. Cash only huffed and shut his eyes.

I gathered my clothes and used the washroom, splashing cold water on my face, then padded into the kitchen. I hesitated, unsure what to do. Stay or go. I knew yesterday had been an oddity for Hunter. He made it clear we were simply scratching the proverbial itch for each other, and I hadn't expected yesterday at all. It had been a wonderful day, though.

Aside from my brothers.

I shook my head as I made a pot of coffee. I would have a cup then leave, sparing Hunter the need to find an excuse to ask me to do so.

I tried to ignore the flash of pain it caused me thinking of that. He was more wonderful than I expected. I loved our sparring. How he made me laugh. His silly dancing when a song came on he really liked. The strength of his arms when he pulled me in to dance with him. How it felt when he was inside me—the passion and need that shone in his beautiful eyes as we...fucked? Made love? I wasn't sure how he'd refer to it, but I knew it was amazing.

And despite what he claimed, he was caring. I ran my finger over the little petals of the flowers he'd bought me. The way he'd read to me last night, his quiet worry when he spoke of me needing help on occasion. He was correct about that. I hated asking. I hated anyone thinking I was anything less than in complete control. I worked hard—and at times, endlessly—to get the job done. I wondered what the group would say if I suddenly told them I needed help. I shook my head at the thought. I was fine. They depended on me. I would make it through the next while then take a little break and come back strong. We had a lot of irons in the fire right now, and I was simply feeling a little burned out. It had happened before, and I'd made it through fine and no one knew anything was the matter.

It seemed odd that a man who was almost a complete stranger noticed that about me when my own family seemed oblivious.

I sat down, pulling one leg close to my chest, and sipped my coffee. I thought of what Hunter had revealed to me last night. His nomadic lifestyle. Growing up that way. Never settling, never developing long relationships. Never planning to. Cash was his only concession. He had been serious, his words honest.

Yet, the man I'd had glimpses of this weekend wasn't the same man he described himself to be. If he were, he wouldn't care if I looked tired. He would have walked away when my brothers approached. I had expected him to take Cash's lead and be out the back door before Ronan had even walked in the house, but he had stayed. He'd let my mother and aunts into his house and accepted their clucking and casseroles. He'd good-naturedly tolerated Liam's teasing.

He'd bought me flowers.

I pursed my lips, wondering if I was the first person to notice those things about him. Maybe, like my family, others accepted what we let them see. Somehow, though, we had both seen something under the façade we presented to the world.

Hands on my shoulders and a set of warm lips ghosting up my neck startled me. Hunter's palms were warm on my skin as he bent close. "You did it again."

I turned my head. "You were sleeping so well I didn't want to wake you. I made coffee, and I was going to bring you a cup."

And leave before you woke up, since I'm not sure how to do this, I added silently.

He poured a cup of coffee, and I ogled his form. He moved with a sensual grace, the strength in his torso and arms evident in the way his muscles flexed and tightened. He flipped the chair around, straddling it and laying one arm along the top as he sipped his coffee and regarded me with his intense gaze.

"I call bullshit on that. You were going to leave without waking me." He indicated my bag by the door.

I sighed. "I thought it might be easier for you if I were just gone."

"You know what your problem is, Little Dragon? You think too much. Your brain is on overdrive every moment of every day. No wonder you're so exhausted."

"It's my job to be thinking. I have no choice but to overthink. I need to be one step ahead of everything and everybody all the time."

He nodded. "That's your job," he agreed.

I threw up my hands in frustration. "What are you saying?"

"You need to relax in your personal life." He reached over and took my hand, forcing the fingers apart. I hadn't realized until he did how tightly I had been clenching my fists. "Think about yesterday. No plans, no demands. You relaxed for the most part and just enjoyed the moment. You need to do that more often."

"What does that have to do with me getting out of bed?"

"If you'd stayed, I would have woken you up with my mouth and my cock. Relaxed you into the day. Walked you to your car and kissed you." He paused. "Asked if maybe we could do this again."

A smile tugged at my lips. "Really?"

He stood and held out his hand. "Let's try it."

"You-you want to go back to bed?"

He pulled me to my feet. "Yes. I want to go back to bed. With you. I want to fuck you with the sun coming up and my name falling from those pretty lips."

I let him lead me back to his room. I couldn't deny either of us.

Later that morning, I unpacked my groceries in my quiet house. My body still felt Hunter's possession from earlier. The way he'd touched me everywhere. Kissed me. As promised, he'd made me come with his mouth, his fingers, and finally, his cock. The power and passion in his thrusts. His low moans and satisfied grunts and curses as he shook with his release. How he soaped my body in the shower and insisted on towel-drying my hair.

He had carried my bags to the SUV, setting them in the back seat, then turned back to me.

"Thank you, Little Dragon."

I nodded, my throat suddenly thick. I swallowed. "Have a good week, Hunter."

He laughed low and slid his hand around the nape of my neck, yanking me to his mouth. "I will now." He held open the door, waiting until I climbed in.

"Try to have a good week, Ava. Tell them all to back off if it gets too much."

I managed a smile, wondering why it was so hard to leave him.

"I'll see you around," I managed to say.

He tilted his head, studying me, then winked.

"You can count on it."

Then he disappeared into the house, Cash following him.

For some unknown reason, tears coursed down my cheeks on the short drive. Wiping them away, I shook my head at my behavior. I was being silly. It had been a great, unexpected weekend. It was exactly what I had needed, and we had agreed on the rules. It was only supposed to be one time. That became one night, which stretched into two.

Still, a small part of me wished it didn't have to end.

I tamped down that silly voice. That wasn't how life worked. At least not for me.

⸱ ————————

I carried my plate to the sofa, setting my coffee on the table in front of me. The room buzzed with voices, lots of various conversations happening around me. Once a month, we had a group brunch—it was casual, whoever wanted to come could. Usually, the same people joined us, but today, there were more than normal, and the place was full.

Watching everyone settle into their groups, I felt a strange pang. Everyone seemed to be a couple today. Liam and Paige. Ronan and Beth. Paul and Diane, Jeremy and Kim. Brayden and Addi. Gracie and Jaxson. Theo was laughing on the sofa with Anne. Reid and Becca's daughters, Lily and Melissa, had their boyfriends with them, and they were in the first stage of love, sitting close together, gazing at each other with adoration. Both Michael and Timothy seemed like nice guys, and I was happy for them. Even quiet Shelby had her boyfriend with her. Simon Kent owned one of the small art galleries in Toronto. He had been in love with her for ages, but she never noticed—until the day she did. Since then, they'd been inseparable, and I had a feeling another wedding would happen soon. The way he looked at her, hovered close, and paid attention to her made my chest ache at times, even though I was thrilled for her. He got along well with everyone—especially his prospective father-in-law, Maddox. They were both businessmen with a head for numbers and a shared love of Shelby. She looked happy and more at ease than ever.

I heard Heather's loud laughter and Reed joining in before the only other single person flounced over and sat beside me on the sofa. I grinned at Sammy Morrison, Reed's sister.

"Is he being a brat again?"

She flipped him off, settling herself and taking a bite of toast. "Being his usual self, yes. Such a pain in my ass," she grumbled. Then she winked. I knew how much the two of them adored each other. They were incredibly close but loved teasing and sparring. Much like my siblings.

"Where's Mila?" I asked.

"Deep into edits. She's up against a deadline."

"When does the book come out?"

Sammy pursed her lips. "November. There is already talk about it. Her publisher is very excited."

Mila was Van's youngest daughter and had always loved writing. She used to make up stories and tell them to us, reading as she said from the "pages in her head." She was quiet and shy until she began to talk about her work. She had written several novels and had been picked up by a publisher, who purchased her series in a rare, lucrative deal. She was excited and nervous and working very hard to learn the ropes of the industry.

"Me too. I can't wait to read it. How are things with you?"

"Busy."

"Done any cool projects lately?"

"I converted a loft. It was stuck in the seventies. It'll be featured on the show in a few months."

Sammy worked independently. She was incredible. She could build anything, design, renovate, fix, and change spaces so you didn't recognize them. She'd inherited her design talent from her mom, Liv, and her dad, Van, had taught her everything when it came to construction. He was incredibly proud of her.

On occasion, she did work for us, but she preferred the freedom of choosing her projects. She was featured on one of the renovation channels on occasion—again, choosing which ones she took on. Her work took her all over the country, and it was rare to see her at one of the brunches.

"What's going on with you?" she asked.

"Not much. Busy. Same old, same old."

"You looked sad when I came over. Are you okay?"

"Sad? No."

"Maybe not sad. Pensive."

I shook my head. "Just looking at all the new faces."

"I know. So many." She winked. "What about you, Ava? Got anyone hidden away? Someone you're having fun with but not introducing to this crazy lot?"

I blinked at her. "Why-why would you say that?"

What had Ronan and Liam been saying?

She laughed and nudged me with her elbow. "Teasing. I wouldn't blame you if you did. Introducing anyone to this bunch would be overwhelming. You'd have to be pretty damn certain of a future with them."

I relaxed. "Right. Well, no chance of that."

She nodded and finished her meal. "I hear you. I need a refill. You want anything?"

I looked down at my still mostly full plate. "Nope, I'm good."

"Okay. How about lunch next week? I'm in Toronto on Wednesday. Uncle Bent has a project he wants me to look at."

"Sounds good. Call me in the morning."

With a fast kiss on the cheek, she was gone, flitting away to visit with her parents or Nan and Pops. She was like a butterfly, alighting somewhere briefly, never staying long.

Somehow, that made me think of Hunter. He never stayed long either. Apparently, it was his mantra. I tried to imagine him here, in this group. He would hate it. The laughter and camaraderie. The oversharing. The sheer number of people gathered around with one common denominator—the love of family.

Yep, he would hate it.

I looked down at my plate, my appetite off. Strangely what I wanted was some of Hunter's slightly burned toast. I pushed down the feeling of sadness once again and picked up my fork, knowing I needed to eat or questions would be asked.

Suddenly, the cushions on either side of me depressed, and I found myself in the middle of a Liam and Ronan sandwich. I rolled my eyes, cursing the fact that I had sat on the center cushion.

They each rested an arm over the back of the sofa, effectively caging me in.

"Hey, big sis," Ronan uttered with a grin. "How's it going?"

"You look lonely sitting here all by yourself," Liam added.

"Sammy just left, so I am hardly lonely." I stuck my fork into the hash browns and lifted it to my mouth. My aunt made awesome hash browns, and they were my favorite. "Feel free to go away."

"Where's the boy toy?" Ronan asked in a low voice. "Waiting at the house?"

"Shopping for dinner?" Liam chuckled.

"I have no idea what you're talking about."

"Lemme refresh your memory. Hunter Owens," Ronan whispered. "What the hell is going on between you two?"

"Nothing. I told you. Cash got loose, and I helped him."

"You helped him grocery shop too?" Liam interjected.

"I was being nice."

"Nice enough he left beard burns on your neck. Don't try to pretend with us," Ronan drawled. "The sexual tension between you two was so thick, I could cut it with a knife."

"Your imagination is running away with you," I said as firmly as I could.

"Really?" he challenged me. "You're telling me you're not playing hide the salami with the guy?"

I tried not to laugh at his description. "Is that what you and Beth do?" I asked. "Hunter's more of a bucking bronco kind of guy, if you must know."

He looked squeamish. "Jesus, Ava. TMI. You could have just nodded."

"You brought it up. Not me."

"I don't want to think about you doing that," he hissed. "You're my sister."

"Then you shouldn't have asked."

"I'm sorry I did."

I had to laugh at his horrified expression. I rubbed his arm. "It's okay, Ronan. I'm only joking."

"I doubt it."

"I guess you'll never know."

"Is he renovating to live there?" Liam asked quietly.

"No. He plans to lease it, I think. Use it on occasion. I'm not involved in his decision-making in regard to the future."

"So, this, whatever it is between you, is casual."

I met his eyes. "On both sides, Liam. I'm a big girl, and I can look after myself."

"I'm aware. I don't have to like it, though."

I shrugged. "My private life is just that. *My* private life. I didn't interfere when you married Paige a few weeks after you met her." I glanced at Ronan. "And I supported you even when you were being an asshole with Beth. So, stay out of my business."

Ronan snorted. "You went behind my back and talked to Beth."

"Which got you back together. Hunter is Mr. Owens's grandson. He's fixing up the place and going to move on. I've tried to be helpful. What happens is between us. No one else. Leave it alone."

"We're just worried," Liam admitted. "We don't want to see you hurt."

"Like I said, I'm a big girl. I can take care of myself. If I choose to have or not have a casual relationship with someone, it's not your concern."

"It is," Ronan insisted.

"Why?"

"Because you deserve more than casual, Ava. You deserve the whole thing."

I stood and looked down at my brothers. Their sincerity was evident, their need to look after me strong. I adored them, but I needed to make sure they understood.

"I'm not like you. I don't want the 'whole thing.' I like my life the way I like it. Just let it go and let me live my life the way I want. I promise you, I know what I'm doing."

"Do you really?" Liam asked. "Or is that what you tell yourself to make it easier?"

I shook my head. "I love you two, but I need you to butt out. Do you hear me?"

They both looked frustrated but nodded. I dug into my pocket and handed Ronan a folded piece of paper. "See if you can do anything with that, okay?"

He opened it. "This is the house Hunter is working on?"

"Yeah. He is going to need an architect's drawings for the addition."

He huffed a sigh, and I bent and kissed his cheek. "For me, Ronan. Look it over for me."

"Fine."

I patted his shoulder and kissed Liam's cheek. "Thanks. Now, go back to your wives, boys. Stop worrying about me."

"Not likely," Ronan snorted. Liam nodded in agreement. "What he said."

I picked up my now-cold coffee and headed to the kitchen.

A while later, I found Nan sitting in the library sipping a cup of tea. A warm shawl was tucked around her shoulders, and her cane rested on the arm of her chair. But her eyes were bright and her smile welcoming. I sat across from her, and we chatted about a few projects ABC was working on.

She studied my face. "You look tired, Ava."

I shook my head in denial. "I'm fine. Busy."

"Is the office too much?" she guessed shrewdly.

I waved off her concerns. "It'll pass. It always does."

She frowned and took a sip of her tea. "It is always acceptable to ask for help."

"And I will if I need it."

She pursed her lips and changed the subject. "I hear you met the Owenses' grandson. He told us you helped him." Then she lifted one eyebrow. "He also informed us you were bossy and ate his potatoes."

I laughed. He was right on both counts. "Something like that. But he's one to talk. He's pretty bossy himself."

"He is an interesting young man. Too young to be so jaded."

"Do you know, Nan? What happened? Why he's stayed away?"

She sighed. "Not entirely. They were always private. I know the daughter was a handful. A free spirit. She left home when she was young. She came back for a while, then disappeared again. One day, Jordan and I were out past the trees picking wild blueberries. We heard an argument—not the words but the loud voices, and we saw Jack and his daughter Nina outside. She was yelling and pushing at her father. He wasn't reacting, but when she disappeared and came back, dragging a little boy behind her, he tried to stop her. There was more yelling on both their parts, and she put the little boy in the car and drove off." Nan paused. "The little boy didn't seem to want to go."

"That was Hunter's mother taking him away," I surmised.

Nan nodded. "Gail never spoke of it, but she always looked sad. The few times I was in their house, I noticed all the pictures of their daughter were gone. There was one of the young boy. I had seen him in town with Gail once. He had a head full of dark hair and those eyes. So unique. But neither Jack nor Gail talked about them." She finished her tea. "I don't think they ever got over losing them."

"She never came back?"

"Not that I know of."

I thought about what Hunter had said—that he never had a home. That they moved and traveled all the time. I could imagine him as a young boy, always on the go, never really happy or settling. That would certainly affect a person. I also remembered his words, *"It was the only way I knew to live."* Was he really going to live that way the rest of his life?

"He seemed like a pleasant young man. A little guarded, but nice," Nan mused. "Stubborn as hell. Independent."

"I think he had to be."

She nodded. "One would have to be patient and let him see there are different ways to live," she said, meeting my gaze. "Especially if one cared about him."

"I was only asking," I replied.

"Of course you were." She patted my hand. "I didn't think anything of it."

She left me sitting there, staring at the water. I sighed and decided to head home. I had things to do today since I had spent the entire day yesterday with Hunter and Cash.

I had to ignore the urge to forget my responsibilities and go back to Hunter's. I wasn't certain I would be welcome, and I didn't want to risk it.

No matter how much I yearned to.

I wiped the mirror after my shower, toweling my hair briskly. It had been a productive afternoon. The house was tidy, I'd made some meals, done a little work, and even managed to sit on my deck and paint my toenails. I wiggled them, the bright purple shining in the light. Drying off, I headed to my room, slipping into a pair of comfy sweats and a big sweatshirt that once belonged to my dad. It had been washed so often, it was thin and soft, the logo barely visible on the front. It hung off my shoulder and the hem was misshapen, but I loved it. It was still warm and cuddly.

I padded into the kitchen, glancing at the time. It was only eight, which left me lots of time to relax for the night. After making a small pot of decaf coffee, I carried a cup to my favorite chair. The table was empty, and I realized I had left my book at Hunter's. For a moment, I stood, recalling how his mouth felt on my neck when he woke me, his need evident after reading the spicy part of the book.

Laying my hand on my neck, I remembered his whispered words, his low groans of satisfaction, and his incredible skill when he touched me. Simply thinking about it made me ache with want for him. With a low groan of dissatisfaction, I reached for my

Kindle, grateful I always kept it charged and bought both the physical copy and e-book. I could keep reading, and I would ask Hunter for my book back the next time I saw him.

I pushed down the feeling of sadness when I realized I wasn't sure there'd be a next time, although I hoped there would be. Despite what I said to my brothers or Nan, I did want to see him again. I liked spending time with him.

I liked it too much.

Sitting down, I found the place I'd stopped before. I had been so tired, I couldn't recall what Hunter had read—I'd enjoyed listening to the timbre of his voice, but I couldn't recall the words, so I began over again. Oddly, I found it hard to concentrate on the book. I was distracted and stared into space. Thinking about Hunter. About the day we spent together. I was so lost in my thoughts, I startled when I heard a heavy knock on the back door.

I sat up, my heart rate kicking into high gear. No one used the back door. My family always came to the front. There could be only one person on my back step. I stood and heard the telltale signs of Cash's excited pacing and saw the outline of Hunter's broad shoulders filling the window.

I flung open the door, and our eyes locked. His gaze was turbulent, the silvery blue a maelstrom of color. He gripped the doorframe, his knuckles white. He had my book fisted in one hand.

"You left this. I thought you might want it," he rasped, taking in the sweatshirt hanging off my shoulder.

I could only nod in silence, words freezing in my throat. There was something different about him tonight. Tension rolled off him like a wave. He was overwrought, almost angry.

Was he angry at me?

"Tell me that shirt once belonged to a member of your family," he growled.

"My dad," I managed to whisper.

He lunged, his hand cupping the back of my neck as he dragged me to his chest. "Thank God."

Then his mouth was on mine, and suddenly, everything was right in my world.

CHAPTER 12

HUNTER

It started in the early afternoon. A slight hum under my skin. Annoying but easily ignored. As I worked, pulling rotting deck boards off the front, at times I stopped, idly wondering if somehow there was an unseen electrical current under my feet I kept stepping on. But I found nothing.

I continued working, trying to disregard the slightly anxious feeling that seemed to seep into my chest. I blasted the boom box, choosing classic 80's rock to drown out the staccato sensations, but even after getting all the boards off and grabbing a beer, the feelings lingered. Grew, in fact.

It was as if I were longing for something. I wasn't hungry or thirsty. Cash was right by my feet. Music was playing, the sun still shining, yet the feeling gripped me harder. I had never felt anything like it.

I went inside, Cash following me, and headed to the bathroom, deciding a hot shower would clear away the odd sensation. I washed and rinsed, the warmth feeling good on my shoulders. I rubbed my hair dry, trimmed my beard, and headed to the bedroom with a towel draped around my waist.

As I stepped into the room, the sensation increased as I inhaled. All I could smell was Ava. Light, sensual and feminine, her scent saturated the room. I hadn't noticed it until now. The closer I got to the bed, the stronger it became. I lifted a pillow to my face and inhaled. Every moment of the last couple of days hit me. Her smile. Her laughter. How she felt underneath me. How she tasted on my tongue. The silken warmth of her mouth. The feel of her soft skin under my fingers. The way she teased me. The serious look on her face when she informed me that, yes, she did order a dinner for four for herself to eat because it had her favorites and why deny herself?

She was unlike any woman I had ever known. Certainly none of them had ever caused this sort of physical reaction before. Simply sniffing her pillow, and I was aching for her. Thinking of making love with her made me hard, and the towel I was wearing tented, my cock desperate as I thought about the way her muscles gripped me as she climaxed. Her throaty moans and pleas. How we moved together and the strength of my orgasms.

With a start, I realized I was *missing* her. How the hell was that possible? I'd never missed a single person in my life. Not a family member, a friend, or a lover. Ever.

Certainly not a woman I had barely known a week and spent a couple of nights with.

Yet, once I thought about it, I realized that was exactly what I was feeling. I wanted Ava back here. I wanted to hear her laughter. Inhale her perfume. Taste her mouth. Bury myself inside her.

I dropped the pillow and backed away from the bed, accidentally kicking something on the floor. I bent and picked up the book she'd brought with her. The one I'd read to her. The one I'd kept reading, then woke her to fuck her because I wanted to. Because I couldn't resist the urge. I had wanted her more than any woman I could recall.

I shook my head. I didn't form attachments. Especially with women. I needed to stop thinking this way. It had been a long time since I'd been with anyone. It was that simple. I was still horny. It had nothing to do with her beautiful eyes or the way she cocked her head while listening to me. The way she touched me or made me laugh with her teasing. Her over-the-top need to organize and fix things around her to make life better. It certainly had nothing to do with the fact that when I was with her, I felt more settled than I ever had.

Nothing.

I tossed the book aside and got dressed, determined to get those thoughts and her out of my mind.

I paced the room, unable to settle. I ate dinner standing, brooding, and staring out the window. The food tasted like ash. I slammed back a shot of tequila, thinking it would jolt me out of whatever-the-hell this was, but it tasted sour and bitter. I glanced at the clock, barking out a humorless laugh. It was barely after eight, and I wanted the day over with. A good night's sleep would shake these maudlin thoughts from my head. Reset my body so I felt calmer.

I cursed under my breath when my inner voice laughed.

I stubbed my toe and cursed again—loudly. Cash lifted his head, his ears laid back in confusion at my anger.

"Sorry, boy." I bent and stroked his silky fur. "Bad day."

He stood, stretched, and padded to the door, pawing at it.

"You wanna go for a walk?" I nodded in agreement. "Good idea. It'll wear us both out."

I went to the bedroom and grabbed some socks, sitting on the bed to pull them on. As I stood, Ava's book slid to the floor, and once again, I picked it up. I stared at it. Maybe she was looking for it. I should probably return it to her. After all, I had no need of it. I had basically read the whole damn thing last night. Dirty parts and all—and there were many of those. Having her beside me had been convenient. Recalling how she had responded, even half asleep, made my dick twitch. I ignored it.

Maybe if I gave the book back to Ava and got it out of my house, saw her for a moment or two, this itch, this constant craving that was clawing at me, would ease.

I grunted in satisfaction. That was the answer. I would leave it on her back porch, knock, and walk away. She'd find it, it would be out of the house, and I'd get back to normal.

Except the feeling didn't abate. If anything, it burned hotter the closer I got to her place. Cash trotted in front of me, already knowing where we were headed. His tail wagged furiously in delight. My cock lengthened, desire racing through my blood as we stood at the edge of the trees and looked at her house. The blind was up on her window, a dim light from somewhere in the house casting its glow on the glass.

"I'll just give her the book," I lied to myself. "Just the book," I repeated, ignoring the fact that I had stuffed a few condoms in my pocket as well as a handful of treats for Cash in the other. My breathing picked up as I approached the door. She might not be home. She might have one of her family members visiting. But I peeked through the glass and saw her curled up in the chair by the front window. She was motionless, her chin resting in her hand as she gazed outside.

She was breathtaking.

I rapped on the door harder than I intended, causing her to jump. She hesitated before approaching the door, our gazes locking through the glass. She wore an old sweatshirt, so large on her it slid off one shoulder, the fabric faded and worn. Casual pants hung low on her hips. She wore no makeup, and her hair was damp, a dark curtain around her shoulders.

She opened the door, the color on her cheeks high. I gripped the doorframe to stop myself launching at her. The yearning sensation was so strong I shook with it.

"You left this. I thought you might want it," I said, my voice sounding strangely rough and my eyes glued to the creamy exposed skin on her shoulder.

She nodded, swallowing several times, but not speaking.

"Tell me that shirt once belonged to a member of your family," I growled, unable to stop the caveman inside me from roaring in jealousy.

"My dad." Her voice was a whisper. Then she licked her lips. Her plump, full lips I wanted underneath mine. I had no thought before I moved, grabbing her, and hauling her close as I cupped the back of her head. "Thank God."

Everything eased as our mouths fused together. The itchy, tearing sensation left my body, and my muscles relaxed the closer I pulled her to me. A different sensation replaced it. Hard, needy lust. I needed her naked. Under me. Over me. I didn't care. I had to be inside her.

Our bodies melded, her breasts pressed against my sternum, her nipples hard points on my skin. She whimpered as I sank my tongue into the sweet warmth of her mouth, and she gripped the back of my neck. I had no recollection of moving inside, but the door slammed shut behind me and Cash trotted past us, heading for the living room. I knew, without a doubt, he would jump into the chair she'd just vacated and sleep there. I slid my hand under Ava's curvy ass and lifted her.

"Bedroom," I mumbled against her mouth.

"Hall. Left."

I tossed her onto the bed, not taking the time to notice the details of the room. All I could see was her. I yanked my shirt over my head. "Dammit, Ava. All day." I shucked off my sweats, my erection hot and heavy against my skin. "All day, I haven't been able to stop thinking about you."

She whimpered, sitting up and peeling off the sweatshirt. Her nipples were rosy peaks, and she cupped her breasts in her hands.

"Yes. Touch yourself. Pinch your nipples. I'm going to suck them until they're aching. Until you beg me to fuck you. Understand?"

I pushed her back against the mattress and tore off her pants. Her toes curled on the white cover, the purple of her nails glittering in the light. I lifted a foot to my mouth, kissing the arch. "Pretty little toes, baby. I'm going to make them curl really tight. I'm going to make you come so hard, you won't remember anything or anyone but me. You won't recall how it felt to be with anyone but me. Not in the past. Not ever again."

I had no idea where those words were coming from. I barely recognized the growl of my own voice. I was on her in a second, our mouths fused together. I had my hands all over her. Stroking her soft skin, cupping her full ass, teasing the juncture of her elbows with my tongue. Pushing her knees apart and burying my face into her center. I couldn't touch her enough. Taste her enough. Feel enough of her warmth to satisfy myself. The more I touched, the more I wanted. I kissed every inch of her. Licked the fragrance of her skin. Explored the heat and velvet of her mouth. Feasted on her wet, ready pussy. Swallowed her cries. Relished in the feeling of her nails on my back, the way her tongue felt on my skin, the bite of her little teeth on my nipples. How hot her mouth felt wrapped around my cock. I groaned and hissed, muttered curses and worshiped her name.

I sank inside her, the heat and ecstasy of her clutching me. We were like animals. I drove into her powerfully, pushing her knees against her chest as I took her. She rolled on top, riding me wildly, crying out in pleasure. I pulled out and pushed her onto her stomach, driving in deeper than ever, rolling her clit between my fingers and hitting her G-spot. She came hard, milking me, one orgasm bleeding into another. I pulled her up to my chest, thrusting endlessly, the pleasure spiking and receding until, finally, I exploded in a burst of fiery lava, the ecstasy so intense it hurt.

I wrapped my arms around her, dropping my face to her neck. We were both panting hard, the force of our chests drawing in the needed oxygen raspy and loud in the room.

I had one arm banded around her breasts, the other cupping her, my finger still stroking her clit.

She whimpered as I strummed her, one final, rippling orgasm winding its way through her. She stilled, and her head fell to her chest.

I kissed the side of her neck. "Hi," I whispered.

She laughed softly. "What the hell was that?"

"I have no idea. Pretty fucking awesome, though."

"If that's how you return a book, Hunter, take the whole shelf. I'll add late fees if you want."

I laughed and tenderly eased her away, laying her on the mattress and rubbing her legs. I kissed her lightly and met her eyes. "Can I stay awhile?"

She cupped my cheek.

"Yes."

I opened the door, glancing behind me. Ava leaned on the counter, peering at me over the rim of her mug. She was sleepy, tousled, and sexy. Her hair was a mess, her neck was red, and there was more than one bite mark on her shoulder. I had noticed her teeth marks on my chest and neck earlier. Our coupling had been intense and addictive. I had kept her up most of the night. In fact, I was surprised she was standing. My lower back ached, and I needed a long hot shower before I started working to ease the dull throb. I wondered how she'd make it through the day.

We'd gotten up early, had coffee, and I was leaving to go home so she could get ready and go to work.

The temptation to ask her to stay home and come with me was strong, but I tamped it down. I had no clue where all these odd impulses were coming from, but they needed to stop.

"Have a good day, Little Dragon."

She laughed, the sound husky and low. "I doubt it will compare to last night, but I'll try."

I winked and walked onto the back deck. I took the steps two at a time, landing on the damp grass and heading toward the forest.

"Hunter?"

I turned at the sound of Ava's voice.

She was leaning on the doorframe, a smile tugging her lips.

"Yeah?"

"Remember 0611."

I frowned. "What is that?"

She tapped the number lock on the door. "In case you need to return anything else. The code is 0611."

A grin split my face. "Okay, I can do that."

She waved and headed inside. I joined Cash waiting for me on the trail, wondering what the hell I was doing and, for the first time in a very long while, not really caring.

AVA

I was grateful for the pile of work on my desk. It kept me busy and my thoughts off Hunter. At least, most of the time. When I stretched to grab a file, my muscles protested a little. When I sat down, I felt a dull ache between my legs, a sure sign of his possession.

He'd been intense and passionate last night. When I opened the door, his expression reminded me of the day I met him—the banked fury in his eyes and his tense body language. But it hadn't been anger driving him last night. It had been need. One that matched my own. As soon as he dragged me into his arms, everything settled in me, and my focus narrowed down to him. Us. The fire that his touch lit between us. I had never experienced anything even remotely similar to the passion he ignited in me. I had thought perhaps I was the only one who felt it, but given his sudden appearance last night and his actions, I knew he was feeling it as well.

What it meant, I had no idea. He wasn't staying. He didn't do long-term relationships. It would probably burn itself out soon enough. It had been a while for both of us, so it was probably fairly normal.

Except, the way Hunter made me feel didn't seem normal.

A knock on my door brought me out of my thoughts, and I lifted my head. Addi came in, smiling and carrying a cup of herbal tea. She sat across from me, looking at my desk.

"We have you snowed under, don't we?"

I chuckled. "Lots of work."

"We're hiring you an assistant."

"Pardon me?"

"You're working too hard, Ava. You're here all the time. Yesterday, you looked exhausted. Dad commented on it." She smiled. "Pops advised me it would be for the best to get you help. No one knows how much work is involved behind the scenes to keep things running as well as he does." She studied me. "You still look tired."

I focused my gaze on the desk. I wasn't sure how to tell her the reason I was tired had more to do with the sexy man from the bluff and his insatiable sexual appetite than my job. Still, the thought of some of the load being taken off my shoulders wasn't unwelcome.

"You tell me what you need, Ava. Do you want an office assistant? Someone to do the filing and upkeep here? Run the paperwork around so you can concentrate on the overall planning?"

I frowned in concentration as I mulled it over.

"Or if you want, we can hire someone to handle the crews…if you're finding it too much?"

I met her gaze. "Too much, as in I can't handle it?"

She shook her head. "No, I know you can handle it, Ava. Maybe you don't want to." She lifted her shoulders. "I would hate to have to deal with the never-ending arguing and pushback."

I laughed. "You do that every day, structuring deals and meeting with prospective buyers. We both do it because we're good at it. It has nothing to do with our gender."

"Of course, it doesn't to us. It often does to the men we deal with."

My lips quirked into a smile. "Not for long. Not if they want to deal with ABC."

She grinned, then became serious. "My job is tough, but yours is tougher. Money talks for me. You have to deal with chauvinistic attitudes on so many levels. It must wear on you. Maybe if you didn't have to handle it all the time, it would be easier."

I blew out a long breath of air. "I appreciate your words and your concern, Addi, but I am fine. Really, I am. I'm not looking for easier. I love my job. I'm a bit tired because of the amount of work, but I'm not overly stressed by any one thing. I would love it if I could concentrate on the more important details and have someone here doing the office part. Maybe I could slowly bring them along, and they can take some other things off my plate when needed."

She nodded. "You might want that once you get married and start a family."

"That isn't going to happen," I assured her firmly. "That ship has sailed."

She frowned. "Ava, I know you went through a bad time after—"

I held up my hand, cutting her off. "I don't want to talk about it."

She leaned closer. "All I was going to say is, you are better than him. He knew how to hurt you—exactly where to cut you so the scar lingered. Don't let him win. You deserve to be happy."

"I am happy."

She shook her head. "I'm not talking career-wise. I mean personally. You deserve what Bray and I have. Gracie and Jaxson. The right person changes your life. Ask Ronan or Liam. They'd be only too happy to tell you that."

For some reason, her words brought Hunter to mind. He made me feel different. Special. But it was only temporary. We'd made that clear to each other from the start.

"Not everyone is so lucky," I said softly.

"I wish you'd talk to me."

"I'm fine. Nothing to talk about. But I will accept your offer of some help here."

She pursed her lips. "Should I mention the accrued vacation time you have?"

"Nope. When I need it, I'll let you know."

She stood, brushing her skirt. "You're as stubborn as your brothers."

I grinned widely. "Thanks."

She rolled her eyes. "I'll send you the applicants. I'll narrow them down, and you can be in on the interviews."

"Sounds good."

With a wave, she left, and I propped my chin in my hand, staring blindly at my desk. I had lied to Addi when I told her I was happy. Lately, I found a lot of my job a struggle. I was tired of having to prove myself. Fight with foremen and contractors who thought because I had a vagina, I had no brain. That because I had breasts, they could walk all over me. I had to put on a front every time I stepped into a meeting, submitted paperwork, or drove to a jobsite. At times, it was wearing.

Memories of the past weekend drifted through my head. I hadn't had to pretend to be anything with Hunter. He accepted me for exactly who I was. He even looked after me, allowing me the space I needed to just be Ava. I recalled the way he took me to bed and read to me. His odd moments of gentleness when he simply watched me. It had been a long time since anyone had done that. Even my own family sometimes forgot I was only Ava underneath all the no-bullshit bluster I put on during the week. Sometimes it was nice to be less in control.

I shook my head and picked up a new file. Those cases were rare. Today, I had to be Ava Callaghan, ball-breaker. I flipped open the file, losing myself in the details, my pen already scratching out the issues to be dealt with.

This was my life, the one I had chosen, and I had a job to do.

The other side of Ava had to be put aside.

CHAPTER 13

AVA

I worked late on Monday night. So late that all the lights were out in the compound when I finally pulled my SUV into the garage. Inside, I kicked off my shoes and padded over to the fridge, suddenly starving. I grabbed a container of cut-up veggies and cheese and stood at the counter, eating. My hunger abated, I headed to my room and changed, brushed my teeth, and slipped into bed. I rolled over, grabbing the pillow, and Hunter's scent hit my nose. I inhaled deeply, shocked at how the smell relaxed me. I curled into a ball, thinking the only thing that would make it better was if he were beside me. I had to admit, I had slept so well in his arms the past three nights, and it felt wrong without him with me. I huffed a sigh, burrowing back into the pillow. His scent would have to suffice.

Except a few moments later, I heard the beeping noise at the back door of the lock disengaging. I sat up, startled, but before I could call out, Hunter appeared in my doorway, and I relaxed.

"What are you doing here?"

He stalked over to the bed, pulling his shirt over his head. "I've been waiting for you."

"Um…"

"I've been here twice. How late do you work, woman?" he asked, shucking off his pants and shoes and climbing in beside me.

"Late," I replied, still in shock. "I-I wasn't expecting you."

"I wasn't expecting to be here either, but I can't seem to stop myself." He pulled his pillow away, tucked it under his head, and yanked me into his arms. "Go to sleep, Little Dragon."

"Where is Cash?"

He snorted. "Asleep on my bed, hogging the whole thing. I had no choice but to trudge down here to sleep."

"You could have moved him off."

"He was in a grumpy mood. Vicious, even. I didn't dare."

"And the bed in the other room?"

"For one thing, it's over fifty years old and lumpy as hell. For another, I don't even want to imagine the things my grandparents did in it. I'd be scarred for life."

A little giggle burst from my lips. "I see."

He nipped my ear. "You want me to leave?"

"No."

He stroked his hand up and down my back. "Stop talking and go to sleep, or I won't be responsible for what happens."

I snuggled closer, feeling exactly what he wanted to happen. "I'm tired."

He kissed my head. "I know. Just let me hold you."

I yawned, suddenly too exhausted to keep my eyes open. "Okay."

I woke alone in the morning, wondering if I had dreamed the whole thing. Hunter appearing so late. Holding me. Making love to me in the early morning hours when the world was still dark and quiet. Kissing my head before leaving my room.

I sat up, running a hand over my head. Had it been a dream? I glanced at the other side of the bed and knew it wasn't. I could see the indent of his head on the pillow. My body still felt his possession. He had shown up, checking until I was home. Held me.

I was unsure what to think. Too scared to hope that it meant anything aside from a warm body and a comfortable place to sleep.

I got up and got ready for the day, rested and in a good mood, despite the long day yesterday and the agenda ahead of me. Idly, I wondered if he would show up again tonight.

I certainly hoped so.

It was almost nine when I got home again after a long, arduous day. I had dealt with a new foreman at a jobsite. He'd talked over, around, and at me, without listening or bothering to realize he worked for my company, not me for him. He was rude, overbearing, and made his dislike for me plain. By the fifth time he'd ignored me, I'd had enough. He had a problem with the contract dates and decided he could rearrange them to suit his time frame better. I didn't like his attitude, how he spoke to the crew or me, and I certainly hated his obvious distaste for woman superiors.

"Mr. Kurtz," I interrupted.

He kept talking, his voice getting louder. I had no choice. I put my fingers between my lips and blew. My whistle was loud and shrill, effectively cutting him off.

He glared at me, and I smiled benignly. "Now I have your attention, I need to point out that you are, in fact, incorrect. The start and end dates are clearly stated in the contract. You work according to our schedule. We hired you. You work for us."

"I don't take orders from a woman."

I feigned shock. "You were hired by one, and I run this end of the company. If you have a problem with it, you can be replaced."

He crossed his arms, trying to look menacing. "Is that a fact?" he challenged.

I was done with his shit. I pointed at another man who had been watching us and, more than once, had rolled his eyes when I was interrupted by his boss. "You. What is your name?"

"Peter Watson."

"You've just been promoted. Mr. Kurtz, you're relieved of your duty. HR will be in touch."

I turned my back, refusing to watch or listen as he yelled obscenities and stormed away.

I tapped out a message to Addi, telling her what happened and that I was managing it. I looked up at Peter. "Can you handle this?"

"Yes, ma'am. I've overseen crews before. I know these guys. We can make it work."

Another man snorted. "Anyone would be better than Kurtz."

I bit back my smile. I would have to talk to whoever hired this crew and get it fixed. I didn't want to see Mr. Kurtz again. "Then I suggest you meet with your new crew and get to work."

I kept my composure, and no one knew the effect the showdown had on me. It wasn't until I was alone in my SUV that I let my emotions out. I gripped the steering wheel and took in several calming breaths, my body shaking with the aftereffects. It never got easier, no matter how often I faced this situation. It wasn't only because I was a woman—I knew Jordan had often fired foremen, replaced overseers due to bad attitudes, but men like Mr. Kurtz made it especially distasteful since they never hid their lack of respect. I hoped it didn't cost us too much, but in the end, it would be worth it. The crew would have been run badly, and we never allowed that. It was for the best.

Still, hours later, I felt the tension in my shoulders. I went inside, stopping at the sight that greeted me. Hunter was in my kitchen, sitting at the little table, his arms folded on top, a beer by his elbow. I was certain it was one of the Creemores I had in the fridge. I lifted one eyebrow in question.

"Cash steal your bed again?"

"Greedy, furry bastard," he said, straight-faced.

"A little early for bedtime, isn't it?"

Ignoring my words, he stood and went to the stove. "Your stomach grumbled all last night. You didn't eat dinner."

"I had some crackers and cheese. Some cut-up veggies."

He snorted and opened the oven door, sliding out a large pizza box. "I've seen your appetite, Ava. That's a snack for you. I brought dinner."

He looked up at my shock and shrugged his shoulders. "Someone needs to make sure you're looking after yourself," he mumbled.

He slid the box onto the table and opened the fridge, pulling out another beer. "Go change and come eat." He stopped in front of me. "From the look of you, I'd say you need food, a neck rub, and some sleep."

I blinked at the sudden dampness in my eyes.

He frowned, looking startled. "Hey, none of that. No tears, Little Dragon. I only brought dinner because I was hungry too."

"And you only plan on sleeping here because your dog took your bed again?"

"Unless you plan on making me walk through the dark, scary forest back to my house alone?" He tucked a stray piece of hair behind my ear, his eyes filled with amusement. "You wouldn't do that, would you, Ava?"

I sniffled. "No, I'll let you stay."

He surprised me with a kiss to my forehead. "Good. Now, go. I'll be here when you get back."

———

I wiped my mouth and sat back, replete. The pizza was delicious, the beer cold, and I gulped down two glasses of ice water thanks to the spicy sausage Hunter had added to the pizza.

It had been a good dinner. I'd told Hunter about what occurred earlier, and his reaction had made me smile.

"I've worked for assholes like that. Good riddance." He winked. "Big balls, Little Dragon. I would have loved to see you in action again."

I shrugged and he chuckled.

"You are a force to be reckoned with."

I kept eating, although I felt my cheeks color at his praise.

I burped, covering my mouth with the napkin. "Whoops."

He threw back his head in laughter. "I like that about you, Ava. Sexy, shoot-from-the-hip businesswoman by day, teenage boy by night at the table with your love of food and belching. The perfect combination."

"Sorry," I uttered. "I was hungrier than I thought. And beer makes me burp. So does soda." I grinned. "And spicy pizza."

He shook his head. "Don't apologize." He indicated the empty pizza box. "I like that. I like you're honest and yourself. No hiding, none of that 'Oh no, I'll only have a salad' shit. I never understood that."

"Most men prefer it that way."

He shrugged. "Prefer what? For you to hide who you are? I don't. I like you just the way you are."

"Really?" I asked, the feeling of insecurity only this subject could cause swarming up in me.

He stood and took two more beers from the fridge, setting them on the table. He slid one my way and met my eyes. "Really," he stated firmly.

"Hmmph," I breathed.

He swallowed and wiped his mouth. "You sound as if you don't believe me."

My grip on my beer bottle was tight, but I shrugged, trying to look nonchalant. It didn't fool him for a moment.

He sat back in his chair, crossing his ankles. "Who was the asshole that hurt you, Ava?"

"Who says there was one?"

He sipped his beer, contemplating me. "You are one of the most confident women I have ever met. I've watched you in action myself. I know what happened today. The responsibilities you carry on your shoulders. Business-wise, you're a force. Yet every so often, I sense fear when it comes to yourself after hours. You doubt your own strength and beauty. Something or someone put that fear and doubt inside you. I assume some asshole is responsible for it."

For a moment, I was silent. I met his gaze, surprised by the gentle patience I could see.

"Why do you want to know?"

"I don't know," he said honestly. "I just do."

Strangely enough, I wanted to tell him.

"I haven't had a lot of relationships," I confessed. "In university, I dated a guy who broke up with me because he said I was just too much. Too bossy, too opinionated, too everything. He said I embarrassed him." I barked out a humorless laugh. "He said a lot of other things, but that hurt the most."

"Sounds as if he was the one with the confidence problem."

"Maybe. I didn't date for a long time after that. Then I met Ryan, and I really liked him. He was smart and funny. A few years older than me and established. He was in control and knew what he wanted from life. He said he liked my brashness —that he admired it." I paused. "I guess he changed his mind."

Hunter's eyes darkened, but he nodded for me to go on.

"Ryan liked the good life. He liked dinners out and the theatre. Parties. He loved big groups." I paused. "He loved being the star of the show in those groups of people."

"Hmm," was all Hunter said.

"At first, it was fun. Different for me. I was busy at work, learning the ropes, and I worked a lot. Ryan understood since he had done the same thing already. We got along well, and we were pretty serious. At least, I thought we were. I even moved in with him."

"What happened?"

"He changed. Or I changed. He became more demanding, less understanding. Shouting all the time. Suddenly, I couldn't do anything right. The way I dressed, spoke, acted—everything was wrong. I was too loud, too opinionated, too over the top. He wanted me to be more like his friends' girlfriends and wives." I snorted. "I was nothing like them. He hated my *'unfeminine'* job, the fact that I had work boots in my trunk, and that I dealt with contractors and city officials. He used to tell everyone I was a PA."

"Elitist asshole."

"I tried so hard to be what he wanted. I'd rush home early to change. I didn't talk about my job. I went to parties with him, hating every second. I didn't see my family as much. I did everything to try to make him happy. It was always about him. What he wanted, his needs." I scrubbed my face, tired of talking about Ryan. It was still painful to think how stupid I'd been.

"How did your family feel about him?"

I grimaced. "They never fully warmed to him. He liked the *men* in my family but sort of ignored the women. He continually tried to get the dads to talk business with him. He wanted their money badly, which, as it turned out, was one of the appealing things about me. Maybe the only one. Once he realized me in his life didn't guarantee BAM dollars in his pocket, I wasn't as desirable —something I wish I'd seen earlier. But I was in deep and determined to make it work. I didn't want to fail."

"But you weren't failing, Ava. He was."

"Took me a while to figure that out. Addi and Gracie were always there for me. They saw what was happening. Liam saw it. Ronan did too." I swallowed. "Everyone did but me. I tried to change myself and who I was to please him, but there was no pleasing him, and I almost lost myself doing that."

"What happened?"

"The entire cliché of a bad relationship happened. I came home early, planning on surprising him with dinner. He surprised me by screwing one of his associates in our bed. I walked in on them."

Hunter cursed quietly.

"We argued, and of course, he told me it was my fault. All of it. I had driven him to it. I wasn't enough. I wasn't pretty enough, thin enough, *anything* enough. I was too loud, too bossy, too manly, too everything terrible in his books. My family were assholes and refused to give him a chance to prove what he could do for them." I shook my head. "I laughed at him and reminded him they didn't need *him* to do anything. They made their fortune honestly, with hard work— unlike him. He didn't like that," I added. "He was all about parties and networking. As I discovered after, he wasn't as, ah, *solvent* as he led me to believe." I rolled my head on my shoulders, feeling the tension of talking about Ryan.

"The money he perceived I had was a huge draw." I took a sip of beer.

"He said the only thing I was good for was fucking and even that was subpar."

"Liar," he hissed.

"He stormed out, and I called my brothers and packed my stuff. Looking around, I realized how much of myself I had already lost. Nothing there was mine. He'd picked everything out and changed things as the whim struck him. I was simply part of the furniture—something to be switched out when he got tired. All I took with me were the clothes I had brought when I moved in. I left everything he had chosen for me—they were for a woman I really didn't know."

For a moment, the room was silent.

"Did you ever see him again?"

"He came to the office, which was a mistake. He told me I was being ridiculous, and if he was willing to overlook my drawbacks, I could do the same. He told me in no uncertain terms I was getting the better end of the deal."

"Please tell me your brothers escorted him from the building. Preferably unconscious."

I grinned. "He was a little woozy from the right hook I laid on him when he tried to grab me. Ronan might have had to help him out."

He flashed his smile, wide and approving. "That's my girl."

I rubbed my head. "He was the second person I cared about who told me I was too much, yet not enough. I decided to stop look-ing. It took me a while to come to terms with the fact that I am over the top. Bossy. In your face. But I like me. My family likes me. The people I know who are true friends like me. The fact is that I'm not made for a long-term relationship. I am too much, but that's just me."

He leaned forward. "It's not that you're too much, Little Dragon. They weren't worthy of you."

I smiled at his words. His simple, honest words.

"It's probably a good thing we have a time limit, Hunter. You would probably change your mind and grow tired of my 'antics.'" I made quotation marks with my fingers.

He regarded me silently, then stood and pulled me from the chair. "We were supposed to be one night, Ava. It's days later, and here I am. Does that sound like I plan on changing my mind?"

"But you'll leave."

"Yes. I will. But not because of you." He ran his fingers down my cheek. "In fact, you'll be difficult to leave behind," he admitted softly.

"You don't have to go." I clutched his shirt tight in my hands.

He smiled sadly. "I do, Little Dragon. I'm like a rolling stone. I gather a little moss, but nothing sticks. I've been honest with you about that from the start. When I leave, it will be because I have to go—because that's my way to live. I also disagree with you, and I think you are meant for a long-term relationship—just not with me. I'm the one who doesn't do long-term. I have never known that, and I never will. I'm not built that way, but it has nothing to do with you—or your antics, as you call them. I find those charming and droll. I like the fact that you order enough Chinese food to feed a family. Have balls big enough to tell off assholes that stand in your way. I love being able to sit and eat pizza and beer with you and listen to your little lady burps that make you laugh while you inhale half a large pizza. You let me be Hunter. You accept my grouchiness and silence. You don't push." He exhaled hard. "I like spending time with you. I like *you*."

I knew his words didn't come easily. Hunter wasn't big on sharing his emotions. For him to admit he liked me wasn't easy. I wished I knew his story—why he felt the way he did. I wondered if I would ever know it or if he would leave before he trusted me enough to tell me. I also knew the next words out of my mouth were important. We'd drifted into dangerous territory for both of us. The atmosphere was heavy and dark. I needed to lighten it up or he would leave.

"I am also an excellent dance partner," I sniffed. "Despite your unusual taste in music."

He chuckled, his eyes crinkling in the corners.

I gasped as I suddenly found myself swung into his arms, and he turned and headed to the bedroom. "I like both kinds of dancing with you, Little Dragon."

"Both kinds?"

He tossed me onto my bed and hovered over me, leaning on his hands and caging me in. "The regular kind and the mattress dancing. Because another thing that idiot got wrong is there is nothing subpar about your moves. You are the sexiest woman I have ever been with, and I come harder than a freight train every time I'm inside you." He traced my lips. "Any part of you."

I nipped his finger, feeling my body flush in pleasure at his words. "Oh yeah?"

His mouth parted, his breathing picking up. "Yes."

"You gonna back up those words, cowboy?"

He stepped back, dragging his shirt over his head. "Oh baby, I never back away from a challenge. Ever. You wanna ride a cowboy? That's what you're gonna get."

I watched him undress, his erection growing, heavy and thick. His eyes were like ice on fire—burning and intense, never leaving my gaze. They were full of wicked, dark promises. He was going to be all over me. His hands, his mouth, his cock. He was out to prove a point, and he wasn't going to stop until he had.

I was about to get fucked—and hard.

Yay, me.

CHAPTER 14

HUNTER

I slipped away while Ava was sleeping, finding my way home easily in the dim light. I had stood beside her bed looking down at her, confused and torn, before letting myself out, making sure to lock the door behind me.

I had no idea why I returned to her every evening. Why, by the end of the day, I was filled with longing, the need to see her. To make sure she was okay. The first time, I had used the book as the excuse, certain once I had her again, the ache and need would go away.

It hadn't. In fact, it had grown.

It was a shock to realize how much I enjoyed her company. Listening to her talk, hearing her laugh. I liked sharing a meal with her, hearing about her day. She asked questions about mine, seemingly as interested in my banal news as I was in her far more entertaining words. I wasn't used to sharing. Or this endless craving I had to see her.

Every day, I swore I wouldn't allow it to overtake my senses. Every day, I found myself at her door. In her bed.

I climbed the steps to the house, opening the door and letting Cash out. I went in and made a cup of instant coffee, thinking how horrified Ava would be over it. It was easier at times than making a pot, and unlike her, I didn't have a fancy machine sitting on the counter.

I carried the cup outside and set it on the tailgate, watching Cash roll in the grass, stretching his legs out in the sun in contentment. He trotted over, getting some headbutts and attention, then he lay by my feet, gnawing on one of the treats I had gotten him at the pet store earlier in the week. He chewed and I sipped, both of us enjoying the quiet.

I thought about Ava's past she'd confided in me last night. I shook my head in disbelief that a woman as beautiful and confident could be discounted by any man. I thought she was amazing. Strong, fearless, smart, funny, and gorgeous. How she managed to attract two losers who made her question her self-worth was beyond me. She needed someone equally as strong, someone who valued her strength and vitality. Who appreciated her quirks.

Another strange thought came into my head. She needed someone who would look after her. She hid a quiet vulnerability. She worked too hard and in a business that forced her to show only her tough side. She needed a place to be Ava. To be soft and peaceful. She needed to be held and read to. Brought dinner. Tucked into bed to get a good sleep.

Made love to regularly to let her know how incredibly sexy she was.

She needed someone like me.

I stood, shocked at the thought.

I wasn't in the market. Soon enough, I would crave a new place, and the need to pack up and move on would overtake everything else. Even this insane desire for her. I was simply overreacting to the intimacy of last night. Hearing Ava's words. Using my body to show her just how wrong those other men had been.

That was all.

Needing to move, I picked up Cash's favorite stick and tossed it. For the next while, I concentrated only on him and the stick. Pitch and return. Farther. Farther away still. Watching him run, his tail wagging as he raced to find it, his head held up happy and proud as he returned it to me.

Inside my head were a barrage of unwelcome thoughts. Unbidden feelings about Ava. Slowly, I sorted them. I was reacting to my anger. That was all. I found Ava attractive, and I had been without feminine company for a while and was enjoying it. Simple. She was amazing in bed, and I liked exploring that with her. It was natural. The fact that I hadn't been with anyone for a long time was what drove me to her nightly. Totally feasible. I would have to exercise more control about the daily visits, and once I found my balance again, we could see each other every few days. She was enjoying the relationship as well, so there was no need to end it.

Yet.

I simply had to stop giving in to these ridiculous cravings for her.

My shoulders slumped as I threw the stick one last time, this time almost sending it over the bluff. Cash grabbed it and came back, although his pace wasn't as quick as it had been. I glanced at my watch, surprised to see I'd been tossing it for over an hour. I patted his head as he dropped the stick at my feet. "Come on, boy. I need a shower then I'm going to head into town and pick up a few supplies. I'll work all afternoon, and the deck should mostly be done."

I looked at the new structure. It was going to be awesome when finished. The company I had hired had poured the footings for the cedar columns and new framework, as well as completing the installation for the heavy wood columns. Now, I was almost done with the rest of the framing. Once that was complete, I could work on the deck boards, then move on to the extension on the other side of the house.

I headed inside, my day planned. I would grill something easy on the barbecue later and tonight work on the supply list I would need to start the next project—the extension. I still needed to find an architect to draw up the needed plans, and I decided I would make that the next priority.

I nodded, satisfied, as I stepped into the shower. I had lots to keep me busy—right up until midnight. I wouldn't visit Ava tonight. I wouldn't see her for a few days. Break the pattern.

It was a good, solid plan. It just didn't work.

I never made it into town. Instead, I threw myself into work, and I got a lot accomplished in the afternoon. I finished framing the deck and rebuilt the steps. I worked late into the evening until the light began to fade and my body was exhausted. Dinner ended up being a sandwich eaten over the sink and drinking the milk straight from the container. I needed a trip to the grocery store, which I planned on doing in the morning. The rest of the evening was spent in pursuit of mindless endeavors. None of which accomplished what I wanted—which was to stop the nagging desire to head over to Ava's. I glanced through some magazines, not really seeing the pages. I sorted through some drawers in the kitchen, tossing out most of the junk inside them. I paced and tried a couple of shots of whiskey to help calm the nerves that suddenly seemed to be on the outside of my body, taut and exposed. Flipped through the few TV channels available, thinking I needed to upgrade the TV and the Wi-Fi here. I played music but somehow had no desire to dance. I looked at the clock, convinced it had to be after midnight, shocked to find it was only ten. I gave up and went to bed, planning on sleeping hard and getting up early.

I spent the night tossing and turning. Pulling the pillow Ava had slept on close to my face and catching the faint whiff of her perfume. Wondering if she was sleeping. Contemplating what she would do if I showed up at three a.m. and climbed into bed with her. I moved to the sofa, thinking it would be better. It wasn't. Eventually I drifted, but my sleep was far from restful.

In the morning, I went to the town hall and spoke with Milly, asking if she could recommend a local architect.

"Mr. Shuman is retired but still does some work," she replied, pursing her lips. "I'll give you his number. He tends to be hard to get a hold of since retiring, though."

"Anyone else?" I asked.

"Not local. But I can give you the number of a couple of places. One is in Mississauga and one in St. Catharines. Of course, there are others, but I know these names off the top of my head." She paused. "Ava Callaghan's brother is an architect. A very good one."

I smiled grimly. "Yes, I was told that."

I accepted the paper gratefully. In my truck, my stomach growled, and I headed to the diner, deciding breakfast out would be good. Then I would do my errands and head back to the house and work on the deck. The weather was perfect to be outside. Not too hot, with a light breeze. It made the grueling task of handling the big project on my own easier when I wasn't sweating and having to stop every few moments to wipe my head or get a drink. I parked my truck and began to head inside when I saw her.

Ava was at a booth, sitting by the window. She had a file open, a cup of coffee in one hand. Her hair was down, brushed to one side, the deep sable color glinting with the purple streaks in the sun. She wasn't looking at the file, though, but staring into space. She looked…dejected. I stopped, simply staring, then before I could help myself, tapped on the window.

She glanced up, startled, a smile clearing away the sadness. She lifted her eyebrows and tilted her head in a silent invitation, and I was powerless to refuse it. I headed inside and, without thinking, slid into the booth beside her. It was natural to press my mouth to her cheek, remembering where we were.

"Hey, Little Dragon," I breathed against her skin.

"Hi," she responded. "What are you doing here?"

"Just came from town hall. You?"

"I have a meeting at eleven. I decided to treat myself to breakfast before heading to it since my day is booked solid. Not sure I'll have a chance to eat again."

Connie came over and smiled at me. "You staying or just visiting?"

I laughed. "Staying. Coffee and the special, please. Over easy."

"Got it." A mug appeared, and I sipped it with appreciation.

"You look tired," Ava said, not meeting my eyes.

"I did a lot of work on the deck. Finished the framework and steps and plan on starting the boards today."

"You didn't come over last night."

Her words hung between us. For a moment, I was at a loss, then I cleared my throat. "I fell asleep on the couch. I was whacked. Never made the dinner on the barbecue I had planned either." It was a partial lie, but it was all I could offer her. I had no plans on telling her how strong a hold she had on me. I could barely acknowledge it to myself.

"So, you've come seeking sustenance."

"And I got you too." I nudged her with my elbow. "Double bonus."

"I missed you," she whispered.

I wasn't sure how to respond, but I dropped my hand to her leg, found her fingers, and squeezed them.

"The couch wasn't as comfortable as your bed," I admitted.

She rolled her eyes but, Ava being Ava, let it drop. She asked about Cash, the next step in the renovation, and entertained me with more stories of her work escapades.

Our breakfasts came, and I had to laugh as she slipped one of her eggs onto my plate and scooped some potatoes from mine without asking. I had no objections since I preferred the eggs over the spuds, but it seemed such an oddly intimate thing between us. She already knew my likes and also knew I wouldn't mind.

We ate in companionable silence for a few moments. I was starved, and the food was good. Simple, but tasty. I finished my toast, and Ava slid hers my way, letting me take a piece to finish off my eggs. I grinned at her, laughing as she speared the last potato from the edge of my plate.

The harmony of the moment was interrupted by two large bodies sliding into the booth with us. We were startled and looked up, meeting the wry grins and dancing gazes of Ronan and Liam. They filled the booth, barely fitting on the bench. The look of sheer delight on their faces was enough to make me groan.

Ava spoke. "What are you two clowns doing here?"

"We came for breakfast," Ronan replied. "Imagine our shock when we saw our sister having breakfast with her neighbor."

"Showing him around again, Ava?" Liam asked.

"He saw me here and asked to join me. No point in the two of us eating breakfast alone. Not that it's any of your business," she added haughtily.

Her tone didn't make them back down.

"Oh." Ronan looked at Liam then cast his gaze around the booth. "Are we sitting on imaginary friends that joined you too? I assume that's why you two are fused at the hip on the same side of the booth."

Liam smirked. "And sharing food. Isn't that so..." He trailed off as Ava glared at him. "*Kind.*"

Ronan nodded, leaning back in the booth. "Neighborly. She's a great neighbor, Liam. The best, I'd say."

I wanted to tell the two of them to fuck off. Except it was too funny. They both knew what was going on. They weren't trying to be assholes, simply humorous. And the bottom line was I didn't care. If they didn't give me a hassle, I wouldn't be rude. I knew how much her family meant to Ava, and although I didn't understand it, I could respect it.

"She *is* the best neighbor," I agreed. "She already told me not to expect too much from you two slackers in that department. She explained she was the responsible, polite one in the family."

For a moment, they were silent, then they began to laugh. I joined in, shaking my head.

"You want coffee?" I surprised myself by asking.

Somehow I wasn't shocked when they said yes.

Connie brought the fresh mugs, filled up mine and Ava's, and left after assuring Ronan that, yes, they had the grilled cinnamon bun and she would bring him the biggest one they had. Liam ordered one as well, and Ava piped up, saying she and I would split one.

Apparently breakfast had two courses today.

Over the delicious buns and coffee, Ronan asked about the house. I told him what I told Ava, adding in the fact that I was going to call Mr. Shuman about the plans.

"Good luck." He grinned. "He's probably fishing. He's always fishing."

"Well, I'll try the places she gave me numbers for."

He nodded. "They're decent, but you'll wait awhile."

I shrugged, unsure what to say.

"You could let me have a look," Ronan offered quietly. "I'm good."

I felt Ava's eyes on me, and I sensed her sudden tension.

"If you wanted to, I suppose I could."

"Great. I'll come over later and check it out."

"Sure."

They finished their snack and coffee and stood to leave. "See you kids later." Liam winked.

I chuckled as Ava flipped him the bird. I grabbed the bill before they could, shaking my head. "On me," I insisted.

They thanked me and left. For a moment, I contemplated moving to the other side of the booth, then changed my mind. I liked sitting beside her, feeling her leg pressed against mine. Ava finished her coffee, then wiped her mouth.

"That was unexpected."

"The visit, or the fact that I didn't shut Ronan down?" I asked honestly.

"Both."

I drained my mug. "I'm just letting him have a look. No harm in that. He's your brother. Even Milly mentioned him this morning."

She turned, meeting my gaze fully. "Thank you."

I shifted. "It's just a look. Don't expect anything."

"I don't. I don't expect anything from you. I know you're only passing through and what is between us is a for-now sort of thing. But I still appreciate you bending on this."

Her simple acceptance made me smile. "Why is this so important to you?"

She shrugged. "I've always loved the property. I just want to make sure it's given the best. And Ronan is the best."

I wasn't sure how to respond. Her words were honest and real. Her next statement surprised me with its intuitiveness.

"You can visit anytime, Hunter. And I want to see you when I feel like it too. It doesn't mean I think there's more between us than there is. It just means we like spending time together. Nothing wrong with that. We're big people, and we both know what's happening."

She glanced at her watch. "I have to go."

I paid the bill and followed her out. She dug in her purse for her keys, looking up when I grasped her elbow. "I missed you last night too."

She smiled, although it looked forced. "Well, you know where I am." She pressed a kiss to my cheek. "Thanks for breakfast. Have fun with Ronan."

I snorted and watched her drive away.

I felt conflicted as I slid behind the wheel of the truck. She was basically giving me permission to fuck her anytime with no strings. And telling me if she was in the mood, she'd visit me for the same thing. She knew we had an expiry date, and she was okay with that. It was a perfect scenario.

Why, then, did I feel so torn up about it?

I finished drilling a deck board in place and lifted my water, draining the bottle. As with every job I was doing on my own, it took longer, but in the end, it would be worth it. The house would be fixed up and should provide a nice income for me, plus a place I could return to if I wanted. I wiped the sweat off my brow. I'd never had a home base. A steady source of income. I had done a lot of research, and properties around here fetched a good rate for summer and fall rentals. I would have to hire a company to look after the paperwork and keep the place clean, but there would still be money coming into the bank.

The thought of leaving did something odd to my chest. I had to admit I liked it here. The peace and quiet. The water. Even the little town.

And there was no denying the biggest draw of them all. Ava.

Leaving her behind was not going to be easy, but we had no future. She loved her family, her life, and her job. She was settled and content. I had no idea how to be part of a relationship, never mind a family. I never settled anywhere. My life was a string of endless jobs, people I met but never got to know, and no roots. The only things I could count on were my truck and Cash—and even those wouldn't be around forever. I also knew once I left, even if I came back, there would be no picking up the threads with Ava. Whether she knew it or not, she wasn't that sort of woman. She needed someone who fit into her life. Who would meld into her family.

That certainly wasn't me. I knew it and accepted it, but still, the thought of not seeing her left me with a strange feeling.

I shook my head to clear my thoughts. That was a few weeks, maybe months from now. I still had a lot of work ahead of me to get this place done.

After we'd finished eating, she went off to her meeting, and once I finished my errands, I came here and started working. I enjoyed the unexpected chance to see her again. Even though it had only been a short time since I'd seen her, I liked having a meal with her and talking. Even if her pain-in-the-ass brothers showed up. They were decent guys.

I headed to the pile and grabbed the next board, getting ready to cut it. A truck pulled into the driveway, and I stopped, watching as Ronan and Liam climbed from the vehicle. I shut off the saw and waited as they approached. Ronan carried a clipboard and a laser measure, a pencil tucked behind his ear. They had changed and were both in T-shirts and jeans.

I nodded as they came close. Cash wove around their legs, accepting pats and attention like it was his due. The damned dog seemed to love Ava's family. Traitor.

Ronan whistled. "Wow, that is some porch. Love it."

"Thanks. Want to make the most of the space and view."

"Absolutely." He indicated the house. "Show me."

For the next half an hour, I showed him and Liam the house and the plans, including the ones Ava had sketched out. Ronan was quick to see what I was trying to accomplish and added a few of his own suggestions. His hand flew over the paper on his clipboard, and he showed me a few ideas. I was impressed with his instinct and had to admit I liked his concepts. Inside, he had some thoughts.

"You should blow out that wall and add to the guest room. Extend the porch so it wraps around the whole house. Take advantage of the views there too." He scratched his neck. "Ava says you plan on renting the place. Views sell."

"Hadn't thought of that."

"I know our rental units that do best lean toward luxury rustic. The cabin feel, but with all the amenities. Views, screened-in porches, modern appliances. The hot tub will be a big hit." He gazed around the property. "No room for a pool, but there is the beach." He indicated the small patch of sand and rock on the opposite side of the bluff.

"It needs a set of stairs to get to it," I pointed out. "My grandfather never developed it. It'll have to wait awhile since it's not in the budget."

"I assume you'll advertise it as an adult getaway?"

I nodded, reluctant to talk too much about my plans. I had no idea that the company they had held rental properties.

Ronan let it go, not pushing me. "Let me have a few days, Hunter. I'll show you my ideas on paper. If you like them, great. If not, no worries."

"You sure you have time?"

He smiled, the brilliance of it reminding me of Ava's beam. "This is easy. Move a couple of walls, throw up a few others. Now, if you wanted a whole new house, that would be different. And your spec drawings help a lot. I'll do a basic draft, and you can look it over."

I hesitated, my instinct about never accepting help, never trusting anyone, kicking in. Then I thought of Ava and how much it would mean to her. "Okay."

"Great." He clapped me on the shoulder, and we headed outside.

Liam, who had been quiet in the house, spoke up. "A little grunt work out here could make this a nice space. Clear out those dead trees, add a little patch of cedars here, maybe some flowering bushes over there. Some easy to care for planters on the deck and porch would add a nice touch."

"Thanks for the ideas."

They walked toward the truck, and I was surprised when they tossed the clipboard and other items in and both snapped on tool belts and headed back toward me. I narrowed my eyes.

"What do you think you're doing?"

"Helping you with the porch."

"I didn't ask for help."

Ronan shook his head. "We know that. But think of how much quicker it would go. Liam can cut, you and I can install. Three sets of hands will make it go three times faster."

"Maybe I like to work on my own."

Liam scoffed. "We get the loner aspect, Hunter. But we're not trying to encroach on your property. We're not here to twist your arm or get you to sell to us. We understand you're not interested. We're here as neighbors and Ava's brothers."

"Ava and I are not a couple."

Ronan snorted, covering his mouth and coughing something that sounded like bullshit into his hand, then he shrugged. "Whatever you are is between you and my sister. But we're still neighbors, and that's what neighbors do. Help one another. Plus, it's a great afternoon, and I feel like swinging a hammer and sweating. You gonna let us or what?"

"Fine," I agreed grudgingly.

"Great. Hit the tunes, and let's get at this."

CHAPTER 15
HUNTER

At eight o'clock, I stood under the hot spray of the shower, grateful as the warmth sank into my tired muscles. Ronan and Liam were surprisingly easy to work with, and we got along well, the afternoon flying by. I was shocked when I realized we'd finished all the boards and reattached the wide steps I'd built the day before. Another pleasant surprise was the fact that neither of them were chatterers. They concentrated on the job. Often the only sounds aside from the music I had playing were one of us calling out measurement confirmations, the occasional grunt, and the noises of the saw and drills. I did chuckle a few times when I noticed we all had the habit of singing along to the music. At six, pizza arrived I hadn't ordered, and Ronan lifted one shoulder with a smirk.

"Gotta fill the tank."

I was pissed he refused to take money for the pizza, but they gratefully accepted the cold beer I brought outside.

"Creemore." Liam hummed in pleasure, taking a long swallow. "My sister get you onto this?"

"Yeah."

He nodded, wiping his mouth. "It's a family favorite."

At my look of surprise, he shook his head. "What? You think we're too rich and snobby to drink beer?" He laughed. "My dad drinks beer, eats tacos, loves to go bowling, acts like a teenager around my mother, and still cannonballs into the pool. We all had a pretty normal upbringing. We're just people."

"Except Bentley," Ronan deadpanned. "He's a bit snobby."

Liam laughed. "It's an act. He's as much of a goofball as the rest of them."

Ronan met my eyes and winked. "Snobby," he mouthed. I held back my laughter. The two brothers reminded me of Ava.

We ate in comfortable silence, the beer disappearing fast. I brought out more, plus extra waters, and once we'd polished off the huge pizza, we finished the deck.

I refused to let them help with the cleanup, more than grateful for their efforts for the day. They waved as they left, Ronan assuring me he'd be in touch soon.

I put away the tools and climbed the sturdy, wide steps, already moving ahead in my mind to the cedar railings and posts I would add. The dark color of the boards and the red of the cedar would make a great color combination as accents. I planned to replace the old siding with a fresh, modern look, and I wondered what color to choose. I had a feeling Ava would tell me her ideas without much prompting.

I washed my hair, rinsed off, and headed to the bedroom, throwing on a fresh shirt and sweats. I was still towel-drying my hair as I walked into the living room and found Ava sitting on the sofa, Cash lying across her feet. I bit back my grin as a pleased feeling washed over me.

She had come to me tonight. I liked that.

"Little Dragon." I winked. "Can't stay away?"

She ignored my words. "You got a lot done out there today. Eating your Wheaties, Hunter?"

I laughed. "Your brothers insisted on donating some manual labor. Three sets of hands made it go fast." I sat across from her in the old chair, first leaning down to brush a kiss to her tempting mouth. "They know their way around tools."

She smirked. "Van—my uncle—is in construction. He built all the houses at our place. We all loved hanging around. He put us to work. My brothers, cousins, my dad, and uncles all pitched in. He taught us a lot. He still oversees all the flips Bentley does and helps out as foreman at ABC on occasion."

"Huh."

"Assumed the worst again, didn't you? No one in my family is lazy, Hunter. We all have our skill sets, and none of us is afraid of hard work. Even Bentley can swing a hammer or throw up a wall. He's a firm believer in understanding what goes on behind what you do. He can spot a weak foundation or a bad roof as fast as any contractor. Some of my best memories are all the dads and uncles working, framing a new house, joking and laughing. Van showing me how to use a hammer and a drill. Jordan teaching me how to plan out a project."

"Is that how you got into your career?"

She hummed. "It certainly planted the seeds. I've always been highly organized. Mom says I wrote lists from the time I was a child. I would tell her what I wanted to do the next day, and she would write it out for me before I could do it on my own. I always found myself calmer when I knew what I was going to do. I think I got it from my dad. He's always been big on lists, although he uses his voice to make his. He's dyslexic, and he finds it easier."

"Wow, that must be a challenge, given the business world."

"It is, but he handles it well." She looked sad for a moment. "He was always so glad none of us had the same trait. He never wanted any of us to struggle the way he did." She met my eyes. "He had a really rough start in life. I'm grateful he is the amazing man he is. He swore he would never allow his children to go through what he did. All the BAM men are the same way. They support countless children's charities and programs."

"Impressive."

She nodded. "They are. They all are." She leaned forward, eager. "Maybe you could see for yourself."

"Sorry?"

"Come meet my family. No one is going to try to buy your land or make you uncomfortable. They aren't the enemy, Hunter. I swear."

"Meet them," I repeated.

"Yes. Two weeks from now, we're having a barbecue on Sunday. It's relaxed and fun. The men grill too much food that still gets eaten. We all pitch in and make munchies, salads, and desserts. The pool will be open. There's music and fun. You can bring Cash."

She looked so hopeful and earnest, I didn't have the heart to tell her no. I was always shocked at how much I wanted to please her. To make her smile.

"I'll think about it."

Her eyes widened in pleasure. "Really?"

"Yes, really." I stood. "Now I'm starving." Despite the pizza earlier, I was hungry again.

"I brought burritos from that little place in town."

I glared at her. "You've been sitting there, yammering away, when there're burritos waiting?" I pulled her from the sofa. "You better have gotten chips and salsa too."

"As if you can eat burritos without them," she scoffed.

She followed me to the kitchen and pulled the bag from the oven. Then she grabbed some bottles of Creemore from the fridge that she'd picked up as well, the bottles glistening with cold.

I grabbed her and kissed her. She really couldn't be more perfect.

I ignored the little voice that added, "more perfect for me," in my head—even though a huge part of me agreed with it.

I didn't know what to do with those words.

Ava left before dawn, the sound of her SUV engine fading away. Although as I sat on my deck sipping coffee, I swore I heard the faint sound of it drifting across the open area between us as she arrived home. It was probably my imagination. She had stayed, and the night had been different from the other nights we spent together. I had been sore and aching, and she insisted on giving me a neck and back rub. Afterward, she lay on my chest, and I read to her, stroking my hand over her hair as I spoke the words of the murder mystery aloud. It was a book I'd found on the shelf in the living room. I had already figured out it didn't matter what I read, the sound of my voice and the caresses I gave her helped to soothe and relax her. I didn't wake her to fuck her, instead quietly switched off the light and resettled her on my chest, falling asleep with her draped over me. It felt more intimate than sex with her somehow. The need to care for her, to watch over her as she slumbered, were new and different feelings for me. I wasn't sure how to handle them any more than the need to see her all the time.

Stopping my inner musings, I finished my coffee and got to work on the railings. They were a simple, easy design, and I lost track of time as I measured, drilled, and put them together. The sound of a truck in the driveway made me look up, and I frowned as Ronan climbed out of the driver's seat and walked toward me. He carried a takeout tray of coffee and a bag.

"Hey."

He waved. "Looks good."

"What's up?"

"Oh, I needed to check a couple measurements I had for an idea. Mind if I go in?"

"Help yourself."

"I brought a snack."

"Okay, do what you need to do, and I'll finish this railing."

"Great."

A few moments later, he sat beside me on the steps and offered me a coffee. I sipped it gratefully and munched on the fresh Danish. "Good," I mumbled around a mouthful.

He chewed and swallowed. "Another family tradition. Lemon Danish is our favorite." He flashed me a grin. "We fight to the death over the last one, no matter how many Mom buys."

I laughed. "Who usually wins?"

"Ava. She fights dirty."

I laughed. "My Little Dragon. I shouldn't be surprised."

He quirked his eyebrow at my nickname but only grinned. "She is a dragon. She breathes fire when she's pissed."

"It's a cover," I said without thinking.

He paused. "A cover?"

"Your sister isn't the big bad wolf she likes people to think she is. Those moments she breathes fire take a lot out of her."

He leaned back on his elbows. "And you know this because…"

I scoffed. "Because I'm looking. She handles a lot of shit, Ronan. It exhausts her. Last night, she burrowed so tight into me while she slept—" I shut up as I realized what I'd said.

"Keep going."

I stared at the water for a moment. "She needs a place to just be Ava sometimes. Not the project manager, not the perfect daughter she wants to be, not the big sister with all the answers. Just Ava."

"You're right." He finished his coffee, dropping the cup into the paper bag. "I went through a bad time, feeling invisible in my family. Being a triplet, you tend to be part of a group all the time, you know. Ava understood that, and she supported me even when I was an idiot. I know she's not as tough as she lets on, and I know how hard she tries to be what she thinks she has to be. I try to help her. So does Liam. They're close. But you're the first person outside the family who has ever seen that about her. Whom she has gotten close enough to and allowed to see it." He sneered. "That idiot she was involved with a few years ago certainly didn't. He had no idea what he let go. Jackass."

"I worry about her. The responsibilities she carries," I admitted, unable to keep the words to myself.

"Addi is hiring someone to help her. And she plans on getting a third person in to take off more of the load." He met my gaze. "We aren't as blind as you think."

"Good."

He stood, brushing off his pants. "Lemme help you install a couple of those railings. You can add the posts by yourself later."

I hesitated and he laughed. "Wow, you are a tough nut to crack. Just like your grandfather. Accept the help, Hunter."

Grudgingly, I stood. "Fine."

We worked in companionable silence, the railings going up fast. His phone went off, and he checked the screen. "Shit, I gotta go."

"Thanks for your help."

"No problem. I love working with my hands and enjoy the chance to be outside."

He headed toward his truck, stopping and turning around.

"Thanks."

"For?"

"Worrying about Ava. Seeing her."

I shrugged, unsure how to answer.

"I wonder if you realize how blind you are, though," he mused. "You might want to think about that."

Then he left, his words making me frown.

What the hell did he mean?

I got a text from Ava around nine. We had finally exchanged numbers a few days prior, but this was the first time she had used the digits.

> **Ava:** *Drinking with the girls.*
> **Hunter:** *Are you drunk?*
> **Ava:** *I can't feel my toes.*
> **Hunter:** *I'll take that as a yes. Be safe, Little Dragon. Have fun.*
> **Ava:** *I like it when you call me that.*
> **Hunter:** *I like calling you Little Dragon.*
> **Ava:** *Sleeping at Addi's.*
> **Hunter:** *Good.*

I smiled as I rummaged in the fridge to find something to eat. I was glad she was with her family and having fun, although part of me was disappointed I wouldn't see her.

My phone buzzed.

> **Ava:** *When I'm drunk, I get horny.*
> **Hunter:** *Good to know.*

Ava: *I'm drunk.*
Hunter: *LOL. So, you're horny? I can't help you.*
Ava: *Dammit.*
Hunter: *I'll make it up.*
Ava: *Good. Will you do that thing with your tongue? I really like that.*

I burst out laughing.

Hunter: *Whatever you want.*
Ava: *I want that. I want you. Your big cock inside me and your mouth on mine.*
Hunter: *And my tongue doing that thing?*
Ava: *Yes.*

I had to adjust myself at the thought of being inside her. We fit each other well. In fact, she was perfect around me.

Hunter: *Tomorrow, Little Dragon. Tomorrow, I'll be all over you. As long as you're not hungover.*
Ava: *I'm wet, Hunter.*

I dropped my head, shaking it and groaning.

Hunter: *Jesus.*
Ava: *I want you. I want you all the time.*
Hunter: *I can't show up at Addi's for a booty call.*
Ava: *She wouldn't mind.*

Once again, I began to laugh. She was incorrigible. But I sobered at her next message.

Ava: *I had a bad day.*

Hunter: *Why?*
Ava: *Another asshole. He called me a C U Next Tuesday. I hate that word.*
Hunter: *Give me his name.*
Ava: *No.*
Hunter: *Give me his name, and I'll get Ronan and we'll pay him a visit.*
Ava: *I love that you and my bros are buddies.*
Hunter: *Name.*
Ava: *It's fine. The girls and I are drinking the day away.*

I drummed my fingers on the counter, the rage inside me shocking. I wanted to find this idiot who upset her and teach him a lesson. Drive my fist into his face and wipe the no doubt superior smile off it. He needed someone to teach him some manners.

I was glad that Ava was with people who cared about her, although a huge part of me wanted to trudge through the trees and knock on every door there until I found out which house was Addi's and bring Ava back here with me. I'd make her forget about that asshole. I'd make her forget about everything but me. Us. Our bodies moving together, slick with sweat and desire. My cock buried so deep inside her, she'd feel it for days.

I shook my head. What was it about this woman that made me want to protect her? To say to hell with everything and everybody and go find her? I wanted to wrap her in my arms and hold her until the distress faded. Kiss her until she forgot about the day. Be the one who made her feel better.

I looked down at the screen, seeing she had sent another message.

Ava: *I'm fine—really. I shouldn't have said anything. Having fun.*
You sleep well. I'll see you soon. Night.

I smiled grimly as I replied.

Hunter: *Count on it.*

AVA

I walked home in the early dawn, enjoying the fresh air. My head
ached a little, but otherwise, I felt fine. Maybe a little tired. I ran
a hand through my damp hair. I'd grabbed a shower at Addi's
and wore the T-shirt Brayden had loaned me, plus a pair of
Addi's leggings after I spilled wine on myself. I carried my soiled
clothes under my arm. Thank goodness for favorite cousins who
lived close. I approached my little house tucked up against the
backdrop of the towering trees. I'd left my car in the driveway,
planning on going to Hunter's later, when Addi pulled up and
told me to get in the car and took me to her house. There Gracie,
Heather, Paige, and Beth waited, bottles of wine open and my
favorite Chinese takeout on the table.

It had felt good to sit with them and shake off the day. Addi had
been in the meeting where I had once again been subjected to
name-calling. Not only had she immediately put a stop to any
dealings with the company, but Ronan and Brayden had escorted
Mr. Edgington none too gently from the building. I tried to hide
it, but it upset me. I was used to dealing with tough men. Men
who tried to intimidate and talk down to me. Quite often, I
ended up winning them over, earning their grudging respect.
Sometimes I wasn't successful. I was used to that. But it felt lately

as if the insults had taken on a new level. The disparity nastier. More personal.

Or maybe Hunter was right when he said he thought I was tired. Maybe I needed a break. A holiday.

I glanced at my phone, slightly embarrassed I had texted him. I had to admit, rereading the texts this morning, I felt a delight at his teasing and a thrill at his instant protectiveness. Ronan had told me the two of them were getting along well, and it pleased me. A part of me, way down deep inside, hoped if he made friends with us, if he saw how great living here could be, he would stay. That I wouldn't have to say goodbye. That the part of me that was growing more attached to him wouldn't have to feel the pain of his leaving.

I sighed as I approached the door. I needed to tamp that down. He had made his position very clear. Still, a girl could hope.

My heart sped up as I opened the door and found Hunter sitting on the sofa, his long legs crossed at the knee, his foot bobbing impatiently. An empty cup of coffee sat in front of him. He'd obviously been here for a while.

He regarded me, his eyes lit with anger and determination, icy blue flames that mesmerized me.

"Um, hi," I squeaked. I literally squeaked, my voice was so high. "I didn't expect to see you here."

He unfurled himself from the sofa. "Really? You were pretty plain last night. You wanted to be fucked. By me. And I'm here to deliver." He paused. "Me and my tongue."

"Ah," I managed to get out through my suddenly dry throat.

"And then we're going to discuss the asshole that made you drink."

"Brayden and Ronan kicked him off the property," I said after clearing my throat. "I-I think they had a lot to say to him. Addi canceled the contract."

"Good. I'm glad to know your family is protecting you. I guess that leaves me with the other job."

He crossed the room in three long strides and swooped me into his arms.

"What job?" I asked, breathless.

"Fucking you into oblivion." The anger in his eyes had been replaced by a scorching heat, a raging inferno of blue and silver lava. "It's a dirty job, Little Dragon, but someone's gotta do it."

"I hope it's really dirty," I replied.

He grinned suddenly and leaned close, his mouth hovering over mine. "Filthy."

I woke up, warmth surrounding me. Hunter had me held tight to his chest, his arms banded around me, his leg over mine, keeping me close. For a moment, I didn't move, enjoying being so close to him. Gradually, I shifted and blinked in the bright morning light. Behind me, he grunted.

"You're finally awake."

I swallowed, wriggling from his hold and reaching for my bottle of water. I drank deeply and turned to look at him. "That's what happens when you get fucked into oblivion." I air-quoted the words and grimaced a little as I moved. "You did your job well."

He crossed his arms under his head. "I figured that out by your screams of pleasure."

"I didn't scream."

"Well, you groaned and called my name. Loudly. God and a few other deities too. You curse like a sailor when I fuck you." He lifted one eyebrow. "Did you use to be one?"

I nodded. "I should have mentioned that."

He threw back his head in laughter. "I see."

I pushed him back and straddled his legs, running my hands along his bare chest, letting them drift lower, grinning as his dick began to thicken. "Permission to come aboard, Captain?"

He gripped my hips. "Permission granted. Both of them. Climb aboard and come. Hard."

"Aye-aye."

I was alone when I woke the next time. I slid from bed, my muscles protesting, and padded to the shower, letting the heat ease the ache. I dressed and put up my hair, then headed to the kitchen. The only evidence of Hunter being there earlier was the washed coffee cup in the drainer.

Well, that and the pleasant hum between my thighs.

I made a cup of coffee, frowning as I opened the fridge and saw the pot of sauce and meatballs I had made earlier in the week and never eaten. Glancing at the clock, I felt an idea form, and I pulled the pot from the fridge and set it on the stove to reheat. I drank my coffee on my front deck, waving at Liam as he went past in the golf cart, piled high with dirt and plants. Lucy was beside him, a big hat on her head, and she waved wildly as they drove by, a small shovel in her hand. The two of them would no doubt have a grand time digging in the dirt, with Lucy asking a thousand and one questions that Liam would patiently answer as he tried to make sure she didn't drown his seedlings or attempt to bury her prosthetic arm and see if it would grow too. She was a constant source of amusement to everyone, and we all adored her. Liam especially so. Every time she called him Daddy, his face melted and he was putty in her hands.

A fact she was well aware of.

Inside, I boiled some noodles, tasted the sauce, and grated a huge pile of Asiago cheese. Once the noodles were cooked, I combined them with the sauce and meatballs, piled on the cheese, and put on the lid. Then I headed through the forest and toward Hunter.

CHAPTER 16

HUNTER

I knew she was coming before I saw her. Cash stood at attention, his gaze focused on the tree line, his tail wagging madly. I paused in my task, watching, my anticipation almost as great as his. She appeared between the break in the trees, her hair piled on her head, dressed casually. Her hands were encased in oven mitts, and she carried a large pot. She made me grin with her random appearances and offerings.

She approached me with one of her shier smiles—one I had a feeling few people ever saw. Despite her bravado and snark, she was surprisingly reticent about sex outside the bedroom. She actually blushed after we'd been together, our bodies still hot from our joining, the air around us sizzling with the heat of our efforts. I had made an offhand remark and been fascinated as the color crept into her cheeks and gradually went down her neck, tingeing her breasts pink. I found it endearing. Charming. Somehow it made her even sexier.

"Come bearing gifts, Little Dragon?" I asked, eyeing the pan in her grip.

"Spaghetti."

"You made spaghetti?" I set aside the nail gun and stood. "Really?"

I freaking loved spaghetti.

"Yeah. I made the sauce a couple of nights ago but hadn't gotten around to eating it. So, I thought I'd share. I figured, I was hungry, so you must be too."

"I am."

She set the pot down on the second step, disappeared inside, and returned with two forks and some water. She sat down and placed the pot on her lap, protecting her skin with the big mitts. She tilted her head, indicating the spot behind her. I didn't need a second invitation, sliding onto the top step and caging her between my legs. She lifted the lid, and the aroma hit me. Spicy tomato sauce, cheese, oregano, and garlic wafted up, making me groan. She handed me a fork and draped a tea towel over her shoulder.

"Dig in."

I leaned over her shoulder, twirling the pasta, chewing it slowly. I speared a meatball, humming under my breath at the delicious taste.

"So good," I mumbled, grateful for the tea towel when some sauce dripped. I caught it with my finger and bent close, kissing the side of her neck, enjoying the shiver.

I knew we could go inside. Get bowls. Eat like normal human beings. Except, I liked this. Her tucked in front of me, sharing a pot of pasta, enjoying the fresh air, the aroma of her meal, and the scent of newly cut cedar.

We ate in silence, aside from my grunts and mutterings of appreciation. She leaned against me, relaxed and at peace. We had a couple of fork fights going after the same meatball, which made me laugh. She threw Cash a meatball, which he gobbled down then waited hopefully for more. Instead, she dug into her pocket and tossed him a dog biscuit she'd obviously brought with her. He happily caught it and lay in the sun, chewing on it.

The sound of a truck in the driveway made us look up, and she groaned and dropped her head.

"Fuck's sake," she muttered as Ronan got out of the truck and approached us with a wide, shit-eating grin on his face.

"You take this whole neighbor thing to another level, Ava. Now you're teaching him to eat pasta? Wow. Just wow."

Chuckling, he walked up the steps and passed us, going inside. Ava peeked up at me, and I shrugged, twirling more spaghetti. Ronan came outside and sat beside Ava, sticking a fork into the pot and twirling a massive amount of pasta and adding a meatball, then shoving it in his face and chewing.

"Help yourself, please," I deadpanned.

He nodded, his mouth full. He chewed and swallowed, reaching over for more, batting Ava's hand out of the way when she tried to stop him. "I'm hungry," he protested.

"You have Beth. She'll make you food."

"She's out with Evan." He nudged her. "Unlike some people, she was home at a decent time and not drunk."

I chuckled as I twirled more pasta. I had a feeling the bastard was going to eat way too much of my meal, and I really didn't want to share it. I looked around, trying to see where Ava had put the lid to the pot but couldn't spy it.

Ava sighed. "I did have a little too much last night."

Ronan stopped eating and looked at her. "I'm only teasing. You needed to relax last night." He looked up, meeting my eyes. "She tell you what happened yesterday afternoon?"

"Yeah."

"Motherfucker. No one calls my sister names. You should have laid one of your karate moves on him, Ava."

"You know karate?" I asked, surprised.

"I have a black belt," she confirmed.

I was impressed. "Holy shit. Remind me not to piss you off."

She patted my knee. "I'll be gentle." She turned to Ronan. "I just wanted him gone. If I had engaged, it would have escalated. And if I'd flipped him, which, believe me, I wanted to, he would have sued. I think you and Brayden made your point. And Addi, when she tore up the contract."

"I sort of roughed him up a little in the elevator. Brayden might have covered the camera," he confessed. "He'll think twice about calling anyone that name again."

My respect for Ronan grew, and I stopped looking for the lid. He deserved some of the delicious pasta. We ate for a while, then I spoke.

"So, are you stalking me now? That's three days in a row you've been here, Ronan."

"You track my sister's visits too?"

I lifted one eyebrow. "For totally different reasons."

"Ew. Never mind. I brought a set of plans to show you."

"Already?"

"I had time. Beth was out last night, so was Evan. They left again this morning, so I had lots of free time. And like I said, your plan was pretty simple. You can look it over, I'll make any changes needed, and you can submit for approval." He winked in a conspiratorial way. "Once they see my name attached to the plans, it'll be pushed through fast."

"Such humility."

He stretched out his arms. "Just speaking the truth."

"Okay, let's see these plans." Without thinking, I kissed the top of Ava's head. "Excellent spaghetti, Little Dragon. Thanks."

Ronan laughed as he stood. "It was awesome, *Little Dragon*. Just what I needed."

"Shut it and go get the drawings," she muttered, pushing him off the steps.

I leaned down, pressing my lips to her ear. "Hide the spaghetti while he's busy."

Her giggle made me smile.

"These are awesome, Ronan. Exactly what I pictured. I even like the deck extension wrapping around the house."

"You don't have to extend the roof over the deck. Add a pergola around the back half and run it along the side. Use some climbing vines, and as they fill in, the shade will be there. That way, you can start the foundation. Save yourself a ton of cash."

"Great."

He shut the computer. "I'll print these up with the specs and drop them off Monday. You can take it to Milly and get your permit. Who are you using to pour the foundation?"

"I spoke to Smithers Corp and Davenport Co."

"Davenport is better. Local, straightforward."

"All right. Thanks for the tip."

"Roof?"

"I'll do it myself."

Ronan lifted one eyebrow but didn't say anything. "Framing?"

"You're looking at him. I'll hire a couple guys to help for the heavy stuff and finish it on my own."

"Big jobs."

"I know what I'm doing," I informed him.

Ronan laughed. "No doubt. Still, big jobs to tackle on your own. Get my number from Ava. Call me. Liam and I will swing by and help. So will Paul and Jeremy. Happy to help a neighbor."

I hesitated, my irrational need to say no immediately hitting me.

Ronan held up his hands. "No pressure. But many hands and all. And free labor as long as there is beer and pizza." He nudged Ava. "Or spaghetti."

I smiled although it was forced.

"Aylmer's Electric does good work. Again, local. Honest. Tell Hank I sent you. He'll look after you."

"Okay."

He stood and hugged Ava quickly, then headed to the door.

"Enjoy the rest of your day, kids."

He left, the sound of his engine fading away.

Ava looked at me nervously. "He was just trying to be helpful."

"I know."

She sighed. "You don't trust many people, do you? Especially my family. Why?"

I blew out a long breath. "Long story."

"I'm not in a hurry to leave. Unless you want me to go."

I met her gaze. "No."

She reached across the table and gripped my hand. "I just want to understand."

I laughed. "I'm not sure I understand myself."

"Try me."

"I've never told anyone about my past. Not a soul."

"I think I might be a little different from just *anyone*, Hunter."

She had a point. What she was, exactly, I couldn't say, but she was different. Still, it made me uncomfortable.

I stood and paced, already feeling my nerves stretching taut. "My mom was a wild child, from what I understand. I guess she gave my grandparents a lot of trouble." I indicated the room. "My grandparents lived in town and owned this place. They used it as a cottage. They moved here when she was about twelve, hoping that a little distance from town and some open space would help her." I barked a laugh. "It didn't."

Ava stayed silent.

"Long story short—the trouble kept happening. Then when she was sixteen, she got pregnant with me."

"Ah," Ava breathed out.

"Now, I got all this from my grandfather's attorney, so some of it is pretty sketchy. He could tell me what little he knew but not the whys."

"What happened?"

"Same old story, told a thousand times. She planned to give me up for adoption, but when I was born, decided to keep me. She stayed here with my grandparents for a while, then found a job and moved closer to Toronto. That failed, and she came back. Then another opportunity and we were gone. Then back. It continued until I was five." I ran my hand over the mantel. "I have vague recollections of being here. Sitting by the fireplace, hearing my grandfather talk. The arguments between him and my mother. My grandmother in the kitchen. Just fleeting, fast moments. Nothing concrete. I wasn't even sure who the people were until recently."

"Oh?" Ava hummed the question.

"Too many people have come and gone from my life. Most of them are just shadows of memories—especially when I was little. One memory I have, though…" I rolled my shoulders as the anxiety built. "One day, there was a huge fight. I remember the shouting. It scared me, and I hid under the bed. My mother came in and dragged me out, tossing me into the car. There was more yelling, and my grandmother was crying, my grandfather trying to open the car door, but my mother drove away. It was the last time I was here until now."

"Wow. Where did you go?"

I grimaced. "I have no idea, Ava. The list is endless. My mother —she was unable to settle anywhere for very long. Ever. I can't tell you the string of cities and places we lived. Never more than a few months. Six, I think, was the longest. The number of men that came and went. The long list of promises of 'This time, it will be different,' I went through. My mother was distrustful of everything and everyone." I pushed off the mantel, pacing around the room. "We lived in apartments, trailers, run-down houses, fancy places, hotels, motels, even tents. Whatever broken-down piece of shit she was driving at the time. An old RV for a while. Endless changes of addresses. Most of the time, living hand to mouth. We'd land somewhere new, and she'd get a job and make the same promise that we'd found the right place. But invariably, we'd pack up and be gone in the middle of the night, leaving behind debts, lies, and little pieces of a broken life."

I stopped in front of Ava, tugging a hand through my hair.

"What about school? Friends?"

I barked out a laugh. "I have no idea how many schools I went to and got pulled from. I never finished a grade—ever. Because of my age, they'd just push me ahead. I never made any friends. There was no point. I knew we'd be gone before too long."

"How did you survive?" she asked.

"By relying on myself. I learned to cook basic foods. Toast or eggs if we had them. I would sneak a buck out of her purse and get a box of macaroni and cook it. Hide it so I had something to eat for a couple of days since most of the time, she forgot about that sort of thing. I washed my clothes in the bathtub—if we had one. I went to the local library and taught myself. I learned to cope. The few times we had a place that was decent, it was usually because she met someone—" I held up my fingers in quotations "—'special.'"

I shook my head. "They never lasted. She drove them away with her paranoia, distrust, and demands. Then the cycle would start again."

Ava reached for my hand that was clasping and unclasping on my thigh. She pulled me onto the chair beside her. "Keep talking," she pleaded.

"When I was sixteen, I had enough. She had enough. She told me it was time to be on my own. I remember laughing and telling her I'd been on my own for years. We argued and I left."

"Where did you go?"

"I did what I knew best, Ava. All I knew was to be a rolling stone. I went from place to place, picking up skills and trades. I worked in car washes, construction sites, restaurants, whatever I could do to find work. Landscaping, picking crops, anything. I worked all around Canada, in the States, I even went to Australia, working my way there on a boat. I stayed there for a year, doing odd jobs. I came back to Canada and got my GED." I offered her a sad smile. "Probably the oldest graduate in the country."

She squeezed my hand. "Still, you got it." She paused. "Why didn't you come here to see your grandparents?"

"Two reasons. One, they were really just a dim memory. I had no idea where this place was or who the people I remembered were. They could have been one of the hundred places we stayed at." I huffed out a long exhale. "Two, my mother told me her parents kicked us out and that they didn't want either of us. I was about twelve and asked about them. Then later, she told me they had both died. She told me we had no family."

"Why?"

I shrugged. "Maybe she was punishing my grandparents by keeping me away. Maybe something else. I have no idea."

I stood and circled the room again. "She died when I was in my late thirties. All her things went into storage. There wasn't much, but I couldn't bear to even look at it. Our relationship had dissolved into a polite call or letter once a year checking in, and usually it was me reaching out to her from some deep-seated sense of obligation. After I left, she stayed in Canada. She kept a PO Box in Alberta, and I had a cell phone so she could get in touch. I would write her on occasion to let her know where I was. The calls were sporadic and painful. I was working in the Northwest Territories when I got a call saying she was ill. She died not long after."

"Did you see her?"

"No."

"Do you regret that?" she asked, her voice low with care.

"No, Ava. My relationship with my mother was messy and complicated. I was never a kid or allowed to be one. As far back as I can remember, I was considered a burden, just something she had to deal with. I was never taken into consideration or felt as if I mattered. I went where I was told to go, did what I was told to do, and learned from her never to trust, build relationships, or depend on anyone." I ran a hand through my hair. "I never understood why she kept me. It wasn't as if she loved me. She should have given me up."

There was a beat of silence, then Ava cleared her throat. Her voice sounded thick.

"What about your grandparents? How did you discover they were alive?"

I grimaced. "I discovered too late. I finally went to collect the things I'd put into storage. I decided it was time to put the past to bed. There wasn't much, but I went through the boxes. It was mostly junk, but I found a package of letters she'd kept and I opened them. They were from my grandfather. There weren't many, but the last one was dated a year before she passed. I realized she'd been lying and my grandfather, at least, was alive. I looked up the address, but there was no phone number. I wrote a letter to the address, and a few weeks later, I got a call from my grandfather's solicitor, saying he had passed recently and my grandmother had passed years prior. He informed me that I was in his will. He had left me this place, and it was being held in trust for me for ten years. I came here to see it."

"What would have happened after ten years?"

"There was a second beneficiary. It would go to them."

"I see."

"There was no mention of me in the letters. Nothing. I guess I meant as little to them as I did to her. I have no idea why he left me this place." I scoffed bitterly. "No wonder I'm so screwed up. I have no idea how to be normal."

"You *are* normal, Hunter."

"No, I'm not. I don't connect with people or places. I don't have roots or a history. Just a lot of bad memories. She really messed up my thinking, Ava. I don't have any of the usual desires other people do. Family. Kids. A spouse. A home. I find trust hard. Half the time, I have one foot out the door before I've even said hello." I locked gazes with her. "It's part of my makeup. It's who I am."

"No. It's who you thought you were. You can change that."

I shook my head in disagreement. "No, I can't. I don't have the emotional depth."

She jumped to her feet. "Yes, you do! You look after Cash. You care about me."

I waved her off. "Cash is an animal. That is different. And you..." I sighed as I traced my finger along her cheek. "While you are special in your own way, you have a time limit too, Little Dragon. Everyone does. I'm not equipped to deal with it. To stay anywhere. I don't know how."

"You could learn," she insisted stubbornly. "If you wanted, you could learn."

"Maybe," I said slowly. "Maybe—I don't want to learn."

Her eyes widened, and I saw the flash of pain in them. Still, she grabbed my hand. "Don't. Don't let her win, Hunter. You can overcome this. All of this. There has to be a reason your grandfather left you this place. Maybe he was trying to give you roots. A place to call your own."

I smiled ruefully. "Maybe he felt guilty. Or maybe he had no one else to leave it to."

"You said there was a second beneficiary. Is it a relative?"

I met her eyes. "No. It was you, Ava."

CHAPTER 17
AVA

I stared out the window at the water, pulling my legs up to my chest. I wrapped my arms around my knees, laying my cheek on them. From the great room, I heard laughter and the snippets of many conversations. I felt removed and tired today.

So tired.

I still had no idea what to think about Hunter's announcement yesterday. That his grandfather had listed me as a beneficiary if he never showed up. It also explained the way he hissed, *"You're her,"* the day I introduced myself.

Why would Mr. Owens list me as the second beneficiary?

I had always tried to be nice to Mr. Owens. I checked on him, made sure he had supplies. My family looked after him behind the scenes, but he never shared anything personal. Never told me about his grandson. He would talk of his wife, Gail. Share the occasional story. At times, seem lost in memories. But Hunter's name never passed his lips. His plans for the house were never brought up.

I sighed, shutting my eyes and rolling my shoulders.

Hunter's words, his story, kept flitting through my mind. The pain he kept hidden. The emotional toll his childhood had taken on him. His refusal to even consider that he could have a different kind of life, that he was different from his mother. He couldn't see it. He couldn't see how incredible he was or how capable he was of caring. Loving.

I wiped the tears that kept coming, drying my face with my sweatshirt. I had done exactly what I swore I wouldn't do. What I never planned to happen. I was falling in love with Hunter Owens. Despite the difference in our childhoods, the ten-year age gap between us, how we viewed things, somehow we fit. I felt different in his company. He had a way of making me feel safe. Protected. Yet not in an overbearing, coddling way. He let me be me. He loved my bossiness and quirks. But he also made me safe enough to show my weaker side. Nothing felt as good as lying on his chest, listening to his low baritone voice as he read to me. Feeling his arms around me in the night when I would wake up. His humor and the sound of his laughter that seemed to surprise him when it happened—as if he weren't used to hearing himself amused.

And the way he saw *me*. He knew when I was tired. When I needed to be held. He saw through all my defenses and underneath the bluster I had perfected to the real me. And he allowed me to show it, and in his own special way, he surrounded me, helping me find my strength.

Except, maybe I had pushed him too far. After telling me his past yesterday, he had shut down. He stood and went outside, working on the railings. I joined him, but things were strained. I wasn't sure if he regretted telling me, if he felt I had overstepped, or if he simply needed some time to process the entire conversation. When Gracie had texted me, asking for some help, he seemed grateful for the reprieve. He kissed me and sent me off with a smile, but his lips had barely brushed mine, and there had been no indication of any plans to see me later. After I walked out of view through the break in the trees, I had paused. There was no sound behind me, no nail gun, nothing. I stepped off the path and peeked through the trees. Hunter stood, bent over the railing, his head hanging down, his shoulders hunched in defeat. I waited, wanting him to come after me, to call out—but he didn't. I was desperate to go back to him and wrap my arms around him, but I knew he wouldn't like it, and I couldn't bear the rejection that would follow. My footsteps dragged all the way back to my house.

He hadn't called or texted, and my back door hadn't opened all night. I spent the night tossing and turning, and this morning had dragged myself from bed, looking haggard and feeling lousy.

A cup of coffee appeared in front of me. I lifted my head and met my mom's worried gaze. She sat across from me, sipping her coffee in silence. Finally, she spoke.

"Are you all right, Ava?"

"I'm good. It was a long week."

"So your brother told us. Your father is worried."

I shrugged. "It happens, Mom. You know yourself, dealing with people is hard. Some harder than others. I've had a bad stretch lately."

"Maybe you need a break."

I gazed past her to the water outside, mesmerized as always by the variant of colors in the lake as the waves rolled.

"You haven't taken a break in a long time," she continued.

"Things have been too busy," I agreed.

"Ava."

Her tone caught my attention, and I met her gaze. She looked concerned, her green eyes clouded with worry.

"Life is too short to do nothing but work."

"I know."

"Ronan said you're getting some help. You need to take advantage of that and have a holiday."

I rubbed my temples. "I'll talk to Addi about it."

She leaned close, laying her hand over mine. "Is there something else?"

I forced a smile. "What else could there be?"

"Maybe a certain neighbor has caught your attention?"

"Ronan has a big mouth," I groused.

She shook her head. "Ronan didn't say anything. I see the way your gaze looks in that direction. I've dropped by a few times, and you're not home but your car is there. Once I came, and I heard the sound of a male voice—" she held up her hand before I could protest "—and a dog. Hunter has a dog." Then she smiled, her voice filled with affection. "And I know my daughter. You've been crying, and that is unusual. Something is troubling you. Something is on your mind. I think the same thing that was on Hunter's mind the day I saw him. Each other."

I sighed. "Mom, it's complicated."

She waved her hand. "This entire family thrives on complicated."

"He doesn't want to be part of this family. Part of *any* family. It's not serious between us. It's just a 'for now' thing." I smiled ruefully. "I know it's not what you want to hear, but it's the truth."

She regarded me shrewdly. "Is it?"

I looked down, picking at an imaginary thread on my shirt. "It is for him."

"But for you?"

"It doesn't matter. I agreed to the terms. He was very clear."

"People can change their minds."

I shook my head, sadness wrapping around my heart. "Hunter is steadfast in his determination. He-he's damaged, Mom. His upbringing was as bad as Dad's. Very similar to Maddox's. Neglect and pain. He's convinced he can't love. That life holds nothing for him but an endless trail of searching."

"Then help him find what he is searching for."

"He won't let me." I swallowed. "I think, maybe this time, love and patience aren't enough."

"Only you can decide that. I hate to see you suffer."

"I hate seeing him suffer when he doesn't have to."

She took my hand. "I can't tell you what to do. But I will say this. Love doesn't always have an HEA like the books we read. If this relationship hurts you, you need to step away. If he can't return your feelings, he isn't the one for you. But if you want to fight for him, then fight. But don't fight forever. Nothing and no one are worth that sort of pain. As hard as it is, you have to decide what is right for you. But don't lose yourself doing it. Because you are too special, my girl. And if Hunter can't see that, then the problem is his, not yours. Don't let him rob you of that."

She stood and kissed my forehead the way she had when I was a child. I inhaled her comforting scent of jasmine and floral. She patted my cheek and walked away, leaving me alone with my thoughts.

I only wished they weren't such a jumbled mess in my head.

───────

Monday and Tuesday were endless. I felt as if part of me were missing. I longed to hear Hunter's voice. To see his face, feel his touch. I didn't know if telling me his history had been too much for him or if it all had been too overwhelming. Me, my brothers, the house. Or perhaps, as he suggested, his need to move on had hit him and he'd decided to distance himself now.

I went through the motions. Attended meetings, interviewed some candidates for my assistant plus the extra body Addi wanted in the office to take care of all the filing and general work that needed to be handled for all of us. He or she would help out in all areas, going where required, and learning about all aspects of the business.

"I liked him," Addi mused, holding up a résumé. "He was a straight shooter. Open." She smirked. "Outspoken. He'd represent us well." She flipped the page. "With his experience, he'd take a lot off your plate."

"Yes, I liked Robert too. He's used to much more responsibility, though. Will he be happy being part of a team?"

She regarded me quietly, a small frown pulling down her lips. "He's looking to cut back since his wife gave birth. He was honest about that. I think he'd be thrilled to be part of a great team here." Addi's short nails made a clicking sound as she tapped them on the top of her desk. "And frankly, you need the help. And a holiday."

I met her concerned eyes and shook my head, silently begging her not to go there right now. She frowned again but nodded. "We also need to hire a couple of good foremen and create some new teams. I am tired of the bullshit we're going through hiring outside teams. I know it saves us money with salaries and benefits, but I'm not happy with the attitudes and problems we're running into. I discussed it with Dad, and he agrees."

"I agree."

"Okay. I'm calling Robert in for a second interview. We'll get him settled plus another body for more office staff, and I'll get Ronan and Brayden to start fleshing out teams. I think two smaller ones would be good. We have enough projects coming up, we can use them."

"Sounds good."

I stood to leave, getting to the door before Addi called my name. "Ava."

I turned, meeting her gaze.

"I'm here. If you want to talk. Anything. All you have to do is ask."

All I could do was nod.

I pulled into the driveway, leaving the SUV there. I rarely parked inside the garage during the summer. I headed inside, dropping my purse on the bench and kicking off my shoes. Padding toward the kitchen, I stopped at the sight of my pot sitting on the counter. The last time I had seen it had been at Hunter's. My gaze flew around the room, and my shoulders dropped when I realized he wasn't there. He had brought it back and left.

Dejected, I turned to go to my room and change.

Except, the back door flew open, and Hunter stood there. He looked unkempt, his hair wild as if he'd run his fingers through it a hundred times, his beard longer than normal. His eyes were intense, the icy blue a scorching inferno of anger and frustration. He walked in, slamming the door behind him. We stood separated by ten feet, yet I felt his touch as sure as if he were right in front of me.

"Goddammit, Ava," he growled, stalking toward me.

I couldn't speak.

"I can't get involved with you. Not the way you want. Don't you get it?"

"Get what?" I managed to ask.

"I will use you until I'm done. Then I'll walk. And I can't do that. Not to you."

"Why?" I whispered.

He gripped my arms. "Because I *do* care. Somehow, you've gotten under my skin. Your toughness and your smart mouth. Your fucking delicious spaghetti. The way you make me laugh. I fucking crave you. Every minute you're not within my sight, I want you back." He shook me slightly. "Physically, I can't get enough of you. But I can't give you more. I care, but not the way that you want—that you need—me to care." He barked out a bitter laugh. "I care just enough to not want to hurt you. Which hurts me."

I dared to cup his cheek. "It hurts me too."

"I've struggled to stay away from you. It's better that I do. I only came to bring back your pot. But when I came inside, all I could

247

smell was you. Inhale the fragrance that is *all* you. I heard your car, so I left. But I couldn't go." He leaned into my hand. "Fuck, I couldn't go."

I moved my fingers on his skin, skimming over his cheek and the roughness of his beard. "But you can't stay either?" I asked.

He met my eyes, and I saw the sorrow in them. "No."

I made a decision.

"Then stay for now. Let me have you for as long as you can stay. Give me that, at least."

"But—"

I silenced him with my finger. "The future will be what it is. But I want you while you're here. When you go, I won't beg. But right now, I am begging. Begging for you to stay with me now. Just for now."

He crushed me to him, his mouth covering mine. Instantly, all the pain, confusion, and loneliness evaporated. He wrapped his arms around me, his embrace tight, his kiss passionate and possessive. His tongue slid along mine in sensuous passes, and he lifted me, one hand on the back of my neck, the other cupping my ass. I felt the urgency in his touch, the power in his kiss. The way his fingers stroked restlessly on my skin. The rumble of satisfaction in his chest. I ran my fingers over his neck and shoulders in a long, repeated pattern, sliding them into his hair at the nape of his neck, pressing them into the tight muscles. He relaxed under my touch, his kisses becoming more leisurely, less urgent. But no less drugging.

He dragged his mouth across my cheek, down my neck, his tongue hot and wet on my skin. He tugged on my earlobe. "I want you, Little Dragon. Can I have you?"

"Yes," I answered simply. I would take what he offered. Whatever he offered. When it was over, I would deal with the aftermath then. But for now, he was there. With me. That was all that mattered.

He swung me into his arms, carrying me down the hall. The whole time, he kissed me, his mouth hard on mine, trailing over my skin, down my neck, his breath hot against me.

In my room, he set me on my feet, still kissing me, our hands tugging and pulling at the clothing that separated us. The sheets were cool under my sensitive skin as we fell onto the mattress, his weight pinning me down. He felt hot, his touch urgent. Everything was magnified. How he tasted, the way his hands felt gripping my hips, his deep breathing. I cried out as he drew a nipple into his mouth, sucking and biting. He used his lips and tongue on my skin, lavishing me in caresses. He stroked me with his fingers, finding my center and sliding along my clit with a deft touch. I arched into him, begging and pleading. For what, only he knew, and he gave it to me.

We were all over the bed. I was under him, on top, pressed to his chest, then finally on my stomach. After grabbing a condom, he drew up my hips and entered me from behind, the angle intense, the feel of him acute. He began to move, kissing my back and neck, turning my head to capture my mouth. He slid his fingers back to my clit and strummed in time with his thrusts, ramping the pleasure so high I wept. My orgasm bloomed, unfurling low in my stomach, its tendrils far-reaching. I gripped the sheets, pushing my body up closer to the pleasure as I came, trembling, crying, and moaning Hunter's name. He sat up, taking me with him, my back pressed to his chest. He pressed his lips to my ear, groaning and cursing, his frame vibrating as his cock swelled inside me, setting off yet another orgasm that shook me to my core as he thrust wildly, his release a long, drawn-out sigh escaping his mouth.

He dropped his head to my shoulder, our heavy breathing the only sound. My tears dripped heedlessly down my cheeks, landing on his skin. He reared back, turning my face to his.

"No, no, Little Dragon," he crooned, shifting us so he wrapped his arms around me, holding me tight. He dropped kisses to my face, brushing away the tears. "No crying. Please. Are you hurt? Was I too rough? Tell me," he pleaded, running his hands along my arms and torso. "Where—tell me where?"

"Not-not hurt," I assured him. I had no idea how to tell him. What to say that wouldn't push him away. How did I tell him I was so happy he was here with me? That he filled a need within me I didn't understand, and I knew would be empty once he left. That I was certain I would never recover from, yet was powerless to resist?

"Just overwhelmed," I whispered. "That was intense."

He lay back, taking me with him. He kept me close, pulling a blanket over us.

"It's always intense with you." He pressed a kiss to my head.

"Don't stay away again," I said quietly. "I know it's not forever, but I have you for now and—"

He stopped me from saying anything else with a press of his fingers on my mouth.

"I won't," he promised.

I settled back to his chest, feeling safe.

"Sleep a bit, then we'll talk," he promised. "We can go see Cash. He's missed you."

I felt sleep pulling me under as he spoke again, the words so quiet, I wasn't sure if they were real or not.

"But not as much as I did, Little Dragon."

―――――――――

The pattern of my life changed in a subtle fashion over the next while. I went to work, handling my job with a renewed sense of purpose. I issued orders, filed plans and paperwork, and attended meetings, my head somehow clearer. Taking a page from Hunter's book, I focused on now. Nothing else.

Addi hired Robert, and I was looking forward to his starting with the company. Having some help would remove some of the stress from my plate. It would take him some time to settle, but I was sure he would fit in well.

The biggest change was the end of my workday. I was never certain when I opened my door if Hunter would be waiting. Leaning against my counter, lounging on the sofa, stretched out on my bed. I never knew where I would find him. If he wasn't there, I knew he was waiting at his house, and I would change and make my way up the path to his place. Cash always greeted me with excited woofs, a wagging tail, and his favorite game of trying to trip me as he wound his way around my legs over and again.

Hunter always greeted me with one of his slow grins, a tight embrace, and a kiss deep enough to make my toes curl. Every night was spent in his arms. My favorite part of the day was resting on his chest, listening to his rich voice read out loud. The day, the worries, everything faded away as I lost myself to him, his voice, and the stroke of his gentle touch.

I pulled up to the house and went inside, the silence telling me Hunter wasn't there. But on my bed was a note, and I picked it up, scanning it quickly.

> ***Busy day.***
> ***Can I interest you in a late dinner for four for two?***
> ***I promise to fill you up an hour later...***
> ***H***

I grinned at his words, then changed, heading toward the back door. A knock on my front door stopped me, and I retraced my steps, opening the door to admit Gracie. She grinned at me.

"I thought I saw your car."

"Come in," I offered.

"No, just wanted to make sure you were still okay for tomorrow?"

At my blank look, she chuckled. "The barbecue on Sunday. You, Addi, Paige, and I are in charge of appetizers and snacks."

"Right. My goodness, the last couple of weeks have gone by fast," I mused.

"So, we need to go shopping and do the prep tomorrow."

My heart sank, knowing I would have to leave Hunter sooner than I planned. As well as Sunday since it was always an all-day thing with the family barbecues. I hadn't mentioned it to him again, and he hadn't brought it up. Either he had forgotten, or he was simply avoiding the subject. I had a feeling I knew which it was. I forced a smile to my face.

"Okay, what time?"

"I thought midafternoon. We can grab what we need and get it done. Maybe watch a movie and have wine after? Jaxson is going to take care of Kylie."

"Sounds good."

"We're sticking to the menu we planned, right?"

I grabbed my phone and looked at my notes, scanning the items. Neither Gracie nor I was fond of cooking, but we did rock the appetizers.

"I think this should work. I already have the chicken in the marinade in the freezer, so that saves us time."

"I made the stuffed mushroom filling today. Jaxson found these huge mushrooms yesterday, so that's all done," Gracie said.

"Then we're ahead of the game. How about I pick you up at three?"

"Sounds good." She paused. "Any plans for tonight?"

"I'm having Chinese with a friend."

She bit back a smile. "The friend I saw peek through your back window a moment ago?"

"Ah." I cleared my throat. *Hunter was here?* The thought that maybe he was as anxious to see me as I was to see him made my heart rate speed up.

"Did you invite him to the barbecue?"

"He's not much for family stuff."

"This family or any family?"

"Any."

"But you're having dinner with him."

"We're friends."

"Friends?" she asked, her eyes dancing. "*Close* friends?"

"Temporary friends. He'll be leaving soon."

She pursed her lips. "That's too bad."

"Why would you say that?"

"I assume he's the reason behind the bounce in your step lately. The way you smile more."

I shrugged, not wanting her to know how deeply I felt for him. I had to keep that piece of information to myself. If she knew, if somehow Hunter found out… No, I had to keep it hidden.

"We scratch an itch for each other."

She laughed. "That's what Jaxson thought."

"You're different."

"If you say so." She kissed my cheek. "Go and have a nice dinner. I'll see you tomorrow. If you're a little late, no big deal." She winked and left, laughing as she shut the door behind her.

I hurried to the back door and pulled it open. Hunter sat on the step, turning as I came out. I settled beside him, and he bumped my shoulder.

"Hey, Little Dragon."

"You could have come in," I told him.

"I didn't want to interrupt."

"More like you didn't want to meet another member of my family."

He chuckled, but he didn't deny it.

"I have to go shopping with Gracie tomorrow and make some stuff for Sunday."

He stared straight ahead. "Right. Sunday. Your family barbecue."

I hummed and waited for him to say more.

"What time do you have to leave tomorrow?"

"I have to pick her up at three."

He stood and held out his hand. "Well, let's go. I'm starving."

I let him pull me up, not asking the burning question.

I was too damn scared to hear his answer.

We slid into a booth at the restaurant, and Hunter grinned. "Should I bother looking at the menu?"

I laughed. "The dinner for three is okay too, just not as good. No shrimp."

"God forbid."

Mrs. Yeo came over, smiling. "Ava, how good to see you." She glanced at Hunter. "Who is your friend?"

"This is Hunter. Ah, he's my neighbor."

She lifted her eyebrows. "I wish I had a neighbor like him."

Hunter laughed, not at all taken aback by her teasing.

"Nice to meet you."

"You too." She glanced at me. "Usual?"

"Yes."

"I have beans tonight. Asparagus too."

"Oh, add those, please!"

She walked away laughing, and Hunter chuckled. "More food?"

"Her spicy green beans and asparagus are to die for. She only adds them to the menu when she can get them fresh. I can't pass those up."

"So, dinner for four plus two extra dishes."

I shrugged. "I worked hard today. Built up an appetite."

He eyed me slowly, leaning low over the table. "I've got an appetite too, Little Dragon. You gonna satisfy that later?"

"If you're lucky."

He sat back, grinning. "Oh, I'm feeling it tonight."

I grinned back. I had a feeling he was right.

CHAPTER 18

HUNTER

I wandered the house after Ava left the next day, restless and edgy. We'd eaten dinner, brought home leftovers, then spent the night playing backgammon and Scrabble at the kitchen table. She made simple, silly things fun. I couldn't recall the last time I'd played anything but a game of poker with some guys I was working with. But when she saw the games I had found in the cupboard, she was delighted and insisted we needed to use them, not throw them out.

"You have to keep them, Hunter. If you do rent the place, they're great pastimes for people when it rains."

She had a point. But when she opened the backgammon and found it in perfect, although slightly dusty, condition, she wanted to play. It turned out my Little Dragon was competitive and fierce with board games. She loved trash talk and strategizing. Taking my men. Her intelligence was evident during Scrabble. Her love of the triple word score abounded. I challenged her often, making her look up words only to piss her off. I insisted she had to use the dictionary I found with the games and not her phone, in keeping with the theme of the night of old-fashioned fun. She would squint as she looked up the word, her beautiful eyes flashing in triumph as she read the definition and used the word in a sentence.

When she stood to dance yet another victory, I chased her to the bedroom and tackled her on the bed. The laughter soon became something else entirely. Late in the night, I woke up and found her in the kitchen, sitting on the counter in my T-shirt, eating Chinese food. I stood between her legs, letting her feed me bites, then finally carried her back to bed, holding her close until she slept again.

She was quiet in the morning as we moved around. She helped me sort a closet in the guest room, discovering a few more things she insisted needed to stay. A pile of barely looked-at magazines, some old-fashioned glassware, and a popcorn maker for a fire.

"You never know what you're going to find," she enthused. *"All hidden treasures."*

We took Cash for a walk after lunch, and when we got back, she paused on the porch.

"I should go."

I nodded. "Okay." I already knew I wouldn't see her tonight and probably not tomorrow. I hated the thought of it. I also hated the fact that I hated it.

She pushed her hands into her back pockets. "Um, the invitation is open, you know, in case you change your mind and want a swim and some food. It's really casual. You can bring Cash if you want."

"Thanks," I said, unable to refuse her outright. We both knew I wouldn't go, but neither of us wanted to acknowledge the fact that I was that much of an asshole.

"Okay, there's some Chinese left for you."

"I'm good, Little Dragon. Enjoy your time with the girls and have fun." I didn't add *"tomorrow,"* but she knew.

A sad look crossed her face, and her bright eyes dimmed a little. But she didn't falter, leaning up and kissing my cheek. "See you later," she murmured.

She didn't look back, disappearing down the trail.

I missed her the moment she was out of sight.

Now unable to settle, I searched for something to do. Knowing I had to clear out the master bedroom before demo started, I grabbed some boxes and sorted through the surprisingly large closet. Most of it was being tossed. Old clothes, shoes, hats, and such. I found a couple of plaid shirts, never worn, with the prices still attached. I tossed those on the bed, knowing they would come in handy. There were some file boxes on the top shelf I pulled down. I opened the lids, quickly looking inside. One contained paperwork I decided I would go through. Another was tax returns, and the third contained piles of envelopes, the edges of some yellowed and curled and others looking newer. They looked more personal than business-related, so I assumed they were letters to my grandmother from when they were young, as well as other correspondence. I decided to put them aside until another time, and I spent the rest of the day sorting the other two boxes. I started a fire, burning everything I had no need or interest in keeping. I cracked a beer, watching the flames flicker and eat the paper I patiently fed to it. I tried not to think of Ava, but she popped into my head without trying. Her smiles and laughter. Her wit and intelligence. The way she wrinkled her nose when concentrating. Her unapologetic appetite.

How she felt in my arms. How I felt when I was with her. The way we moved together.

How empty my bed would be tonight.

How lonely I would be again when I left this place, left her, in the not-too-distant future.

I pushed those thoughts out of my head.

That was my life. It was all I knew.

I had no choice.

At least, that was what my head kept saying.

The next day, my restlessness grew tenfold. I was up early, working, clearing the back, getting ready to have the foundations poured. As soon as I got my permit, I needed to get it done. I worked under the heat of the sun, sweat pouring down my back as I used the chainsaw to clear away branches and the ax to chop at the undergrowth. I paused to wipe my brow, draining a bottle of water. I noticed some pieces of shingles in the pile of undergrowth, and I stepped back, peering at the roof. Cursing, I grabbed my ladder and climbed to the top, walking carefully on the spongy surface. Near the center, I discovered a missing patch of roofing, as well as another one farther over the peak. Luckily, rain wasn't forecast for the next few days, but I was going to have to get some tarps and cover the holes. The whole thing was coming off once the extension was done, but I would need to protect the gaps until that happened. We'd had a storm last week, and the shingles must have come off then. I recalled Ava blaming Cash for spilling his water bowl, but eyeing the missing shingles, I realized the water had come in from the ceiling, not his bowl. I walked the entire roof, pausing at the top to glance toward Ava's. I realized I could see the houses of the compound up here. At least a few of them. I could see her roof and the huge structure she called the Hub that stood closer to the water. I stretched as high as I could, curiosity filling me. I wondered if she was home now at the center of the place where they would gather for the barbecue. I glanced at my watch, surprised to see it was already past twelve, and Ava had said they usually started around eleven. I squinted, pretty certain I could make out the building where they would be. I thought I saw people gathering, even heard the sounds of music drifting across the open space, but I decided it was only my imagination working overtime.

With a huff, I climbed down the ladder. I'd have to go and buy some tarps this week. I went inside and showered. I began to get dressed, ignoring the constant pull in my chest. I looked in the mirror, staring at my reflection. I could see the yearning on my face, feel the need building inside me. For a moment, I didn't move, then I groaned.

Fuck it.

AVA

I set out the two huge platters of appetizers, knowing they would be cleared in a flash. We had tons more inside. I sniffed the air, smelling the chickens on the spit and the large roast beef Van had been cooking since eight o'clock. The air was rich with the scents of the cooking meat. The rec center fridges held platters of burgers and sausages. Up at the Hub were massive bowls of salads and tables of desserts. Buns and all the condiments were in coolers. When we were ready to grill, the golf carts would be loaded and the food transported here in quick succession.

There was a large bar set up, coolers of iced beer, wine, and soft drinks cold and ready to drink. Lots of alcohol and mixers on hand. We had spiked iced tea and lemonade, as well as plain variations available, the tall glass beverage holders glinting with moisture in the heat.

It was a beautiful day with a nice breeze. The sun was out, with only a handful of puffy clouds visible in the sky. But it wasn't too hot yet, which was great. The men had erected canopies, so there were lots of places to sit and get out of the sun if it got too much. The glass doors to the rec center were all pushed open, and you could sit inside and still be part of the party.

It was one of my favorite get-togethers of the year. Most of us tried to make it, so the place was usually jumping. I always enjoyed it.

But today, my smile was more forced than usual. My laughter not as easily found. As I looked around at my family, I felt slightly cut off. Not everyone had a partner, but most did. A few not-married had boyfriends or girlfriends with them. I was the oldest one without a partner. It had never bothered me before.

But that was before Hunter Owens entered my life.

I hated leaving him yesterday. He didn't say it, but there was a desolate look in his eyes as he waved me off, pretending to be cheerful. Once again, he chose to be alone. It didn't have to be that way, but it was what he thought was needed.

He'd texted me once last night, saying he hoped I was having a good time. I'd texted him back, telling him I was but was thinking of him. He never responded.

I had hoped to hear from him this morning. Hoped that somehow, the scent of the meat roasting would drift to his bluff, and he would regret his decision and join us. Relax and discover my family were awesome people. That perhaps he would unwind a little and see how he could fit in—that maybe, just maybe, he didn't have to leave. I hoped in vain since my phone never rang, and eventually, I stopped feeling anticipation when a vehicle would pull into the compound. He wouldn't change his mind.

I went inside to apply some more sunscreen and, if I was being honest, hide for a few moments. I looked in the mirror, grateful for sunglasses and the hat I was going to wear. I looked dejected, which was silly. He had to live his life the way he saw fit, and I had promised not to push. He wouldn't be comfortable here, and that was the end of the story. I had to put him out of my mind and enjoy the day.

Determined, I finished applying the sunscreen, fixed a smile on my face, and headed outside. I went to the bar, pouring one of Maddox's spiked iced teas. They were delicious and refreshing and, if you weren't careful, would knock you off your feet. I took a sip of the cold beverage, turning around to call out to my dad.

I froze at what I saw, a small gasp escaping my mouth. From the direction of my house, Hunter was walking slowly toward the rec center, Cash trotting beside him, his tail wagging furiously. Hunter was dressed in a pair of cargo shorts, with a tight gray T-shirt stretched across his torso, showing off his arms and pecs. He wore a baseball hat and sunglasses, and in his free hand, he carried a case of Creemore. Cash barked excitedly at seeing me, and everyone turned in the direction of the sound.

"Who the hell is that?" someone muttered.

My mom appeared at my elbow. "Go and welcome him, Ava. He must be second-guessing his decision already with this lot staring him down."

Before I could move, Ronan and Liam were headed toward him, slapping his back, taking the beer, and unclipping the lead on Cash's collar. My feet moved of their own accord, and I stopped in front of him.

"You came," I breathed out, crouching down to stroke Cash.

Hunter smiled and knelt beside me. "I did." He glanced toward the group behind me. "I might already be regretting it."

"Don't," I pleaded. "Come meet them. Have something to eat. A swim. It'll be fun. I promise."

I was shocked when he held out his hand, taking mine and squeezing it. "Okay, Little Dragon. I'm holding you to that."

We stood and headed toward my family.

HUNTER

I had no idea why I decided to come. All I knew was I wanted to be where she was—wherever that was. Before I could change my mind, I put on some decent shorts and an unwrinkled shirt, grabbed the unopened case of Creemore, and snapped on Cash's lead. As I wound my way down the path to her house, my feet never paused. Whether that was because Cash was pulling me along as fast as he could go or because I was as anxious as he was, I didn't know. At her place, I skirted the house and stopped in the front, for the first time hesitating. I wondered how her family would react. How I would react to them. It wasn't hard to find the party once I was close. I could smell the food, hear the laughter. I rounded the corner, approaching the pool, the large building behind it open and filled with Ava's family. I spotted her immediately, getting a drink from a glass jug. I tried not to laugh at her outfit. A gray T-shirt and long shorts looked effortlessly sexy on her and matched mine. Her hair was tucked under a hat, and she wore sunglasses. Someone spotted me, and there was a lull in the conversations as the group stared. For a moment, nothing happened, then Liam and Ronan broke away and came over to greet me. They were friendly and welcoming, but I only had eyes for the beautiful brunette headed my way. Her brothers relieved me of the Creemore and unclipped Cash's lead.

"He's safe here," Ronan assured me. "And welcome." He slapped me on the back. "As are you."

Ava came over and kneeled in front of Cash, giving him the affection he loved from her.

"You came," she whispered.

"I did."

Part of me was already regretting it, but she asked me to stay even for a little while, and I couldn't say no to her. As we headed toward her family, I wondered if that would ever change.

Up close, her father and uncles were a scary lot. But their hand-shakes were firm and their smiles friendly.

Ava introduced me simply as Hunter Owens. "Our new neighbor for the time being. I thought he might enjoy a day away from all the work he's doing up at the house."

Bentley Ridge nodded. "I hear you've been busy."

"Yes, I have," I agreed.

"Great view from that angle," Maddox Riley stated. "Peaceful and private."

"Just how I like it," I replied.

Aiden, Ava's father, grinned at me. "Your grandfather liked to chase me off his property with a shotgun."

"I've heard. It wasn't loaded." I laughed. "Even if it had been, I doubt he could have hit the side of a barn at fifty paces. His eyesight was for shit." At least that was what his lawyer had told me.

That made everyone laugh, and I felt as if I had passed some sort of test.

I was hugged by the women I had already met, plus a few new ones to add to the confusion. I lost count of the names and relationships—who belonged to whom, kids, grandkids, cousins—it was all a blur.

It took me a while to figure out why people were grinning until I realized I was still holding Ava's hand, mine wrapped tightly around hers, gripping it hard.

Cami smiled, her kindness hard to resist. "There are some munchies out. The real food will be about another hour or more. Help yourself."

I let Ava drag me to the table, and I reluctantly released her hand so she could fill a plate.

"I thought these were munchies?" I asked, eyeing the towering plate. It was overflowing with sticky ribs, chicken strips, stuffed mushrooms, steak bites, spicy sausage slices, as well as cheese, crackers, dips, and veggies.

"They are. We can share." She led us to one of the many tables, where Liam, Ronan, and their wives waited. Ronan pushed a beer toward me.

"You probably need this."

I accepted it gratefully, swallowing the cold brew. I dared to glance around, surprised to see I wasn't being stared at—at least not openly. I was sure I was being discussed, but I felt comfortable at this table. I saw Cash with a few of the guys, playing frisbee, catching and returning it, in his glory.

"He'll end up in the pool," I said dryly, tucking into the delicious repast in front of me.

"No worries. It's all good," Liam assured me.

"No other dogs here?"

"At times, we've had hamsters, fish, dogs, cats, even a goat once," Ava explained. "Reid and Becca still have a couple of cats. Van's dog died about three years ago. He's never had the heart to get another one. So, right now, Cash is on his own."

I laughed. "And loving it."

I finished the last item on the plate, and Ava began to get up. I placed a hand on her shoulder. "I'll get it, Little Dragon. I didn't come here for you to wait on me."

I headed to the table and began filling the plate again. I was going to need to run or swim before I could eat again, but I didn't care. Everything was delicious.

A large shadow appeared beside me, and I met the gaze of Ava's father. I noticed his different colored eyes, the green and brown irises bright in his face. I had observed Cami's bright-green gaze the first time I met her. I could see how Ava got such unusual eyes now.

He regarded me steadily. "Can I get you anything?" he asked.

"No, sir. This is an amazing feast. I appreciate the invitation."

"My wife likes you."

I wasn't sure how to respond to that. "Ah."

"Ronan and Liam say you're very talented. Lots of construction experience."

"Yes, I've done it for a lot of years."

"They seem to like you as well. They've mentioned you often."

"They've been very kind, helping me at times."

"Ava invited you over today?"

"Ah, yes?" I said, my reply sounding more like a question.

"Oddly enough, Ava has never mentioned you to me. Not directly. I wasn't aware of your, ah, *friendship* until a short while ago."

I felt the back of my neck prickle. "Oh," I managed to croak out. "She helped me at city hall. We've run into each other a few times, and she's been very neighborly."

"*Neighborly*," he repeated. "Is that what they're calling it these days? Huh."

The prickle became an irritating itch. I had to stop myself from rubbing the back of my neck to relieve the tic.

"Her silence says more than words, Hunter." He smiled at me, his hand on my shoulder. "I love my daughter."

"I'm sure you do. She is a great friend."

He nodded slowly. "Friend." Then a grin crossed his face. "You know, I heard history repeats itself. This is just too funny." His slaps to my shoulder were heavy. "Too fucking funny. I'm going to like this. Enjoy the food. Plenty more to come." He walked away, shaking his head. He stopped and murmured to his wife, who also chuckled, then slapped his hand. He rejoined the men at the circle of barbecues and smokers and said something. They all laughed raucously, and I had a feeling it was directly to do with me. I returned to the table with another plate of food.

"What did my dad say to you?" Ava asked, looking anxious.

"I'm not sure. Except he made my neck sweat, and I have a feeling it's not over."

Ronan heard me and laughed. "He does that. Ignore him. Dad loves to tease."

I forced a grin and picked up another rib. I had a feeling it was just beginning.

A strange feeling followed me all afternoon. The fact that my presence made Ava so happy somehow made me happy. Between the munchies and the late lunch, we took a walk, and Ava showed me the property. The houses were well-built, the land used wisely. None of them was showy or ostentatious but built with natural elements—lots of stone and wood on them, fitting into the background. A few were larger, but most were an average size. The Hub was impressive, as was their rec center. I smiled at the golf carts I saw being driven around, picking up food to take to the barbecue. From their beach, you couldn't see my place, but Ava showed me the rocky cove that separated us and the steep path she'd taken the first day to bring Cash to me. I could see why she preferred using the longer but easier path through the woods. You could see the house was there, but the trees protected it from a full view. I took complete advantage of the fact that we were finally out of sight of her family, and I dragged her into my arms, kissing her until the need that buzzed under my skin settled and she was breathless. I knocked off her hat, her hair spilling over her shoulders. I buried my hands in it, kissing her again, drinking in her sweetness.

"I still can't believe you're here," she murmured against my mouth.

"I couldn't stay away," I admitted.

"Good."

"The barbecue smelled too good to resist," I teased. "I was hungry."

She gasped in outrage and bit my lip playfully, moaning as I yanked her back to my chest. "You're too good to resist," I whispered.

She wrapped herself around me. "I know."

The meal was spectacular. I ate three helpings, and Ronan declared me to be part Callaghan. I laughed at his teasing, surprised to realize how much I was enjoying myself. I couldn't recall doing so—ever. I helped with cleanup, grinning at how everyone pitched in so it was done quickly. Leftovers were covered for snacks later, and everyone found a place to relax. I talked to Ava's brother Paul about his environmental passion. To Jeremy about his interior specialty. I noticed how families seemed to congregate together to eat and relax, and I was able to piece together groupings easier. The way they all got along fascinated me. I had never experienced anything like it. They seemed to have genuine affection for one another. The older mixed with the younger, laughing and talking. Beth's brother Evan had a special relationship with Ronan and Aiden, never straying far from either of them. Lucy was like a magnet to Liam's side, and I was shocked to find out she was adopted and not his biologically. She resembled him closely.

They were all real, decent people. Not an asshole in the bunch. They were friendly, kind, and warm.

Until the games started.

Then all gloves came off, and suddenly, I understood Ava's competitiveness.

Croquet, horseshoes, wiffle ball, pool volleyball—all were taken seriously. And everyone, aside from Sandy and Jordan, joined in. The grandparents kept score, called fouls, and tried to keep everyone in line.

They failed.

I had never laughed so hard in my life. Misdirected croquet balls, hip checks that sent the horseshoe flying anywhere but the stake, cannonballs and dunking during the volleyball—nothing was sacred.

And I loved every moment.

Later as darkness fell, fire pits were lit, hot dogs were brought out to roast, and all the ingredients for s'mores appeared. Mounds of marshmallows, chocolate, and graham crackers were piled in bowls. I had been certain I wouldn't eat again, but I managed some of the still-delicious leftovers plus three hot dogs and at least half a dozen marshmallows. I settled back against the lounger and sipped some ice water, strangely content once Ava joined me, resting her back pressed to my chest. It seemed as soon as she was close, I wanted her closer. Her family knew we were more than friends, but no one had gotten in my face about it, and somehow that made me even more relaxed.

I pressed a fast kiss to her head. "Good day?" I murmured.

"The best," she confirmed. She found my hand in the darkness and squeezed it. "Thank you."

I squeezed back. "I had a great day." I chuckled. "So did Cash. He's passed out over there with the kids." I shook my head. "He's going to find me boring company after today."

"He can come back anytime. You can too."

I felt the stirrings of something. Panic, worry, sadness—something. I took a sip of my water, trying to find the right words to say.

"I just meant if you want a swim or something. It's always open," she added. "After a long day of working on the house, it might feel good."

"Thanks."

I was conflicted. These people were nothing like I thought they would be. They were warm, open, and friendly. Not once did they mention my property or buying it. A few had spoken of my grandfather but only in the kindest of terms. I was beginning to wonder if he had been wrong. If what Natasha had told me was simply malicious gossip and not fact.

"Do you, ah, know Natasha Mayor?" I asked Ava.

She snorted. "Yeah, we all do."

"I assume you don't like her?"

She shrugged. "I don't really know her well. She had a thing for Liam in high school. Lied and told people they were together, even though Liam barely spoke to her. She wasn't very nice in high school, and he wasn't interested. She didn't like it when he set the record straight. She's been bitter since that day. I don't think she has much good to say about us. Any of us."

I shut my eyes in shame. I had listened to her and made a judgment before meeting Ava's family.

"Why?"

"I met her at the lawyer's office. She seemed a little angry."

"She's been angry for years. Ignore whatever gossip she's spouting these days."

That was good advice. From this day on, I would make up my own mind about the BAM family.

Ronan strolled by, grinning down at us. He sat on the chair beside me. "You ready for me to come help with the house?" He opened his arms. "You got a whole crew with experience here."

"No, I'm good, thanks."

He didn't push it, sitting back and crossing his leg. "You change your mind, let me know."

I nodded.

Ava yawned, and I nudged her. "I should go. You need to get to bed. Monday is going to come early."

She smiled. "I have the day off. We all do. BAM and ABC stay closed on the Monday after our family barbecue." Then she lowered her voice. "You can come back to mine if you want?"

The thought of being alone with her, being able to touch her sun-drenched skin, kiss her marshmallow-sweet mouth, and bury myself inside her was too much to resist.

"Take me home, Ava," I whispered, nuzzling behind her ear. "Now."

She shivered.

"Okay."

CHAPTER 19
AVA

Tuesday, I hummed under my breath as I sat at my desk, going over my list of things to do. I studied the list then marked which ones I could hand off to Robert and which I needed to finish or, in a few cases, start. I didn't want to overwhelm him his first week, but I was looking forward to having a couple fewer responsibilities on my plate.

It meant I could spend a little more time with Hunter.

He'd stayed at my place all day yesterday, leaving early this morning. We had coffee, then he kissed me until I was a shaking mess, stepped back with a wink, and called for Cash. I watched the two of them disappear into the trail, my fingers on my lips as if holding his kisses there.

We hadn't done much on Monday except concentrate on each other. To my surprise, Hunter asked some questions about my family, making sure he had all the "clans," as he called them, straight. He was fascinated by Ronan's and Liam's relationships with Evan and Lucy. Laughed hard when I told him about Grace and Jaxson's beginning, and seemed confused by Addi and Brayden.

"I can't imagine forming an attachment that early in life," he admitted. "I can't form one at this stage either," he had muttered, staring into space.

I refused to let those words dampen my mood. He *was* forming an attachment. To me. To this place. I had seen a different side to Hunter on Sunday. More open and receptive. Relaxed. I had to figure out a way of allowing him to show that side more often.

A knock on my door brought me out of my musings, and I looked up to see Robert waiting. I smiled and beckoned him in.

He sat across from me, laptop open, notebook in hand.

"You ready to get started?"

He nodded. "Hit me."

Later that day, I walked out of city hall, permits secured for an addition to the winery. Addi would be pleased, and we planned to break ground late in the fall and have it completed for the busy spring/summer season next year. The addition would increase business and be a great boon to our bottom line. I was so deep in my thoughts, I didn't notice the truck beside my car or the handsome man leaning against it, watching me.

"Excuse me," a voice I would recognize anywhere drawled. "I'm a little lost, and I was wondering if you could direct me?"

I looked up, meeting Hunter's ice-blue gaze. Heat flickered in the depths of his stare, and I felt myself responding instantly.

"Hi," I said, my voice breathless. "What are you doing here?"

He looped an arm around my waist and pulled me close. "Waiting for you."

His mouth covered mine, possessive and firm, his kiss sparking the flame that never completely went out for him. It was always just below the surface, hot and simmering, waiting to ignite.

Everything and everyone around us disappeared when we were this close. All I could see, hear, and feel was him.

Until a car honking brought me to my senses, and I stepped back, blinking. I touched my fingers to my lips, and Hunter cocked his head to the side.

"You do that every time."

"What?"

"You sigh when I kiss you, and you touch your lips as if you still feel me there." He grinned. "I like that."

I shook my head to clear it and slapped his arm. "What are you doing here?" I asked again.

"I was in town getting some tarps, and I saw your SUV. I decided to wait for you." He winked. "You okay with that, Little Dragon, or are you gonna pull some of your karate moves on me and accuse me of stalking you?"

"I'll let it pass this time."

"You got time for coffee?"

"Actually, I was going to head home."

He frowned, glancing at his watch. "It's four o'clock. You playing hooky?"

"No, my new associate, Robert, is handling things at the office, so I am not needed there." I smiled widely. "He is pretty awesome already. I like him a lot."

"*Robert*," he repeated, narrowing his eyes. "Exactly how much do you *like* him, Ava?"

His voice was low, the tone off. He sounded…almost *jealous*. Hunter wasn't the jealous sort.

Or was he?

"A lot," I confessed. "We get along so well. And his smile. It's so contagious. He's going to be my favorite coworker. I can tell."

His eyes were almost slits as he glared. "Is that right? And why *exactly* would that be?"

I couldn't contain my laughter. He was being ridiculous.

"Because he has experience, understands the business, is as organized as I am, and took this job because he wants more time with his *family*." I stressed the word. "Once he's up to speed, it's going to make a huge difference for me."

Hunter stepped closer. "You're going to pay for that little stunt, baby. You like riling me up?"

I slid my hand up his arm and around his neck, playing with the back of his hair. "You were awfully sexy, all pissed off and high-handed."

He gripped my hip. "I plan on showing you pissed off and high-handed later. For now, I want you to get into that SUV and go to my place. I'm gonna feed you, then we'll talk about your—" his gaze was icy hot, and he ran his tongue along his bottom lip "—teasing. We'll talk about it *my way*. Later."

"Feed me?"

He pulled me to the driver's side door, opening it and waiting until I was inside.

"You're going to need your strength." His grin was wide and wicked. "Every ounce you have." He began to shut the door. "Be naked when I get there."

"I thought we were eating?"

"Oh, we are. I just want you naked. It'll make dinner so much more interesting."

And he walked away.

I waited on his porch, fully clothed, certain he was teasing. I heard his truck along the road, and he pulled up, yanking off his sunglasses and shaking his head. He climbed down, patting Cash's head and tossing him a new treat he'd bought him. He picked up a bag on the passenger seat and walked toward the house.

"You don't take direction very well, Ms. Callaghan."

"I assumed you were kidding."

"You assumed wrong."

"You really want me to eat naked?"

"I really want to eat *you* naked," he replied.

I blinked. "What?"

"You heard me. Lose the clothes and come…for dinner."

"What about you?"

"What about me?"

"Are you going to be naked too?"

"Depends how nicely you ask."

I turned and headed inside. I was sure he was still kidding, but to call his bluff, I pulled off my dress and sat at the table, my legs crossed primly.

He came inside and set down the bag on the table. "Do you always have this much trouble with authority?"

"I took off my dress. These chairs are rough. I might get splinters."

"We're not eating at the table. We're having a picnic on the floor." He took a thick quilt off the sofa, spreading it on the rug in front of the fireplace. I watched as he toed off his boots, undid his jeans, and yanked his shirt over his head. He lifted one eyebrow in challenge.

"I never took you for a coward, Ava."

Glaring, I unclasped my bra and dragged my underwear down my legs, going as slowly as possible. I felt his hunger from across the room. Felt the heat of his stare. With a bravado I wasn't feeling right then, I walked over and lowered myself to the blanket, sitting cross-legged.

His jeans disappeared fast. He sat across from me, opening the bag. His knees pressed into mine, his erection tenting the front of his boxers. He lifted out some containers, handing me one. I opened it, revealing a thick, juicy, double cheeseburger from the diner.

"Oh God," I muttered. "I always make a mess. I use about a hundred napkins when I eat one of these."

"I know," he said, his voice gruff. "But today, no napkins. Every time you drip something, I'm going to use my mouth on you."

I almost swallowed my tongue. "Pardon me?"

"You heard me." He pushed the container my way. "Eat up. I put gravy on your fries too."

"Where is yours?"

He winked. "We're sharing. You're my plate, Little Dragon."

"You are one kinky son of a bitch, Hunter Owens."

"Eat."

It was the longest, messiest dinner I had ever eaten. Every bite oozed ketchup or mustard. Grease dotted my chest, no matter how careful I tried to be. Hunter's mouth left a blaze of fire on my skin as he licked and nipped at my skin. He took bites from the burger, holding it over my legs, licking off the condiments with a wicked smile. He held up the fries, watching with glee as the gravy slowly slid from the end of the French fry to my thigh. Then he pulled a large, icy cold vanilla milkshake from the bag, and he dripped the sweet concoction on me, lapping it away with his tongue until I was going out of my mind with desire. I needed his hands on me. I wanted his cock inside me. I was wet and aching, my body ready for him, my need growing by the minute.

His erection never abated during "dinner." It was hard and tempting, and he avoided my wandering hands, never allowing me to touch him.

"Nuh-uh, Ava," he chided gently. "You teased me. It's my turn."

"Not fair," I pouted. "I have to be naked. You don't."

He met my eyes. "If I were naked, I would have fucked you twice by now. I'm holding back."

My breath shuddered.

He finished the last of the milkshake, replacing the lid and adding it to the bag. His tongue flicked out, wiping his lips. My eyes never left his mouth.

"Ava," he whispered.

I looked at him.

"I have never wanted to fuck someone the way I want to fuck you right now. Right here. On your knees, bent over, screaming my name as I drive into you. On my lap, my cock buried so deep you'll feel me for days. With my mouth, so I can taste you for hours afterward. On your back, so I can feel your legs wrapped around me and watch your face as you come."

His words lingered in the air.

"Now?" I asked, almost panting in my desire.

His eyes gleamed.

"Is that what you want?"

"Yes, for the love of God, yes."

He lunged.

I lay in Hunter's arms, aching, tired, and sated. The room was silent, the muted sounds of the world outside dimmed by his heart beating under my ear. He stroked up and down my arm in long, unhurried passes of his hands, his fingers barely touching my skin, yet warming it with the soft touches.

He had been equally demanding and gentle. At times almost rough, yet the edges tempered with tenderness. He was commanding but giving. Fierce in his passion, but never once was I afraid or worried. He gave me such pleasure, his desire for me evident in every touch, every stroke of his tongue, every movement of his body. I lost count of my orgasms. How many times I cried out his name, begged for more, heard his voice moaning my name in a long gust of air. *"Ava."*

"So, who's your favorite now?" he murmured, his tone teasing and low yet still raspy.

I hummed against his warm skin. "You were always my favorite."

"I guess you won't be teasing me again."

I propped my chin on my hand, studying him as I rested it on his chest. "If what just happened was meant to discourage me from teasing, your thought process is off, Hunter. Way off."

He pushed my hair away from my face, running his hand along my shoulder. "You drive me crazy, woman. I've never wanted anyone the way I do you."

"Right back at you."

His eyes shone a silver gray in the dim light. "I wasn't too rough?"

"I liked it. Every single part. Well, except the end."

"The end?"

"I feel so connected to you when we're together, Hunter. Once we're done, I feel you withdraw a little. I don't like it."

He grimaced. "I'm not sure how to respond to that."

"You don't have to. I just wanted to tell you."

A rumble of thunder in the distance made him frown. "Damn. I never got the tarps on the roof. It wasn't supposed to rain."

"I think just lightly. Heavier rain in a couple of days."

"Well, it's too dark to try to get them up now. I'll do them tomorrow."

"Won't the rain make the roof slippery?"

"I have lots of experience, and it'll be fast."

"Maybe you should ask Ronan or Liam to help."

His reply was swift. "No. I can do it on my own."

"I know you can. But they—"

"I said no."

I sighed and sat up. "Letting them help you isn't a sign of weakness. Asking for help doesn't make you indebted to someone."

He stood, his expression closed off now. "It does in my world." He held out his hand. "Case closed. Come for a shower with me."

I knew not to argue with him. I didn't understand his thinking, but then again, I couldn't comprehend his upbringing. His mother had instilled such strong tendencies not to accept help or comfort from anyone. To never get close. To walk away first before the other person did. I hoped to break that pattern, but I had to be patient.

We showered, getting the last of his "Ava picnic" off my skin. I dressed in one of his T-shirts and a pair of leggings I'd left there one day, and I padded to the living room. He was in the kitchen feeding Cash. He'd been quiet in the shower, his mood darker than earlier. Wanting to distract him, I noticed a file box on the floor.

"What's this?" I asked.

"I was cleaning the closet, getting it ready for the reno," he explained. "I spent hours going through a couple other boxes of mostly junk, but I hadn't gotten to that one."

I flipped open the lid, taking in the piles of envelopes tied with ribbons. "They look like letters."

"I think they might be. I'll probably burn them as well."

"Can I look?"

He shrugged. "Knock yourself out."

I carried the box to the old coffee table, perching it on the top. I dug into the box, pulling out a bundle and selecting an envelope. It was a letter from Mr. Owens's wife to him from a time I assumed when they were younger, dating, and they were apart. It was sweet, full of news and tidbits of the place she was visiting, and signed with lots of kisses. I refolded it, tucked it back in the envelope, and read another one, this time from him to her. It was shorter, less newsy, and the last line made me smile.

I miss you. Come home to me. Always, Owen.

"Love letters between your grandparents," I confirmed. "Why did he sign his letters as Owen?"

"He was a junior. He didn't like his name much, so he went by Owen. At least to her."

285

"Ah."

I flipped through the small pile, then tucked it back in the box. I went to the next pile, this one held together by an old elastic, brittle and dull with age. I frowned at the single name written with a dark scrawl on the envelope.

Hunter

In the corner was a date. I shuffled through the envelopes, noting each one was the same.

"When is your birthday?" I asked.

"September twelfth. Why?"

I was quiet as I checked the next few piles. All dated, all addressed to Hunter.

"These are yours," I said.

"What?"

"These are all addressed to you. There is one for your birthday and Christmas every year."

He came over, holding out his hand. I placed a pile in his palm. He tore off the elastic, his movements jerky. He scanned the envelopes, his frown deepening. "I don't understand."

"He wrote you. Every birthday. Every Christmas."

He looked confused. Upset. Conflicted. Then he dumped the letters in the box and shut the lid.

"Aren't you going to read them?" I asked.

"Later." Was his terse reply.

"We could read them together?" I replied, thinking it might help him.

"No. They're personal."

Those two words stung unexpectedly. They were clear in their intent. The letters were personal—and I was not. I had to blink away the tears that hit hot and fast. I stood and turned, wiping my eyes so he wouldn't see how he'd hurt me. "I see."

He didn't say anything. The air in the room was now heavy with tension. Laced with uncertainty, the intimacy of earlier evaporated. I bent and stroked Cash's head, his fur soft under my hands.

"Maybe I should go," I offered, hoping, praying he would say no. Pull me into his arms and tell me he simply wasn't ready to see the letters. Tell me he didn't mean it the way I thought. I needed to hear him say I did mean something.

But instead, he nodded.

"That's probably a good idea."

I picked up my dress and shoes and grabbed my purse off the hook where I'd left it earlier.

"Be careful on the roof."

He never replied.

CHAPTER 20
HUNTER

All night, I prowled the house, too keyed up to sleep. The sound of the rain that came and went agitated me. The box sitting on the coffee table mocked me. Ava's words echoed in my head on a persistent loop.

"He wrote you. Every birthday. Every Christmas."

That information shocked me. My mother had told me all my life my grandparents wanted nothing to do with me. Later on, she said they were dead. I was still grappling with that lie, and now there was a very good chance she had lied again.

Maybe everything she had ever told me was a lie.

I stared at the box, my feet refusing to take me closer.

What was in those envelopes?

Why had my grandfather written me so many letters?

I scrubbed my face as the most burning question blazed through my brain.

Why had I sent Ava away?

I should have told her another time or that I wasn't ready. She would have shut the lid and left it alone. I knew that. But I had reacted to the panicked, sick feeling in my stomach and lashed out.

The hurt on her face had been obvious. My choice of words couldn't have been deadlier. With that short sentence, I had devastated her.

"No. They're personal."

The words had come out without thinking. My usual way of avoidance. Push people away. Don't let them get close. Never show your emotions.

And I feared the contents of that innocuous-looking box would break me, and I didn't want her to see that. I let her walk away. Blow my entire world apart. And somehow, I knew she wouldn't return.

And I wasn't sure how to deal with that either.

I drained the coffee cup in my hand and set the mug down with a loud thunk.

I picked up the box and carried it to the table. Swallowing, I opened the lid, staring at the envelopes. I lifted out the first pile, noting the date in the corner. Slowly, I sorted the envelopes. There was one for my birthday and one for Christmas every year, starting when I would have been six and going until I turned twenty-one. After that, there was one a year, those envelopes different-looking. They resembled a letter, slightly thicker than the others. Once I was finished, the box was empty except for a larger manila envelope dated last year and the small pile of letters between my grandparents.

With shaking hands, I opened the first envelope. It was a child's birthday card with a fire truck and colorful words on the front. Inside was a crisp five-dollar bill, the paper currency no longer even in circulation anymore. It was signed by my grandfather with a simple message.

We love you and miss you, Hunter.
Gram and Gramps xx

The Christmas card was much the same. Another short message, but this time a crisp ten-dollar bill.

We hope to have you with us soon.
All our love, Gram and Gramps xx

I opened all the cards slowly, taking in all the details. They changed to reflect me growing older. By the time I would have been sixteen, the fives had been replaced with tens, and the Christmas cards contained crisp twenties. But there was a card to mark each passing birthday and Christmas. Each one a hopeful note of seeing me soon.

None of this made sense. I didn't understand. If they had loved me, why would my mother have told me differently? She never seemed to want me, so why didn't she leave me here with them? I knew I had lived here, at least for a short time. She could have gone on with her life instead of dragging me around with her. She never really made a secret that, at times, she found me a burden. Why had she told me they were dead?

I shook my head, rubbing my eyes. A headache was beginning to form. I looked up, surprised to see how many hours had passed since I started looking at the box. The early morning sun was weak, barely breaking through the clouds, but the rain had stopped for now.

I stood, looking at the cards. I had them open on the table, displayed like you would on your birthday. The bright colors mocked me, out of place with the drab surroundings and my fractured mood. There was a small pile of cash and more envelopes to open, but I felt weary. Worn-out as if I'd been running a marathon.

I needed a distraction. I needed to get the tarp on the roof. I knew the rain would get heavier later, and water had already pooled in the pans I had set out. I didn't want any further damage to have to repair. I would do the tarps, then have a shower and go back to the envelopes. The air outside would help clear my head so I could concentrate again.

I strapped on my tool belt and yanked a hoodie over my head. Cash, who had been sleeping while I sat at the table, stood by the front door, his tail wagging. He didn't like the rain much, but he'd wander the yard a little, then sit on the porch while I was working. I slipped on my sneakers, needing the grip the soles would provide.

The air outside was heavy with humidity, the branches on the trees dripping with moisture. I turned on the boom box on the porch, the sounds of Hall & Oates filling the air and breaking the perpetual silence around me. I set up the ladder, grabbed the tarps, and headed up.

The roof was slick, and I carefully made my way over to the damaged area and began to work. It was slow going, the wind just annoying enough to pick up the edges and move them as I drove nails into the tarp to keep the protective layer in place. The drizzle began again, and I cursed under my breath every time I slipped on the wet tiles. Once again, Ava's words came to mind, and I recalled rejecting her offer of asking Ronan or Liam for help. The job would have gone faster.

I finished the largest problem, then carefully made my way over to the other one. Smaller, but higher on the peak, it would be even more difficult. The wind began to pick up, the rain becoming heavier. I shivered as my clothing grew damp and the wind blew the rain into my face. Knowing it was only going to get worse, I cursed again but kept going. Slowly, I fitted the tarp over the damaged area, nailing as I went. My hands grew tired, and my mind drifted. I kept seeing Ava's face. The hurt I had caused her. The fact that I had let her walk away. I should have called after her. I should have dragged her into my arms and begged her forgiveness. Allowed her to see the real reason for lashing out. Shared my fear. I constantly underestimated her. She would have understood and forgiven me. She would have sat with me while I opened the cards. Being Ava, she somehow would have helped me find the joy in the contents of the box instead of only adding to my confusion.

I was so deep inside my thoughts, I made a mistake. I stretched to nail a section I had missed, allowing my foot to rest on the tarp instead of the roofing tile. The slick, wet surface moved under my weight, throwing me off-balance. I grabbed for the chimney that was close by, the brick crumbling under my fingers. For a moment, I teetered, then stumbled, falling to the roof and hitting my head. I tumbled and rolled, grasping at air. The force of my body hitting it sent the ladder flying, and then I was airborne, the cold all around me. I braced for impact, the breath leaving my body as I hit the ground, my ankle twisting under me. Pain exploded in my torso, extending down my arms and legs. My head felt as if it had been struck with a sledgehammer, and for a moment, the world around me faded and grew black.

The feel of Cash's great head nudging me and his distressed whimpers brought me around. I blinked, pain hitting me. With a groan, I slowly pulled myself onto my knees. I lifted my head, the agony making me hiss. I was in front of the house, about six feet from the porch. Beside me was a sawhorse I had narrowly missed landing on. Even as I used it, it took everything in me to pull myself up to my feet, the torture of the movements bringing tears to my eyes. I knew I had to get inside. My left arm hung useless at my side, and I was pretty sure I'd broken some ribs. I felt the blood dripping down my neck, and I lifted a shaky hand to my head, wincing at the cut I could feel. My ankle felt as if it was on fire with every tentative step I took. I dragged the sawhorse with me, needing to lean on it to go forward.

I looked like a drunk trying to reach the porch, the ground swaying before my gaze. I stumbled and shook, finally making it to the steps. Cash was beside me, his whimpers growing louder.

"So…s'o-okay…boy," I stuttered. "Good. We're…good."

I managed to climb the steps, grunting and groaning at the pain. I only had to get to the door and inside. My cell phone was on the bench, charging, and I would call 9-1-1 and get help. Everything would be fine.

Except my foot caught the edge of the top step, and I went down like a sack of potatoes. I hit the edge of the table as I went over, the boom box hitting the steps as it fell, the music becoming disjointed then silent as it sat in the rain. I lay on the porch, shivering and unable to move. Cash's whimpers grew into sharp, frightened barks. I attempted to lift my hand to touch him, bring him comfort, but the action was impossible.

With a low groan, I succumbed, and the world around me went dark.

AVA

I blinked, my eyes feeling heavy. They were dry and weary. I tried to concentrate on the words on the page, but they floated away, much like my concentration.

I hadn't slept much after leaving Hunter's. I showered when I got home, needing the heat. Hoping the water would wash away the feeling of rejection. But I felt it staining my skin. He went so quickly from being a teasing, warm lover to a man encased in walls so thick, I would never be able to penetrate them. I didn't understand.

I didn't know if I ever would.

My phone rang, and I answered, hearing the pleasant voice of Milly Johnson on the other end.

"Ava, dear, you left an envelope behind yesterday. I'm sorry I've been so busy I haven't called until now."

"Oh," I responded. "I was wondering where that was," I lied. I hadn't even opened my bag this morning. I glanced at the clock. It was already past one. I had accomplished nothing, done nothing this morning but stare at my desk. I shook my head to clear it.

"I'll pop around this afternoon and pick it up."

"All right."

I hung up, making a decision. It was an awful day outside. Blustery and cold. The rain was hitting the window not in drops but waves of water. It matched my mood.

I slipped on my coat and poked my head into Robert's office. He looked up from the files he was studying. "I'm going back to city hall. I left a file there I need. Then I'm going home to work. I-I have a headache," I lied again.

"You look pale," he agreed. "I think everyone is hiding with this weather today, so it's quiet. You head home, I'll hold down the fort. We have nothing scheduled this afternoon."

"Great. See you tomorrow."

I managed to get out of the office without running into Gracie or Addi. They'd know I was lying, and I didn't feel like talking. Talking would lead to crying, and I had done enough of that.

The parking lot was deserted at city hall, and I rushed in, the rain never letting up. Milly handed me my envelope with a smile.

"I'm sorry I didn't notice yesterday."

I shook my head. "It's fine. Gave me an excuse to get out of the office."

"I expect to see your neighbor today. I called him to tell him his permit was approved and ready."

I forced a smile to my face. "He must have been pleased."

"He didn't answer his cell phone. I left a message. He's been so anxious about it, I thought he'd be here right away. The rain must be keeping him inside."

"I guess so."

I left and hurried back to my SUV. I pushed aside my worry. Hunter always kept his cell phone on him. He also forgot to charge it at times, so he might have missed the call. I glanced at the sky. Surely he wasn't out there working in this weather?

I shook my head. Hunter was a grown man, and he knew what he was doing. He was probably busy inside somewhere. He always stayed busy.

I drove home and parked in the garage, entering the house. I kicked off my shoes and quickly changed into warm sweats and a long-sleeved shirt in my room. I tugged a cardigan over my arms as I padded toward the kitchen. I needed something hot to ward off the chill.

But as I plugged in the kettle, I heard a commotion on my back steps. Startled, I turned to see Cash jumping at the door, barking and whining. I opened the door, and he burst in, his fur wet, winding around my legs, obviously agitated. I dropped to my knees in front of him.

"Cash. What is it?" I ran my hands over him, but he seemed to be unhurt. He growled low in his throat, pushing at me. I glanced over my shoulder, a feeling of dread washing over me.

"Is it Hunter?" I asked.

Cash's ears lay flat, and he barked, the sounds frantic. I pulled on my sneakers and grabbed a rain jacket off the hook, remembering my cell phone.

I followed Cash as fast as I could go with the ground so wet. I cursed myself more than once. I should have driven, but I was so panicked I wasn't thinking straight.

The first thing I saw as I rounded the house was the ladder lying on the ground. Then the boom box in pieces scattered on the grass. I headed to the porch, gasping in horror at the sight in front of me.

Hunter, unconscious, his clothing dripping with rain, blood on his head and clothes. I dropped to my knees, running my hands over him, calling his name. His lips were blue, his skin a pasty white. I felt along his neck, finding his pulse. Weak and slow but it was there.

"Stay with me, Hunter," I begged. "Please." He didn't stir.

I was shaking so hard, I dropped the phone twice before I was able to punch in 9-1-1. I managed to tell the woman who answered the address and what I thought had happened.

"He fell off the roof. He's unconscious and not responding. Please," I begged. "He's so cold and needs help."

"The ambulance has been dispatched, ma'am. Do you have a blanket you can put on him without moving him?"

"Yes." I rushed inside, grabbing the blanket that still was on the floor from last night. I draped it over him. I dropped my cell phone and leaned close.

"Help is coming, Hunter. I'm here. I'm right here, baby. Stay strong."

He didn't move or respond. Tears filled my eyes, and the sound of an approaching ambulance broke through my muddled mind. "You're going to be fine," I assured him, wiping my eyes. "And when you are, I'm going to kick your ass for doing this."

I watched, anxious and fearful, as they examined Hunter, started an IV, and carefully placed him on a stretcher. I was certain I saw him grimace as they moved him. As they loaded him into the ambulance, I put Cash in the house, quickly toweling him off, then I hurried to get inside the ambulance with Hunter. I held his cold hand the entire way, leaning close to whisper to him that everything was going to fine and I was there. I had no idea if he heard me, but I kept talking.

At the hospital, I stood in the waiting room, dripping water on the floor, shaking from cold and worry. A kind nurse came over and handed me a dry blanket. "Someone will be out about your fiancé soon, dear. We need his health card and some other information, though."

"I'll get it," I whispered. I wasn't sure how, but I would.

I stood, facing the doors they'd taken Hunter through, knowing I should move. Aware I needed to put the blanket she gave me around my shoulders. But my feet wouldn't move.

Until I heard a voice say my name.

"Ava?"

I turned and met my brother Ronan's confused gaze. He was with Beth, and they were frowning as they looked at me. In fast strides, Ronan was by my side.

"Why are you here? Are you hurt?" He took the blanket from my hands. "You're wet." He draped it over my shoulders, using the end to blot my hair. "Ava?" He looked at Beth, worry etched on his face. "She's not talking."

"She's upset, Ronan," Beth assured him, taking my arm and leading me to a chair. "Ava, what happened?"

My teeth began to chatter. "Hunter. Hunter is hurt."

Ronan crouched by my feet. "What happened?"

"He-he fell off the roof, I think."

Ronan cursed. "What the hell was he doing on the roof on a day like today?"

Tears filled my eyes, and I shook my head. "I don't know. I have to get his health card. And Cash is alone. My car is at home." A sob escaped my mouth. "I don't know how badly he's hurt."

Ronan straightened and said something to Beth. He sat beside me, pulling me into his side. Beth hurried down the hall.

Ronan hugged me close. "It's okay, Ava. We're here, and we'll figure it out."

I burrowed into his side, his warmth welcome. A few moments later, Beth appeared, a bag in hand. "Here is some coffee and a set of dry scrubs. You change. Ronan will go to Hunter's and get his ID and Cash. He can stay with us. Evan will love it." She spoke to Ronan. "Go to Ava's and get her dry clothes and shoes. Socks too. I'll sit with her until you come back."

He pressed a kiss to my head. "Any idea where I'll find his wallet?"

"It's always by the front door or on his dresser. It's brown."

"Okay. Give me the keys."

I handed him the keys I'd taken from Hunter's front door. He knew the code for my lock.

"I'll be back soon."

Beth tugged on my arm. "Go change before you catch pneumonia. I'll be here."

I nodded and shuffled to the bathroom. I used the blanket to dry my skin, shivering as I tugged on the scrubs. My socks were soaked, so I rolled them up with my wet things. The sneakers were wet as well, but there was nothing I could do about that right now.

Beth was waiting when I returned, another dry blanket in hand. "Take off your shoes and sit with your feet under you. You'll warm up faster."

I did as she instructed, grateful for the warm blanket. I sipped the horrible coffee, ignoring the taste and appreciating the heat.

The nurse I had spoken to came out to tell me the doctors were with my fiancé and they were doing some tests. I told her my brother had gone to get the health card for me. She left, promising me an update soon.

Beth tucked the blanket back up around my shoulders. "Your fiancé?" she asked quietly. "Is there something I should know?"

I shook my head. "That was the only way they would let me in the ambulance or tell me anything."

She nodded, watching me closely.

"But you love him," she said simply.

I met her eyes, her dark-brown gaze soft and sympathetic.

"Yes," I admitted. "I do."

She patted my hand.

"We'll get through this."

I nodded, praying she was right.

Ronan returned, and I gave the information to the desk. I was able to fill in most of the questions, although a few I was unsure of. I couldn't recall seeing any medications in his bathroom, nor could I recall him mentioning any allergies. I only prayed I was right. I confessed we'd been together just a short time and I was unsure, so she made some notes on the chart.

I felt better, dressed in my own clothes and fresh dry socks and shoes. I was calmer knowing Hunter was being looked after by professionals.

I convinced Ronan and Beth to leave, promising I would call. They had to get home to Evan and look after Cash. When I inquired why they were in the hospital, it turned out Beth had burned her hand and Ronan wanted it looked at, the overprotective husband he was. She held up the appendage, showing me the bandage.

"Hardly needed," she whispered. "I think they just put it on to shut him up."

"I heard that," he said dryly.

"You were meant to. You scared them, I think, acting all big and hulky."

"Hmmph," was his only reply.

"You call me when you're ready to come home. I'll come get you," Ronan assured me.

I waved them off and sat in the waiting room. I paced a bit, sat, checked my phone, stared at Hunter's cell phone, which Ronan had grabbed. It was password-protected, but the lock screen made me smile. It was a picture he'd taken of me sitting on the porch with Cash beside me, my head leaning on him. It occurred to me that meant something. What, I wasn't sure, but somehow, I knew it did.

They finally came to get me, and I was able to speak with a doctor. In Hunter's room, I swallowed my nerves as I looked at him. His head was bandaged, his arm in a sling, and there was a boot on his leg. His face was bruised and swollen.

I stood beside the bed, aching to touch him, terrified to hurt him. The doctor introduced himself.

"I'm Dr. Michaels. Your fiancé has suffered a major fall. His shoulder was dislocated. He has two broken ribs, a badly sprained ankle, and a concussion. Not to mention the contusions and cuts from the fall itself. His core temperature was low when you brought him in, indicating he'd been lying outside for a few hours in the cold." He closed the tablet with a snap. "He's lucky it's not worse and you found him when you did. We brought up his temperature slowly, and he's woken up a few times. He knew his name, although he was a little fuzzy on other details. We'll monitor him for the next twenty-four hours."

I laid my hand on Hunter's uninjured arm. "Oh, Hunter," I whispered. "You foolish man."

Dr. Michaels smiled at me. "He did say your name a few times. Talk to him. Let him know you're here. It will bring him some comfort. I'll check in again in a short while."

"Thank you," I said, not looking up from Hunter's bruised face.

The doctor left, the door swinging closed slowly behind him. The only sounds in the room were the low beeps of the machines, Hunter's slow, steady breathing, and my own short breaths. Seeing him like this, lying there hurt and bruised, scared me. He was always so vital and strong. Independent and in control. He was going to need help to recover. To be cared for and looked after.

And I was going to be the one to do it.

No matter how hard he fought against me.

HUNTER

My eyes fluttered open, taking a moment to focus in the dimness around me. The room was unfamiliar, the dull beige walls and industrial ceiling not those of my bedroom. I peered around, taking in the machines, the IV, and the medicinal smell.

This was a hospital room.

Why was I in a hospital?

Fractured memories hit. The roof. The tarp. Slipping. Rolling. Grasping at air. The green of the ground as it rushed up to meet me. The impact. The long, painful process to get to the porch.

And then nothing.

Except, in my mind, there was a voice. A sweet, warm voice I knew. Telling me she was there. That everything would be okay. Begging me to stay. Whispering...*I love you?*

Slowly, I turned my head, and there she was.

Ava.

She was asleep in a chair close to the bed, her hand wrapped around mine, her other arm tucked under her head. She looked like a pretzel in the chair, and I could only imagine how stiff she would be when she woke up.

How long had I been here?

I swallowed, my throat feeling thick and dry. I attempted to lift my arm but realized it was in a sling. I groaned as my body reacted to my movement, and Ava sat upright, instantly alert.

She stood, hovering over me, our eyes locked. Hers were red-rimmed and weary, the usually bright hue of her irises dull and worried. Her face was pale, and her bottom lip looked as if she'd bitten it for hours on end.

"Hi," I managed to rasp out.

"Hunter," she whispered, her hands fluttering as if wanting to touch me but unsure. Strangely, I needed to feel her touch. I needed her to connect me back to this moment.

"Please," I asked, unable to say the words.

She cupped my face, her skin cool against mine. I sighed in relief and leaned into her caress.

"Wh-what happened?" I asked.

"You fell off the roof. I found you," she said simply.

I cleared my throat, closing my eyes in gratitude as she slipped an ice chip between my lips. The cold eased the dry feeling, and I opened my eyes. "More."

She fed me a few, waiting patiently as each one melted before giving me another.

"You found me?" I asked.

"Cash showed up at my back door. He was frantic. I followed him to your place and found you on the porch—" she swallowed deeply "—ice cold, bleeding, and unconscious." She had to swallow again. "I called the ambulance."

The lingering fear and worry were plain in her voice.

"I'm sorry."

She lifted her gaze to mine, her eyes blazing. "Once you've recovered, we're going to discuss you being up on the roof on a rainy day, alone, without a safety harness. But not now." She patted my arm. "Right now, I'm simply grateful you're still here." She straightened. "I'm going to go let them know you're awake."

"Ava—"

She cut me off. "They think I'm your fiancée. It was the only way I could stay here. So, until further notice, we're engaged. You got that?"

I blinked at her words. "Okay."

"I told them you weren't on any medications I knew of and you weren't allergic to anything. Was I wrong?"

"No."

"Okay. I'll go get the doctor."

I captured her hand before she could leave. "Tell me what my injuries are. I have a massive headache, so I assume a concussion?"

She nodded. "Broken ribs, dislocated shoulder, sprained ankle, concussion, contusions, and cuts." Her voice shook. "If I hadn't found you, Hunter…" Her words ended on a sob.

I tugged her closer, trying not to wince at the jolt of pain it caused. "I'm sorry, Little Dragon. I didn't mean to scare you."

She pulled against me. "I have to get the doctor."

"No, wait a second. Just stay with me for a minute. Please."

She sat down, wrapping her hands around mine. She rested her forehead against our clasped fingers, and I knew she was crying.

"I'm sorry for scaring you," I repeated. "And I'm sorry for being an ass to you." I flexed my fingers, even that simple action causing me pain. "I do that."

"You mean, act like an asshole?" She sniffled.

"Yes."

She wiped her cheeks. "You do it well."

I met her eyes. "I'm sorry, baby. I really am."

She stood. "Actions speak louder than words. If you're sorry about being an asshole, there's a simple solution. Stop being one. I'm going to go get the doctor."

I watched her leave, my lips quirking of their own violation. She was pissed at me.

With a groan, I closed my eyes. I was pissed at myself. I never should have been up on that roof.

Now, I was injured. But the question was, what was next?

I had my answer fairly quickly. Dr. Michaels went over my injuries in more detail than Ava, his manner calm and direct.

"You'll be out of the sling in a few days, although the shoulder will ache for a while. The ribs will take six to eight weeks to heal. Your ankle, four weeks. We did a CT scan of your head and it looked fine, but you'll probably have a headache for several days. I won't lie. You're going to feel like you got hit by a freight train for the next while. Your recovery will be a slow one. We'll keep you another day, then you can be released to your fiancée here, who assures me you'll be well cared for. We'll follow up as an outpatient."

Hearing the word fiancée was a jolt even though Ava had explained her reasons to me. It was his other statement, though, that hit me.

"How slow will this be? When can I walk?"

"No weight-bearing on the ankle for two weeks."

"It's a sprain. I've had them before."

He shook his head. "This is a bad one. I'm shocked it's not broken. You will recover from all of your injuries, Mr. Owens, but they're going to take time. You rush it, you could do further damage. Believe me, the first time you try to move, you'll understand."

He paused by the door, talking to Ava in a quiet voice. I blew out a long breath. If I was being honest, I already understood. Lifting my head felt as if a marching band were inside my skull. As I tried to shift, my entire body ached. My shoulder felt as if it was on fire, and my ribs screamed if I took in too deep a breath. I could only imagine what fun sitting up was going to be.

Gentle fingers across my brow brought me out of my musings. Ava peered down at me. "Do you need more pain meds?"

"I think so."

"Okay, I'll ask the nurse for some."

She began to leave, and I grabbed at her hand. "You're coming back, right?" I asked, suddenly anxious.

"I am."

"Good. That's good," I mumbled, letting my eyes shut. The darkness was a relief. The feel of Ava's lips on my cheek was soft and fleeting, but intensely comforting.

I couldn't delve into the reason behind that comfort. At least, not right now.

I slept on and off, immediately looking for Ava when my eyes would open. She was always there, sitting in the chair, her knees drawn up to her chest. She would take my hand in comfort as if sensing my need.

My head felt clearer later in the day, and when I woke, Ava was speaking with a woman. She held a clipboard and was asking Ava about my situation when I left the hospital. Ava's voice was firm when she spoke.

"He'll be staying with me. Any therapy or appointments he requires will be looked after."

Neither woman noticed I was awake. I wanted to speak up and object to Ava's remark, but I stayed quiet.

"He'll need a lot of care at first," the woman pointed out.

"I'm aware. It will get less as he heals. I'll get additional help as needed."

They went into the hall, and I frowned. Ava was going to look after me? I wanted to tell them I didn't need help, but I knew that was a lie. I couldn't move without pain, and there was no way I could look after myself. But I didn't want that burden on Ava either.

She came back into the room, meeting my eyes. "You're awake."

"I can't ask you to look after me."

"Good thing you didn't ask, then."

"Ava—"

She held up her hand, stopping me. "Hunter, you can't go home. You can't be alone. I have a guest room with a walk-in shower. I can work from home most of the time and there are lots of people in the compound who will step in when I have to go to work."

"You expect your family to care for me?" I shook my head. "Not happening."

She leaned over me, her gaze serious, her tone firm. "It can happen and it will. You can't be alone. How would you even care for Cash? Stop being so stubborn, Hunter. You won't be able to walk on your own for a while. You can't use crutches until the shoulder heals. And then how would you get around? Your ribs will be so sore, you won't be able to cook or get dressed on your own. So, it's either a rehab hospital in Toronto or at the house with me. They'll send someone to bathe you for the first while. In a few weeks, once you've recovered, we'll see what happens. But until then, I'm in charge. Got it?"

I wanted to argue, but everything she said made sense.

"After the way I treated you, why would you want to?" I asked.

She sat down, shaking her head. "I don't know, but I have to. I can't tell you what it did to me seeing you lying on the porch, bleeding and injured." Her voice broke, and she was quiet for a moment. "I don't understand you sometimes, Hunter. But frankly, I don't think you understand yourself either."

She slipped her hand into mine. "You're hurt, and that hurts me. I want to help you get better because I care. I care about *you*." She met my eyes. "We need to leave it at that for now. You won't be released until at least tomorrow, and you're coming home with me."

I hated seeing the worry in her eyes. Knowing how upset she'd been. How strong she was *being* for me. "Okay, Little Dragon. I don't think I'll be a very good patient, though."

She rolled her eyes. "I already figured that out."

I sighed, shocked at how much a simple conversation sapped me of my strength. I felt Ava's fingers stroking along my brow. Her touch was light and gentle, bringing with it relief and warmth. I leaned into her caress, drifting.

She touched her lips to my cheek, the scent of her chasing away the medicinal smell and replacing it with the lingering notes of flowers, citrus, and her.

It lulled me back to sleep.

AVA

I peeked in on Hunter. He was asleep, his head turned into the pillow, the rise and fall of his chest steady. He had been a surprisingly docile patient since I'd brought him home with me four days ago. He slept a lot. His body needed to rest to recover. He hated being reliant on me—on anyone—for help, so he asked for very little. It zapped all his energy to get out of bed and be helped to the bathroom for a shower. Ralph, the nurse who came to help him, was friendly and pleasant, and Hunter was polite, although I could tell he hated requiring the aid. I knew once he got stronger, he would refuse it.

I sat at the kitchen table, looking over my lists. Addi had been shocked when I'd informed her I would be working between home and the office for a while, although she understood when she heard about Hunter's accident. I had spoken to Robert, who assured me that between us, nothing would get missed. My parents had been to the house once they found out, checking in on Hunter and making sure we were all right the first day I brought him home.

"All of us can help," Mom soothed me. "You figure out your schedule. There are enough of us, we can sit with Hunter while you go to work or do errands." She reached out, clasping my hand. "You have to look after yourself as well."

"I know," I assured her. "I am."

"You look tired."

"It's been a little stressful."

She squeezed my fingers. "I know." She met my eyes. "Seeing someone we love hurt is always difficult."

I felt a tremor go through me. "Am I that obvious?" I whispered.

"No. But I know my daughter. I see a lot of myself in you. A lot of your father in him. He is not an easy man to love."

I shook my head. "That's the problem, Mom. He is easy to love."

"I suppose it's not easy for him to accept it, then."

I nodded, then felt the tears I'd been holding back gather in my eyes. "I was so scared, Mom. Seeing him lying there, how still he was. The blood. How frantic Cash was." I wiped my eyes. "I thought—" I swallowed. "I thought he..." I couldn't even finish the sentence.

"I know, but he's not. He's here, and he'll be fine, thanks to you."

I nodded. "He will be."

Dad walked in, bringing Cash with him. He'd taken him outside to throw a ball with him for a while. Cash was wagging his tail, his head up. He'd been so excited to see Hunter, making whimpering noises in the back of his throat and wanting Hunter's attention.

"We need a dog, Sunshine."

"Maybe when you retire. In the meantime, you can look after Cash."

I smiled at the memory. By the next day, my fridge was full of casseroles and easy dinners. There was a list of people wanting to take Cash for a walk or to play with him, and I had no shortage of bodies willing to sit with Hunter when I had to go to the office or run errands. My family rallied, the way they always did when someone needed help. I was grateful, and Hunter…well, Hunter was confused. All the caring and generosity were alien to him. He was polite with everyone, but he held himself back. A part of me wondered if he would be comfortable in a place that was home to me. If he would ever find a place to be comfortable enough to call *home*. The thought of him leaving, wandering to yet another destination, searching for something he couldn't put into words hurt my heart, but I knew there was nothing I could do to hold him. If I held too tight, he would leave all that much sooner.

I heard movement down the hall, and I rose from the chair, shaking my head to clear my thoughts. I stopped and poured a glass of the iced tea Emmy had brought. Hunter loved it, and I was going to have to call her and ask for more.

I peeked into his room with a smile. Cash was next to the bed, his great head resting on the mattress as Hunter stroked it. Cash had rarely left his side since they were reunited. Cash's relief and joy were evident at seeing Hunter. He sensed, as animals did, that

Hunter was hurt and stayed close. In turn, Hunter had praised Cash quietly, thanking him for coming to get me.

"You saved me, boy. You saved me," he murmured, patting his haunches and stroking his head. "Good boy."

I tapped on the door, and Hunter looked up from his half-supine position on the bed. I knew how much effort that small movement cost him.

"It's your house, Little Dragon. You don't have to knock." He smiled easily, his smile growing as he saw what I was carrying.

I stepped in, handing him the iced tea and sitting in the chair beside the bed. "Just being polite."

He drank deeply, his eyes crinkling in enjoyment. "I have no idea what your aunt puts in that, but I swear I'm addicted."

"She adds a bunch of fruit juices. Bentley is crazy about it—we all are—she makes it all the time." I took the glass from his hand and put it on the table. "She'll bring more."

He smiled, and I leaned over, brushing the hair off his forehead. He seemed to love my touches, always leaning into them as if he wanted closer. He watched me all the time, his gaze following me around the room, his attention focused on me whenever I was close. His color was better today, the bruising already fading thanks to the cream I rubbed on his skin.

"How are you feeling?"

"I'm fine."

I lifted my eyebrows and pursed my lips. He chuckled.

"I'm okay. The ankle isn't hurting as much, and my shoulder feels okay. I think we can get rid of the sling today."

"Tomorrow. The doctor said tomorrow."

Hunter shook his head, stubborn and determined. "He said sooner if it felt better. It feels better, and I want the damn thing off."

Our eyes locked in a battle of wills.

"If you don't help me, I'll do it myself."

I rolled my eyes. He would.

Standing, I unclipped the band around his neck and helped him ease his arm out of the sling. He grimaced a little then relaxed against the pillow. "That feels better."

"Don't try to do too much."

He cracked open an eye. "What do you think I'm going to do, Ava? Jump out of bed and start swinging a hammer? I know I can't do anything much. It's just a relief to have that thing off my neck." He sighed. "The crutch is next. I can't do much about the ribs, though."

"They will heal. You have to give them time."

He stared out the window. "I know." His gaze drifted to mine. "Did I hear Ronan's voice earlier?"

I swallowed. "Yes."

"Why do you look so guilty?"

"He finished tarping the roof for you."

Hunter frowned. "Oh."

"I didn't want you to worry about it. More rain is forecast."

He was quiet, then nodded. "Thank you." He took my hand. "I mean it. Thank you." He hesitated. "Did he, ah, go inside?"

"Yes."

He grimaced.

"So did I. The other day when I went to get you some clothes."

"Oh," he said again. "So, you saw them? The cards?"

"Yes. I knew they were private, so I gathered them up with all the money that was there and put them back in the box." I indicated the door behind me. "It's in the closet over there, safe. Ronan didn't see them."

"Okay. Good." He fell silent for a moment. When he spoke, his voice was quiet.

"Every year," he mused. "Every birthday, every Christmas. Why would he do that?" He met my eyes. "I don't understand. If he didn't care, why would he do that?"

"I think the point is that he *did* care, Hunter. He saved them for you, hoping he could give them to you one day."

"Why would my mother lie about that?" A frown marred his face. "She never really wanted me, so why didn't she let them have me if they did care?"

"I don't know." I paused. "I saw you hadn't finished opening the envelopes. Maybe the ones that look like letters would explain things?"

"Maybe."

"I could get them for you if you wanted."

He shook his head, suddenly looking exhausted. "Not now. I can't right now."

"Okay."

I stood, running my hand across his brow. "Okay. Rest. We can talk about it later."

He closed his eyes and sighed. "Later."

The next moment, he was out. I kept stroking his head, wondering if there would be a later, or if, like other things, he would choose to ignore what was staring him in the face and continue on a path he thought he *had* to be on. I stepped back and left the room, pulling the door closed behind me. Only time would tell.

HUNTER

I sat up slowly, trying not to groan. My room was dark, and a breeze coming in the window felt good on my skin. Cash raised his head, looking at me, then with a huff, lay back down. I wondered what day it was. Time had ceased having much meaning. It felt as if it had been months since I'd left the hospital, even though I knew it had only been a matter of a couple of weeks. I rolled my shoulder, still feeling the tweak of pain from the healing injury. I tested my ankle, grateful to be out of the boot, even though the limb continued to protest when I walked. I still relied on the crutch a great deal of time. The cuts and bruises were healing thanks to whatever stuff Ava insisted on rubbing on them daily. The worst part was the ribs. They would be the slowest thing to heal and caused me the most pain. Any sudden movement, any unexpected cough or sneeze, caused a vortex of pain I had never experienced before. The doctor told me I was lucky that a rib hadn't pierced my lungs or done further injury. That I should be grateful I hadn't done permanent damage to my spine. He had lectured me about being on the roof and cautioned me about wearing safety equipment. Ava seemed pleased at my dressing-down, but it was nothing compared to her lecture once she took me back to her house and got me settled. I knew it was brewing in the car on the way to her place and braced myself for when she blew.

It started off calmly enough.

"So, while we're on the subject, why did you choose to go on the roof on such a rainy day?"

I lifted my eyebrows. I hadn't been aware we were on that subject. Or any subject, really, since she hadn't spoken to me since we left the hospital.

"I needed a distraction."

Her voice dripped with sarcasm. "And you thought the best distraction was to climb a ladder during the rain and nail down tarps on a slippery roof?"

"It wasn't raining when I went up. It was a fast job—or at least it was supposed to be. I didn't want the water seeping into the house again."

"And God forbid you ask for help. Call my brothers, who offered. Because asking for help makes people think you need them, and you can't have that— right, Hunter?"

There was no mistaking the anger in her voice. I chose to ignore the last part of her sentence.

"I really didn't think I needed any help. Fifteen minutes, job done. I didn't expect to fall. I've done things a lot more dangerous than that."

That was the wrong thing to say. She slammed her hands on her hips and didn't stop talking for ten minutes. I let her talk, knowing she needed to get it out. I listened to her lecture about safety on the jobsite. Never working on projects alone. The precautions her company insisted on taking with every crew member. She knew what she was talking about. I agreed with her on all points—which only seemed to make her angrier.

"I agree with you. It was stupid. But I didn't plan on falling."

"I didn't plan on finding you covered in blood and unconscious either," she snapped.

I held out my hand. "Come here, Little Dragon."

"No," she refused.

"Please."

"I'm not finished."

I crooked my fingers. "Please."

When she was close enough, I took her hands and pulled her down beside me on the bed. She sat gingerly, always concerned about causing me pain by jostling me.

"I'm sorry. I didn't mean to frighten you, and I know I did. I wasn't thinking clearly, and I shouldn't have been on the roof. I wish I could take it back, but I can't. Trust me, I'm paying for it. But you can't keep being mad."

She sniffled a little. "I want to kick your ass so bad."

I slipped my fingers under her chin. "When I'm healed, I'll let you. Until then, what can I do to make it up?"

She looked away, then stood. "If I can't be mad, you can't be mad either."

"Why would I be mad?"

She took a deep breath. "I picked up your permit and sent a crew to your house to do the work."

I gaped at her. "What?"

"You can't do it. Not now, not in a few weeks. You were going to hire an outside company to do some work. I hired us on your behalf. Van is overseeing it." She crossed her arms and narrowed her eyes, waiting for the fight.

I waited for my explosion of anger. For the words to fly from my mouth that would hurt her. To deny her the assistance we both knew I required.

But nothing came. There was a strange relief in knowing I wouldn't have to face the roof before I was ready. To climb a ladder before my leg was strong and my ribs healed. An odd sensation flooded my chest. I felt cared for. Seen. It was as if Ava somehow knew my worries and simply took care of them.

"I'd like to talk to Van. Ronan, as well."

She blinked. "I can arrange that."

I held out my hand again, waiting until she took it.

"Thank you."

Her smile could light the whole city.

"You're welcome."

The conversation drifted through my head as I sat in the dark. I still couldn't explain my lack of anger. Ronan and Van came to the house, and we talked. Agreed on a figure. A timeline. I was shocked when Ronan showed me pictures of what had already been done. He grinned.

"Van and his boys don't mess around. Our crews are the best in the business."

I was very calm about it all.

The reason had to be Ava. How could I possibly be mad at her? From the moment I had woken up in the hospital, she had been

319

there. At my side. Caring for me like no one had ever done in my life. She fussed and worried. Her family did the same. Some days, the house felt as if it had a revolving door of people coming and going to check on me. On her. On us. I should hate it, yet I didn't. It confused me, filled me with a sense of awe. Ava accepted it as normal. It was as abnormal to me as caring for someone. And I realized, I did care for Ava—more than I expected to. More than I wanted to.

And she was the reason I wasn't asleep. I couldn't stop thinking about her. Knowing she was down the hall, close, yet not close enough, was keeping me awake.

I needed to see her.

Carefully, I eased off the bed, holding in the moan. Even after many long days of recovery, I shuffled like an old man down the hall. I refused to use the crutch since I didn't want to disturb Ava. I only wanted to see her.

Except, before I made it to her door, she was there, worried and anxious. "Hunter, what's wrong?"

The words were out before I could stop them. "You know why I sleep so much in the daytime?"

"Because you're recovering?"

"Because I know you're close. You'll come check on me. Talk to me. I lie in that bed every night, wishing I could see you."

"Why didn't you call me? Ring the bell?" she asked quietly. "I would have come to you."

"I won't use a bell to call you. I just wanted to look in and see you."

She shook her head. "Stubborn man." Taking my hand, she tugged. "Come on."

She led me back to the room, lifting the covers. I slid in, a groan escaping at the movement. She didn't say anything but went to the other side of the bed and crawled in, lying beside me but not touching.

"Better?" she asked.

I found her hand, enfolding it in mine. "Almost. Can you come closer?"

She slid over, careful not to press on me. She laid her head on my shoulder and found my hand again, entwining our fingers. "Now?"

I turned my head and breathed her in. "Much better."

The room was quiet for a moment.

"You know, coming down the hall to look at me is a little stalker-ish, Hunter."

"I need something to fill the time. Stalking seemed easy. We're both in the house, so I don't have to go far."

She chuckled then became serious. "You really can't sleep because you're longing for me?"

"*Longing* for you? That sounds a little old-fashioned."

"Ah, the heroes in my historical romances often long for their ladies. Pine for them. One of my favorites is Demon Winter in *Winter's Widow*. His longing for his ladylove is quite touching."

The name of the book was familiar, so I had probably read it to her one night. Historical romance. I knew she loved it. All the women in her family did. She loved it when I read them to her, and I had to admit, they were pretty steamy, although some of the heroes made me laugh. Love like that didn't exist.

"Sorry to kill your buzz, but I'm not *longing,*" I snorted.

"What would you call it?"

"I'm...horny."

She burst out laughing. "Horny? If I so much as tried to *touch* you, you'd scream."

"I could hold still. Let you do all the work." I was teasing, having only wanted to change the subject from longing, but it was back-firing on me.

"Hunter, you are never *still* in bed. Ever. Even when your cock is in my mouth, your hips and pelvis move, your back arches, your legs shift and bend, and your arms are in perpetual motion. Never mind the shivering and shaking." She tapped the air like a touch pad. "Scream, scream, scream. And not one pleasurable one in the lot."

She was right, of course, except talking about my dick in her mouth made me harden.

"I really move that much?"

She pressed a light kiss to my shoulder. "You do. It's incredibly sexy the way you express yourself with your body."

"Well, now I am *really* horny. I was just teasing before."

"Something to shoot for, then," she murmured. "Your dick in my mouth." She yawned. "Incentive."

The room grew quiet, and soon her breathing became deep and regular, wafting over my skin. Her hair tickled my shoulder, and the soft, sexy scent of her filled my nose. My body relaxed of its own accord, feeling her warmth soaking into me. She was right. I moved a lot during sex. Sex with her. Everything was heightened when we were together. Touches, scents, tastes. My body felt alive under her touch. She brought that out in me. Once again, she was unique.

And right now, she also brought me peace. That feeling was even rarer.

I closed my eyes and fell asleep.

CHAPTER 21
HUNTER

Three weeks later, I walked into Ava's house, my gait back to normal. Her car was in the driveway, so I knew she was home. She was sitting at her desk, mumbling to herself.

"The doctor said six to eight weeks. It's been three. Most normal men who fall off a roof and break their ribs stay *down*. But not when you're the invincible Hunter Owens. No, you go back to the jobsite. Right back to where you got hurt. It doesn't matter if it's his house or his job. I don't care what he says. Stubborn, pigheaded idiot."

She was so deep into trashing me she didn't even hear me come in. I leaned on the doorway, listening to more of her muttered rant.

"See if I run to the hospital when he gets hurt again. I'm not taking him any damned iced tea either. He can stay thirsty."

"Now, Little Dragon, I know you wouldn't let that happen."

Her beautiful eyes went wide. "How long have you been standing there?"

"Just before pigheaded idiot."

She lifted her chin and tossed her hair. "Well, you are."

I crossed the room and sat in the chair by her desk. "Ava, I was going stir-crazy. I was driving *you* stir-crazy."

She didn't say anything but tapped her fingers on the desk. I noticed it was a thing with the women here. They did it to make their partner nervous, make them confess some great sin. Start spewing confessions just to stop the eternal silence and narrowed gaze directed at them. I wasn't falling for that shit.

Except the room seemed a little hotter and the back of my neck prickled.

"Really, I'm fine. I'm not doing anything. I swear. I can't. Sitting hurts—I certainly can't shift drywall or use the nail gun. I'm just there for advice. Guidance." I took her hand, stopping the tapping. "I'm not putting myself at risk." Bravely, I met her gaze. "Honest, baby. You can call Van."

Shit. I caved.

After two weeks of being a patient, I became impatient. I could walk again without much trouble. Lift my arm and use it thanks to the exercises Aiden coached me on. My ribs were still sore, but they were better. I could move without wanting to cry like a six-year-old who'd just lost their balloon in the park. Most of the time.

Once I started feeling better, I asked Ava about going back to the house. I didn't need as much care now, and it seemed to be the right thing. She looked at me askance.

"Hunter, with all the dust happening, are you crazy? You'll cough and sneeze and reinjure your ribs, or worse. You're not going anywhere," she informed me.

Her words made sense, and I had to admit I was relieved. I liked being with her. I enjoyed her company, our varied conversations, and especially having her next to me at night. She'd slept beside me ever since the night I told her I needed her there.

And I had to admit, I even liked her crazy family, although they took some getting used to. I never knew who would show up, how long they'd stay, or what they would say. I played a lot of cards and board games with the mothers, and Sandy was especially fond of jigsaw puzzles. The men tended to drop by with updates on the house or to check in. Their visits were shorter, and they never brought baked goods or iced tea with them. I preferred the women.

Once I was able to move around, I had Ronan take me to the house, amazed at the progress once again. Beams, posts, and foundations were done. Exterior walls and roof extension done. The roof was being completed as I watched, feeling grateful I wasn't up there. I walked inside, seeing the new addition changing the entire flow of the house. I started finding my way there whenever Ava was out of her house. She could leave me for longer periods and go into work. It was all going great until Cami ratted me out and Ava arrived at the house, walking in and meeting my startled gaze.

"What are you doing here?" she asked.

"Ah, Cash got out and headed here. I had to follow him?" I said, knowing I had just blown it.

"Is that what happened yesterday too?"

"Oh, um…"

Van appeared beside me. "Give him a break, Ava. You think I'd let him do anything? It's the man's house. He wants to look around, he can. Besides, he's been a great help."

"If he's not doing anything, how is he helping?"

"He's overseeing. In fact, Hunter, I was thinking it was time you took the project back. You're great with the crew. I'll check in if you need something, but you could oversee it." He looked at Ava. "No work, just pointing. Making a few calls. Telling the men what to do. Like most of our foremen."

That made her smile. "Not really."

"No, but in this case, it works."

Ava tapped her fingers on her arm, and she nodded. "We'll discuss it at home." She opened the door to the SUV. "You coming?"

Van turned to walk away and met my eyes. He winked, his gaze amused. "I suggest you do everything she says right now."

"Right."

I got in the SUV, Cash jumping in the back seat, his tail wagging hard. He loved being in a vehicle. For him, it was a new adventure waiting to happen.

For me right then, not so much.

"We agreed on this, Ava. It's time."

I was shocked to see her lips quiver.

"Hey, hey. What is this?" I asked, slipping my fingers under her chin and making her meet my eyes. "Everything is fine. I am not overdoing. I'm making sure the house is built the way I want."

"I just worry."

"You can stop worrying now. Soon, I'll be one hundred percent."

She huffed through her nose, making me grin. When she did that, she suited the nickname I gave her. I swore, if she could, she would breathe fire.

"Who said you were ever one hundred percent before?"

I laughed, the sound loud in the room. I tapped her nose playfully. "You got me there, Ava. You got me there."

AVA

The crew made huge progress on the house. I walked around, taking it all in. The outside was complete, right down to the painting and trim work. Inside, plumbing and electricity were complete, walls were up, the new cupboards in, and work was almost done on the bathrooms. It was looking great. Another couple of weeks, it would be ready for paint and furniture.

I paused as a thought hit me.

What would happen then?

I heard his voice talking to one of the crew, its distinctive timbre carrying through the walls. I had heard the same voice groaning my name the past few nights.

With his recovery going well and his strength returning, so had his libido. On the weekend, he'd pulled me onto his lap, kissing me with all the pent-up longing and passion he'd been feeling. His tongue was demanding, his mouth hard on mine, and he roamed my body with shaking hands, fisting my shirt, delving his fingers under it to cup my breasts and play with my nipples.

"I don't want to hurt you," I protested halfheartedly.

He pulled me down on his erection. "Does this feel like I hurt?"

"Your ribs—"

"I want you." He silenced me with another kiss that curled my toes.

We ended up on the bed, me hovering over him, our eyes locked as I slid down on his sheathed cock, inch by inch, until we were flush. I shut my eyes at the feeling of him inside me again. He gripped my hips, his voice pleading.

"Please, Little Dragon. Move for me. I need you to move."

I wagged my finger. "Let me 'do the work.' You stay still." I began to move —long, slow rolls of my hips. He cursed, holding my hip tighter, fisting the sheets with his other hand.

"You feel so fucking good," he groaned. "We're so fucking good."

I rode him to an intense orgasm. He cried out my name, his hips arching to get closer, groaning in a combination of pain and pleasure. After, I lay beside him as he stroked my hair.

"Are you okay?" I asked.

He grunted. "More than okay."

"It hurt?"

"A little. Well worth it. And I bet once we practice a little more, the pain will go away."

And we'd been practicing daily.

We felt like…a couple. Sharing our days, sleeping close at night. Against his will, I was certain he was growing fond of my family —some members more than others.

Yet, the future remained up in the air. He hadn't talked about leaving lately, and part of me dared to hope he no longer wanted to. That he would settle here and make a life—with me.

He walked into the room, catching my eye. Van was with him, and he kissed my cheek. "Hey, Ava. Place looks good, right?"

"Awesome. I love the reuse of the wood and the stone on the fireplace."

Van nodded. "It's coming together." A huge smile crossed his face. "And here is the woman who can provide the finishing touches."

I turned and met the smiling face of Liv, Van's wife. She had been the head designer at BAM before she retired. Her taste and eye for detail were impeccable. I was pleased to see her in on the project. She would make the house lovely. She stopped and brushed a kiss to my cheek.

"Hello, Ava."

I smiled. "Liv." She headed to Van, stopping to pat Hunter's arm. She knew he wasn't much of a hugger, although he was better than he used to be.

Van greeted her as if he hadn't seen her for months, not hours. He swept her into his arms and kissed her, his eyes dancing. "Hello, wife."

She laughed and pushed him away. They were like my parents. Like all the second gen, they were openly affectionate and still deeply in love.

I met Hunter's gaze, trying not to laugh as he rolled his eyes at their display of affection.

"I'm going to look around while you chat with Liv."

I walked through the empty rooms, noticing the new windows that let in the light and how the porch wrapped around the entire house. The patio doors in the guest room, a late addition to the plan, added a nice focal point. In the master bedroom, I gazed at the back deck, imagining sitting out there watching the water and the sun, enjoying the peace. It was still my favorite view anywhere. The French doors were a great feature on the new wall, showcasing the surrounding nature.

As I was standing, lost in the view, I heard Liv.

"Tell me your style, Hunter. What you want in the house."

"Does my style really matter?"

Her voice was surprised. "Of course it does. Your home needs to feel like you. What you like. The colors you want on the walls. The type of furniture you prefer."

"My style is simple, I guess. I want neutral colors and sturdy furniture." He paused, and I could imagine him scratching his head in confusion. His next words shocked me, and I had to grab the wall to stop from falling. "But it's not my home—it's going to be a rental property most of the time, so I need easy maintenance and durable."

There was a beat of silence, then Liv spoke, her voice smooth.

"Maybe something with slipcovers, then. Easy to wash and get out marks. Washable rugs. Simple lighting. Heavy tables."

"Yes."

My heart thumped erratically in my chest. *Rental*. He was still planning on leaving. He simply hadn't mentioned it. He knew he was going—he'd never made a secret out of the fact—so he'd stopped bringing it up. I'd taken his silence to mean something else. I thought he was settling, when in reality, he was simply going forward with his plans.

I had misconstrued it all. My feelings for Hunter were far stronger than his for me. I knew he cared, he'd admitted that much, but the bottom line was, he didn't care *enough*.

I wasn't enough. Usually the men in my life told me I was too much, but this time, I was lacking.

And he would leave me.

Hunter strode into the room, his ankle fully healed. "There you are. I need your help, Little Dragon. Liv is bringing out swatches and catalogues. I can't with that stuff. Come rescue me."

I blinked, looking away, not wanting him to see the hurt on my face. "Sure," I managed to get out.

He frowned. "Are you all right? You're pale." He stepped closer. "Really pale."

"I'm fine."

"Ava—"

I waved him off. "I said I'm fine. Let's go see what Liv has up her sleeve."

I brushed past him, his scent swirling in the air.

I would miss that. I would miss him.

I wasn't sure how I was going to survive his goodbye.

HUNTER

Something was off with Ava, but I couldn't figure it out. The past few days, she'd been quieter than I was used to. Almost withdrawn. She smiled at the right time, laughed if I made a joke, but she wasn't herself. Her smiles didn't reach her eyes, her laughter sounded forced and hollow to my ears. In her bed, she was right there with me, but her lovemaking had an almost desperate feel to it. I was certain I had heard her crying in the middle of the night, but when I reached for her, she was completely still, not reacting to my touch or my quiet whisper of her name. She'd always been so open and honest with me, and I was puzzled.

"Hey," Van greeted me as he walked in.

"Hi."

"Liv is coming over in a bit to show you some stuff she picked. If you like it, she'll order it."

"Great." I was pleased that Liv was going to help put the place to rights. It was looking better than my expectations had hoped. It would be a warm, welcoming place when it was complete. I was surprised at my lack of enthusiasm about the project finishing, though. My main focus since I arrived was to get the house done and move on. By the time this was done, I would have been here for a lot longer than I planned. It was time to go.

"So, you're not staying on?" Van asked, leaning against the counter.

"No. My goal was to get this place done and rent it out as much as possible."

"That's a shame. I thought you'd be around longer."

"Hmm," I murmured, unsure what to say.

"I was going to recommend you to Addi. Get you on as one of the new foremen ABC is looking for. Great future with that company." He paused. "Plus, you know…Ava."

"Ava and I have an understanding."

He took a sip of the coffee he had brought with him. "I guess I thought that had changed. You two seem so close." He shook his head. "Too bad. You'd have a great life here. Good job, a woman who loves you, a family that would add something to your life you didn't even know you were missing."

The sound of a car pulling up made him smile. "Here's Liv. I'll go say hello."

I watched him walk away, my mind racing.

He thought things had changed?

Ava's withdrawn behavior suddenly made sense.

She thought things had changed as well. She'd overheard me confirming with Liv that I was leaving. No wonder she'd been so pale when I went to get her. I had just dropped a bombshell on her I knew nothing about.

The past while, we'd been acting like a couple. And I allowed it because the truth was that I fucking liked it. Being part of Ava's life. Basking in the feelings she brought forth in me. I let her care for me. I stayed with her when I should have come back here, regardless of the dust and mess. Now I was at home with her. Cash was settled.

But it all had to stop.

The bottom line was, nothing had changed. I didn't know how to love. Not the way Ava deserved or needed to be loved. I could fuck her, make her laugh, and for a while, we'd be golden. But I would leave because it was all I knew. The urge would grab hold, and I'd have to go. The longer I stayed, the harder it was going to be for both of us when I left.

I had to leave her before I destroyed her. Once I left, she would see she was better off without me.

I ignored the voice asking me if I would destroy myself by doing so. One thing I knew for certain was that I would never be better without her.

"Did you think I was going to stay?" I asked Ava.

She was sitting across the table from me, a glass of wine by her mostly uneaten plate. She'd used the excuse of being tired, work was crazy, and a late lunch every night this week. But now I knew what the problem was. It was me. I couldn't take the pain in her eyes anymore, and I decided to address it.

Her eyes widened at my blunt words.

"Sorry?" she whispered.

"You thought I'd changed my mind. That we were a couple."

She straightened her shoulders. "Yes."

"Nothing's changed for me, Little Dragon. I don't *stay*. Anywhere." I folded my hands on the table, wondering why they were shaking. "You knew that."

"I thought things were different since your accident."

"In some ways, yes."

"Which ones?"

"I understand you more. I see that families can be real. I'm grateful to them for their help. It was hard to accept it, but you were right. Accepting help doesn't make me any less a person." I paused. "And I learned what it's like to feel happy. You made me happy, Ava. I will always remember you for that."

"That's all? That's all you'll remember?"

"No. I'll never forget anything about you. But, Ava, I'm not the guy. I can't settle. I don't know how. I don't want to know how. I come and go. It's what I do."

"What if I said I wanted to go with you?"

I shook my head, even as her words caused my heart to beat faster. "That's the biggest difference between us. You need your family. They're a huge part of you, and you would be lost without them."

"And you don't need anyone?"

"No," I lied. Somehow, somewhere along the line, I had started to need her. But it had to stop.

"Everyone needs someone," she protested. "Everyone needs a place to belong. Hunter, stop running. Look around you and see what you have here."

"What I have here is a house I'm going to rent for income. A place I might visit on occasion but never stay. A group of people I was lucky to meet." I sucked in a deep breath. "And a woman who will be hard to say goodbye to." I met her pain-filled eyes. "But I'll still do it."

"I love you," she whispered.

Her words tore through me. I had never heard those words spoken to me before. I knew I never would again.

"No, you love the man you think I am. I'm not him, Ava. I'm not your knight. I'm just a fucked-up version of him." I stood. "I have to go."

"What? Where?"

"I'm going back to the house. I never should have stayed. I let you think it meant I would stay forever."

"You won't even try?"

"I can't."

I began to walk away when she spoke. I didn't turn around, letting her words hit my back like sharp knives piercing my skin.

"You're a coward."

I didn't reply. She was right.

"Love is always scary, Hunter. Staying is always scary. I think you love me. I think that's why you're leaving. Not because you have to but because the thought of admitting you love me, admitting you need me, frightens the shit out of you. And instead of admitting it, you're walking away."

I glanced over my shoulder. She stood, her chin lifted, her shoulders back. My fierce Little Dragon. Brave and strong. She'd survive this. Survive me.

"Take care of yourself, Ava."

This time, she turned away.

CHAPTER 22
HUNTER

The next two weeks passed in a haze. The days started to wind down, the house project coming to an end. Everything was almost complete. Ava had been right, as she always was, and Liv had done a great job. She found a local furniture maker and bought an entire line of display model samples. They were crafted of wood, resembling Stickley furnishings with the heavy wooden bases and thick, padded cushions. The sofa and chairs were comfortable, durable, and attractive. The tables reflected the heavy wood trim on the furniture, giving the house a masculine appeal, yet not over the top. The king-size bed in the master bedroom was a sleigh bed she had painted white to "soften it." We reused the dressers that were in the house and upgraded the handles and painted them to match. The guest rooms had queen-sized beds, wrought-iron headboards, and simple furniture. The scatter rugs were soft underfoot and easily cared for. Practical dishes and glasses were in the cupboards, and the necessities were in place. I had to admit, it was a style I liked a lot and could easily live with. Somehow, Liv had nailed it on the head without much direction from me. Ava would love it.

I hadn't seen her since I'd walked out of her house that night. I'd packed my duffel bag, took the filing box from the cupboard, and left. She had already disappeared, and I knew she was on the beach, no doubt staring at the water and cursing the day I entered her life.

I would always feel the opposite. I was blessed to have met her.

I missed her more than I ever expected to. It wasn't a feeling I was used to experiencing. I had never cared about anyone enough to miss them. I felt a continuous hollow feeling in my chest, and the yearning for her, instead of diminishing as I thought it would, only grew daily. I had to keep Cash tied on his lead to stop him from going to her house. At times, I wished someone would do the same for me, the desire to head down the path and be with her overwhelming me to the point I would find myself at the trail behind the house, unsure how I'd gotten there.

I ran a hand over my face, the silence around me deafening. The boom box was unrepairable, and the bottom compartment that held my small collection of tapes had broken open as well, the rain-soaked cassettes unusable and dead.

Much like my heart.

The sound of footsteps made me rush to the front door, wondering if it was Ava. But the footsteps were too heavy, and when I opened the door, I wasn't surprised to find Ronan there. I waited, wondering if he was going to punch me, but he brushed past me.

"You look like shit," he muttered. "Even worse than my sister."

"Is she ill?" I asked, feeling panicked.

He looked over his shoulder. "Only for you, asshole."

I followed him, not commenting.

He set down a file on the table. "I have your bill, including Liv's portion."

"Okay."

"I expect full payment before you leave."

"I'll have it tomorrow."

He asked the burning question I knew he had been wondering since the project started.

"How are you affording all this, Hunter?"

"My grandfather left a nice chunk of change to me, as well as the house. I figured it was as good an investment as any."

"So, you're not leaving because of money."

"No."

He leaned on the chairback, looking at me. "You're throwing away the best thing in your life. The best thing you will ever find."

"I'm not good for her."

"Bullshit. Right now, I want to put a beating on you so bad, your broken ribs will feel like a tickle. I promised my sister I wouldn't touch you. But I can speak my mind."

I owed him, so I remained silent.

He stared at me, his shoulders suddenly losing their tension. His voice was surprisingly kind when he spoke.

"Hunter, what are you doing?"

"What I should have done months ago. I'm leaving."

"Why?"

"I can't be what she needs. What she deserves. All I have to offer her is a bunch of promises we both know I'll break." I met his eyes. "I don't know how to love, Ronan. How to stay."

"Ava would show you."

"She shouldn't have to do that. I can't be fixed. My mother broke that part of me long ago."

He opened his mouth, then shook his head. "My dad almost lost my mom because of a stupid idea in his head. You have the same one, and I wish to God I could get it out of there." He slammed his hand on the chair, frustrated. "I like you, Hunter. My family likes you. My sister is suffering, and she won't hear a word against you. You are throwing away the one woman who could fix you. She already has, but you're so stubborn, you can't see it."

"She's better off without me. If I stay now, I'll only leave later." I stood. "I want to ask you a favor."

He lifted an eyebrow. "You have some balls."

"Look after her. Make sure she finds her smile again. Once I'm gone, it'll be better."

"And this place?"

"I'm going to leave it to a rental company. They can handle the bookings and the care and send me my share." I looked around. "I always thought I'd come back, but I don't think so anymore."

"We can do it."

"What?"

"We have a leasing division. They can handle it for you."

"Why would you want to do that?"

"Because Ava loves this place. I want your word, if you decide to sell, we get first dibs. Until then, it will be well looked after."

"Deal."

"I'll bring the papers tomorrow."

"Fine."

I signed the papers and handed them to Ronan. He wasn't as confrontational today and said nothing about Ava. He shook my hand and assured me they would list the property and keep me informed.

"When do you leave?"

"A couple of days."

I was surprised when he stuck out his hand again. "Safe travels, Hunter."

"Thanks, Ronan. Thanks for everything. I mean it."

He turned to go, and I noticed a white envelope on the table. I picked it up. "You forgot something."

He shook his head. "No, it's for you."

I turned it over, recognizing Ava's flowing script on the front.

> **For your travels, Hunter.**
> **I hope you find your place.**
> **Ava**

I looked up, puzzled, but Ronan was gone. I set down the envelope, unable to face opening it right now. I felt hollow. Empty. The usual spark of adventure for the next leg of my journey was absent. The urge I thought would hit me was gone. I only felt regret.

I went to the guest room where I had been keeping my things. I didn't want to mess up the place, so I'd been sleeping on the sofa and using the smaller bathroom. Beside the bed were my duffel bag, a suitcase, and the two boxes I planned to take with me. I kicked at the one box, then bent and removed the package of envelopes that contained the letters I hadn't yet read from my grandfather. Maybe before I left this place, so I could leave it all behind, it was time to read them. I needed to open the last of the envelopes that tied me to this place—including Ava's.

I poured some whiskey into a glass, took a bracing sip, and began to read.

AVA

I sat on the rocks, facing the water. I felt tired. Weary—right to my bones. Hunter was gone. Ronan had told me he was leaving in a couple of days, and this morning, I had walked over to say goodbye, but his truck was gone and the house locked. It looked deserted without the truck in the driveway or the porch door open. I hadn't wanted him to leave on bad terms, but I was too late.

Defeated, I had come here to the hidden inlet, knowing it would be uninhabited.

We used to play on these rocks as children, but rarely did anyone come here anymore. The sandy beach around the bluff was a much nicer place to sit and spend time.

But this was the place I came to when I wanted to be alone.

I stared at the water that hit the rocks with loud slaps today. The wind was strong, and storm clouds were beginning to gather in the distance. I wondered if Ronan would be bugging Beth to show him with the telescope he had given her all the variations in the clouds. He loved the fact that she was a meteorologist and was always asking her "cloud questions."

I looked down at my feet, noticing my toenails were chipped. I never let that happen. I liked to keep my toes neat and pretty, but I hadn't felt much like soaking in the tub or giving myself a pedicure. It would allow too much time to think. So, I worked. I was in the office early, stayed late, and participated in every meeting I could. I pasted on my smile, made funny jokes, and hoped like hell none of my family saw through my façade. If they did, they were too polite to tell me so.

A bark made my head snap up. I was shocked to see Cash bounding toward me, his tail wagging, his head high. When he reached me, he was so excited, he almost pushed me off the rock. I stroked his head, accepting his wet kisses.

Hunter followed him slowly, standing a few feet away from me. I met his eyes, the color of them bright in the light. Ice glowing inside fire. He looked as weary as I felt, the dark shadows under his eyes a direct contrast to his pale irises.

"I thought you left. I was at the house, and your truck was gone."

"Someone cut their leg on a broken tree branch this morning. We were at the vet." Hunter indicated Cash's bandaged leg.

I rubbed Cash's head again. "Poor baby," I crooned softly. "Will he be okay?"

"He'll be fine."

"So, you're leaving soon?" I asked, not looking at Hunter. It hurt too much.

"I planned to. But…" He tapped something on his hand, the motion causing me to glance up. He had the envelope I'd given Ronan in his hand. "You made me these."

"For the road, yes."

"When did you do this, Ava?" His voice was raspier than usual. I wasn't sure if it was because he was tired or another reason.

"Over the last little while. It took me a long time to find all the songs."

"How?"

I shrugged. "You had the tape cases with the song titles listed on the bookcase. I took a photo of them and then searched for all the songs listed and burned you some CDs since your tapes got ruined. I noticed your truck had a CD player, and you can probably buy yourself a newer boom box to play them if you wanted."

His voice was quieter, and I realized he had stepped closer as I kept my gaze focused on Cash.

"Why?" he asked.

"I know what they meant to you. I wanted you to have them."

The words hung between us.

"They are the only good memory I have of my mother. The only positive thing she ever shared. Those tapes, that music, was the one thing I had that made me smile from my upbringing. I thought they were gone, and you gave them back to me."

I stayed silent, unsure how to respond.

"I read my grandfather's letters."

"Oh."

His voice shook as he spoke. "They *did* want me. My grandparents. My grandfather explained my mother took me away because she was angry at him. I did live here with them for a while, but then they had a fight and she left, taking me with her because she knew that would hurt them. My mother never forgave him. He begged her to let them have me, but she refused." He barked a bitter laugh. "She would have been better off without me. I would have been better off without her. *Everyone* lost because she was pissed and held a grudge."

I heard the pain in his voice. "I'm sorry."

"My entire life has been a lie. Everything. She made me feel unloved. Unwanted. She told me no one had ever loved me. She made me feel as if I was as broken as she was. She refused to let me feel safe."

"Hunter," I whispered.

"I learned a lot about my grandparents in those letters. Their story, their life I missed. My grandfather knew how kind you were to him, Ava. Your family as well. He regretted his attitude, but his pride stopped him from admitting it. He was sorry for the way he acted. For the things he said to them, and for refusing their compassion." He shook his head. "He said a lot of things to

346

people about your family which he regretted but, again, was too stubborn to correct. That's why I reacted badly the first time I found out who you were." Hunter paused. "I never apologized for that."

He met my eyes, and I nodded in understanding.

"He had a lot of regrets in his life. He told me not to follow in his footsteps."

"Good advice," I whispered.

"I read a few of her letters to him he kept. She taunted him about me." He shook his head in frustration.

"I've never felt anger and loathing toward someone as I do her now. My grandparents searched, hoped, prayed I would come back. They wanted me to have a stable life, and they knew, with my mother, I wouldn't get that. His letters apologized over and over for failing me." Hunter's hands clenched into fists. "He isn't the one who failed me. She is."

His pain was evident, his distress acute. He shifted from leg to leg, his shoulders tense.

"I've always prided myself on my honesty. It was something I could hold on to. Even if it wasn't pretty, I told the truth. I'd been lied to so much, I swore I would never do that." Suddenly, he began to pace, moving over the rocks, prowling like a restless animal. He stared at the water and pivoted toward me. "And I kept my promise. Until you."

"Wh-what?'

"You were right. I am a coward. I lied to you. I told you I couldn't love you. I told you I couldn't stay here."

It was my turn to ask the question. One small word that held such potential for the future.

"Why?"

"Because I was fucking terrified, Ava. I still am. Of the way I feel about you. How much I need you. I have never needed anyone. Ever. My mother taught me that lesson, burned it into my soul. But you showed up in my life, and suddenly, I needed you every fucking day. Nothing seemed complete or right if it didn't involve you—no matter how I tried to fight it. I even lied to myself, thinking you were just an itch I needed to scratch. Someone I could walk away from."

His intense gaze locked with mine, and I couldn't tear my eyes from his.

"I need your smile, your sass. I need you to put me in my place. Tease me. I need your touch. Jesus, you make me feel so much with just a touch." He shook his head. "And your family. Your fucking wild, intrusive family. I've never wanted to be part of something as much as I want to be part of them. To be accepted and be in on the family jokes and stupid barbecues."

I was stunned. Unable to speak.

"You make me weak. You make me want things I was told I can't have. Things I didn't think I deserved or even existed." He pointed toward the bluff. "I read those letters last night, then opened your envelope. All of them contained love. For me. For over thirty years, my grandfather hoped I would show up. He loved me that whole fucking time, and my mother stole that from me. You loved me all these months without asking for anything in return."

Tears formed in my eyes at his words. He was pouring out his heart to me, but I still wasn't sure why. Was this an apology? Was he still leaving?

"I opened your letter from my grandfather too. He knows everything you did for him. He made you the second beneficiary and left you the house in case, eventually, one day, I did find my way back—even after the ten years had passed. He told you to read all the letters so you would understand me." His voice caught. "He said if I showed up, he hoped you'd love me. He asked you to give me a chance. He thought maybe I'd be difficult, given how I was raised." He drew in a long breath. "I think his words were, 'Given his DNA, he'll be a pigheaded idiot.'"

A giggle-sob escaped my mouth. "They were not."

"Swear to God, they were."

"What else did he say?"

"So much. I have so much to tell you. So much I want to share. If you agree."

"Agree?"

"To give me a chance."

"You need to say exactly what you mean, Hunter."

He dropped to his knees in front of me. "I want to grow old with you. Eat dinner for four every Friday and get sucked into your family so deep, I don't remember anything about growing up. I want to belong to you. For this place to be *where* I belong. I'm tired of being alone." He cupped my face, his hands shaking. "You're my beginning, Ava. I want you to be my end and everything in between. I love you, Little Dragon. Everything about you."

I clutched his wrists, desperate to believe his words. "Am I enough for you?"

"You're perfect for me."

"Tell me what you want."

"I want to stay. *Let* me stay, Ava. Hold me and never let me leave."

I flung my arms around his neck.

"Yes."

HUNTER

Ava lay in my arms, the storm outside beating against the windows, the waves crashing on the rocks and sand below. The wind was so loud it roared in its ferocity, shaking the glass and bending the tree branches low to the ground with its anger.

But inside the house, we were at peace. After we left the beach and came up to the house, we talked. I showed her the pile of letters. Let her read the one my grandfather had written her.

She giggle-snorted at his request to try to love me.

"That would have been awkward if you'd shown up with a wife and kids."

I had to laugh as I kissed her. "Pretty sure he knew that possibility was low."

We were both exhausted, so as the clouds gathered and the light turned gray, I pulled her to the bedroom and tugged her into my arms on the new bed.

"The house is so lovely," Ava murmured. "Liv did a great job."

"You like it?"

"Yes."

I didn't hesitate. "Enough to live here?"

She tilted up her head. "What?"

"Would you leave your family's compound and live here with me?"

"You want me to live with you?"

"Among other things, yes."

"Other things?"

"I never want to be without you again. I never want to be alone again. I want to marry you, Ava. Then I want to take you away with me. I want to show you some of the places I've seen. I want to share them with you."

She blinked, her mouth forming a small O.

"Too much?" I asked.

"Hunter, I thought I lost you. Now you're talking moving in, marriage, and travel."

I pulled her closer, our bodies aligning perfectly. My ribs had healed to the point that now I felt only the slightest ache when I moved. "Okay, let's break this down. Can I convince you to take a few weeks off work and go away with me? We both need to rejuvenate."

I loved the way her eyes lit up.

"Yes."

"When we get back, would you live here with me?"

"Yes."

"When I ask, will you marry me?"

"Why do you love me?"

"Because of your heart. The way you love me. Accept me. I love your feisty business side, but I adore the vulnerable, soft side you let me see. I like the fact that you need me as much as I need you. I love your laugh, your directness, and your sweet soul. All of you, Ava. I love all of you because you were made for me. You are the gift I've been given to make up for everything that came before. I'd do it all again if it meant I got you."

Tears filled her eyes.

"I know you worry about what happened before. The men who hurt you. I promise never to do that again. You will never be too much, or not enough. You are perfect for me. I'm only sorry I was too scared to admit it."

Her lips quivered, but she smiled. "Okay, then."

"Okay, you'll marry me?"

She nodded.

I reached into my pocket and held up a ring. "This was my grandmother's. It was in the last envelope. My grandfather hoped I would give it to the woman I loved." I slid it on her finger. The dainty band was scattered with tiny diamonds and probably wasn't worth much monetarily, but sentimentally, I knew Ava would know its value. "Wear this until we can pick out something together. You can wear it as a band if you want or on your other hand."

"It's so pretty."

"It marks you as mine." I met her beautiful eyes. "You are mine, right?"

"Yes. And you belong to me."

"I've never belonged anywhere before."

She pressed her mouth to my lips, her voice a gentle hum to my ears.

"Welcome home, Hunter."

EPILOGUE
THIRTEEN MONTHS LATER

HUNTER

I carried a tray into the bedroom, smiling at my wife as she slumbered. Sundays were still her day to sleep in, and usually I made sure she wasn't disturbed, but today was a special day. I slid the tray on the table, sitting beside her on the mattress. I swept away the hair that had fallen across her face, running my finger down her cheek.

"Wake up, Little Dragon."

She frowned, pursing her lips and burrowing back under the covers.

I leaned closer. "Baby, I got bacon."

Her eyes opened, the unique blend of greens, golds, and browns sleepy and soft. "Bacon?" she asked, her voice raspy but hopeful. Ava was crazy for bacon, swearing it belonged in its own food group.

I kissed her. "Sit up."

With a grimace, she pulled herself up to lean against the head-board, and I slid the tray onto her lap. There was the promised bacon, toast, and coffee on the tray. I had picked a rose from the garden and put it in a glass since I wasn't sure where the vases were. She grinned as she looked at the tray, picking up a piece of bacon. "Mmm," she mumbled. "Delicious."

Laughing, I did the same. I lifted my coffee cup and waited until she picked up hers. "Happy anniversary, my Little Dragon." We clinked cups, and she smiled before taking a sip.

"I thought you'd sleep in today too," she said, nibbling on some toast and sliding another piece of bacon into her mouth, thinking I didn't notice. "Not get up and cook. You had a crazy week."

"It was busy," I agreed. I had accepted the job with ABC as a foreman. I loved the work, the people, and the satisfaction I got over a job well done. Their expectations were high, and I strove to make sure they were maintained. Van still did some work with both companies, and I enjoyed working alongside him. We had just finished a flip in town, the deadline threatened because of supply issues. But we sourced, found, and brought in what was needed and made it just under the wire. We worked double shifts to make it happen.

I leaned forward and kissed her. "But I didn't want to spend the day sleeping. I wanted to make you breakfast then take you out on the boat. I want you all to myself today."

"Hmm, the boat," she replied. We loved spending time on the boat. Exploring the marinas and inlets. Just us. It wasn't a big boat, but it was comfortable and was a great escape for us. My need to move still hit me on occasion, and getting out in the boat scratched that itch. Ava loved spending time on the water, and Cash was a huge fan.

She hummed against my mouth as I kissed her again. I would never tire of kissing her. I smiled as I drew back, watching with amusement as she took another piece of bacon. The plate was going down fast. She even had the nerve to narrow her eyes as I took a second piece.

"A year has gone by so fast," she mused.

"It has. Best year of my life." I tilted my head. "You were so beautiful on our wedding day. You took my breath away."

Aiden and Cami hadn't been happy with our idea of eloping.

"Liam already did that. I want a wedding for my daughter."

"You had three weddings, Mom," Ava argued. "Ronan, Paul, and Jeremy all had traditional weddings."

"You're my daughter," Cami stressed. "I want to be the mother of the bride. I want to see your father walk you down the aisle." Her mouth had quivered, her eyes misty. "You're my little girl."

I couldn't stand seeing her upset. I also saw a flare of something in Ava's eyes at her mother's words. She wanted more as well.

We compromised.

We had the wedding by the pool. Just family, which with this group, was a big enough crowd. Cami designed Ava's dress—a knee-length froth of lace and silk that exploded from her waist and left her neck and shoulders bare. I needed a suit and made the mistake of asking Aiden where to get one. I spent an afternoon with Bentley, Maddox, and my soon-to-be father-in-law in a high-end shop in Toronto being fitted for one. Liam and Ronan arrived not long after we did, and by the time the afternoon was done, I was drunk on whiskey, the owner of not one but three suits, plus shirts, ties, vests, and the oddest socks I had ever seen. The shoes that went with the suits were so shiny, I swore I could see my reflection in them. I had no idea when I would wear the clothes, but I was assured I would need them. The BAM men insisted the clothes were their gift to me, and I swallowed my objections and accepted their generosity.

Our wedding day was bright and sunny. Ava was a vision, with her hair swept up and her dress swirling around her legs as she walked toward me on Aiden's arm. We said our vows under a huge, canopied tent, festooned with flowers and even a temporary dance floor.

I spoke my vows in a clear voice, Ava's replies quieter but firm. Once we were declared husband and wife, the party was on, and I was officially welcomed as a member of the family.

And for the first time in my life, I was part of something. A group of people not all related by blood but related by love. There were times I found them overwhelming, but most of the time, I enjoyed being part of the craziness and affection that surrounded the group. I had friends, something I had never allowed myself until I met Ava. I had become especially close to Ronan, Liam, and Aiden. Van was another man I looked up to. All great examples of good husbands, fathers, and friends. I strove to follow their standards.

"It's been amazing," Ava agreed, her voice bringing me out of my memories. She tapped the small envelope on the tray.

"What is that?"

With a smirk, I held it out to her. "Your gift."

She took it eagerly. Ava loved gifts. I loved giving them to her. Small things, like her favorite chocolate bar, flowers, some piece of bric-a-brac that caught her eye. Never anything over the top or expensive. She was amazingly low-maintenance.

I had a feeling she would like this one, though.

She opened the flap and read the words. "Australia? Really?" she squealed.

"Our honeymoon was short, and we never left Canada. I want to take you away from everything."

She clasped my hand. "I loved our honeymoon."

It was just us and Cash in the truck, my CDs she'd made me ready to play, and no destination in sight. We stayed at cottages, quaint little motels, and resorts. I showed her places I'd worked, towns I'd discovered, and spots I had been to and loved. I could finally share them with someone. I made sure she napped and slept in every day. We made love as often as possible. The two weeks flew by far too fast.

Now I wanted her to really get away, and she'd mentioned how much she wanted to see the rugged beauty of the outback. The map on our kitchen wall had lots of bright red pegs of places she wanted to see. My goal was to change them all to blue for the destinations we had visited.

"I did too. But you'll love this as well. It's all arranged with Addi and Robert. You're covered. Your parents will look after Cash. We leave in two weeks."

She pushed the tray away, climbing onto my lap. I pulled her into my arms, our mouths fused together. Kisses of salty bacon and sweet coffee were perfect when shared with my wife.

"I have a present for you too."

"You?" I asked hopefully, running my hand up her leg.

She laughed, taking my hand. She slid it under the T-shirt she wore, resting it on her stomach and covering it with hers. "Guess what?"

"You want the shirt off?"

"No."

"You're trying to distract me to get the last piece of bacon?"

She laughed, then became serious. "Your hand is covering your gift."

It took me a moment, then her message became clear. "Little Dragon, are you—are you pregnant?"

"I am. We're going to be a family, Hunter."

I had her wrapped up in my arms again in a second. Another astonishing gift from my wife. I was going to be a father.

Eighteen months ago, I was alone. Adrift without roots. Lost and searching for something I would never find because I didn't know what it was.

Now, because of the woman I was holding, I was a husband, a friend, an adopted son. I knew I had been loved and wanted by someone in my childhood. I had memories and laughter. Love that surrounded me. A home. A wonderful life. And soon, a child to share that with. A tiny being I would already give my life for.

"Is everything okay? You're okay?"

"Yes. You can come for the ultrasound."

"I'll be there for everything. I swear I won't let you or our baby down."

"I know. You're going to be a great daddy, Hunter."

Daddy. What a beautiful word. *Family* was another one. And right now, I was holding my entire family, my world, in my arms.

I looked at Ava, tears in my eyes. "Best gift ever."

She smiled, her happiness reflected in her beautiful gaze.

"Your dad and mom will flip. That secures my place as favorite son-in-law."

She laughed, not pointing out the fact that I was the only one. Instead, mischief danced in her eyes.

"Does this mean I get the last piece of bacon?" She grinned. "The baby wants it."

I offered her the plate. "Anything."

A year later

The world was still around me. I looked over the water, the sun not even rising above the gently moving waves. I rocked slowly, staring down into the sleeping face of our son. I'd loved him the entire time Ava was pregnant, talking to him, reading him poems and funny books, putting headphones on her stomach so he could hear my favorite songs. But the moment they placed him in my arms, something in me settled. The last, final piece to the heart I thought I didn't have.

Love, so infinite and strong, seeped into my body. Drip by drip, it filled up all the tiny cracks that still lingered. The healing Ava had started finished with Austin Jackson Owens.

I ran my finger down his downy cheek, marveling at him. He was perfect. The best thing I had ever done in my life.

He snuggled closer, and I smiled down at him.

"Let me tell you about your mother. You are going to love her."

AVA

I woke up to an empty bed. I wasn't surprised. Hunter was no doubt in the nursery with Austin. He was fascinated by him.

But as I slowly eased from the bed, I heard Hunter's voice on the deck. I peeked out the door, trying not to cry at the sight. He was wrapped in a blanket, our son cuddled to his chest, and he was talking to him.

"You have a great family around you. They're the best. A little loud, but the best. And the best of all of them is your mommy. You are so lucky to have her. We both are." He was quiet for a moment. "Your mommy is a walking contradiction. All women are, but that's a subject for another day. Your mother is a tough, smart businesswoman. She can work a boardroom, run a jobsite, and flip any asshole who dares to cross her. I am unbelievably proud of her." He pressed a kiss to Austin's head. "I can say this now because you can't do anything to stop me. She is damn sexy in a skirt." Hunter laughed. "In anything, really, but one day you'll get it."

Hunter rocked for a moment. I tried to wipe away the tears, but they kept coming. I had been like this since Austin was born—my emotions were right at the surface.

Hunter started talking again. "Your mommy has this soft side. She needs to be held and taken care of—that's my job. I think you and I are going to see it a lot the next while. I like the fact that I know about it. She hides it. It's sort of our secret, although the family knows she is pretty sweet—they just pretend to be afraid of her." He stroked Austin's back. "You hit the jackpot with Mommy. I'm glad I have her to help me with you. She is way smarter. Prettier too. And she smells really nice. She'll teach you all the good things, and I'll show you power tools and base-ball. We're a good team that way."

I couldn't help the sniffles that happened. My tears were like a fast-flowing river down my face. Hunter looked up with a smile and extended his hand. "Come see the sunrise with us, Mommy."

I padded outside, and he opened the blanket. I took Austin, then curled up on Hunter's lap. He enveloped us in the warmth of the material and his arms. He kissed my head.

"Heard me, did you?"

"Yes."

"I was just telling our son a few things. He needs to know how awesome you are. He's going to have a great life."

"His daddy is amazing too. He's strong and caring." I cupped Hunter's cheek. "You took such good care of me during my pregnancy. You were a rock."

He turned his head to kiss my palm. "You were easy to take care of. As long as I had bacon on hand, you were good."

We both laughed. My craving for bacon had been endless. And peanut butter sandwiches. Hunter made sure both were well stocked at all times.

"Austin is lucky to have you," I whispered.

Hunter shook his head. "I'm the lucky one. I get both of you."

I snuggled closer. "Always."

"I love you," he breathed against my head.

"I love you."

The sun rose, its rays filling the deck with light. Hunter's embrace tightened, and I sighed in contentment. His love was an all-encompassing entity, wrapping itself around me in every aspect of our life. It now grew and encircled our son. Bonded us as a family.

Hunter had found his place to belong. It was with me. My family had adopted him, giving him a foundation. And now, we had our own. Together we were strong.

I lifted my face to the sun.

What an age to be alive.

Thank you so much for reading AGE OF AVA. If you are so inclined, reviews are always welcome by me at your book retailer.

Grumpy vs sunshine is a trope I enjoy to write. Add in two characters who know what they want and you get combustion whenever they are together. Hunter and Ava were magic to watch fall in love as I typed the words to the page. I hope you loved them as much as I do.

If you would love to read another grumpy/sunshine story from me, check out Maxx and Charly's story in REVVED TO THE MAXX.

If you'd like to know what happened on the shopping trip with

Hunter, click below to read all about the gentlemen's adventure-Bonus Scene AGE OF AVA available at Bookfunnel: https://BookHip.com/MPVHCCW

This is the last ABC Corp book for 2021. But stay tuned for more of your favorite BAM family in 2022.

Enjoy reading! Melanie

ACKNOWLEDGMENTS

Thank you to my wonderful readers who asked for this story and waited patiently.

I hope I did it justice. Your support and love mean the world to me.

You are the reason why I do this everyday.

Lisa—what can I say that you won't silently correct in your head? LOL.

Thank you for your brilliance and humor.

You make the editing so easy and I look forward to your smart ass comments.

Beth, Trina, Melissa, and Deb—thank you for your valuable input, your keen eyes, and encouragement.

Your comments make the story better—always. Your support makes me smile.

Thank you to Avery and Carol for the extra help. I appreciate it greatly.

Karen—my bookmark, my center, my right hand.

Probably even my slightly useless but needed left one.

You rock every day. Love you to the moon and back

Kim—thank you for all you do.

Your humor and constant support is appreciated more than you know.

My reader group, Melanie's Minions—love you all.

Melanie's Literary Mob—my promo team—you do me proud and I love our interactions.

Your support is amazing and humbling. Thank you for asking for this story.

To all the bloggers, grammers, ticktok-y-ers. Thank you for everything you do. Shouting your love of books—of my work, posting, sharing—your recommendations keep my TBR list full, and the support you have shown me is deeply appreciated.

And my Matthew—my soft spot.

I love you. Forever.

ALSO AVAILABLE FROM MORELAND BOOKS

Titles published under M. Moreland

Insta-Spark Collection

It Started with a Kiss

Christmas Sugar

An Instant Connection

An Unexpected Gift

Harvest of Love

Titles published under Melanie Moreland

The Contract Series

The Contract (Contract #1)

The Baby Clause (Contract #2)

The Amendment (Contract #3)

Vested Interest Series

BAM - The Beginning (Prequel)

Bentley (Vested Interest #1)

Aiden (Vested Interest #2)

Maddox (Vested Interest #3)

Reid (Vested Interest #4)

Van (Vested Interest #5)

Halton (Vested Interest #6)

Sandy (Vested Interest #7)

Vested Interest Box Set (Books 1-3)

Vested Interest/ABC Crossover

A Merry Vested Wedding

ABC Corp Series

My Saving Grace (Vested Interest: ABC Corp #1)

Finding Ronan's Heart (Vested Interest: ABC Corp #2)

Loved By Liam (Vested Interest: ABC Corp #3)

Age of Ava (Vested Interest: ABC Corp #4)

Men of Hidden Justice

The Boss

Second-In-Command

Mission Cove

The Summer of Us

Standalones

Into the Storm

Beneath the Scars

Over the Fence

My Image of You (Republishing Soon)

Changing Roles

Happily Ever After Collection

Revved to the Maxx

Heart Strings

ABOUT THE AUTHOR

NYT/WSJ/USAT international bestselling author Melanie Moreland, lives a happy and content life in a quiet area of Ontario with her beloved husband of thirty-plus years and their rescue cat, Amber. Nothing means more to her than her friends and family, and she cherishes every moment spent with them.

While seriously addicted to coffee, and highly challenged with all things computer-related and technical, she relishes baking, cooking, and trying new recipes for people to sample. She loves to throw dinner parties, and enjoys traveling, here and abroad, but finds coming home is always the best part of any trip.

Melanie loves stories, especially paired with a good wine, and enjoys skydiving (free falling over a fleck of dust) extreme snowboarding (falling down stairs) and piloting her own helicopter (tripping over her own feet.) She's learned happily ever afters, even bumpy ones, are all in how you tell the story.

Melanie is represented by Flavia Viotti at Bookcase Literary Agency. For any questions regarding subsidiary or translation rights please contact her at flavia@bookcaseagency.com

Connect with Melanie

Like reader groups? Lots of fun and giveaways! Check it out Melanie Moreland's Minions

Join my newsletter for up-to-date news, sales, book announcements and excerpts (no spam). Click here to sign up Melanie Moreland's newsletter

or visit https://bit.ly/MMorelandNewsletter

Visit my website www.melaniemoreland.com

facebook.com/authormoreland

twitter.com/morelandmelanie

instagram.com/morelandmelanie